LEGENDS ON THE
PRAIRIES

A SACRED LAND STORY

ALSO BY TANYA REIMER

GHOSTS ON THE PRAIRIES
A Sacred Land Story

CAN'T DREAM WITHOUT YOU
FROM THE DARK CHRONICLES

LEGENDS ON THE PRAIRIES

A SACRED LAND STORY

TANYA REIMER

Elsewhen Press

CONTENTS

For my brother, Ricky.

At its core, this story is about brothers helping each other through dark times and it reminds me of that time we were stuck in a somewhat different dark place. Despite my panic and abandon… and me shoving you into the wall… you got us out.

So, thanks for being there, my brother, always.

–Prologue–

1882, Sacred Land—

Drugged, Sacri stumbled on the open Plains.

She had to fight but her muscles were exhausted. Burning.

Edgar brought the knife to her neck, and the cold metal jarred her to her feet, reminding her that she had to stand up and defend against him.

"Where are my diggers, savage?" he demanded, in French.

The diggers were never his, but the protest was lost on her dry, swollen lips. The world blurred in front of her, the knife cold against her skin as she remained silent.

He cut the leather strap on her necklace and the golden cross glimmered as it twirled out of reach, landing in the long grass.

Edgar shoved her to the ground. With her hands tied in front of her, Sacri tumbled into the dirt.

No more energy to fight, she rested, attempting to gather strength from the earth, but the drugs forced the sacred soil to ignore her plea for help.

Edgar picked up the necklace and studied it.

Her necklace. She mustn't die without the pendant on. Her brother Silver promised that the symbols on it would protect her. Without this defence, if Edgar killed her on Cursed Land, her soul might shadow him and that would be the worst way imaginable to spend eternity. She trusted Silver about such things since he had the gift of Sight and could see these shadows or spirits or maybe they were ghosts.

She tasted the dirt as her lips pushed against it. A lot of good she did. She'd led these slave traders right to the tunnels running across the border. Now they knew how she freed slaves.

This was not her destiny. Sacred Land would not be lost because of her. She forced herself up, but she moved too slowly and took a kick to the gut that flung her over.

It hurt to breathe, yet she sucked air in.

She lifted her head to see Edgar's brother Bellecoeur join them. Bellecoeur said, "Come. Your boy found another tunnel." Silver had warned her that Bellecoeur's soul was rotten, too. Having lost their wives, these men dragged their children around to smuggle slaves they intended to sell in their illegal trading. *Idiots.*

She needed to run.

First, she needed to breathe.

Her eyes were too heavy to keep open. Her body was suddenly pressed to the earth. Shaking her head, she tried to clear the ringing, but passed out.

When Sacri woke, the world was out of focus, but children sat beside her. A boy and girl played with the cross she needed for protection.

Sacri struggled to sit. Pain throbbed throughout her but she ignored it. Her hands and feet were tied, forcing her to painfully work on untying her feet, teasing the knots.

"Do you like my necklace?" she asked the children, surprised by the smoothness in her voice. Maybe she'd be fine.

The boy was about seven summers old, the girl a touch older. They were in fancy garments, their skin sparkled it was so clean.

"A story goes with the necklace. This pendant is one of two crosses used to protect warriors from a curse. Would you like to hear about such magic?"

They glanced over their shoulders then at each other, excited. The girl wore a dress with layers of expensive fabric, yet she sat in the dirt with them and nodded. "I love stories about magic, but daddy says such things are what fools believe."

Sacri tilted her head to better study the child. "It only matters what *you* believe." She glanced around for the men, but they'd left her alone with their children.

She sat straighter, prepared to teach while she freed herself.

"Sacred Land is a place where spirits connect to the earth. This land is surrounded by the Cursed Lands and if the curse fails to protect the land, legends say a hero will show. The last time Sacred Land was threatened by settlers who disrespected it, the spirits haunting these burial lands cursed them, proving the legends are real. Only two settlers survived. They were each wearing a cross, the one you hold and another. I am Sacri, protector of that cross."

"I'm Clement." He had a black eye and swollen lip.

"Did your father hit you or did you fall onto his fist?"

He glanced away, but the girl said, "I'm Mattie. Clement won't talk about it but he took a whopping this morning for talking to the servant." She leaned in and whispered, "Wanna meet him? He's about your age."

"I would love to, but I doubt your fathers would approve."

"I wish mine was dead," Clement snapped with a strange rage that she found distressing coming from a child.

Sacri placed her tied hands over his. "Sometimes a father leads you to water. Drink not. Swim not. Remember where the water is and is not."

"And when he pushes you in?" Clement asked.

"A father's love can be confusing. No one asks you to understand. Your job is to learn."

"He doesn't love me."

It was her way to teach and not correct. "In our tribe, if a father fails his children, he is asked to leave and another teaches them, raising them as his own. I do not know how things work in your tribe. Since you have no mother to request this, I could request this for you."

Clement's eyes lit up and he undid her wrists. "Yeah? Could I go home with you?"

"He won't let you go," Mattie pointed out.

Sacri's hands were free and she worked on her legs.

Clement's shoulders slouched forward as he held the loose ropes in his hands. "He might."

"I will ask. It is a hard thing to do for a father."

Clement said, "I would love my son enough to give him to a better father if he asked me. But I'll love him so much, he won't ask."

Mattie handed her the cross. "He can live with me. I

wouldn't mind. So…if there were two crosses, where is the other one?"

"No one knows where the other cross went, but some say when Mother calls the Man of Legends to protect Sacred Land he will be wearing it, a symbol of his power over the Cursed Lands." Sacri stood, ready to leave with the necklace.

"What do you believe?" Clement asked.

She tied the necklace on and scanned the prairies. Her brother was crouching in the long grasses. Silver was not pleased that she spoke with the children. Nothing she did pleased him. She spoke to him with her hands, telling him that the men were in the tunnels. He nodded and went after them.

She faced the children and whispered, "I saw the Man of Legends in a dream. He is the man I wish to raise my children with."

Clement's green eyes lit up and he shot to his feet, too. "Would you marry me if I found it?"

Sacri chuckled. "You are a brave boy, but I wait for this hero promised to me."

Mattie jumped up. "Oh tell us about him." She pulled her skirt around her. "I want to marry one, too. How can I have a dream about a hero?"

An exciting chill swept down Sacri's spine and to her thighs. "In my tribe, when a girl becomes a woman she is left alone for one entire day and night with nothing to eat but sacred plants. If she is lucky, she will get a vision to guide her journey. You could try this. Maybe you'd see something."

Clement pulled back his shoulders. "Tell us what you saw in your dream."

Pride swelled inside her as she planned her future. "I saw damaged grasslands. Life was lost in a tormented dark past. A shadow of a man…" She closed her eyes remembering the details of his pain as it stung her deeply. "I showed him that the fires did not run deep. New life grew. This was hope. He then exploded magic in his hands and symbols burst from them, caressing my skin. Each one was a jolt, images full of stories, and he gave them to me like a present." On her knees, she slowly drew them in the dirt, arranging them just so.

"These are the symbols from the necklace. How would he know them unless he has the other?" She joined the symbols and a new picture formed: the symbol of hope, the Sacred Oak. "And only the Man of Legends should have the cross."

The children got down with her to see her work. Mattie fidgeted around her. Sacri was not used to this much movement from children and waited for Mattie to settle before saying, "The pendant has many of these symbols, but this final one is the promise linking us." She pointed to the tree of hope she'd made. "This is a special symbol to me because, unlike others in my tribe, I was born above ground, under the Sacred Oak." She peered into the distance but they were too far away for her to point the oak out to them. "It lies at the heart of Sacred Land. Its roots link our life with our afterlife."

Clement studied the symbols. "I don't get it. How did dreaming about these symbols mean you'll marry a hero from a legend?"

No one ever believed her when she told them, but she knew. "Our stories about The Man of Legends are endless. But one story claims he won't be born on Sacred Land. He will travel here searching for something important, but what he will find is something of even greater value."

"Like a treasure?" Clement asked.

Mattie let out a long sigh, sitting back on her heels. "Love?"

Sacri shook her head. "No one really knows what, but my dream..." She pointed to the symbol for hope. "This is what I think he will find and he cannot find it without me."

Clement frowned. "A tree?"

She smiled. "Hope. Once he finds this inside himself, he will be ready to fulfill the promise and save Sacred Land."

"So will he be some brave warrior?" Again, Clement sat taller. "It might be me. I'm brave."

Sacri was lost in the storytelling. "He will be planted like this oak, protecting us, and nothing will move him. He will suffer his last breath at one with the soil he saved." She closed her eyes and the peace from her dream washed over her.

"So his hands will be full of magical symbols?" Clement

studied his own hands. "Shouldn't a warrior do something?"

Sacri nodded. "Oh yes! Legends foretell that he will fight the most feared mud monster the earth can summon. He will send ghosts on their way and be so strong that from the earth he shall raise a house. Warriors will lay down their lives for him."

Clement crossed his arms. "No one can fight a mud monster and there is no such thing as ghosts."

Mattie hit him on the shoulder. "That's what makes him legendary, goof."

Suddenly, Edgar towered over them. Sacri was so involved in teaching the children she had forgotten to watch for him. He stepped on her symbols and snagged her by the hair.

"Why are you brats talking to this mutt? Get or I'll smack you both."

The children scattered, but didn't go far.

Edgar tossed her, but Sacri was quick to her feet.

"Edgar, they have no mother to request their freedom but you and your brother have failed teaching these children. I ask for them; let another from your tribe raise these children. One who will give them the happiness they deserve."

He smacked her.

Sacri stumbled back, shocked by the hit. Her cheek stung, but she forced herself to face him again.

"Leave her alone!" Mattie yelled and rushed toward her with Clement tight on her heels.

Edgar glared at Clement. "Get her out of here." He faced Sacri again, pulled her up by the hair, and held a knife to her throat. She gripped the cross, prepared to die.

"This is the last time I ask before I cut limbs. Where are my diggers?"

She had no idea. They were long gone. Once they left the tunnels, they could end up anywhere.

She spat at him.

Small hands yanked his face back and Edgar let her go to wrap his hands around the boy clawing at him. Fast, Clement slipped out of his reach. Edgar chased after him, forgetting about Sacri while he pinned the boy.

"Mattie, you wait here." Sacri rushed to his aid.

Silver would have ended his life, but Sacri wished to save

this man's soul. "Face me and let the boy go."

His leg came up unexpectedly, slamming into her. She rolled as he attacked. Having never seen a man fight this way she wasn't sure how to defend herself. Her kicks and squirming did her no good, he'd strangle her with his powerful bare hands. When their eyes met, Sacri saw her past and her future, which forced her to reach for the comfort of the cross.

Edgar's eyes grew and he dropped her.

Quickly, she scrambled out of his reach. Edgar sucked in a strange breath and fell forward, struggling for air. As he tumbled forward, she saw why: he had a knife in his back.

Clement pulled the blade out and plunged it in again with a wild rage.

Mattie caught his hand before he could stab his father a third time. Blood was smeared on Mattie's dress and Clement's face.

Clement stared down at him calmly, Mattie at his side, even calmer.

Fear washed over Sacri. What was wrong with these children? Were they cursed? Was this normal in their tribe? Already the shadow clouded Clement's eyes. The anger she'd seen earlier... How would Clement fight such violent urges if his ruthless father shadowed his soul?

Sacri fell to her knees, praying for Mother to spare him. "He is a child," she wailed.

Silver would know how to remove the evil from him. She would drag him to Silver. He would help her protect the boy. Then they would teach the girl to sing to release her pain.

A strange nagging promised her this type of healing wouldn't be enough. She should kill them, yet Sacri pushed the notion away. They were children. She had to save them.

There had to be a way.

PART ONE

TEN YEARS LATER

"I cannot scream and yell for you so I sing my song of sorrow, unheard."

–Lacey

–ONE–

1892, Québec—

Alex and Wali crossed the bridge to Alex's new house. He couldn't wait to show Wali where he planned to live with Mattie, across the river, out of town, all hidden away in the bushes. They wouldn't need horses. It wasn't much farmland, so he'd be able to work it by hand. *Everything was perfect*, he lied to himself, hoping he'd soon believe it.

As they walked, Alex tilted his hat to Bellecoeur's strange nephew, Clement. The boy was always around Mattie but he never said much, just stared at the cross around Alex's neck as if he might one day snatch it.

Clement rushed over the bridge with his hands in his pocket, ignoring them.

"Is Mattie at the house?" Alex asked him. "I wanted you both to meet my friend, Wali."

Clement kept on walking.

"Come on, Clement, at least try. For Mattie."

Clement glanced over his shoulder, ready to say something.

Wali grabbed Alex's arm to keep him back since he was used to Alex fighting to make a point.

Clement's piercing green eyes bored into Alex. Then he rubbed the back of his left hand, showing off the strange teardrop tattoo he never wanted to discuss. Mattie said the marking was a curse made by a wild woman from when they'd travelled with their dear old daddies as children. This gal apparently killed Clement's father and Bellecoeur had vowed he'd destroy their entire tribe. Alex didn't doubt that, one day, he would. Bellecoeur was great for biding his time and waiting out his revenge.

After his intense stare, Clement left.

Wali whispered, "You sure got that boy all riled up. Who's the brat?"

Alex watched Clement trudge off. "Mattie's cousin. I told you about him. Bellecoeur raised him when his old man was murdered by some tribals. He has a servant who shadows him and as far as I can tell, he gets everything he wants. I'd like to tell you he's a spoiled brat, but…" Alex sighed. "I feel sorry for the guy. I told Mattie he could hang around since she's tight with him, and I hoped he'd warm up to me but he never says boo, as if talking to me is beneath him."

"Maybe you scare him." Wali chuckled.

"He told her once right in front of me that I was not her man of legends, or something weird like that." Alex forced a lump down his throat. He knew Mattie could do better. His gut tightened because no matter how she pushed him, inside, Alex knew who he really was. "Like everyone else, that cousin of hers thinks I have no future. Guy freaks me out, if you must know, but I try."

"For Mattie?"

"For him. He lost his pa and I know how that feels. We have something in common I hope will eventually bond us. I won't give up on him. He'll come around." Alex smirked. "I found his weakness the other night: he likes stories from the Bible. Come on, he must have walked Mattie over early." The air entered his lungs easier. "I can't wait for you to meet her."

"Whoa." Wali grabbed his shoulder. "Not so fast. This is our last week together as single men. I have a few things I'd like to talk to you about." Wali leaned over the railing of the bridge to peer at the foggy creek. "I know I've been busy these last few months, working weird hours at the distillery, then spending more time than usual volunteering at the clinic, but mostly just staying out of your way…"

Great. He planned to share his doubts about the wedding, too.

Alex leaned on the railing by Wali and watched the water ripple peacefully.

"I wish you'd wait a bit longer and make sure this is you thinking and not responding. This feels so…rushed."

"No fun in that. Besides, I worked hard to win this one over, and she likes me for me. She doesn't care about the drinking or all that past stuff. She sees me, not who I used to be."

"Used to? You've gone three months without booze, drugs, or an array of women, and you think you're a new man?"

His jaw tightened. "I am." Alex couldn't tell his best friend what had pushed him to stop drinking.

Sure, quitting was hard, but he was doing it, he lied to himself: something he was getting very good at doing. "Since I quit drinking, the world is a sharper place, full of new discoveries." He forced a smile, used to repeating this phrase to Mattie, but truth was, he dreamed about booze. He felt sick all the time. The world was not a sharper place—*he hated it*. He was drowning in his fears and failures. Alex desperately needed a drink and he was so weak, that when Wali turned to him with his sweet whiskey breath, he actually paused to smell it.

These doubts shadowed him. He wasn't good enough for the life he planned and it was only a matter of time before Mattie realized that. "No sex or booze for a few months will do that to a guy. You should try it."

Wali rolled his eyes. "Yeah, right. Not gonna happen. I like sex as much as I like my booze. Thank you very much." Wali was half-Chinese and looked Chinese, except for his sparkling blue eyes. The trait was the Montague family pride, and Wali liked to brag that such a blue meant they were trustworthy.

"You sure she isn't using you to annoy the old man? I mean, we work for the asshole. I know how wonderful telling him off properly would feel. If you go through with this, I will support you, but I want you to really think about it."

Alex translated for Bellecoeur, but Wali worked in the distillery, which meant he'd never actually met Bellecoeur, but he was victim of his poor wages and terrible working conditions.

"Bellecoeur was a wild man when he found out she'd agreed to marry me, but...I'll win him over, too."

"That is not a reason to marry her. Give me a better reason."

Alex was used to Wali's blunt ways.

"We're twenty-seven, Wali. Isn't it time we settle down? Shouldn't we do something with our lives that matters? This feels like it."

"Frankly, I'm tempted as hell to tell you to run. Something inside you doubts. I see it in the way you talk about her. You can't get your head out of her bosom long enough to admit it. I'm sorry, Alex, but you've been with her for three months and you've changed your entire life, which is fine, but not once have I seen love in your eyes."

"Love? What the hell is that? Grow up, Wali. Is that what you're waiting for? Guys like us, we don't get love. I'm lucky she even *likes* me. She looks at me and sees hope. I like the guy she thinks I can be."

"I know love. I know what it feels like to matter to someone. I promise, when someone loves you, they won't expect you to be someone else, you already are that guy." Wali's crystal blue eyes swelled with tears. Alex pretended he didn't notice. Wali had never admitted to finding love before and Alex wondered if this was a recent development. Maybe they were growing up.

Alex peered into the fog and confessed, "I like this guy standing here. I feel grounded. Happiness will come later."

Wali placed a hand on his shoulder and they stood like brothers, staring at nothing, yet somehow their past hung between them.

"Then introduce us. Maybe I'll change my mind once I meet her properly."

They walked south toward his land and Wali asked, "Do you smell…nothing, forget I said anything."

The fresh air was nice, but Wali was right, the skies had a bit of an unnatural, smoky haze that made Alex uneasy. His parents had died in a fire when he was a young boy. Everyone knew how nervous he was around fires. Wali especially didn't mention smoke. Of course, guys like Bellecoeur called him an over-sentimental fool and would light fires in his office fireplace to watch Alex squirm.

"They have some type of mill down the creek, must be from there. Hopefully it's not year round."

Wali slapped Alex on the back. "Despite my reservations,

I'm proud of you," he told Alex, a hanky to his nose. Wali had been sick for years and he'd taken all sorts of medication. The idea of losing him terrified Alex. Wali was the only real thing about his life.

Alex watched his friend pretend he was fine, as Wali wiped the blood from his nose.

"A man must grow up and get married eventually."

Wali chuckled. "I suppose most do, but I meant because you went through the entire day without beating anyone up. Not that shopping should be an adventure, but normally any outing with you is."

They'd had only one close encounter today but, sober, Alex had found the right words and hadn't needed to use his fists to protect his friend. "Someone has to stick up for you. Why are you always making yourself such an easy target? A guy like that only saw the bills in your wallet."

Wali shrugged. "He can have them. What do I need them for?"

"I don't know, food maybe."

"I've been saving up for a while, Alex. I sold a few paintings for a bit more than I thought I would, yet I see that money and wonder what the heck am I keeping my merger savings for? Might as well make someone happy with the little bit I do have." Wali lived with a carefree attitude that Alex envied.

Well, things were about to change. He gripped the keys, proud to start his perfect life. And every breath with Mattie would be perfect, he lied to himself again.

"I have better things to do with my hands these days than fight, so you better look out for yourself," Alex said. "You can't just invite anyone into your life or your bed. Think. If they come with a sob story or a great big WANTED poster on their back, walk away."

Wali frowned, serious. "I don't know how to tell you this, Alex…"

"Spit it out, we tell each other everything."

Wali nodded. "I'm leaving."

"Where to? For how long?"

Wali stared ahead, not talking while they walked.

Alex fished in his pocket to show Wali what he planned to

give Mattie. "While you gather your courage to tell me about your next misadventure, look at this." Alex pulled the gold cross from the lined box and dangled the chain for Wali to see. He'd decided to give it to Mattie for their wedding since she was always asking him to share stories about it. "My father's gold cross. My family heirloom will mean more than the stupid ring Bellecoeur told me to give her. I was too embarrassed to show you that paperweight."

The cross twirled in front of him.

"I bought the gold chain today. It's my wedding gift to her. The most important thing I own. Think she'll like it?"

Wali nodded without conviction. "I guess it's a good enough idea. Why not paint her something? Or carve her some candlesticks? A handmade gift would mean more."

"She never gets too excited about my paintings and carving sucks without you to chat with. I might give the hobby up."

Wali gripped Alex's arm. "You paint well. It's good for you to let go of your pain. Remember that."

"What pain? I'm content."

Wali opened his mouth and closed it again. Then he said, "You should paint more. I like how you mix in the symbols from your cross into images you see. At least promise me you'll hold onto something that made you who you are."

"Why? That me was a fool."

"This new fake you I can do without." He shook his head. "When life gets ya down, you reach into yourself and pull out an amazing person. In those paintings and carvings, I see your faith, I see your dreams, and I see your sorrows. Hell, I see myself in them. You matter, Alex, and don't ever think otherwise. You matter to me. Don't let her kill your soul. Someone who loves you would encourage your talent, because watching you create things with your hands gives me hope."

The cross was still in Alex's hand. Each engraving etched in the gold was a symbol, a language he wished he knew. "Hope?" he asked, doubtful. Hope felt like something impossible to create with his hands.

"Yeah. Think about it. What do we know about our history? Writers, artists, poets, and songwriters pass down our stories and have the power to shape them and see them anyway they want. Like some artist did with this cross you hold. They can leave us with an image of hope or despair. We can screw up, and make countless mistakes, but if you record just one moment when we were heroes, that's all anyone will ever know. When you carve and paint, I see a trace of who we want to be and you're leaving that behind." Wali shrugged. "Maybe it's me, and all the death I've been thinking about lately, but I like the idea of knowing that one day I might be gone from this world, but you'll leave my story behind in a hopeful way like that."

"Wow. Thanks, I guess. I've been singing," Alex confessed. "Mattie likes it. Kinda said the same thing as you, but sexier." He raised his eyebrows playfully.

"What'll Bellecoeur say about you giving her your cross?"

"Oh he'll hate the idea. Every time Bellecoeur sees it, he demands I toss it. So..." Alex smirked. "Since it drives him nuts, I'll give it to his daughter and sweetly ask her to wear the pendant all the time."

"Sounds like love. You enjoy torturing him far too much and now, you're playing on her young ignorance," Wali teased, since Mattie was eight years younger than they were. A guy could get into a lot of trouble in eight years.

Alex gently placed the antique in the box before he slipped the case in his pocket. He liked the idea of having won her over despite what Monsieur Bellecoeur had told her about him. "I feel good about this, Wali," he lied, because he had terrible doubts about everything. "Wait until you see the house Bellecoeur sold us. He's charging me a fortune to live there, but since he pays my wages, I figured I have to give his daughter the best."

"The oaf is charging you? All his money and he can't cut you some slack? Damn, I can spot you a bit of cash if you need it."

"I don't need your money, Wali. I'm fine." Another lie. He had to give Mattie every last cent he owned to pay for the wedding and the furniture. He didn't even have enough to pay for the gold chain he'd charged.

The smoky stench grew stronger. They marched on, not talking. Something was burning.

When they rounded the corner to his place, smoke rose out

the north side of his new house.

They ran toward his future home as flames consumed the entire right side of the house.

Alex could see Monsieur Bellecoeur's face and hear his cursed words: *I don't expect anything good from a drunk like you.*

Alex fell to his knees. He'd been close to proving him wrong. So close.

Wali placed a hand on his shoulder. "Breathe, Alex, it's fine. I'll run with these horses and get help. We'll snuff the fire out. The barn's standing. The buggy and horses are fine. There's furniture in the wagon. You guys will live with me until we fix this up again."

They watched the flames for a moment, helpless, then Wali added, "That creepy brat we passed on the bridge, you didn't tick him off to the point where he'd do something so…"

"Clement!" Alex jumped to his feet. "Mattie was with him!"

Alex scanned the farm for her. She'd be out here. "Mattie!" His scream vibrated over the rush of growing flames.

–TWO–

Two weeks later—

Alex met his friend's eyes, unconvinced. Wali rolled the paper out flat on his kitchen table—the table Alex had built as an engagement present for Mattie. Alex bit back the thought. Mattie was gone.

Alex pushed the two empty bottles of whiskey out of the way to look at the stupid handbill that had Wali so excited.

Everything was a bit blurry. Alex didn't understand what Wali was showing him with the handbill. It announced something about settling land out west. Something he didn't care about.

His friend sneaked a sip of Alex's whiskey before saying, "See how promising the District of Assiniboia is? How peaceful? If I stay in Québec, I'll have to break land, haul trees…you know, crap I don't need to deal with. On the prairies, the worst things I'll break my back over are a few rocks the Good Lord left for my house."

"You're moving?" Was this what he'd been trying to tell Alex on the bridge?

Wali stole another sip. "Damn, you have tasty whiskey. This from the distillery? No wonder Bellecoeur is swimming in cash. And just so you know, I sold two more paintings and told him to shove his job."

"I stole the bottles from him the day Mattie…" He couldn't bring himself to say 'died'. Instead, he studied the label. He'd drawn the design one night while he fought the cravings. It had the symbols from his cross, arranged around Bellecoeur's name. Mattie had been so proud; she'd given his work to her father, only he wouldn't use it until she told him that she'd made it. "Nothing belongs to me. Not sure how it happened." Alex shoved the paper toward Wali. "Look, I don't know what you want from me, but this is a stupid idea. You're not going west to farm. Sit and carve with me. I need to do something with my hands."

"Carve? You can't handle a knife. You're so blasted you can't even see me. And since when is farming a stupid idea? It was your idea."

"When I had a future, a wife to help me, and land. I don't know what I want, Wali, but it's not this life."

"You have land. Instead of a wife, you have me…a brother who is willing to take you on an adventure. You're suffering, but last time I saw you like this, my dumb idea worked. Do you trust me to get you out of this dark terrifying place or not, Alex?" His blue eyes promised fun.

Alex smirked. "We built your mother a house the last time you said I was in a dark place."

"We did because guys like us, we can do anything. I won't let you suffer this alone." He dropped their carving tools on the table. "For when I get back later. If you clean up while I'm out."

Alex touched the closest knife as if their friendship shimmered in the blade. The idea of being alone terrified him.

"We'll change the world into something better, but not with this." Wali pointed to the booze. The bottle grew between them into a giant shadow.

Alex needed to do something with his hands. "I wouldn't mind painting, but it's such an effort to get my things together." He took a deep breath. "I haven't even paid anything on my place, yet."

"Good. Let the lot go and buy land with me on the prairies. Think about my idea. An adventure beats sitting here getting stinking drunk."

"Since when do you farm?" Alex demanded.

"Since I saw this ad. Won me over, it did. Can you imagine? We'll start our own town with our own rules and values… A place we can call home." Wali grinned from ear to ear. "No bosses, no one judging us, just us conquering the New World."

"Sounds like running away to me," Alex mumbled to a bottle on the table.

Wali lifted one of the empty bottles. "I guess it is, but I figured you're first-class at running from things. It's fine. We'll stay and…and what, Alex? Drink ourselves stupid? We need a better plan."

"I had a plan."

"So did I, yet look at us."

Even though they lived together, Alex had no idea what his friend had been up to while he'd been winning Mattie's pa over. "What did you do these last few months? You were hardly here. Only slept in your bed about a dozen times. You find someone? Is this what you wanted to tell me on the bridge?"

"Just getting out of your hair so you could be alone with the boss' daughter."

"It wasn't like that," Alex lied to himself. "She was innocent and I promised God I'd change my ways for a perfect life with her."

"Yeah right. You telling me you never slept with her? Not once?" Wali winced.

Alex bowed his head, ashamed.

"Cripes, if you must lie to me, at least make it a lie I'll buy into."

"Don't talk about her." Alex threw the closest bottle of whiskey at the wall behind Wali. It shattered. Wali never even glanced at the mess.

"Breathe, buddy, get control of that temper. Maybe I should have invited some dames over for you and forgot the farming bit."

"There won't be another, Wali. I can't be trusted around women." Had Wali heard her cry out? "She said I was too rough," he admitted shamefully.

"So, you'll be a priest? Because throwing your cross to a lost cause like Bellecoeur might offend the Bishop."

Alex instinctively touched his neck for the cross. It was gone. Bellecoeur had his pendant. For months, Bellecoeur had nagged him about wearing the symbol of his faith. Told him only a fool invested his energy in a thankless God. Of course, when he proved to be right, Alex threw the pendant at him, chain and all.

"Just leave me alone."

"She's gone, Alex. She might have been shocked by how wild you are, but I happen to know a few gals who say no one compares to Alex Depaix in the sack. Want me to see what they're up to?"

The old Alex would have already brought them home. This new Alex had no idea if he could ever trust himself with a woman again, especially not if he was drinking.

"Damn, she messed you up good. We both need a break from this life. At least come see what type of trouble I get into." Wali pointed to the handbill. "We can do this."

Alex eyed the picture on the crumpled paper. A man held his wife around the waist. Smiling. Happy. It was not an image Alex needed and he pushed the paper off the table.

It floated silently to the floor.

Wali sat back in the wooden chair. Alex stared at the chair as memories haunted him. During the cold winter nights, while talking with Mattie, Alex had carved images on each spindle. Her cousin had chaperoned. Everything in the room reminded Alex of happiness he never did deserve.

He sipped the whiskey and offered Wali another round, then Alex peered out of the window at the trees. Trees he'd slipped away in with Mattie when Clement was busy and Wali was out.

He hated those trees. Everywhere he looked: Mattie. She haunted him, and nothing he'd ever done had been right for her. That hurt him the most; she'd deserved better than him. He gulped the whiskey. The burn it usually packed didn't affect him anymore. The sweet fuzziness he'd enjoyed last week was harder to find. He watched the booze swirl in the bottom of his cup, well, Wali's cup. Maybe the intoxicated feeling he craved was another form of escape.

He slammed the cup down with a crisp shake. No more running.

"What I see on this stupid piece of paper is empty promises. Night skies full of mosquitoes. Not worth the fight. Think about it. What would you do if you came face to face with a bison? They're enormous, Wali. Huge."

"Once upon a time, you were a guy who told me a dream

was always worth a fight. That guy was my best friend. I would have died fighting by him. I don't know who this guy is." Wali snagged the cup and looked at the whiskey in it, ignoring him. "I know you had a rough go lately. But no more booze." He pounded the last sip back so Alex couldn't. "If farming isn't it, we can do anything else. I'm up for any adventure. I have nothing keeping me here."

"Then go."

Wali took a fake swig of imaginary whiskey and peeked in the cup. He whispered, "Bellecoeur blamed you for her death, and you let him talk to you like that when you were with me all day. You know damn well you had nothing to do with the accident. The Alex I know would have punched him."

Wali let those words settle on the table before continuing. "I want you to come with me, to prove to yourself that you're not the mess Bellecoeur sees. Fighting will do you good. Since you met him, you're so focused on pleasing him, you don't see what's right in front of you. I tolerated your strange sucking up when Mattie was around because I thought you might be on to something, but I won't let the bastard bring you down anymore."

Alex leaned forward, his elbows on the table, something Mattie hated. Maybe Wali was right. He should have smoked Mattie's pa in the kisser. Why was he still trying to please the old grump? Why did he ever want to please him?

Eyes down, Wali picked up the handbill. "We need out of here. A fresh start." Wali tapped the paper in his hopeful way while he arranged it in front of Alex.

Alex shook his head. "From what I heard, the land is too tough to settle. The folk in Winnipeg aren't even brave enough to tackle those prairies and they are the toughest in the country. You're not looking well." Frankly, Wali was skin and bones. "I'm not stupid enough to get myself killed for land no one wants. You go if you're so excited about it. I'll go to work tomorrow."

"Work? You can't go back to work for her father. Have you lost your mind?"

Alex tightened his jaw to prove he didn't run from nothing. "I'll face her pa." He'd said that for two weeks, but each morning, the idea of facing Mattie's father made him pour another glass of whiskey. Maybe Wali was right, where had his fight gone? Had he ever had any? Sticking up for Wali wasn't much of an accomplishment, but it was about all he'd ever done that was worthwhile.

Alex took another sip but the cup was empty.

"You know what, Alex, if you go to work in the morning, I'll forget this entire idea."

Alex picked up the handbill and stared at it. Then he crumpled and tossed the paper toward the garbage. He missed and the paper ball bounced off the wall. It annoyed him that Wali bothered him with something so stupid. Go West. Why? Alex glanced in his cup and slammed it down when his stomach turned. Stupid.

"Mattie wouldn't want you to drink yourself away with booze you stole from her old man."

"You have no idea what Mattie would want."

"Considering you ain't drunk a drop since your first date, I have a good idea it wasn't to see you boozed up."

Guilt swelled inside Alex. On their first date, he'd taken Mattie dancing but got into a fight. She was upset with him and he'd wanted to prove that he was fun, so he brought her back to his place for a wild adventure… Only she hadn't told him that he was her first.

Most women liked how aggressive he was in the bedroom, but she had been innocent and he'd felt like a schmuck. More than anything, he'd wanted to make that night up to her. He'd wanted everything perfect for her so he promised to quit drinking and wait until they were married to sleep together again.

"You're a translator for a man you can't face and should have knocked out months ago," Wali complained. "I get that you were trying to win him over, but man, he was dragging you to a bad place. The snake is up to no good. Come with me. Let's find out if there is more to life." Wali was ready to leave, but he stopped in the doorway and peeked in the garbage can. "Remember when we were little gaffers and you punched that big bully who shoved me down 'cause he said Chinese folk belonged in the dirt?"

Alex had no idea where his friend was going with this. "I tend to block out my moments of intense rage and live in a blissful paradise of joyful illusions." He pointed to the bottles messing up their dump. "Clearly."

"Well, you were happy back then. Had things figured out. Do you remember what you said to him when you shoved *his* head in the dirt?"

A smile crept up on Alex even if he didn't want to feel happiness. Yeah, he remembered. "A fool spends his life pushing people in the dirt; a hero is just pleased he has dirt." Alex chuckled. "The expression was my pa's. Felt fitting." His dad had been an amazing farmer. Maybe wanting to follow in his footsteps explained why he'd hoped to farm with Mattie so desperately. Maybe he'd been searching for one idea that was his, that gave him a sense of himself in her list of rules for who he had to pretend to be.

"You smiled." Wali grinned back. "Come with me, we'll search for happiness in the dirt. Can't find more beautiful dirt than this place they call District of Assiniboia."

Guilt flashed over Alex for laughing. He shouldn't be happy. "Happiness was within my reach, and I lost it."

"Mattie—"

"Don't talk about her." Alex's entire body tightened as grief invaded him again. He'd had his life planned out and God had stolen it. Gone. God played with him, torturing him for pleasure.

"How you handle her death is the testament of who you want to be. Think about your actions. Be the man she was proud to call her future husband, not the drunk her father sees."

"I feel like a ghost, not a man. All wispy inside, as if I don't exist anymore. I want the grief to end," he finally admitted. "Yet I won't let her go."

Wali shoved his hands in his pocket. "You mad at God for taking her from you?"

"Now you bring God into this?"

"Are you?"

Alex inhaled deeply, touching his neck, used to finding the comfort of the cross around it, but it was bare and this bothered him.

Wali watched his fingers. Alex wondered what Wali thought behind those lively blue eyes. Did everyone blame him?

"Yeah. I hate God. I wish He'd take me, too. You happy now? Bellecoeur was right. I was a fool to believe in such things."

"I sat where you are, Alex, and I hated God, too, then a good friend of mine, God rest his soul, said hating God wasn't an option, accepting His challenge was the only way to fight back. I figured you'd understand something that serious."

Fighting back against God? The rage burned up in him. Yeah, getting even did sound like something Alex wanted. "Your friend died? Who? Is this who you were seeing? Who you fell for?"

Wali clenched his jaw, the pain of his loss close.

"I'm sorry, Wali. Was it Ben?" He'd only met him once. He'd picked Wali up in one of those steam-powered vehicles. "What happened to him? He looked tough enough to fight a pack of wolves."

"Yet a cough did him in."

"Why didn't you tell me? Why do you insist on cutting me out of your life sometimes? You're a brother to me, Wali. Do you think I care if you have other friends? The idea of you finding even a moment of happiness means the world to me."

Wali faced the wall, studying a picture Alex had drawn. Mattie must have pinned it up. Familiar shapes mixed on the canvas, telling a story about a boy surviving a fire because of his best friend. His story poured out in images of flames, games, grass, tears, and a kind mother watching out for him. Wali's mother would have liked the picture and Alex had remembered her while painting in a wild drunken bliss one evening. He had no idea where Mattie had found it. Or maybe Wali had dragged it out.

"We were more than friends, Alex." Wali was clearly crying as he faced the picture. Alex hadn't meant to hurt him.

He brought a bottle to Wali. "It helps to pitch these at the wall."

Wali yanked the bottle from him and placed it gently on the counter.

"I'm sorry. How can I be there if I don't know? You should have told me. When did he die?"

"I don't have to tell you anything, Alex. Friends are just

there when they need each other." He faced Alex. "Ben needed someone to sit with him while he died. I didn't need to drag you into our grief before your wedding. I… One day I hope my best friend will sit with me, but this requires a strength I don't see in you." He stormed out, slamming the door. Alex didn't run after him, the guy was more resilient than Canadian thistles and clearly all this death had worn him down. He'd come back.

"You can find a better companion than me for your adventure," Alex called after him. "And for your dying days." He ran his hand over his unshaven jaw as his thoughts jumbled. When was the last time he'd shaved? He couldn't remember. Ate? Probably longer.

Alex picked up the balled up handbill that had Wali so excited and tossed the paper in the garbage. Then he stared at it. An envelope along the side of the trash caught his attention. He snagged it. Wali had printed WEISSES BLUT on the back then scribbled over the words madly. Alex had no idea what those words meant, but an uneasy dread washed over him as he realized this was from a doctor. What if Wali was dying?

Confused, terrified, he stumbled out to the creek that ran by their place.

It was almost sunset, and every night, as the sun set, he sang to Mattie by the water's edge. He had no idea what he'd sing, but when he settled in, the words would come. He'd chant of sorrow, of ideas, of dreams, he'd sing in any language the fit took him, and his words would be for her because she had loved it when he sang to her. He was too shy to sing for anyone else.

Tonight, he gathered by the water and told her through song how terrified he was that Wali might be dying. The words rolled out in a melody, pulling the grief from the depth of his soul, and placing his sorrows on the creek to float away. When he finished, he fell on the muddy bank and let the cold earth ooze around his fingers. If only the earth could suck away the aches inside him and bear the grief for him.

He had drifted off when Mattie's sweet voice whispered, *"The cross. You will need the protection it offers."*

-THREE-

Monsieur Bellecoeur pulled Alex into his office. He shut the door and motioned for Alex to sit. There were three seats. Alex normally took the hard uncomfortable one reserved for translators. A creature of habit, he perched on the edge of the seat, waiting for Mattie's pa to sit across from him.

He was a snake of a man and his shadow loomed over Alex, but he didn't sit. He coiled in the corner, ready to strike. In French, Bellecoeur said, "Things have changed around here. It's best if you moved on."

Looking at the desk, Alex digested this news.

Fired.

How would he pay for his land if he didn't have a job? A well-paying job like this would be hard to find.

Oh. The truth tightened around him, suffocating him. On top of everything else, he'd have to give the land back.

"I know how hard things have been for you, son." His voice slipped on 'son', as if he regretted saying it, but the word was out, a habit Monsieur Bellecoeur had grown accustomed to over the last month, especially around clients. "My nephew will replace you."

"Clement? He doesn't even speak, how can he translate for you?"

"I don't need a translator. I have land that savages won't give up and he has something they want. Nothing for you to do around here anymore. I'm packing up and moving my operations to Moose Jaw." A long pause followed as Bellecoeur slithered around the room, judging him. "I was in Moose Jaw this past week and they need a guy to shovel coal. The pay is half what you made, well, maybe less than half. I wouldn't slip in a good word for just anyone, but *my* Mattie would want me to do well by you. Despite the religious crap you had her believing and despite my warnings about dirt like you."

Alex was used to Bellecoeur calling down his religion and well, everything about him. Frankly, his fearful attitude used to amuse Alex. Now, the mocking stung. Guys like Bellecoeur were good at squeezing the life from him. The fact that Alex didn't jump up to set him straight was a cold reminder of how beaten he felt.

"I regret hauling you out of the bar to work for me."

And there it was. He liked to rub it in Alex's face that when Bellecoeur found him, he was stone drunk with his hand up a blouse or two. Bellecoeur had reminded Mattie every time he saw her, too. Snakes were helpful like that. Lucky for him, Mattie hadn't cared about his past, even though Alex had a hard time letting those memories go.

"I've come a long way since then," Alex reminded him. "Despite your beliefs, I held firm to my own."

"See, that's part of the problem. I chose you. I wanted a guy to shut up and do the job. Who better than the local drunken Romeo? I did not get one decent reference for you. Yet you surprised me and I am not easy to surprise. When you sobered up, it was clear you thought for yourself, then Mattie was in the picture and I couldn't toss you out without a scene."

Bellecoeur liked to maintain a thoroughly respectable image. Alex had no idea who he tried so hard to impress. If Alex wanted to stay, he could throw a fit, yell about being fired after losing his almost-wife. Bellecoeur would backtrack to the shadows to save face. Yet his pride forced him to sit like a lump while Bellecoeur stole everything away from him one stroke at a time.

"I have no reason to keep you. Shoveling coal is the best I can offer and where scum belongs."

Alex swallowed the lump in his throat. "In Moose Jaw?" He was being offered a sympathy job.

"It's on the prairies. I'll be there, if you need anything." He handed Alex a bottle of whiskey. "Despite the plans I had for you, I grew to like you, and it bothers me that you're under my skin like this. I had your type figured out yet you did impress me, too bad it didn't last."

Alex handled the bottle, thinking about the story in the Bible where the snake hands Eve the apple that ruins her. It had the newest label he'd sketched. From the *Sacred Land* batch.

"You're selling booze on the prairies?" Alex asked.

Bellecoeur smirked. "Growing the grain there, making my poison there, and storing the cases there, actually. There are rumours of prohibition in the wind and I'm saving my business. Always be ahead of the crowd, Alexandre. The way I see it, this prohibition could go either way."

Was this why he wanted him in Moose Jaw? Did he think he might need him? "I'm confused. If booze is illegal, how do you plan to make such a venture profitable?"

"Only a guy with his head stuck in a bible would see forbidden things as a closed door instead of an opportunity."

Alex understood. If making booze was illegal, and he had a bunch handy, each bottle would sell for double the price. Bellecoeur could shut down his distillery operations and save face with his other businesses while dabbling in underground sales. His regular business deals would look like all was on the up and up.

The guy was so dirty, really, it wouldn't surprise Alex if he'd started the cries for prohibition himself.

Alex shot up and gently placed the bottle on the desk. He faced his almost-father-in-law. Monsieur Bellecoeur gripped the doorknob, creating a lifeline to the real world.

Should he beg for his job back? His cross? Take the job in Moose Jaw? Where was Moose Jaw? Sounded like the last stop on his oblivion ride.

Maybe he should punch him.

It was what he felt like doing so many times but he'd behaved for Mattie. He would have died for her had God given him the chance. His fists clenched, but somehow, a punch would have been stooping to Bellecoeur's level.

He could be a man about this. Chin up, Alex said, "You were like a pa to me, Monsieur Bellecoeur, not a perfect one, but you did fine in your own way. I'm returning your titles. I appreciate everything you did for Mattie and me so we could have a nice life. It would have been perfect." His voice was even and warm, but his insides twisted. "Perfect."

The snake in the grass nodded, his long fingers rubbing together. The crinkles along the side of his eyes slithered inward. "It was perfect, wasn't it? Maybe you learnt something, Alexandre. God didn't promise you happiness. I did. The moment you decided to vow before Him, you lost it all. So I ask you, my boy, where is your God now? You know, if you crawl back to me, I might take pity on you. But I only tolerated the religious crap because Mattie asked me to be civil with you. She deserved one moment of happiness. Saddens me she thought she'd find this joy with the likes of you. Yup. Where is your God?"

"On the prairies." The words poured out before he could catch himself, but his instinct was to snap at Bellecoeur when he called down God. Alex touched where his cross should be, feeling the protection it used to offer against devils like this.

"You should fit right in. I'll stop by to see you when I settle in Moose Jaw. Maybe we'll share a few." He paused, his lips sneering up, reminding Alex that he didn't drink. Never touched a drop as if booze were pure poison. "I'm sure you'll be my best customer." He pulled a paper with an address from his pocket and slipped it to Alex.

Alex didn't reach for it. Instead, his fists tightened. He took a quick breath to keep control, not wanting his last conversation with this man to be one of pity or blame. They would part ways as civilized men.

Bellecoeur shook his head, disgusted with Alex. "It should have been you."

Well, they agreed on one thing.

"I want my cross back."

"I gave your trinket to Clement." His answer was a quick strike.

Alex stepped forward. "Why?"

"Like I said, he's getting land from savages and he needs the girlie trinket to do it." He smirked. "I think he has a woman there. Amuses me, that boy."

"It was a gift from my father before he died."

"Poor man with poor taste."

This deflated Alex's anger. Only a petty man would call down a dead man he didn't know. It wasn't worth the fight.

His father had been ten times the man Bellecoeur was. Alex didn't have to defend his honour; he'd make him proud by living his example.

Alex ducked out without another word, leaving with just the clothes on his back, his fight gone.

Wali wasn't home yet and Alex didn't know where he went anymore. He'd lost touch with his best friend these last few months. How fast life could change.

Alex waited by the creek for Wali, watching the clouds travelling west. Even the clouds thought it was a swell idea.

It was late when Wali joined him. They sat side by side, staring at the water.

"I punched the snake," Alex lied.

"About bloody time you faced your demons and let your fear push you forward instead of down." Wali looked too pleased. "Tell me about it."

"I'm off to Moose Jaw. I swung by the library to find out where this city is. Well… It's on the prairies, by the land you hope to farm. So looks like we're going on your adventure."

"What's in Moose Jaw that has you this fired-up?"

"My cross. I want it back. The pendant was my pa's and the snake gave it to Clement, who is now in Moose Jaw. Bellecoeur can't be right about any of this. He can't."

Wali smirked. "So we'll prove him wrong about his lack of faith in God, or in you?"

"Maybe a bit of both."

"Good. It scares me when you lose faith. It's the only respectable thing about you." Wali clutched a bottle in his hand. He studied it long and hard. "This won't be easy. Think we could make a pact and stick to it? No boozing, no distractions, and by that I mean we keep our pants on."

"You're on. No booze, pants on until we get there." He pulled the bottle from Wali's grip. "For both of us."

"Deal. Come in, I'll make us a bite."

-FOUR-

On the prairies—

Sacri rode with Jon behind her. He clutched around her waist, perhaps too tight.

Shocked by the scene before her, Sacri slowed the mare. Prairie fires had blazed through while she was in Moose Jaw. Much of the Cursed Lands were destroyed. The fire had spread toward Sacred Land. Sacri squinted to see if flames had reached the Sacred Oak, but much to her relief, her symbol of hope stood strong in the distance.

As she studied things, Jon's hands wandered over her breasts. She pushed his hands down and stopped the mare. "Get off," she ordered. He slipped off the horse and offered to help her, but Sacri ignored his outreached hands, taking her time to dismount.

She'd seen many fires over the years, but the destruction she saw before her now was particularly familiar. This was from her dream. She inhaled deeply. The air tasted putrid. She took a second deeper breath. Finally, after all these years, her waiting would pay off. She expected a twinge of hope, or perhaps joy, but she was uneasy and Jon had a way about him that pushed her to rush.

She forced a smile at Jon, ready to teach him about her people.

He sneezed, wiped his nose on his sleeve, and brushed back his long black hair. He was Chinese, from a land far away. Everything about him fell into place.

"How much farther?" he asked.

She waited at the edge of the ruined prairies for him. With an annoyed sigh, he joined her. She taught quickly, because

Jon was impatient. "The blessed lands are divided into many areas, such as Healing Lands or Cursed Lands." She pointed in the direction of each. "Each part of the blessed lands offers bountiful promises to my tribe, but Sacred Land..." She paused for a moment and stared at it. He looked with her. "*Cîpay* are born and buried there."

"What's that?"

"My tribe is known as Ghosts of the Earth. Each of the sacred tribes who live on blessed lands has a different name. Each of these tribes believes that we live many lives until one day we earn the right to be *Cîpay*. We then merge our souls with Mother and live at peace with Her forever, answering Her cry when needed."

"You come here to be born and to die? I wouldn't be telling too many about this, makes you weak."

He was right. They were in trouble because settlers had moved onto the blessed lands. Yet she had to give him hope so that he would fight for her. "Not weak. It is where the ancients meet and ancestors speak. All souls go through this land and make us stronger. Sacred Land is the center of the earth, where Mother rests."

"Well, your land is in a shit mess." He shook his head disgusted.

"It is not lost," she promised him.

"I suppose not." He fell to his knees beside her and Sacri prepared herself. This was it. The moment from her dream. He would move aside the damaged grasses and discover new life.

He ran a hand up her naked leg and slipped under her pelt skirt. She jumped and pulled away. "What are you doing?"

"We're alone. What do you think I'm doing?" He tickled a hand behind her knees and yanked her down, tumbling her to the ground. He squirmed over her.

Disgusted, Sacri pushed him off and he rolled beside her. He had the lace to her dress in his hand and dangled it teasingly. "Want me to tie you up?"

She was horrified. No. This was a sacred moment. They could not do these things until she moved her mat beside his. What was he doing? She pulled her dress together, shocked that he'd undone her straps so quickly. He was skilled with his hands. Of course, she knew the Man of Legends would be. Yet in the dream, there was no touching with his hands, only images. He would kiss her soul with these images. His hands should be full of magic, not want.

She grabbed his hands to check for the magic but a silver flash from Sacred Land caught her attention and she jumped up. "No!"

Jon let out a gasp as his hands flung to his neck. An arrow lodged in it. His eyes grew huge as he fell back, staring at her. Blood pooled around his fingers.

She dropped beside him, one hand over her mouth, the other against her stomach as she watched his life return to Mother.

On her knees, Sacri wept at his side.

Silver joined her but she ignored him, feeling the pain deep in her soul.

"What did you do to your necklace?" Silver demanded of Sacri.

She glanced up at her brother. He glared, blocking the sun. He always seemed bigger when he was angry with her.

"You killed the Man of Legends," she accused him, touching the cross around her neck, wondering what her brother could see.

He didn't acknowledge Jon. "Do up your dress."

She grabbed the lace from Jon's fingers and fixed her dress while her brother went to her horse.

"What did you do to your necklace?" he demanded again. "It has a link to another. Like a fine thread connecting them." He pulled her satchel off the horse and searched it for the other cross.

She'd held them together, to compare them, but that was all she'd done. How did he always know when she hid something from him? "I wanted to surprise you."

He pulled out the golden chain Clement had given her and studied the dangling cross, admiring how the gold caught the sun. The pendant was identical to hers. Only hers was on a leather lace.

"I found it in the Moose Jaw tunnels when I saved Jon." She didn't mention Clement since Silver did not like her talking to Clement. "It is a gift. From sister to brother."

He frowned but gripped the chain. "Who wore this?" His tone implied he was going hunting.

"You killed the Man of Legends. He was to save our most blessed of lands. Look at the horizon. This is the image from my dream. He knelt before the destruction and he..." Nothing else was there from the dream. Hope from the dream had pushed her forward all these years and it was not here. She felt nothing but hurt. "He is gone."

"If this was the man you search for, we are doomed."

She bowed her head.

"Sacri, a man Mother chooses to protect Her land must be weathered, strong, and skilled with his tongue. He must be willing to die for this land. There must be something in his soul that stems from the dawn of our existence. He is a hero who Mother created and will summon to duty when She feels all others have failed Her." He shook his head. "He would not be so easy for me to kill." He gripped the necklace. "In fact, killing him would prove impossible."

She kept her head down. "I planned to make him this man."

"You cannot make someone *Cîpay*. This connection comes from here." He knelt and touched the soil. "This is an honour. This vow comes with responsibility. The earth links to the soul of each *Cîpay*, forcing them to dig down and embrace who they are. When a *Cîpay* ceases to use their body to breathe, it is because the earth breathes for them. They are eternally one with the land we protect. You cannot imagine the strength required for someone not born on Sacred Land to make this connection. He would be a gift from Mother Herself. A true warrior in his heart. There is no hiding who you are inside, not from me. It is why Mother has given me the gift of Sight."

"My dream said he would have a way with words and images not fists. He will be skilled with his hands. He is not a warrior like you, but he'll find this bond. Others less worthy have."

Silver broke into a full smile as if she proved his point. "I respect those with a pure soul and a solid link to the earth. This liar had neither and used you to spy for Bellecoeur. He would not have protected us from droves of white men and had already traded you for money." He dug in Jon's pocket and pulled out bills he tossed to her.

She felt like a fool, but she believed what her brother had seen in Jon's soul, even at a distance.

Silver dropped his bow beside her and sat with her by Jon. His long legs rested on the sacred soil. "Where did you find this one?"

"In the tunnels under Moose Jaw. He worked for half the wages of white men then paid most of his earnings for room and board. He was skilled with his tongue and taught others English. Everything fit with the legend. I have to find him, Silver. Time is running out." Her heart was heavy. Tunnels connected each of the sections of land, allowing warriors from the Ghost tribes freedom to travel in the heart of winter to Sacred Land. If Sacred Land was lost, the souls of her entire tribe would vanish. Now that settlers came in great numbers, they couldn't keep their land safe and, unlike other areas where Ghost tribes could join with other Native tribes, they were alone to protect Sacred Land. There were no others to help them blend in.

"We need someone from their side to explain it to them. Those tunnels are for our safety, but others copy them, use them for not good things. Not good. This disrespect is a mockery of our traditions and it pains the earth the way we mistreat each other."

Silver bowed his head. "Sacri, I had my own vision." The men of her tribe had a different coming of age ceremony. He was only allowed to share the visions or dreams. "A white man will find the ceremonial pipe, then I will die. Not by his hands, but to save him."

Sacri frowned. "Why would you die for a settler?"

"The real question is why would one find the ceremonial pipe when I hide it?" He studied his hands. "I have more blood from their tribe on my hands than any other warrior, yet I know one will be worth giving my life for. The only outsider who could be this is…"

"The Man of Legends." She placed her hands on her stomach. Finding him meant Silver would die. She glanced at Jon, relieved it wasn't him.

"A pipe smoking ceremony requires acceptance from the other warriors. Do you think Menashen or Louis would have passed this guy the sacred pipe?" His eyes tightened as he glared at her. "They would have challenged him and he would be dead by their hands instead of mine."

"Do you believe we will find the Man of Legends?"

"The path is so set, Sacri, that I am already dead."

He was right. The dream had left her with such a sense of fullness. She told herself that finding him would save her tribe, but truth was that she wanted to fill the emptiness inside her. She tried to explain this to her brother, but couldn't because she didn't want to see him die either. "Many ask me to move my mat beside theirs, yet I wait. Because in the dream I was Sacri a woman full of life. The woman before you is dead like these grasses. Like you, when I meet the Man of Legends this me will die and my new life will begin."

"Precisely. Do not insult me by bringing me weeds like this married fool." Silver left.

Jon was married? Linked to another? She bowed her head.

Sacri trusted what her brother had seen and shuffled away, disappointed, leaving Jon's body for Mother to deal with.

The creek was nearby and she rushed to the tunnel.

Maybe there was no man. Maybe Mother forgot to send him and Sacri would have to protect Sacred Land herself.

Sacri rolled into the bushes and took the tunnel.

She planned to surface at the Sacred Oak so she could pray there, where her connection to the earth was strongest.

"Where were you?" Paniya cut her off, with her annoying stance of a Chosen One. "I ran into Silver and he was so furious he wouldn't look at me. You didn't go off on one of your free-the-slaves expeditions, did you?"

Sacri considered setting her straight with a fist then stepped back. She was young and had a lot to learn. Paniya rubbed her growing belly, reminding Sacri of her sacredness.

Paniya hung around Louis. He'd taken to teaching her in a very fatherly way that confused the other women. Should they respect her as a woman or teach her as a child? Most ignored her, in fear that Louis would correct them. Of course, Sacri was not afraid of Louis and if he was teaching this woman, she would, too.

As a Chosen One, Paniya had a tremendous responsibility.

Her child would be a Child of the Earth. A possible leader of the Ghosts tribes. They needed a leader, but it was impossible to believe that this woman would raise such a warrior. She had much to learn before her child was born.

Then again, as a Chosen One, all the warriors would train her child, blessing him or her with the skills of an entire tribe, not one father, but many.

No man was worthy of sharing her mat until the child was born and he would have to agree to let the best warriors train the child.

It was a joke. Nothing about Paniya was chosen. Yet Silver had said this, and he was impossible to argue with.

Still, Sacri knew the truth. Several months ago, shortly after Paniya had arrived, she was picking berries and Sacri heard her scream. Sacri had chased a white man off her. She suspected this was the reason for the growing belly. She had no proof, but she wasn't stupid either. Nukum had told that her children were gifts from Mother, but Sacri knew babies did not grow by a gift from Mother; a man had been needed to grow the baby inside her.

Before she could share this fact with her brother, he announced that the child had been sent by Mother. Silver told her that until the child was born, Paniya was a Chosen One, with life inside her and Sacri was to protect her from anyone who might not respect the vow. He meant the settlers, because the Ghost tribes would respect it. None were foolish enough to disappoint Silver.

"In Moose Jaw, I found a not good man who thinks he owns people. I set him straight and freed his workers," Sacri explained, hoping she would understand the tasks she would soon have to teach her child.

"By yourself? You are foolish. No wonder Silver is constantly shadowing you and has no time for a wife." She leaned in to inspect Sacri's pendant. "It glows. How?"

Sacri covered her necklace. She didn't want Paniya looking at it.

"He's not out there, you know?" Paniya sneered. "This Man of Legends you seek. You'll never become *Cîpay*. You're so stupid you don't even know how to read the dream properly. Everyone is talking about you. Sacri, the stupid legend chaser. They say the man you seek will lure you in with his charm. Give me the necklace. I want it."

"Mind your place." Sacri glared.

"My place? You think you're so noble because your brother is Silver? I begged and pleaded him to accept my mat by his and he wouldn't even look at me." The words gushed out of her and she fell to her knees in tears. "He refused me. You know why, Sacri? Because he has a settler's woman who he steals away with. He dishonours our people."

Sacri chuckled. "I doubt that." Still, she had no idea Silver had turned Paniya down. Was she lying? "You watch your tongue, for you were lured by a demon, and Silver cannot help it if he sees this in you."

"Demon? Sacri, help me. I am confused by your teachings." Paniya cried into her hands then pressed her tear-stained hands into the dirt and wailed for Mother to protect her.

Needing to escape the drama, Sacri left for the Sacred Oak. She wasn't good with other women, especially young ones not raised on Sacred Land. She wasn't sure where Paniya came from but it was from the north. Beyond where she'd travelled.

The men of the tribe were better friends. Except at the end of the day, they always wanted to share her mat, and some were hard to refuse.

She didn't know why Silver had turned away the girl. Normally, if a woman of their tribe carried life, she could pick any available warrior and he didn't refuse. Still, she suspected Silver had refused a few women over the years. Sacri found warriors always waiting for her to choose them and she wasn't even with child. She might not be able to give them a child.

Still, the idea was distressing. What if Sacri found the Man of Legends and this hero didn't want her? Then everyone would know she'd misread the dream.

–FIVE–

Sacri strolled, with her head down, toward the creek. From the shadows of the tunnel, Menashen stepped forward, cutting her off. He was younger than her but always asking to share her mat. "Sacri. What are you up to today?"

He walked with her. She told him about the man she'd found and how Silver had killed him. She tried not to look at him, for Menashen was nice to see.

"Sacri," he grabbed her arm, "why don't you forget this legend bullshit and let me take care of you?"

He was taller than she was, and in better shape than Silver, but she avoided his eyes. When she was with him, she felt excited and sexy, but the emptiness inside her did not change.

She grazed the tattoo for bravery on his chest. "I cannot ignore my destiny, and I do not need you to care for me."

He sighed. "Nichena asked to move her mat by mine. I hesitate because of you."

She knew this day would come. She'd turned down many warriors over the years, but Menashen was the hardest to see go. "She is a wise woman and has chosen the best warrior. Go, be a worthy husband."

He reached to touch her and pulled his hand away in a tight fist. He nodded. "It angers me that another is worthy of you yet I am not. I would give my life for you, Sacri."

"I would never ask this of you."

He gently ran a finger on her chin. "You will never have to." He vanished into the shadows of the tunnel. She was sorry to see him go, but Nichena was worthy.

Still, she stared after him for a long time, in case he came back.

A voice from her right startled her. "Hard to turn some

guys down." Louis was a new bachelor. He was older than she was by three summers. Silver's age. His wife had died during the winter from a horrible cough. Sacri had sat with her but his wife's suffering never let up. He missed her. Sacri missed her. She had been nice to talk with.

Older warriors like Silver and Louis were rare, even rarer that they sought wives. Sacri liked to talk with Louis. His companionship was welcome, and he was smart.

She confessed to him. "I wonder sometimes, if I make mistakes. I will be twenty-eight summers old soon. Already, I have lost a child before he was born. Will the Man of Legends want me if I cannot give him children?" She sighed. "I turn down warriors who make me feel so special. What if he's not this way? Am I foolish to trust in something so impossible?"

He thought about this. "Imagine if he is more than this. Feeling special is good, but we both know Menashen has a lot of growing up to do. You would have spent more time asking me to smack him behind the head than it's worth." He sighed. "Sacri, I have boys to raise and protect. If you want to help me while you wait," he stepped into the thin light so she could see he held food for his family that he'd caught. He was a desirable provider. "Know I will step aside when you ask, but I would appreciate the help."

A frantic need to comfort him swept over her yet she watched him suffer alone.

"I am always here to help you raise your boys. They are family. If they need a mother, I am sure Nichena or Paniya would care for your boys if you are lost in battle."

"They had a mother. Paniya is a child herself and needs guidance, not more responsibility. Nichena will be with Menashen if he ever stops dreaming about you. Besides, I don't want him teaching my boys. He's a dependable warrior, but his pride gets in the way. Not sure he'll ever grow up and see the big picture."

He was saying she was the best warrior to teach his boys and she was honoured. "If I am your choice, you have my word. I will be there for them when you cannot."

"Thank you. This is what I needed to hear. Sacri, I'm terrified to go back into battle, because I can't leave them alone. You could move your mat beside mine without ever sharing mats. I would find comfort in knowing they have someone to raise them. Think about it."

She didn't know many men with that type of self-control yet she trusted Louis and if she moved her mat, others would leave them alone. It wasn't a rotten idea, but she wanted to pray on it.

"They are never alone. We are Ghosts of the Earth, Louis. Linked through the power of Sacred Land. I enjoy your company but I will move my mat once, and this act will be final."

"I respect that, Sacri."

She stepped away and climbed out of the tunnel onto the prairies. She held her hands on the Sacred Oak growing alongside the water. Scarred by the fire, it would survive. She felt safe by the old tree.

Sacri stared at the damage, her prayers lost on her mute lips. This was the image from her dream, she was sure of it. So sure, she expected the Man of Legends to appear on the horizon.

Yet he was not here.

He was never here.

She fell to her knees and cried against the tree where she was born. Her mother's gentle voice comforted her, "*Believe.*"

Believe. In what? A legend? A dream? A stupid story?

Frustrated, she ripped the cross from her neck and threw it in the darkened grasses. All her sacrifices and for what?

She'd lost the chance to have a family, to make friends.

Alone, she cried with her hands in the earth and on the tree. Her tears were flowing freely when Silver placed his hands on her head. The leather lace was in his hand and the cross dangled against her forehead. "Do not remove the cross. It will bring you much joy."

"What does that mean?"

He shrugged. "I explain not what I see, I only see." He brushed the golden chain he wore around his neck. "Who gave you this cross? Your link to him is strong."

She didn't dare lie to him a second time. He had to know it was Clement. "Do you see the link?"

He nodded and raised an eyebrow. "It is a fun one. Makes me want to kill him and hug him at the same time. I was confused at first, but he might be someone I need to meet. A link like this means happiness is in your future."

Fun? He'd never called the link she shared with Clement fun before. In order to save Clement, Sacri had taken the burden of his father's shadow into her by using the *Cîpay* tattoo for judgement. The teardrop tattoo on the back of Clement's hand and the one on her side linked their souls. Silver had been furious and sent Edgar's soul to Cursed Land. She'd tried to explain this to Clement but he'd been so young he'd thought she was punishing him and wouldn't talk to her. To calm him, she promised she would help him be a suitable father to his own son or she would find his children a new father. She was bound to the promise.

Why would their link change? "Explain the link to me."

"A soul has fine threads extending out, and sometimes, those threads grow and embed in others. Sometimes, they find a soul they like and tie themselves to it. This one here," he touched the air, moving his hand over nothing, "this is the link to Clement. This fine line is faded and dark, scary, and troubled, promising hardship and pain. But this one." His hand ran along the invisible cord. "This is magical. I rarely see this type of link in others. So many colours, so full of life. This connection digs into you like the roots from this oak. I want to meet him. This is the soul you should bring to me."

She was amazed that he saw these things in her soul. "I have another link? When did this happen? How?"

He frowned. "You mean you have no idea who? You should, the colours swirling inside you are of hope and love. Whoever gave you this feeling is—"

She shook her head, cutting him off. "He is just a dream. I believe and wish for the Man of Legends so hard, I must have created this when I handled the necklace. I am sorry to disappoint you, there is no man."

He frowned, studying the air. "Let me teach you what I learnt." Silver placed a package between them.

She wiped her tears to see what he'd found. He unfolded the cloth, one corner at a time as if it contained a magical secret. Finally, he revealed a bread.

She tasted the bread, savouring a sweet honey texture. "Did you make this?"

"It was a gift. I was like you; so caught up in my destiny to protect Sacred Land, I almost missed out on something magical." His smile widened, taking her by surprise.

Magical? Had he linked his soul to another? "You look happy."

He lay back in the ashes, clearly pleased, but she didn't understand his teachings.

"Paniya says she chose you and you turned her away."

"She is a Chosen One, off limits. The elders ordered this."

"We both know there are no elders. You invented this lie. You lead this tribe. Admit to the responsibility you have."

"I lied to protect her. She is too young, and no warriors coupled with her. Means someone attacked her. If others learn this, panic will spread. You should teach her how to be a mother. She lost hers when she was young. Her father did not know what to teach."

"What do I know about being a mother? I don't even have a mate."

"I could point out many warriors who think you would make an excellent mother. Perhaps the question is why are you turning away perfectly acceptable suitors like Menashen or Louis?" He didn't wait for her answer. "These are things we have no need to discuss. We know there is more than picking a partner because of convenience or because they are the best warriors or mothers. Sharing their mats does not quench this longing inside. Why? You are like me, Sacri. We know there is a magic our soul makes when it meets 'the one'. I see this connection, but until now, I never felt such magic myself. She is so connected with me, I look at bread and feel her love." He closed his eyes. "Like you and the pendant. His imprint is strong on it, and this is what has created the link you share. A link cannot go to nothing, he exists. Gives me hope when I should be without." He closed his eyes and sighed deeply into the earth.

Sacri watched him. "Who is she?" Seeing her brother so relaxed was strange. She tasted the bread again. It was not bread from their tribe. "You found someone from another tribe?"

"She is a settler's daughter. Remember when you asked me to find Gavin Bernoit and keep him off this land?"

Sacri sat taller. "And did you find him? He had watery-blue eyes," she reminded him. He was the one who'd attacked Paniya. Anger boiled in her at the memory. He had gotten away from her. It troubled her that he might be the father of Paniya's child and Silver called the baby a Chosen One, a possible leader of their tribe.

She was ready to tell him what he'd done to Paniya when it dawned on her what Silver was hinting at. "Not his daughter?"

Silver was still dreaming, ignoring her sudden rage. "I plan to bring her here as my wife."

"You cannot do that." Sacri's tone was firm. "You are leading this tribe. You cannot walk on Sacred Land with a wife from the settler tribes. The daughter of a...*of Gavin Bernoit*. No. I want nothing of his on this land. You must choose one of ours."

"I can't choose something like this, it simply is. You of all people should understand. Besides, I lead nothing. Others turn to me because our leader is not born yet." He sighed, dreamily. "She fills me with dizzy smiles and I turn into mud when she touches me. Frankly, I don't care whose daughter she is. She is who my soul needs to feel right. Louis used to think it was funny that his father gave up his life as a banker to live with us underground, but I would give up Sacred Land to watch her soul dance for me."

She was mortified. Gavin Bernoit's daughter? Should she tell him what he'd done? She studied her dreaming brother. Perhaps telling him wasn't necessary. Silver was normally wary of all outsiders. Clearly, this girl was different. "Where is she?"

His smile faded and he grabbed a rock, clenching it while he sat up. "There is a problem." His voice implied he was at war and she needed to prepare. "Our people are not the only ones who will have a problem with this. Her father sent her to live with her aunt because he caught us together. I found her there, now she says her cousin is escorting her to another relative soon. I will have to find a way to steal her."

"And make a war with a cold man like that? Why? Find a

better way. Make her come to you then vanish her beneath the earth."

Ghosts of the Earth weren't at war with any tribes except the settlers, and this war was more a one-sided battle as they tried to keep the settlers off Sacred Land.

"She cannot be vanished. A woman like her needs to be free. I only want to be next to her soul, to watch it talk to me."

"Is this why I see ghosts searching for us? Gavin Bernoit takes what he wants. Who gave him the idea to come wearing a sheet?"

He tossed the rock in the water. "And there is the problem. Gavin Bernoit, I can handle." His bottom lip quivered and Sacri felt his pain.

"Who has betrayed us?" she demanded.

"Clement."

Oh. Sacri felt the weight of that fall on her shoulders. Because of the link she shared with him, Clement was not someone they could fight. He was one of them.

"He's working for his uncle Bellecoeur. He's been to the surrounding villages, tossing money around that is winning him friends. Clement thinks he's safe if he visits Sacred Land covered in a sheet. Fool doesn't know I see his soul."

"Forget Clement, he's my problem. I will help you, Silver."

He showed her a wanted poster. "Read it. What does it say?"

She'd learnt to read thanks to her friend, the priest. Sacri grabbed the paper to read it to her brother, but the image was distracting. "Is this you? You look vicious."

"This is how I look to them. A savage."

"It says you are wanted for stealing Gavin Bernoit's daughter and he offers a nice reward."

He frowned. "He sends her off and blames me? She was fine when I left her. I did not steal anyone. Yet."

The wanted poster said more. It said to kill him on sight because he was dangerous.

"Silver, this is not good."

"No, it's not. The benefit we had was that the settlers were scattered and working for themselves. Clement uses his uncle's money to gather them. He knows us, our ways, even our tunnels. Worse, I cannot kill him."

"Perhaps we should consider Clement's last deal." It had sent Silver to the Ceremonial Chamber for days. She assumed his uncle was after their land, their tunnels.

Silver got up. He studied the prairies. "His uncle needs access to our tunnels but Clement wants something so valuable it pains me that he could even put a price on it."

"What does he want? Maybe we can..." her voice trailed off when Silver wiped a tear. Sacri stared at him, stunned.

"I kept this from you because he wants something I cannot give and I do not want him to have." He glanced at her. "I was terrified if you found out, you would take him up on his offer, but now that I see the promise of happiness in your soul, I am relieved you won't make that sacrifice for us."

Sacri touched her stomach as fear crept up on her. He wanted *her*? Her voice was soft when she asked, "If I agree, could he keep the settlers off this land? Would he convince his uncle to stop his revenge and forget our tunnels?"

Silver's jaw was tight. "Do not agree."

Clement was in a position to help. He was not someone Silver could kill.

She put her hands to her mouth. "What if he is the Man of Legends?" It never occurred to her that she wouldn't want to be with the Man of Legends. Was this really what her destiny was?

Silver ran his hand over the invisible thread. "Your dream promised that you would move your mat beside the Man of Legends. That he would be real. This means our land will be in danger and it also means..." He stared at her. "You see, Sacri, I know a woman only moves her mat after a link has been formed. I physically see the love that binds couples. There can only be one Man of Legends, yet you now have two links. Before you agree, you must meet this other man."

"Some stranger won't have the power he does. I won't forget my responsibility because of some link you see." She felt like puking. How could she have been so blind? Of course, the Man of Legends was Clement. He could help them, but he wouldn't see this without her.

Silver touched the cross around his neck. "I have to leave. Promise not to talk to Clement until my return."

"I cannot make such promises."
"You must, or I won't return."
She sighed. "Fine."

–Six–

A few days later, there was a buzz underground. Everyone was too busy to talk. When Louis appeared before Sacri in a solemn bow, she wasn't surprised. "Prepare. Your father wishes to speak with you." He looked troubled but left before she could question him.

Her father was dead, but it was common for spirits to haunt Sacred Land. Still, she hadn't spoken to him since his death. Sacri had no idea how to prepare. She bathed with earth and wore her sacred garments. She adjusted her pendant, then relaced the string through the side of her dress. Finally, she glanced down at herself as ready as she'd ever be.

She checked the main tunnel, but the place was deserted.

Sacri rubbed her tattooed arms nervously. Would she be left behind if the tribe left Sacred Land? Her family's responsibility was to protect this land and she was the last in line.

Chin up and shoulders back, she tiptoed into the Ceremonial Chamber, deep underground, at the center of the world. Yet the roots from the Sacred Oak ran through the chamber reminding her how life intertwined. She touched the roots. Her father said she had a sacred bond to the tree since it had protected her when she was born. He swore that her mother's soul had joined with this tree. Which made the oak even more special to her.

Water ran by the chamber, giving the air an earthy taste. This was her favourite room in the tunnels. Her bare feet rubbed the soft earth. This room was cool and moist and she felt at one with the earth. It was a blessing to know the comforts of home.

She knelt when she was as far as she dared go.

Sacri waited.

"*I sense your distress.*" Her father's warm voice filled the chamber, taking her off guard.

"I am troubled these days," she admitted to the invisible presence. His love for her warmed the room and she confessed everything, "Silver has gone missing. I protect Sacred Land until his return. I know of a way to keep settlers off our land, but I have to accept the offer of marriage to someone marked for judgement. I would have to leave Sacred Land." Saying such things felt wrong.

Sacri kept her head down, fighting the bile in her mouth.

"*You are bound to protect Sacred Land until Silver returns. The others leave in search of safer lands and to warn the other tribes that we will need help defending this land. You cannot have this shadow on your soul. You must prepare to fight.*"

She took a deep breath. So they were to prepare for war.

Her shoulders sagged. She had failed her people. Her dream had been so clear, so simple, and yet impossible to make real.

"Honovi, do you believe a Man of Legends exists?" she asked her father.

"*It only matters what you believe. You know this.*"

–SEVEN–

The rest of the tribe had left. Only Louis' boys carved in the tunnel. When Sacri ran into them, they burst into conversations at the same time, trying to share what they had been doing with the tools. Sacri knelt with them and admired their work because, despite her fears, she was a teacher at heart. She taught them the pattern: bird, rock, water, sky, and earth. They copied her teachings in its simplest form.

She left them and ran into Louis. He grabbed her arms. "Sacri, I had no idea what else to do. Silver made me promise not to let you talk to Clement until his return. Means I had to stay, but I couldn't tell the others the truth." He bowed his head. "I'm sorry, I had no choice."

She glanced in his chamber. By his mat was hers. "You moved my mat?"

"Sacri. I could only justify staying if your mat was beside mine."

He'd told the others she'd moved her mat so he could stay behind with her? As if she needed his protection? She glared at him and he dropped his head, ashamed of his actions.

"You know how I feel about this."

"It means nothing," he promised her.

It meant everything.

"I have to stay," he admitted and she softened. "I can't be running with my boys or with Paniya this close to birthing. I was just too proud to admit that to the others."

She tossed his arms off her. "No one moves my mat but me."

She picked the bear hide up and hauled her mat to her prayer room. There she fell to her knees in tears because this was not how her destiny was supposed to go. Her people fled from settlers they didn't understand. How could they? The settlers came in herds like buffalo, but they never left. They grouped houses as if they wanted companionship, yet added fences as if they did not. They even use tracks to travel because horses were not fast enough. Watching was painful, because the respect the earth demanded was not heard. They were too loud, too fast, and too self-involved. Sacri did not like the men moving in, but she disliked their women even more. They did not bless. They did not stand in front of their men but behind them. They were good at eye rolling and talking down to her.

Sacred Land was untouched, but the Cursed Lands, the Healing Lands, and all the others had been invaded. Where would they go? How would she keep them off Sacred Land? How many warriors would return to help her?

She ran her hands deep in the earth to share her sorrow with the Blessed Mother but she paused, sensing a strange new energy coming from the east. A peculiar sensation washed over her.

"Where are you going?" Louis demanded. He'd been standing outside her prayer room.

"Do you sense that?" she asked.

He was quick to touch the walls. "It's warm. A warning?"

Warmth, yes. "Mother is pleased," she said to Louis. "Stay with your boys, teach them, raise them. I will check it out. They need you, I do not." It was her way of saying he wasn't the boss when Silver was gone: she was.

He sighed, clearly not used to staying behind. His boys were at his side.

"I will be quick."

She spent the day with her hands in the dirt, feeling various spots above ground for the warmth. A direct line to the east had formed. Someone was coming. Someone Mother was excited to welcome.

–EIGHT–

Winnipeg—

Alex watched trains come in, while Wali figured things out.

"Mmm, smells fantastic." Alex stared at the approaching train as he waited by an older woman with a basket. Wali walked up to him, so he added, "Then again, everything smells delicious when you're going on two days without food. A guy does what he must to get home to his dying aunt." He wasn't talking to anyone, but Wali nodded as if the comment made a lick of sense.

The woman gasped. "Oh you poor boys. Here." She shoved the basket at Alex.

Alex dramatically pushed it back at her. "Oh, we couldn't."

"I insist. Eat. Be strong for your aunt."

"Thank you. How shall I repay you? A prayer perhaps?"

She nodded and walked off.

Wali said, "Look at you, enchanting old dames. I admire how you work. Is it the smile? Could I pull off a smile like you?" Wali grinned and his crooked teeth had something black in them.

Alex chuckled. "A starving man learns how to charm a woman with a basket of food in a hurry." He shrugged, but truth was, Alex watched people closely and found that few disliked him. Maybe it explained why he had such a hard time with Bellecoeur's open hatred for him.

"Convincing women to give me things was never my strong suit," Wali admitted.

Alex opened the basket. They uncovered bread with a jar of jam stashed beside it. Heavenly. They dived in.

The arriving train caused excitement on the platform. It

wasn't their train but Alex enjoyed the rush created as it pulled up, almost as if the moving cars could suck him in and throw him out the other side, a new man.

"So what's the plan?" he asked Wali, shoving bread in his mouth.

"I'm going downtown for a spell." Wali's forehead was covered in beads of sweat. Alex knew exactly where he planned to go. He refused to let his friend end up at the pub.

"We agreed on no booze. We make a trip straight to Moose Jaw, no distractions."

"I'm going to claim my land. You want some? It's easy to do," Wali said.

"Nah. Let's keep moving. We'll do that when we're in Moose Jaw. Bellecoeur offered me a job."

"We can buy land while we wait here, and head straight to our land, tracks go that way, too. No need to go to Moose Jaw."

"I'm not letting you buy land you've never seen."

"I'm not letting you work for the devil. We'll each claim a quarter section. That's 160 acres."

"What the hell are we gonna do with that much land?"

"Farm it. We'll build a homestead."

Alex shook his head. "We can't afford it."

"It's ten bucks."

Alex chuckled. "Yeah, right."

"I'm serious. All we have to do is build a house and live in it for three years."

"That's it? Sounds too good to be true. You're making shit up so you can grab a drink. If that's how it'll be, I'm leaving you here."

"I'm serious, Alex, didn't you read that handbill? All we gotta do is break five acres and plant crops on them during that time."

Alex crossed his arms. He'd follow him to the land title office if he had to. "Lead the way, but you're full of lies. Besides, breaking land might not be as easy as you think." Alex had travelled to Northern Québec and he'd witnessed settlers break land. The thick forests made the work next to impossible. "We don't know what we'll have to deal with, that's why it's best to head to Moose Jaw."

"I tell you land is ten bucks and you'll pass? You stand here and blame me, pretending I'll get lost at the pub, but that's what's going through your mind. Admit it. You think if we leave the train station, it's over."

"Don't turn this around on me." Alex fished in his pockets in case he had some change kicking around. "I have nothing anyhow."

"You can pay later."

"Ten bucks is cheap for land, but Bellecoeur has a job for me in Moose Jaw. I am so weak that if we passed a pub I might forget I'm at his mercy."

"So you have no money for land, but for booze you do?"

"I just need to find a lonely widow and I'll have all the drinks I want."

"Well, use that charm, maybe you'll convince these guys at the Dominion Office to give you land for your dying aunt." Wali headed out and Alex was quick to follow.

"It sounds like work anyway, and unlike you, I am not a reliable worker. I slip through life with a drink in hand and a lady in my arms. You know; carefree, whispering baskets away from poor ladies."

"These days you do more whining than frolicking. But what do I know?" Wali went down the street, as if he knew where he was going.

"You know where it is?"

"The guy at the station told me the office is about a fifteen-minute stroll this way."

Alex walked with Wali, taking in his surroundings. They weren't far from the river and the air had a homey feel to it. "I like this city," he told him.

Wali turned toward the river. A large white, house-like building was in the distance. The sign in the window read, 'Dominion Lands Office'.

"I'd like you to come with me to see this land, but there won't be people out there, and I know how you don't like to be alone so I understand if at the train station we go separate ways."

"You serious?" Alex demanded. "You brought me out here to dump me? Screw you. I'll go with you. I'll watch you fill a wagon full of crap you won't use, because in a few months, you'll pack up and head to Moose Jaw to work for Bellecoeur with me."

"They wouldn't sell us land that isn't farmable."

"They would." He didn't point out the other swindles Wali had fallen victim to over the years. "Bellecoeur would sell you ice in a snow storm if you were dumb enough to buy it. He's been trading land for years. He probably knows these guys and teaches them how to screw blokes like us over."

"Well, I won't be packing up. If you come, you'd better be prepared to stay. I am not working for the devil again, and I won't let you." He walked through the door but Alex waited impatiently, outside.

Trusting Wali was getting hard. What did he know about any of this? Alex paced the dock, watching the birds on the water. A couple in love strolled by, holding hands, talking softly.

He watched them, feeling so wispy inside. Seeing love planting roots like that gave him an inner warmth he'd forgotten was possible.

An hour later, Wali came out with a man in a three-button suit behind him. "Come in. This guy wants you to sign a few papers." Wali's hair was ruffled and a button on his suspenders was missing. Alex inspected him. He didn't look like he'd taken a shit kicking, but something was going on. Had they roughed him up?

All his muscles tightened. He should have gone in with him. "What for?"

Real close, Wali whispered, "It's all good, but since I don't have a wife, they want to know where my land goes if I die. I want it to go to you, which got me whisked to this side office and..." He met Alex's eyes, panicked. Whatever he wanted to say was too hard so he took a deep breath instead.

"Wali?" Alex frowned. "Did they threaten you? You smell like whiskey."

"It's fine. Just humour me. Sign his papers so we can get the hell out of here."

Alex eyed the guy up. Was he pushing his friend around? Why?

Wali met Alex's eyes. "Look at me. I'm fine. Just needed a drink to take in what we're about to do. Sign the papers." He almost dragged Alex inside, past a line-up of men working at desks, to a side office.

Papers were in a tidy stack on the desk.

"Our own private office?" Alex glanced around and stepped up to the man in the three-button vest as if he might kick his ass. "You had Wali in here alone?"

Wali stood too near Alex. "Alex, Xavier works for Bellecoeur, but is willing to look the other way and let us walk out with land no one else wants."

Ah, crap.

"What do we owe him for this kind gesture?"

"I took care of it. He needs you to sign a few things." Alex knew his friend well enough to know when he lied about something. He probably deserved this treatment for all the lies he'd been shoving at Wali lately.

Alex made a sour face.

The man came closer and smelled Alex.

"What the heck are you sniffing me for?" Alex was ready to hit him.

"Booze. I can't let you sign if you've been drinking."

Clearly, this man had been. "Well, seems I'm the only one in this room who didn't sneak a few today," Alex snapped and bent over the desk to sign the papers where Wali pointed. He glanced at the top contract. The first one was exactly what Wali had said. While he was ready to sign the next one, Xavier handed Wali a pamphlet on how to claim a homestead, along with a map of the area. Alex watched Xavier take a moment too long when shaking Wali's hand. His other hand was on his shoulder, and he squeezed gently. By his ear he whispered, "You need anything else, you come to me. Don't trust any of these blokes. Guys like us need to stand together."

"Wali?" Alex stood, ready to hit the guy if Wali looked panicked.

Wali glanced at Alex, and mouthed the word, 'Sign'.

Alex did, but he kept his eyes on Xavier.

When they left the office, Wali let out a long breath. "We did it. Damn. Thanks for not hitting him. It's done." He held up his papers. "We'll be farmers."

"You're shaking." Alex frowned. "What did you do?"

Wali led them to the train station, head down.

"Did Bellecoeur really warn them not to sell me land? That's low. Does he hate me that much?"

"Doubt it. It's probably a control thing. This way you have no choice but to beg for a job. How he plans to punish you for turning his daughter against him."

"Makes me want to prove him wrong even more."

"Then we need cash."

"Cash? You had over fifty on ya. How much did you give that guy for your ten-dollar land?"

"Been a long trip. I haven't got a cent left. I do have my mother's ring to sell, though. And sorry I had a drink with that guy. I couldn't see a way around it. I had to get him on our side. If you want one we can stop at the pub and get us evened up."

Alex glanced over his shoulder at the office. What the heck had happened in there? He really didn't know a thing about buying land, but this didn't feel right.

"Nah, let's get moving."

–Nine–

Alex shifted on the hard train bench. He sat on his jacket but the seat was still uncomfortable. Needing something to do with his hands, he settled on drawing signs in the air like a madman.

He nudged Wali who slept with his jacket rolled up, against the window. "The train stations are getting shabbier. The last one was some guy's house. You sure we're headed the right way?"

Wali mumbled without opening his eyes, "The rail lines are parallel. We'll walk south to meet with the next set, but those tracks end—"

"They end? Then what? You plan to finish them?" Alex teased.

Wali was always bragging about how they had Chinese help with the tracks because they were the hardest workers. Of course, that's how Wali saw it, since his dad had been one of those workers and he never met him but had grand ideas about what he was like.

Wali smirked proudly. "We'll be fine. Sleep. I packed a notebook in my backpack if you want to draw something."

Alex grabbed the backpack and fished through it. He found the notebook with a pencil on top. Wali must have picked them up when they stopped in Winnipeg. Alex felt better when he brought the pencil to the paper and he didn't even notice that they'd stopped, until a man stormed into the car rudely arguing with his gal. Well, they weren't really arguing. He was tearing into her something fierce. The man had a flask, in his jacket, that he sipped from. The action irritated Alex and he stopped drawing to watch the guy.

Finally, Alex shoved the notebook into the bag and got up.

"Grow up, you foolish girl," the guy squawked at her. "You think he's coming for an ugly sap like you? Enough of your games."

She was silent, peering out the window at a shadow in the distance, riding a horse.

Wali was still sleeping, his head against the window, but Alex suspected he was faking, because no one would be able to sleep the way this guy was badmouthing her.

The loudmouth stole another sip.

Alex focused on her. She wore a bonnet and lifted her eyes enough to glance around the car. Her eyes were a shiny blue. Almost as watery as Wali's which made Alex soften to her instantly. She met Alex's stare then looked back at her feet. Her hands hid in a roll, something Mattie called a 'muffler', or a 'muffet'; he could never remember the names she gave her clothes.

The man carried their only bag. He started into her again about her bare feet. She ignored him and stared at Wali. Wali hadn't moved. He was exhausted lately. His ticket peeked out of his pocket, and this was her focus. Her eyelashes were long. She had an earthly beauty to her long slender face that Alex found intriguing in a woman. The sun had bronzed her skin, but the scars on her neck and cheek told a different tale. Alex tensed with the notion that maybe this guy was beating on her.

Alex pulled the ticket out of Wali's pocket and shoved it in his own pant pocket. He never understood why Wali made himself such an easy target.

The man continued his complaining about her as he tossed the bag on the seat and shoved her beside it. Alex shot toward him without thinking. He slammed him into the doorframe and Alex yanked the flask from his pocket.

He was bigger than Alex, when he swung he caught Alex in the gut and again in the jaw. If he hadn't been taken off-guard, Alex would probably have been beaten senseless but the advantage allowed him to bring in a solid right hook, cracking the guy's head against the doorframe, knocking him out. Then Alex poured the booze out of the flask on his head and left the car without looking around. He'd been kicked off a train before for fighting, so he put as much distance between them as he could.

His jaw throbbed but he didn't dare touch it.

Wali was groggy but he followed him out. "What the hell was that about? You have to hit every guy you meet?"

"I never hit you. Not once."

"Thanks. I guess. How was that any of your business?"

"I didn't like either of them, but when I see a guy going on like that it's instinct. I don't pick which things are worth a fight."

"So you'll fight for some dame you don't know, but your own sanity you let slip away?"

"I'm here, on your stupid adventure. Let it go."

They found new seats and Wali went back to sleep while Alex sat, lost in thoughts about how Wali was right. He needed something to fight for. Hitting the creep had felt good and he almost wished there were a line of men needing a good wallop. He didn't need to know the whole story; he knew the guy was being a deadbeat. If he could have Mattie back for one minute, he'd cherish every breath with her and it saddened him that dirtbags got the girls, and he got broken dreams.

"You thinking about the booze you dumped?" Wali asked him. "Because I am. I need a drink." He had droplets of sweat on his forehead. "I'm shaky. Everything frustrates me, even you."

"Just think about something else." Alex felt his frustration. Out the window, the terrain had changed dramatically. Rocks turned into prairies. Not like back home. This was untouched with a sense of forever, eternity, almost sacredness. "The world is sharper without booze clouding it. Enjoy that." Alex stared out the window, watching the shadow on the horse. He was a silver glimmer in the distance, but he stayed in line with the train. Chasing them. It'd be nice to have that type of freedom.

Alex was lost in these thoughts when the woman in the bonnet approached. At first, he assumed she came to demand an apology for knocking her companion out.

Alex glanced around for her no-good friend. He hadn't followed.

She sat on the bench opposite him with her bag at her side.

Wali shot up from his deep sleep as if his pants were suddenly on fire. She had her eyes down, her hands on her lap.

They sat, her staring down at her muffler-thingy, them not talking. Wali was wide-eyed, on his guard as if she might attack them.

Alex was about to say something to her when he noticed her shoes were still missing and there was a drop of blood on the top of her foot. She wiped it when she caught Alex looking at her bare feet.

When the train stopped, Alex stood. "Coming?" he asked Wali. "This is where they told us to get off. Let's see what the fuss is about."

The girl stood, too. Alex didn't acknowledge her.

Wali asked if this was her stop and instead of answering, she flashed her ticket. It was the same as theirs. For some reason this annoyed Alex, and he went to check their tickets but they were missing. They'd probably fallen from his pocket when he'd hit the guy.

He snapped the ticket from her. Was it one of theirs?

Wali helped her with her bag while Alex slugged from the train not too eager to face the next leg of their journey, even less eager to have this woman, he knew nothing about, following them. If she leeched onto men, he understood why the guy had been annoyed with her. He glanced up at the train from the platform and, to his relief, her drunken companion glared at him from a window in the next car. Alex lifted his cap to him. At least she wasn't a murderer.

The train pulled out, leaving the three of them on the tiny platform, facing an empty prairie.

–Ten–

Nothing else was visible for as far as the eye could see, and his eyes could see far. Alex had never seen terrain like this.

"There is nothing here," Alex commented. He stepped closer to Wali as the solitude hovered around him.

"Nothing, or..." Wali smirked, "a guy could say there is opportunity for everything he wants to do before he dies."

Leave it to Wali to see the joy in everything.

The train left them, taking the last bit of familiar with it. They were three idiots without another soul in sight.

"Your friend didn't join us?" Alex asked her.

She shook her head and pointed west.

"He's going on, is he?"

She nodded and pointed south.

"That's where we're going," Wali said. "You can join us."

Alex shook his head. "Not a good idea. We don't know what we're getting ourselves into."

She stepped back as if it wouldn't happen, which was probably good. They didn't need her tagging along.

Alex stood before the prairies and began to see the world as Wali had. Not a lack of things, but a lack of bad things. No trees to remind him of Mattie, no houses or farms he'd never afford.

In the distance, a deer grazed with two young ones. The prairies were full of life. He'd imagined open prairies of nothing, but Wali was right, this nothing was...everything. Skies that never ended, so blue he saw heaven in the dancing fluffy white clouds. Birds soared. Bushes clustered by a slough about a hundred yards off. Finding this connection to a place so foreign to him left him wondering if he'd been caught in the wrong life, and maybe this place was where he was meant to be.

He just wanted to soak the tranquility in.

When he turned around, across the tracks was a pioneer village with eight houses and a few other buildings scattered about. A woman was outside hanging clothes on a line, otherwise the place was deserted.

Alex glanced at Wali. "What do you think?"

"You like it here." Wali smirked.

"I do. Did you know things were this open? I mean, dang, everything is alive. I hear the earth buzzing. Life itself stems from here." He fell to his knees and shoved his hands in the dirt almost sorry he hadn't bought any land while in Winnipeg. Could a man own land this holy? He had his doubts. He ran his fingers in the soft dirt, enjoying the feeling of dry soil under his fingertips.

"We have to travel about thirty miles south to meet with the next set of train tracks. That's quite a hike. I'll get us a wagon," Wali offered.

Alex inhaled deeply with his mouth open and he choked on a mosquito. He coughed the bug up while Wali chuckled.

"I don't want a wagon. Let's hike it." Maybe the gal would leave when she saw they wouldn't walk an easy path.

"Hike this? Sleep in the bushes?"

Alex confessed, "This is not how I imagined it, but a guy could get used to this. The land is surreal. I want to enjoy as much of the view as possible. It's…crowded."

The girl was beside Wali. She studied the prairies with him. In the distance was a silver streak in the sunlight. Was that the man on the horse? "You guys see that?" Alex wondered.

Wali had terrible eyesight and squinted. "What?"

"Over there, it's a man on a horse." Alex glanced at the woman, wondering if she could see it. Her eyes fixated on the spot and her hand went to her stomach while she stood, a stone statue, not breathing.

"It's fine," Wali told her. "You're safe with us."

She nodded and a huge smile found her lips. She pointed to Alex and to the silver shape in the distance, asking him to lead her there, with her hands.

"I'm Alex."

She touched her throat lightly and smiled shyly before she

cast her eyes down again.

"A mute?"

She nodded.

Wali whispered as if she were a butterfly he needed to catch, "That's fine. Use your hands to talk. Alex is great with languages. Where are you headed?" Wali asked her politely.

She pointed to Alex and linked him to the shadow in the distance.

"Me? You're following me? I'm not taking you to that guy."

She brought out a bill from her sleeve.

Alex shook his head. "Not even for money, and stop flashing those bills, someone will rob you."

She reached under the lace around her neck and removed her golden chain. She dangled it in front of Alex.

At first, he dismissed the jewellery but when Wali gasped, Alex stole a better look.

It was his father's cross, gold chain and all.

"What the heck? Where did you get that?" Alex moved to grab the chain but she dropped it along her neck into the lace. He watched her bosoms heave. Her jaw tightened, daring him to search her for it. Then she pointed to Alex, the shadow, and the necklace she concealed.

"I get it if I bring you to him?" He wanted that pendant, but he didn't like this. "Forget it. Keep the cross." He knew where it was. He had no idea how she'd come by his necklace, but it had journeyed back to him by some miracle and it wouldn't be long before a dame this dumb would be dead and he'd take his pendant off her body. "Whatever."

She glanced down again.

Wali gave Alex a dirty look.

"What? I can't stop her from following me, but I don't have to be friendly."

Wali was furious. "Don't be an ass, Alex. She's not doing anything wrong."

"How do you know? You don't know her."

"I don't have to. She has the eyes of a Montague. I trust that," he said proudly as if that made her family.

"She dangles my chain in front of me. Mine! She knew it could buy me off. Clearly, Clement sent her to mess with us.

We aren't dragging a dame with us to check out land. Bad enough we might get lost or dead out here. I don't need to be responsible for her, too."

"Clement? You mean Bellecoeur's nephew? Why would he care where we are? You're nuts with this. No one even knows we're here. Calm down. Look at her. She's beautiful. Doesn't she make you curious? Are you dead inside?"

Head down, she smiled. Alex grabbed her bag from Wali and handed it back to her. She snagged the old bag and gripped it against her body.

"She has trouble written all over her," Alex said.

Her jaw tightened and the defiance flashing over her gave him pause. Maybe she wasn't so bad. He'd always had a thing for women who were daring enough to challenge him.

"Come," Alex said. "But you stand as our equal. We'll be travelling to unknown parts of the prairies, then to Moose Jaw. Once in Moose Jaw, we part ways. Understand? Keep your paws to yourself and behave."

She clutched her bag, but Wali was quick to pull it away from her. "Let me carry her bag. Geesh. I'm Wali, by the way. What do we call you?"

She touched the lace on her sleeve.

"Lacey?"

She nodded.

"See, Alex isn't the only one who understands you. Come on, I need a drink. Think they have a watering hole in this joint?" Wali studied the town.

Alex's mouth watered when Wali said drink. He stepped away from the town, before the promise of drunken bliss seduced him.

"I'll walk," he told Wali while he headed toward the prairies. Wali wasn't usually one to drink alone. He'd follow.

"What? We're leaving? It'll be dark soon."

Alex stalked off.

"Wait here, I'll get us a wagon."

Alex glanced over his shoulder at the small town. "This town doesn't even have a church. You plan to steal one from the poor woman hanging laundry? Come on. I don't want to walk this alone." Desperation pushed him forward.

"Ah…what are you doing? Town is the other way. There's

a livery barn there. I'm sure we can get a horse or something." Wali pointed to the town.

"I am not riding, Wali, you know that. I won't ride if I can walk."

"Thirty miles is a long hike. A wagon is only common sense—"

Alex cut him off with a glare, too proud to admit he was more afraid of horses than walking the prairies alone. Wali's insistence was strange. He was pale. His hand shook at his side and he had a peculiar bruise on his neck that wasn't there this morning. Alex softened. "I'll walk. I could use the alone time to think about my life. You get a horse for Lacey and catch up. That's a fantastic idea. We'll need them anyway because I might be able to walk this, but a good work horse will be a must for this land you want to work."

"Riding is faster. Especially with a dame. No offence, dear."

She rubbed her bare feet in the dirt without commenting.

Wali added, "If it's money, I'll buy you a horse. Come."

"I won't own a horse. You said it's thirty miles. That'll be what? A good ten-hour walk? I'll hoof it."

"You'll slow us down. It'll be dark soon. Alex…"

Done debating with Wali, Alex stormed off.

After a few steps, Alex stopped to remove his shoes wondering why the girl was barefoot. He felt the blades of grass with his toes and sunk his foot down. The dirt was cool under his feet. He liked it.

"Now what are you doing?"

Alex ignored him, determined to do this. He put his shoes under his arm and kept walking.

"You've gone bonkers? Is that it?" Wali sighed.

A few hours later, Alex heard them approaching on horses, and the relief was enormous. Walking alone was hard and he looked forward to the company.

Much to his shock, Wali rode past. Lacey slowed and handed him a hanky. Not in panic, but in a friendly gesture. In it was a slice of bread. She gave him a depressed sigh and glanced at Wali who was ahead, riding hard.

"He's mad, is he?"

She nodded.

"Better go with him, then. I wouldn't want him drinking himself into trouble without me there to defend him."

She rode off, clearly experienced with horses.

He called a thank-you after her and regretted sending her off. Even if she couldn't talk, she'd be a better companion than the solitude around him.

He dropped his shoes and left them in the grass. He wouldn't need them. Walking with his bare feet gave him a sense of freedom.

Wali was a blur in the dust, leaving Alex alone, but he travelled in the same direction. He'd hit the tracks soon and follow them to town. He didn't need Wali.

Yet he glanced around, nervous. The sun was setting. An orange glow warmed the prairies. Alone wasn't so bad, he promised himself.

There were no people. No signs of civilization. He looked proudly at how far he'd walked. The first step had been the hardest, now he moved fast. He'd be there soon and would probably find Wali drunk or beaten up and he'd have to deal with that.

He admitted to himself that being alone on the prairies without people and booze might actually be a good thing for them.

His father had told him that growing up was not a decision, it was an action. They needed to act grown up and do something. Anything.

Alex paused to enjoy the silent moment as the sun breathed one long final pause, changing the skies to pink. He sat to watch the natural display while he sang Mattie a song. His melody was different tonight, full of promise and hope. Peaceful.

Not wanting the song to end, he sang a second time. This time he sang of their journey. He sang of his pain. He even sang about the woman following them. He sang and sang, until there were no words left in him, then he fell back, relaxed on the grass and whispered, "Peace. Peace. Peace."

Mosquitoes gathered around him. He pulled his hat over his eyes and rested. Strange sounds filled the night. Alex tried to identify them but when he heard a man ask why he had refused the cross, he checked the shadows. "Who's there?"

he demanded.

No one answered. Alex returned to the grass and lay down, sure that his imagination had played a trick on him. He drifted off when a man said, "I was curious, is all. You clearly wanted it." He spoke French, but with a different accent than those from Alex's home. His words were slower, clearer, snappier.

Alex lay still, imagining a bunch of warriors around him. "I refuse to owe her anything," he admitted to the dark. "I told her she can tag along, but she had to hold her own. She your gal? You the shadow she keeps searching for?"

"You should probably keep moving. A cougar hunts this land tonight."

Alex chuckled. Now he was trying to scare him. He sat up and glanced around. "Show yourself." The sky was gloomy, but stars and the moon lit the prairies with a greyish glow.

A gleam in the distance caught his attention. Eyes watching him, not human ones. A soft purr-ish growl shot him to his feet. On his knees, he checked for something to defend himself, but he had nothing except his carving tools. He dug a knife out of his pack and peeked up at the biggest cat he'd ever seen. Her ears flattened and her lips pulled back as she let out a strange warning sound like a violent *mah-ow*, followed by a rumble deep in her chest.

Their eyes met.

Alex was torn between fear and hope. He dropped the knife. It was useless against a beast like this. If she wanted him dead, he'd accept his fate.

The monstrous cat showed her fangs. As she lowered her head, her shoulders tensed to leap. Majestic. A powerful goddess on the prairies.

He didn't move as they stared each other down. The growling groan came from deep inside her and she snarled.

Alex was planted, ready for death. "What are you waiting for? Do it."

His voice startled her, but something else caught her attention and she glanced to Alex's right then vanished in the tall grasses as if something was suddenly hunting *her*.

He wondered why she hadn't attacked. Was God so angry with him, He chose to leave him behind to suffer?

Frustrated, Alex collected himself and shoved his things into the pack. He wore his cap and began his journey again. His heart raced as he forged his way, heading south.

A shadow stepped from the dark and joined him. Alex pretended not to notice.

"You are most brave."

"Brave?" Alex stopped to inspect the warrior by the moonlight. He was in cure-hide pants. He wore no shirt. His upper arm had a tattoo around the muscle. His hair was long and fell loose over his shoulders. On his side was a blade and on his back a bow.

"Some would think it's the coward's way. I accepted my death years ago, but God doesn't want me."

"Or maybe Mother saves you for another purpose."

Alex trudged on while the truth sank in; he'd faced a cougar and lived to tell about it. "I suppose you scared it off?"

"Normally, I would not interfere if a cougar decided to eat you."

Alex's hand shook with the urge to draw. He wanted to recreate the eyes shining in the dark. "Those piercing eyes glared into my soul," he told his companion.

"And what did they see?"

Alex gazed back at the dark path he'd travelled and at the stranger. "I have no idea. I don't have a clue who I am."

"Then be who you want." He smacked Alex on the back of the head. "What is wrong with you? You see a cougar: you kill it. A wild hunter is competition and dangerous. I didn't see any fear in you. What kind of man are you?"

Alex chuckled, comfortable with his new friend. "I'll keep it under advisement should our paths cross again." He shrugged. "You didn't run."

"I killed it. Cougars make comfortable mats for sleeping. I planned to wait for it to eat you and then take my shot, but your courage impressed me."

Before he knew it, they were marching side by side, listening to the world. "I'm Alex."

"Silver. I protect Sacred Land. Lacey says you will take her there."

"Lacey doesn't talk."

"She talks with her soul. A wise man hears with his heart."

Alex glanced over and smirked. "You sound smitten."

Silver sighed, content, and Alex understood what Wali meant about seeing love. He wanted the hope Silver displayed in his step.

They chatted about nothing, Alex sharing stories about his journey here. Silver shared his own tales about his journeys, some on foot, a few by horse, and several by train. He didn't like the train because everyone stared at him.

They were comfortable together, like two old friends. The night passed quickly and before Alex knew it, the first rays of sunlight teased the sky.

A train broke the horizon like a moving enemy. His excitement from seeing it earlier vanished. He'd enjoyed the company of his new friend.

"I will see you later, just follow those tracks west, you should be in Laroche before mid-morning." Silver left him and rushed off silently. He dropped to the grasses and never reappeared, the earth had gobbled him up.

How did he do that?

PART TWO

"My roots will only grow in this soil."
—Lacey

–ELEVEN–

It took Alex a lot longer to get to Laroche. He stopped to eat berries growing in the bushes by the tracks where he dozed off. It was late afternoon when he walked down the main street. He took his time, talking to everyone he met. They were nice enough yet weapons were out in the open, ready to use, and when Alex approached, he wouldn't have been surprised to find a knife to his throat within seconds. He kept his conversations short but he hated how they always finished a sentence with a question mark. *Where are you going? Why? Who sent you? Why? You in trouble? Why? How soon will you be out of here? Why? Where did you come from? Why?*

He missed talking with the warrior. Things were simpler when a man told you flat out that he'd planned to watch a cougar eat you should the fit take it.

It was late when Alex found Wali in the pub, passed out at the table. The place was deserted. Wali still clutched an empty glass. Alex smelled it. Water?

He'd had another nosebleed. His hanky was out and covered in blood. He had more bruises on his neck and cheeks. Alex glanced around, but whomever he'd fought with was gone. The place was dead. Alex sat with him and shook his shoulder. "*Mon ami*, it's best if you get a room. People are on edge in this town."

Wali broke into a coughing fit, so Alex brought him more water.

"I'm not the one they worry about. Apparently, some ghost has them worried. Lacey bought a room, after I told the owner I was her husband, so I couldn't very well ask her to buy two."

"Sleeping in the pub in a town where everyone has a gun

slung over their shoulder isn't the brightest. Come."

"Where we going?"

"To find Lacey."

"I won't scare her by barging into her room." He glanced around. "Well, there's nothing for me here either."

"Trust me. I can charm anyone, even sober." Alex grinned and Wali followed, clearly too tired to argue. Alex was sure she'd let them in.

It had been a while since they had slept in a comfortable place and it might be longer until they got a chance again.

He knocked on Lacey's door. She opened the door a crack.

Alex said, "Wali isn't well. He needs to sleep. Give him a blanket and let him crash on the floor."

"You have nothing to worry about," Wali was quick to confess, "I'm not sure what I'd do with ya anyway."

She squinted and pointed to Alex.

"Oh, he's a danger to ya," Wali teased but Lacey held her bag to her chest, ready to run.

"He's kidding. I lost my wife. I'm grieving and not interested in Silver's girl."

"Silver?" Wali asked, confused.

Lacey's eyes grew huge.

"Yeah, a Native I met while walking here who seems to be a bit smitten with Lacey. He's keeping a close eye on her, yet staying far enough away for some reason. Frankly, anyone eager to marry him is much too feisty for me."

Her face lit up and her bosom moved up with the breath.

"I'm off to church. I'll be back later," Alex said.

She let them in. Alex glanced around. She hadn't settled in. The curtains were pulled open, as if she might climb out…or maybe someone might climb in.

She wasn't his problem, he promised himself, yet things like this had him curious. Of course, he couldn't let her leave with his cross. From a distance, he checked to see if she wore the pendant, but it wasn't around her neck. Once she was asleep, he'd go through her bag.

"See Wali, sometimes, all you have to do is ask." To her he added, "You might want to rethink following us tomorrow. I'm not sure how nasty this will get but from the conversations I overheard, there is nothing west except mosquitoes. And well, if you believe the tales—ghosts." He chuckled when her eyes grew big. "I don't imagine we'll be much protection against those. If you decide not to follow us, that's your business. Let me know where you go."

She peered out of the window, holding her breath. Alex looked down with her while Wali settled in. They were on the second floor and had a spectacular view of the setting sun. Orange and pink hues danced on the prairies. In front of the setting sun was the silver ghostly form again. Alex waved.

Lacey placed her hand to the pane and let out her breath.

"You miss him?" Alex asked her. "Why not go with him? At least sneak out and go see him. Invite him in, it's your room."

She touched her stomach, then her lips, then the pane.

Alex stood behind her, watching Silver.

Silver moved his hands, drawing words in the air in front of him. Alex grew curious when Lacey nodded.

"You understand him? What did he say?"

She poked Alex in the chest and pointed to Silver. Alex nodded. "I'll talk to him." He pulled the curtains shut. "Keep quiet and don't draw attention to yourselves. Something weird is happening in this town."

Wali chuckled. "Alex is always convinced that everyone is after him."

"They usually are." He checked the room but it didn't have much. A bed, a chair, a dresser.

Wali dragged a blanket and pillow to the floor. He fell on it as if he hadn't slept in days.

Lacey sat on the edge of the bed.

Alex ordered her to lock the door and stole the second key that she'd left on the dresser. He slipped out and waited for the click of the lock before he left.

First, Alex found a small slough and sat by it. As the sun set, he sang his song for Mattie, not as heartfelt as the night before. Still, he sang about the girl and how troubled she was. He told Mattie how he didn't want Lacey to tag along, yet he hadn't sent her off so maybe he did. It was reassuring to have a woman in the group, but he didn't know why. He sang about how Wali had him worried. He was growing paler and the nosebleeds lasted longer. He told her about his fears about leaving society behind and heading into the unknown. Then he sat in silence. The evening was grey, the moon bright, giving off enough light for him to find his way back to town.

When he stood, across the slough to his right, the moon passed over a man, creating a shadow.

"Silver. I didn't hear you, but I could use the company."

Silver stood like Alex and the moon found him. A golden chain shone from his neck, catching the light. It looked like a cross. His cross?

"The cross around your neck…"

"When she arrives safely and I no longer need this protection, the pendant will once again be yours." His voice was smooth like the breeze dancing in the grass.

"Arrives where?"

He nodded to Alex and walked off, picking up a bow and quiver set. "I'm not your delivery boy. I have plans, you know," Alex called after him.

He stopped walking and glanced over his shoulder. "I imagine so, but a woman travelling alone will draw attention she does not need. And one travelling with me will be hunted."

Alex frowned, but Silver didn't wait for him to respond. He disappeared into the night.

How he vanished left Alex with an excited feeling. This was an adventure and he'd learn and see new things. Alex was tempted to chase after him and find out where his tribe was, but he decided it was probably best not to chase after a man with a bow and arrow. Clearly, Silver was here for Lacey and she'd given him the necklace for safekeeping. Alex was impressed with her.

It was gloomy and the mosquitoes were plenty when Alex stumbled into the church at the end of the town.

The priest had a shotgun by the door, but he didn't glance at it. He spoke French well and had a meal ready to share.

The priest said, "I've been waiting."

"You knew I was coming?"

"Ah, yeah. I get visits from one of the locals. He's a bright boy but doesn't let settlers past Laroche. He says you're allowed to spend one week on his sacred soil. Not sure what makes you special, but I got the impression it's one of your companions. Got a woman with you he might want?"

"Like a trade?" Alex was mortified. "I'm not trafficking women."

"Whatever, I'm excited someone young and strong plans to settle the land past the fifth creek. The settlers call it ghost country, because of the tribe haunting it, but I went myself to see. The soil is rich, the creek flowing. Life blooms there as if it's the pulse of the world, and anyone who makes a home there will find happiness. I know this in my heart." He glared solemnly at Alex.

"I know nothing about this fifth creek."

He ignored Alex. "I don't promise it'll be easy, because you'll have to learn to live in harmony with the tribe. They've made it clear they aren't leaving."

Guys like Silver were easier for Alex to get along with than the men in this town. "From my experience it's not hard to do. They do their own thing, we do ours."

"Welcome to a new world. These guys don't play nice and they don't understand things like this is yours and this is mine. It all belongs to their mother, although I haven't met her yet. I buried more settlers since I arrived than any other priest." He pulled out a map of the area and pointed to a creek. "Right here we'll make a French town. Since the tribe speaks the language fluently it'll be the common language of the area."

"They all speak French?"

"They speak a few languages. Have a real love for learning."

Alex was excited to learn from them. "What is their Native language?"

"No idea. When they speak it, I recognise the odd Cree word, which I imagine they adopted since that's the closest other tribe to this area and they probably had dealings with them. Funny thing about that though is that when I went to visit the Cree tribe just to the north, they swore there were no tribes in this area. One elder said the land was forbidden."

"And yet you want to build a town there?"

Father cleared his throat. "At the heart of this village I

foresee, we'll build a church. I'll even make the trek to offer mass for you. In time, you'll get them to join our church and they can become a part of our town."

Alex wasn't convinced that this was a brilliant plan. "You tell this tribe about your plan to assimilate them?"

"I want you to. Make it in their best interest. They can't keep settlers out forever and if we don't claim this land, imagine the folks who will. Forbidden or not, they will come."

"Why you interested in settling this particular piece? I mean, there's an entire world out there. Sounds to me like this land should be respected and just left alone. These are not things we'll understand and I don't think guys like us should be messing around on land even the Natives avoid."

He leaned in and whispered, sharing a secret, "A rich bloke came through and offered me money to get the tribe off this land and get some French settlers on it, so he can do business with them. Money will flow. I'll see my people prosper." He sat back, proud.

Alex didn't ask if this businessman was Bellecoeur. Of course it was. He had run from him right into his new dirty plans. Explained what was happening. People were torn between fighting this tribe and the promise of money.

"Well, I never cared about money," Alex assured him. "Sounds harsh to kick these people off their land because some rich pompous ass wants it. He say why he wanted it?"

"I didn't ask. At least check. I know you'll like it."

He didn't bother telling the priest he wasn't staying and had no intention of building a town among locals who didn't want them there. He could go, check it out, and tell him the area was haunted as heck and they had better all stay far away. Silver might like that plan better.

They chatted for a spell. The priest knew everyone and everything that happened in Laroche and he spilled the rumours to Alex as if they were old friends. They shared a meager meal during which the priest poured them shots of whiskey that neither drank. They talked for hours about the land, the potential, then about God.

Alex admitted his lack of faith these days.

"We all doubt, it's in those moments we find what we

really believe."

"I don't know what you mean."

The priest sat back as if he knew the secrets of life and smiled. "You tell me your faith has wavered but you wouldn't be here if it wasn't firm. You'd be down at the pub making trouble instead."

It made Alex feel better. Maybe he couldn't find his faith anymore, but if it was a part of him, he would. He could live with that hope.

Alex felt better when he returned to the hotel. He opened the door a crack to Lacey's room and was astounded to see Wali's hat on the bedpost and his feet sticking out from under the blankets. He debated entering, then figured he'd better at least make sure all was on the up and up, because if Silver decided to kill Wali, he'd have to be prepared to run with him like hell.

Wali opened his eyes when Alex shut the door. He held his finger to his lips, signaling Alex to be quiet. A lantern cast a gentle glow over the bed. Wali and Lacey were fully clothed but she'd passed out against him.

"She was crying so I held her and she fell asleep," Wali whispered. "I haven't the heart to move her, but I could use a new hanky. These nosebleeds are coming more often this week. Must be the change in weather or something." His sleeves were rolled up and he had a large red bruise on his left arm.

"You get in a fight?" Alex handed him a hanky from the drawer.

"Banged it, I guess."

"Hmm." Alex lay on the floor in the mess of blankets that Wali had discarded.

He slept with a warm hope inside. Bellecoeur had told him once that only fools felt hope, men found answers. He wasn't sure the two weren't related because in his hope, he found an answer. He'd settle land with Wali, probably not here, but somewhere. He might not stay long, but long enough to see his friend find happiness.

In the morning, Alex was shaving when Lacey woke up in Wali's arms. She studied him for a long moment and brushed her lips against his cheek while he pretended to sleep.

"I see you decided to seduce my friend and he had no idea what to do with you," Alex teased.

She shook her head.

"Oh? He did know what to do with you?"

She panicked and looked ready to run.

"It was a joke, calm down, you're safe with us. So you gave Silver my cross."

She studied him for a moment then tried to sneak out to find the outhouse. Alex grabbed her arm when she was halfway out the door. He whispered to her, "What kinda trouble are you in?"

She met his eyes and he didn't see the timid woman from the train. He saw a woman ready to challenge him. He let her arm go, impressed. Yeah. He liked her. She was a fighter.

"This isn't a game. Are you in trouble?"

She swallowed and glared at his hand as he hovered it over her arm. She nodded.

"Always be honest with me and we'll be fine."

She touched her stomach and lips, then pointed out the window. He looked at her belly. Was she pregnant? Might explain why she panicked. And why Silver followed them so closely.

He handed her the hanky she'd given him with the bread wrapped in it. "When the trouble appears, you take this hanky out. I don't mind you tagging along, but you'd better not use Wali, or when trouble shows I won't as much blink an eye when I see that hanky. Got it?"

She nodded.

He let her go.

Wali rested in the bed, a dreamy look on his face. "She likes me."

"What's not to like, right? You're all-manly and heroic. But she keeps peeking out this window at the warrior I met, so you might wanna keep your hands to yourself."

Wali smiled. "Oh good, then I won't have to disappoint her. She has a scar on her neck. Do you think someone hurt her? Is that why she can't speak?"

"Probably. Usually how these things work."

"What did the priest say?"

Alex took a deep breath. "We need stuff so I borrowed cash

from him. He'll be by expecting us to pay it back in the fall. We better come up with it because I don't like the idea of owing a priest."

"Where did he get money?"

"Really think I asked where a priest gets his money?"

Lacey stood in the doorway. She looked from Wali to Alex then rushed to her bag and pulled out bills. She handed them to Wali. He took the wad.

Alex shut the door and locked it. He didn't trust anyone in this town, except Silver.

"Holy crap." Wali gaped. "Sorry, I didn't mean to swear in front of you, Lacey. Where in tarnation did you get this lump of grass?"

She made a breaking motion with her hands and cradled her heart.

"Broke?" Wali squinted figuring it out.

"Try stolen bribe money." Alex snapped the money from him and handed the bills back to her. "We are not taking this. There is a lot of Bellecoeur's money floating around here. So be cautious."

She handed the cash back to Wali and smiled a brilliant, innocent grin. Wali almost melted off the bed. Alex rolled his eyes. Couldn't he see she was bad news? Because even if Alex liked her, he was smart enough not to trust her.

"We don't know the story behind this money, Wali. We aren't using it."

"She wants to help. We need a few things. We'll pay her back, eventually."

"I said no. This is the list of things we need." He tossed the list at Wali. "Get them and meet me at the church. The priest will have things arranged so you can charge them to him."

"Where are you going?"

Alex glared at Lacey. "I'm going for a stroll. See if ghosts manifest." He'd find out if there were law enforcers around these forsaken prairies. Somehow, he felt as if he'd been set-up and he didn't understand why. Why did Lacey need Alex and Wali to bring her southwest?

–Twelve–

The hotel owner shook his head. He was short and plump, wearing a dirty undershirt.

As he peered under his building searching for skunks, he asked Alex, "You're going where?"

"They call it the fifth creek."

"I heard you." The guy got to his feet. "I was making sure you heard yerself. Fool. That's ghost country. Boys tougher than you tried to settle the land and came back claiming it was impossible." He rubbed his nose on his hand. "Go that way and make noise. We'll make the skunks run out the back."

Along the other side, Alex peered underneath. Shiny eyes gazed at him. A family. "Nothing under here," Alex lied to protect them. He stood. "I talked to the priest, he thinks it'll work."

The bulky man marched up to Alex. "I said they claimed it was impossible, but I didn't mean aloud. They were dead. The priest lives in a dream. A dream of French settlers taking over the prairies. The land is cursed. This is the end of the land worth settling." He glared at him. "Ya sure you didn't see a skunk?"

"If you're afraid she'll spray customers, just build up the front with rocks and she'll be forced to go in and out the backend. No one will be the wiser."

"I was gonna shoot her."

"She's not hurting anyone. Just show her where to go." Alex began to pile up rocks to save the skunk. "So, I don't see any court houses. What's a guy do when the law gets broken around here?"

"The law?" The owner chuckled. "Most times we settle

things with our fists, our guns, or we let God decide by a good old fashion shaming."

"Shaming?"

"Yup. The locals call it that. They drag the guilty party behind a horse and string him up in front of a church. He's left for God to cast judgement."

"Oh. So you do know the locals?"

"The Cree up north, sure. The ones southwest are known as ghosts, 'cause they haunt the land. I swear I saw one who was right see-through. They are nasty. Kill a guy for walking their soil. We find dead guys out there all the time with arrows in their neck, and well, if yer stupid enough to go out there, that'll be yer fate, too."

"Any wanted posters I could check, because we ran into a few creepy guys along the way? As for this talk about ghosts, well, I need to know what's going on."

"We keep those up at the train station." He placed a hand on Alex's shoulder, but Alex kept piling rocks. "You seem like a smart guy, why ya doing something this foolish?"

Alex glared long and hard at the eyes staring back at him. They weren't judging him. They searched for their own answers. "You know the story from the Bible? The one where God asks Noah to build an ark and fill it with animals?"

"Can't say I do."

"Well, it's more a story about trust. I mean, he does it. He builds an ark, fills it with animals, and waits on his boat for a flood to wash out the world. And it does. It rains for forty days and nights. Imagine how he must have felt. There'd be doubt in this God and cursing Him because He was cold and cruel to the others. Of course, there's the deep question of why me? Why spare Noah and his family? Not to mention the desperation of what was to come next. Yet he believed in a bigger plan even if he didn't know it. His intense faith created a blind trust."

The man squinted, figuring him out. Alex worked, and finally the man joined him.

"I'm not saying I have God pushing me to do this, but I'm drowning inside, and there's something in me that wants to survive this flood. This journey is my ark and I have no idea what kind of world I'll disembark onto, but I have to trust it'll be the one that's right for me." Alex passed him a rock. "God stole everything from me and I hate Him. I curse Him and want to give up. Yet like the old fool, Noah, something inside me believes that if I trust Him, it'll be fine. Then I doubt the hate and imagine it's just me being afraid. And I ain't no coward, so I'll face whatever He delivers. Ya know? Maybe He knows something I don't."

"Like what?"

"Like why it wasn't me. Why did my girl die in a fire?"

"Damn. I am sorry to hear that, but I do like yer story." He stared long and hard at Alex. "I like you. The priest is finding it hard to reach more and more of us. Something has us terrified to breathe. I've been here the longest and I've seen more pack up than I can count. I wish ya luck, young fellow, but I won't be here when you get back. God abandoned this country and I'm heading to Winnipeg on my own ark."

"Safe journey."

"You, too." He continued building up the front and Alex left him to his task, heading to the train station to check the wanted posters.

There were two crude drawings of locals. One stole a horse and the other someone's daughter. The station owner looked them over with Alex. Alex understood what the hotel owner meant about the men being terrified. This guy breathed in quick shallow breaths ready to fight him.

Alex tensed as he stood near him.

"You going alone? You have a gun, right? Savages are always taking our things."

"Savages?" Alex glanced at him, shocked that they called locals this.

"Yup. They live wild on the land. No one wants to continue the tracks. That's why they end here. These guys aren't respecting towns anymore and no one is safe. Gavin Bernoit lost his daughter to 'em."

"They stole a child?"

"She's not much of a looker but my son fancied her."

"So they stole a grown woman?" Alex squinted, confused.

"Sure, right out of her house. She's going on twenty or so, I suppose, looked after the farm for her father since her mother died last spring. It gets rough without a woman around and Bernoit needs his gal to help. When I heard his tale, I dropped my things and joined the hunt. Brought my son along, maybe he'll come off the hero."

"And?"

"And nothing. Broke my heel, but we searched a decent stretch. She's probably dead but I didn't share that."

Alex glanced at the man's shoes. They were old. Dirty. Black. A chunk was missing from the heel on the left one.

He stared at Alex's bare feet.

Alex tried to grasp if these men were afraid because they didn't understand or if there was a secret war between the locals from the southwest and the settlers. "Dead? Why would they kill her? Did he see the locals take her? Are you fighting the locals?" If there was a war going on, he was heading back to Winnipeg. He wanted peace and didn't need to be involved in this mess. This wasn't his fight.

"You don't see the savages. They move like ghosts. Gave us our own ideas. This is our land and if anyone'll haunt it, it'll be us." He had a bit of a crazy look to him. Maybe the hotel owner had the right idea—run.

"So a woman goes missing and you assume the locals have her? I'm confused."

He squinted at Alex. "You'll see. They can't be trusted. If you plan to go on ghost country like everyone says, you'd better be ready to side with us."

"Side? I don't like sides. Last time I was forced to pick sides it didn't end well for anyone." Alex was about to argue that maybe she up and left as gals sometimes do, but decided this guy wasn't worth the argument. He got ready to leave.

"Well, if you see her, she has a scar on her neck. Can't miss her. Or so he tells me. I didn't actually ever see her."

"A scar?" Alex stopped and looked at him. Of course she did.

"You saw her?"

Alex shook his head. "I'm putting two and two together by what you're telling me, is all. I don't like what you're saying." A protective anger flared inside him. He wasn't letting them take Lacey back to that hell.

The man crossed his arms. "And why's that?"

"She has a scar on her neck prior to her disappearance. She worked on a farm her father ran while in her twenties. And you think the locals are to blame for her vanishing? Sounds to me like she didn't like the rules out at good old pa's house and ran off with someone who respects her. I wouldn't waste my time searching for this bloke." Alex pointed to the drawing of the Native. His hair was wild, his grey eyes tight. He looked ready to leap from the picture and kick their asses for even peeking at him. Alex took the poster down to get a better look. On the shoulder was a tattoo exactly like Silver's. Alex glanced around as if Silver might leap from behind the counter and demand Lacey from him.

"He invented this guy to save face." Alex decided to keep the poster. Silver might get a kick out of it. "Bet he's a woman-beater and killed her. The savage you should be hunting is him. He's scaring you with tales of locals coming in his home and taking his daughter. I don't believe that. I translated for tribes in Northern Québec and they didn't think in terms of ownership or fighting for land. They protect, and they belong. I follow three simple rules: respect me, respect you, and respect life. Follow those beliefs and you'll be fine."

"You go around talking like that, you won't make many friends. We have to have each other's back."

And who has their back? Anger exploded in him. "Or we could work with the locals since they know this land better than we do." Alex walked out before he got into any more trouble, but it annoyed him when people blamed others to save face. Yet he couldn't tell him that this woman with the scar was with Wali, and not by his choice, but by hers.

At least he knew a bit more about Lacey. If she stole her pa's money, he'd be searching long and hard for her. Alex wouldn't be the one to turn her in but he wasn't sure how to tell Wali he'd been taken in again.

He was standing at the edge of Laroche when Wali rode up in a wagon. Alex was glad to see him. They needed to get out of this town. Yet Alex took a moment to stare off in the distance, wondering what was out there. There would be no more trains. They'd travel uncivilized terrain. No more towns. Wali said that if they decided to build a homestead on the land, the land title officer had told him it would be the first home in the area.

The idea pleased Alex. He considered building a house for Wali just to see if he could. Really, what was stopping them?

Wali cleared his throat. He sat in the wagon with Lacey beside him, but she wore a veil and a fancy dress as if they were heading for a party. Her hair was done up in braids and she waved a fan that she clutched in her gloved hands. The transformation was shocking. He couldn't even tell it was Lacey.

"You coming?" Wali asked. "Or you gonna gawk at her all day?"

"How much do I owe the priest for this crap?" The amount of stuff they had in the wagon surprised Alex. They even had a cow tied to the back.

Wali couldn't seem to catch his breath. "Well. About that. See, Lacey had money… We told the priest I won it in a gambling match."

"He'll know you're lying."

"I lie to priests all the time, Alex, it happens to be the hazard of being me. Hell, I don't even tell you the truth anymore."

"I mean, a woman with cash is suspicious. Means a man is searching for her. Right, Mademoiselle Bernoit?"

Lacey stared straight ahead, but she took a pistol from her side and placed it on her lap. Wali wrapped an arm around her and pulled her in tight against himself. "We're pretending she's my wife. This way, we'll be left alone. I swear, if one more gal asks if I need her company I will probably flip out."

Lacey sat still, waving her fan, holding her pistol.

"Very well." Alex checked the wagon. This was more than the list. "You plan to bring all this?" Alex was doubtful. "I thought we'd check it out and head up to Moose Jaw."

"Why waste a trip? I don't have time to goof around. If we know what we want, let's do it. This isn't much. A few things to help us. Climb in."

Alex needed to walk and started out. Wali walked the wagon beside him. "You have any idea where we're going?" Alex asked him.

"Yup. Each section of land has markers left by the surveyors. We need to locate as many as we can, but really, we head west and south. Not too complicated. When we stop seeing homesteads, we're getting close."

"Any idea what these markers look like?"

"Posts with numbers on them. Either wooden or metal. They are in the corners of the land. If you plan to walk the whole way, keep your eyes open."

Alex scanned the prairies. Bison were to the north, and a silver streak blurred in the distance to the south, could have been sunlight dancing off the prairies, but he had his doubts.

–THIRTEEN–

Alex discovered that the posts were small markers and they weren't only hard to find, they were almost invisible. They stopped everything when they found the second one. Wali drew a square in the dirt with a rock and tried to place them on the map.

"This is confusing as dirt. These numbers don't make any sense," Alex complained.

"You were never good with numbers and maps. It's fine. Let me worry about it. It makes sense to me. Each section has a number that follows east to west. Each section is divided into quarters identified by their position. Northwest, Northeast, Southwest, and Southeast. They organize them into townships."

Alex glared at him. "How will I know when we're close, if the numbers are all stupid?"

"Just read them out to me. I'm mapping it out as we go."

Alex crossed his arms, doubtful anyone could make sense out of this mess.

"Well…I'm searching for the fifth creek, if you must know." He pulled the folded map from his pocket. "You can see it here."

"So you don't know what these posts mean any more than I do." That made more sense. Alex counted out how many creeks they'd passed. "We passed two. Are we setting up near the creek?"

"Yup. I picked this location because a creek ran by it, and the parcel of land next to it is saved for the school board. It's the prime spot."

"What the heck does that matter?"

"Well, once you have children, you'll form a school board

and buy the land. Then you'll have more land. The board will use the money to build a school wherever you want, and you're laughing."

Alex had no idea Wali planned like this.

They set up camp. The first night, Alex slept under the wagon and the others were beside him as if it were a brilliant plan.

Two creeks later and the second evening, Wali insisted on a fire, so Alex lay on the open prairies watching the flames, in case they spread. Sleep evaded him and he was ready to put the fire out when something moved in the distance. Alex leapt to his feet. "Did you see that?" he shouted to Wali.

"What?" Wali was as fast to his feet.

"I saw something. People-type."

They hadn't seen a soul yet.

"Shadows," Alex said.

"Probably a bear."

"This was a man. Or...a ghost."

Wali glanced around, panicked. He added more branches and twigs to the fire as if that might save them. "Probably one of them bison. Lacey? Where did she get to?"

Alex stayed on his feet looking at the darkness. He strained his eyes to peer into the night but nothing moved.

Wali lit his lantern. "I'll search for her. You coming?"

"Maybe she went for a pee." Alex didn't want them wandering around in the dark. He glanced at the fire, but found no comfort in the dancing flames.

"She always lets me know she's leaving."

"Check by the water," Alex mumbled, fixated on the spot where he'd seen the man.

Wali vanished down the bank. The moment he stepped out of sight, a monstrous man with wild hair rose in the shadows, growing from the earth. The warrior gripped his spear, creating a shiver through Alex.

A second shadow who might have been Silver met him and they vanished over a slight hill.

Alex stopped breathing, waiting. He was sure that if the ghost had wanted him dead, he would be. Every breath felt like hours passed.

"Found her," Wali hollered minutes later. "She was doing

her business."

The ghost appeared again, this time to Alex's right. He tilted his head, studying Alex. Then he jabbed his spear into the ground.

Alex let his bare feet dig into the earth, planting himself. If this ghost attacked, he'd fight.

Suddenly, the ghost melted into the earth and vanished.

Lacey and Wali burst to life behind him, pulling him back from the shadowy dream. He sat beside Wali who insisted Lacey sleep closer to the fire, which only made Alex more nervous.

Had he dreamed it? Alex stayed awake, waiting for the ghost to come back, but there was nothing.

He poked a small stick at the fire, promising himself he was in control of it. He even moved rocks around it to keep the fire contained. Everything felt weird in the gloomy night and he blamed it on the talk about ghosts. He knew the shadow was a man. He didn't believe in haunting spirits.

Yet, glancing out at the dark grasslands...anything was possible.

Alex poked the fire, lost in his musings. There were no logs. The twigs they had gathered burned fast. It wouldn't be long before the fire died and he could sleep. Yet even after he tossed dirt on it, he couldn't sleep. All night he kept Lacey in the corner of his eye. Was she meeting these warriors in the dark? How many shadows were out there?

He must have dozed off because morning was on them. Perhaps that's how things were on the prairies, dark one moment and light the next.

Alex considered the shadow as he made breakfast for them with flour and water. He prepared a tea with brown sugar, too, since he wanted to keep his flask of maple syrup a secret surprise for later in the trip.

Wali stretched. "You look shaken. Did you see something else?"

"Just a shadow, a dream I guess. We'll move out when you're ready."

Wali cleared his throat. "Thing is, ah...this is it. I think. I need to find a marker to make sure, but it seems about right.

The creek up ahead is the fifth one. Somewhere around this creek is the land we're searching for."

"Depends how accurate the map is."

Lacey washed up in the creek, down a path leading from their campsite, through the long grasses to the water's edge. Had such a worn trail been made by animals or ghostly men?

Alex glanced around. The place was different by day. The creek flowed peacefully. Boulders scattered around the area in odd formations. "You want to farm this?" Alex chuckled. "You might be mad. We'll find better land and sell this off to someone else."

"Well." Wali stood beside him. "Thing is, some of this is your land, and some is Xavier's."

"Xavier? The guy from Winnipeg?"

"Yeah, we'll buy the parcel of land back from him for a price. It was all in those papers you signed. I was only allowed so much, so I bought some in your name, some in his. I mean, I was sweet-talking him anyway, why not go for the whole thing?"

Alex frowned, thinking about those papers he'd signed without reading. He'd known better. "Why would you do that? How did you do that?"

Wali held his hanky to his nose. It bled again. "If you're not happy here, come fall, we'll pack up and spend the winter in Moose Jaw or Regina, and it all goes back to him, we lose nothing. Just give it a chance."

Alex glanced at the extra stuff in the wagon. That explained a few things.

"We'll build a homestead?" Alex peeked over at his friend, but he had no idea what to say.

"I messed up a lot of things in my life, Alex, but us, this friendship we share, it was always real, and I want you to know I appreciate that. I told myself if there was one thing I wanted to do this life, it was to see you smile again, and that smile is close."

Alex picked up one of the huge boulders and dropped it. This would take forever to clean up. He'd need a decent workhorse, because this was not something he could do alone. A cart would help.

Squinting toward the sun, he watched the area where the

shadow of the man had appeared last night. Horses wandered free.

"At the titles office, he told me this land was returned a few times because it's haunted." Wali chuckled. "Why I'm not brave enough to live here by myself. Figured how you seem to wisp through life lately that you'd fit right in."

Lacey walked back to them, she had something in her hand. When she was close enough, Alex grabbed a spear from her. The handle was carved with symbols and the tip was dipped in silver. He'd never seen anything like this.

"You found this by the water?" Alex demanded.

She nodded.

Alex said, "Haunted by locals."

"Locals?" Wali glanced around. "You mean like a tribe? Wouldn't we see them?"

"When we do, we better be friendly, because you might have paid for this land, Wali, but God gave every grain of dirt covering it to them. Or...Mother gave it to them. We need to think like them."

"I'll keep it under consideration." Wali shoved a knife along his back so it was easy to grab and Alex held the spear. This was a warning; they were being told to leave.

–FOURTEEN–

It took a full day to find the markers they needed. They weren't all there but by the end of their hunting, they had an idea where their land ran. Wali and Alex stood on the wagon surveying a few of the piles of boulders they'd used as markers.

"That's a lot of land." Alex was stumped as to how they would ever farm all of it. "What will we do with all this?"

Wali smiled. "We'll work the easiest 10 acres; build a homestead for you this year and one for me next year."

"We're too far from Laroche."

"With the land we don't use, in three years we sell it off and build a new town."

Alex chuckled. "We get to choose where a town grows?"

"Why not? The land across the creek is too rocky to work. That's where the church and school can go. Lacey has enough money. I'll ask her if we can buy land in her name. If she's the head of her household, they'll let her do that. She can own the land to the west of us. We'll call our town Montague or maybe Wali. I really want something named after me out here. It'll be perfect. See what she thinks." Wali brought out a flask and took a sip. He handed it to Alex.

Alex laughed at Wali's idea and drank a mouthful from the flask. He choked on it. "What the hell is this? I thought you were sharing your water. If we're to do this, we can't be getting drunk. We agreed."

Wali pulled the flask from Alex. "It's a sip. It numbs my pain. You don't want any, then don't take any. I agreed we'd go without until we arrived. We're here."

It couldn't hurt. Alex yanked the booze away from his friend and took a small sip then a bigger one.

Wali grabbed it back from him and drank the rest. "Where do we build a house?"

Alex glanced around. "This is the best spot for a house. It's high and overlooks the rest of our land. It's in the middle, kinda. Means we'll have the house always in our sight."

Wali nodded, clearly proud that Alex agreed.

Alex added, "We'll need a barn for the horses and oxen."

"Oxen?"

"To break land this rocky it's a must. So where we gonna find wood? Where are the trees?"

They surveyed the area. There were shrubs and plenty of bush area but solid trees for building were few.

"Nothing but rocks," Alex muttered. "It's possible. I mean, we could build everything out of rocks and sod. What we remove from the land so we can work, we use to live."

Wali had a huge grin. "Wow. You're getting into this. Nice to see you're back. I like this you better."

"You have more whiskey?"

—FIFTEEN—

The next day, Alex woke with a headache. Wali had stashed quite a few bottles in the wagon and they'd emptied most of them.

No one was around, but the sun promised noon. Alex forced himself up. Cursing himself for drinking. A blasted wolf could have eaten them. He needed to focus. Mattie would kick his ass.

Mattie was gone.

He stumbled around the camp with a bottle he wanted to finish so he didn't have to look at the booze again. Mostly he paced, planning, thinking, and cursing to himself. He moved a few rocks to outline where he wanted to build, but when he came back to them; they were right where they'd been to begin with.

Was he still drunk?

Something strange was going on. Finally, he decided to clean up. He stripped down and slipped into the cold creek for a quick swim to clear his head. The water was chilly, but crystal clear.

Letting the sun dry him, he lay on the bank, and sipped at the bottle, trying to make it last, watching the clouds roll in. Maybe it wouldn't be so bad here. The place was quiet.

He reached for his clothes but they were gone.

What the heck?

He shot to his feet and raced back to camp. Everything was packed up, even his clothes were folded in a pile on the ground. Horses grazed close by, as if waiting for him to hitch them up to his wagon and take off. Lacey sat on the wagon in her usual seat, her hands tied on her lap. She was dressed in a burgundy skirt that came down to her ankles. Her blouse was grey with long sleeves. She even had an apron on, ready to cook.

Alex rushed to untie her. "You hurt?"

She shook her head.

"Where is Wali?" he demanded, grabbing his pants and slipping them on, used to dressing in front of women, but she didn't even peek which was a sobering slap.

She pointed angrily to the open prairies and grabbed the bottle from him. She dumped the whiskey on his head before climbing from the wagon.

Alex chuckled. "I suppose I deserve that." He glanced at the wagon before following her. "You see who loaded this? What's going on?"

She shook her head while rushing forward. Lacey pulled up her skirt a touch so as not to trip on it and ran faster, in her bare feet.

He kept up with her. "Where were you last night while we drank too much?"

She stopped running to glare at him, then shook her fist.

"I annoy you, do I?" He faced her. "Well, I annoy myself, too." He dismissed her, needing to find Wali and get the heck out of here.

"Wali?" His voice echoed on the prairies. "I'd like to be on our way."

Lacey grabbed his arm and shook her head. She pointed to the ground with both hands.

"Give me one reason why we should stay."

Lacey dropped to her knees. Alex watched her. She placed her hands in the dirt and cried, eyes closed, saying a silent prayer. He watched her lips move. She was praying for someone to help her.

"You're staying here?" he asked.

She wiped her tears before she faced Alex. Eyes on him she leapt to her feet. She stomped her feet and glared at him. Geesh. Her emotions were all over the place.

"Fine, stay." He didn't have time for overdramatic women. "Wali! Where are you?" Alex ran his hand in his sticky hair. He needed another swim in the creek.

"Alex?" The voice was muffled.

Alex looked around. There was nothing but open prairies.

"Alex? I'm in a hole."

Lacey fled west and dropped to her knees. He joined her, shocked to see a hole.

Wali mumbled from below, "I don't think we should drink anymore."

"Looks like a trap. This is manmade." Alex ran his hands along the side of the hole, telling Wali about how their things were packed up and how Lacey was staying if they decided to go.

"Go? This is my land. I never actually owned anything this great before. I plan to die out here. Well, not in this hole. Get me out."

Alex was listening but not completely. The hole had him entranced. Whatever tools they'd used to chip away at this hole would come in handy to build his house. He should talk to these locals.

He glanced around the prairies at their future fields. Why couldn't he see them?

He refused to believe in the stories about ghosts. This was a real hole, dug by a real person.

Wali complained, "What are you doing? Just get me out, will ya? Cripes man, it stinks down here."

"You hurt?"

"A badger chased me in here. I don't remember much. I'm bruised up and my ass is sore."

Alex glanced around "Well, it's gone. Maybe you stepped on its burrow or something."

Lacey shook her head, banged her hands together, and tilted her head. Then, using both hands, she traced the figure of a woman in the air.

"Lacey says she was attacked by a woman. You didn't see anyone?"

"Dang. Is she hurt?"

"She looks fine to me. Better than us." Alex kept his eyes on her just the same.

"What time is it?"

"Late. I'll have to go back for things before I can get you out of there. It might take me a few minutes to put something together. Lacey will keep you company. Share a story or something."

"Bring me something to drink. Water, I mean. I need water. God, I never want to see booze again."

On the way back, Alex checked the ground for footprints. The grasses were different lengths but some places had no grass, just rocks. He was leaving a trail in the long grass and a startled deer jumped across his path. In the distance, some type of dog watched him. He didn't see any other signs of life except birds. The skies were littered with them.

Back at the wagon, Alex considered dumping the booze. Really, it was for the best. If they kept any alcohol, they'd be drinking again tonight. He opened the cap and the sweet smell hit him, making him queasy.

Before he could dump it, he spied movement. A woman. He stopped to watch her. She was alone with her back to him about twenty yards from the wagon. Her hands pushed deep in the soil.

As if she could sense him staring at her, she shot up and marched toward him. Alex checked around for help but there was no one. He clutched the bottle. He never felt so terrified of a woman. She was…a warrior. Like a ghost, she stepped at one with the world. Her strides had purpose, pride, and he was so in awe that when she pulled her bow and arrow out and pointed it at him, he stood there like a fool and gaped.

She yelled something at him, but he had no idea what.

Shaken from his trance, he fell on one knee and bowed his head. He tossed the bottle behind him and placed his hands in the dirt like hers had been a moment before.

She stormed toward him. A soldier of the earth.

He glanced up, then looked back at the ground. Her face was emotionless as she flew toward him in her animal pelt dress. Her hair was loose and long, the darkest black he'd ever seen. She was taller than he was, and graceful.

She stood before him. "What are you doing?"

"Bowing before a goddess of the earth." He had no clue what tradition called for but he bet humble and on his knees was his safest pose. "What were you doing to the earth with your hands in it?" he asked, digging his hands in. "What do you feel when you do this?" He scooped dirt up and smelled it as she had. She hit his hand and the dirt exploded on his face.

He blinked, surprised.

She spoke English again, with an accent that reminded him of when Bellecoeur and Mattie spoke English. "Dis land sacred and you hurt it."

"You were praying?" He gaped at her ankles. She had a tattoo on her leg of one of the strange symbols from his cross. He'd carved it into his woodworking and added this symbol into his story pictures. It was like a house with no bottom and a flat roof with a swirl inside like a ghost. Alex had no idea what the symbol meant, but seeing it run up the side of her leg intrigued him.

"Is this image a word? What does it say?" He almost touched her leg but she backed up.

Alex spoke French but she continued in English. "Dat is my earth mark. I earned it. Your dings are packed. You get your friends and you leave."

"I can't." He stood but kept his eyes down so as not to appear to be a threat.

"You will."

That simple. She expected him to leave. When he glanced up, she was nowhere in sight. Vanished.

"I can't leave," he called after her, wiping the dirt from his face. If Wali and Lacey wouldn't come, he wouldn't leave them.

He had nowhere else to go anyhow.

-Sixteen-

Later that evening, Sacri sat in the long grasses, watching the strange man. He fell to his knees to study something in the dirt, not far from the creek.

The others built things around a shelter or a primitive camp. She paid them little attention. This man fascinated her. Why couldn't he leave? He didn't say he wouldn't leave, he'd said he couldn't. Why had he bowed to her and smelled the earth? His French had a heavy accent. How far had he travelled?

He'd dumped the whiskey—that was smart, it was clearly poisoned. Had turned them into easy targets. She wiped her hands on her skirt. Her palms were sweaty. This was a strange feeling that even affected her breath and her heart—it raced as if she'd been running too fast.

Did he make her feel this way?

She couldn't leave. She was spellbound by him.

Sacri told herself that if he wouldn't go, it was her duty to watch him until Silver arrived and forced him to leave. Besides, he wasn't much of a danger.

The woman stretched and Sacri glanced her way. She was a curious one. She'd been in the tunnels yet hadn't shown the men the entrance. Sacri caught her blessing her face with light dust and when she saw Sacri, she ignored her as if Sacri were invisible. Her light brown curls bounced around her head beautifully. Sacri touched her own grimy hair. She was interested to talk with her.

She liked how this woman's dress fell straight but gave her room to move freely underneath. She wasn't fancy like other women who'd come out here. She was dressed to stay and work with the men. Sacri ran her hands down her own tight dress wondering what it would be like to dress like that. She decided she would like it.

The woman stayed close to the Chinese man and he spoke gently to her, but they weren't a couple. He talked to her like a brother, teaching her things, looking out for her.

The man Sacri watched, the one with the silky voice, got up from the dirt and hauled the ladder away. His sleeves were rolled up and his shirt was filthy. His muscles pushed against the fabric. She wanted him to remove his shirt and make himself at home, which was a wrong thought, but he was exciting to look at and she couldn't help those feelings, they fitted with her.

He'd made a ladder to help his friend. Over the years, when someone ended up in Silver's hole, either they died in it, which made Silver crazy, or their friends lowered a rope. No one had ever made a ladder. He didn't think like others. The ladder had actually taken less time to build than it had taken the others to haul their friends out or die. After he got his friend out, he had gone down the hole himself. It amused her that he had climbed down and talked in Silver's burial hole. Silver wouldn't like that.

She had no idea how to make him leave but she wanted to go up to him and hear him say things again. His French was thrilling. Richer than theirs and not mixed with Cree words. She could learn from him.

After he put the ladder by the wagon, he went down to the creek. All the way. He faced north, away from her and was on his knees in the tall grass. It blew around him, the wind making the grasses dance.

What was the earth telling him? On her knees, she listened with her hands in the dirt, but she heard nothing. Nothing. It was the first time in months that the earth wasn't screaming at her in pain. Mother should be angry, they were building something on Sacred Land, and this was unacceptable.

What was he doing to it? How had he stopped Mother's crying?

She sat cross-legged so her head was out of the grass and she could study the horizon for danger. As the train tracks had approached, the number of visits by settlers increased. Most moved on, but it would only be a matter of time before a group decided they *couldn't* leave.

Louis said he'd seen a crew of six headed this way. They'd be on this land by nightfall. He said they searched for a woman with a scar on her neck travelling with one of their warriors.

On the horizon, Silver appeared. She was relieved to see him. She brushed her lips in a silent greeting. He shot an arrow in the air to the northeast. Sacri leapt to her feet. Danger approached. She was ready to run but he signalled her to protect the three settlers. From the distance, he explained that six ghosts were on their way, and she was to kill them only if they attacked the woman.

With her hands, she let him know she got his message and returned to her hiding spot in the grass. She trusted Silver but he'd never asked her to protect settlers before…

Oh. The girl. Sacri studied her. She was walking to camp with a rabbit she'd caught and a fistful of leaves.

So this was Silver's mate. How would the others react?

He'd obviously taught her things to blend in, but she wasn't one of them. Maybe she didn't have to be. Louis' father had done fine: he'd raised a warrior. Still, this was Silver. Want or not, he led their people.

Sacri checked her weapons, ready to defend. Ghosts didn't scare her. Silver said they were men in sheets, he said they mocked *Cîpay* with their sheets because they said Sacred Land was haunted. Their ignorance made them dangerous, but a danger she could handle.

The ladder-man was by the creek, not moving. Maybe he slept sitting up. Wouldn't surprise her; he was weird.

She marched toward him. When she was close enough, she stopped to listen. He sang softly. Deeply entranced.

His voice soothed her worries. She listened in awe at his story as he shared his tale with the water. His words were from languages she knew, such as, French, English, and Chinese. But he also sang with words she didn't know. It told of winds blowing and mosquitoes biting. A song full of silly words sounding comforting together or jarring into each other to deepen the pain. The melody touched her when his voice softened even more and a smile melted words onto the water. He sang of a seductive warrior who terrified him yet warmed him inside. A hope he wanted to caress and couldn't grasp.

Maybe he sang of her. Maybe she was the painting he wanted to carve on stones. Maybe he'd noticed each breath she'd taken. Sacri glanced down at herself wishing it were true.

What if he sang of her? He'd called her a goddess born from the earth. No one had ever called her a goddess before.

She was drawn in.

Finally, consumed with his agony, she closed her eyes, too. His soft voice carried sorrow over the wind to settle on the water. She brushed his hand and joined his song with her own word, "*Cîwêw*." She wished him peace. Such comfort was all she could do.

He stopped the minute her hand grazed his, and recoiled. He flew back, shocked to see her.

Then he jumped to his feet and left her by the bank.

She trailed behind him, curious.

"Why are you following me?" he demanded in French, not facing her.

She relaxed. Speaking French was her favourite. Questions poured out of her. "Why not leave? Why sing a Song of Sorrow? Who have you lost? Why build a ladder?"

He faced her with a questioning look.

"I don't like you listening to me sing."

She'd insulted him. "Your song was not meant for me. I am sorry I listened, but the melody pulled me. Who is the goddess you met? Who do you sing to like this?"

He stared at her, ready to say things. His mouth opened but no words came out. He frowned and she was sure he would burst into tears like a child but his entire body gobbled the pain up.

She'd never met a man who displayed his grief so openly. She stepped toward him and spoke gently, "The Song of Sorrow is how we heal our pains, by letting our troubles pour back to the earth so Mother can bear them for us. I never saw an outsider do this, never a man. By sharing your pain, I meant to help. Who taught you to sing the Song of Sorrow?"

He frowned and scanned her lips as if they lied. "My... A..." He swallowed a lump. "A woman I was to marry. She loved to sing with me by the water and since her death, I sing to her, for her." He frowned.

Sacri was disappointed. She'd hoped the song was about her, but she couldn't tell him something so foolish. "So you feel closer to her when you sing this way?"

He shook his head. "I lied. I mean, it's the truth, it's why I started to sing, but a weird hope came over me. Maybe it's this place or…" He met her eyes. "Maybe it's you. I was lost in the moment, singing for you then you surprised me. For a moment, I thought maybe I was in so much pain I made you materialize to help me forget."

"I am as real as your pain."

"I see that. Too real. What does *Cîwêw* mean?"

"I wished you peace. I am sorry I stumbled on your moment." Why was she apologizing? This was her land to protect. He should apologize to her. Yet his sorrow flowed so deep, she wanted to see him smile. "I will let you grieve in peace." She prepared to leave but he glared at her in a terrified sort of way.

He marched up to her, too close, but Silver said to stand her ground so she faced him and didn't move, even as his hand came up to caress her. She prepared to flip him if he touched her, but he reached for the cross around her neck.

"Where did you get the cross?" He studied it. "This is mine. What happened to my chain?"

"No." Why did everyone want her necklace? She placed a hand to cover it. "Do not touch me."

"It's mine. Did the warrior with the tattoos on his arm give it to you? Are you Silver's wife? What does he want with Lacey?" He pulled away but was still in her soul space and his energy made breathing difficult in a way that Silver would not approve of. Sacri tightened her fists so she didn't touch his chest to feel him breathe.

"Where did you get it? My father gave it to me before he died. It's mine."

"This is mine," she said. "Honovi gave it to me when I was born."

"Honovi?"

"My father."

"I'll draw every symbol on this pendant and prove to you

it's mine."

She pushed him back. Movement in the distance caught her attention. "Ghosts." She rushed past him to point. "Hide the woman."

"What?" He pulled back when the men appeared, heading their way. "What the hell is that?" He jogged with her.

"Ghosts. They search for a woman with a scar and if they find her, I get to kill them. They mock our beliefs. Stay back."

"Kill? No. You do not kill anyone on my land. If they come in sheets, they're afraid to show their faces. I'll handle them."

"You?" She stopped to inspect him. He was shorter than she was but clearly strong. He had no weapons except a small knife in his right pocket. "What will you do to them?"

"Talk. Ask them to leave my land."

Could he talk to them? Would they listen? He needed to know what to say so she said, "This is Sacred Land, you do not own Sacred Land, you owe it. Tell them this. And know that the boy, Clement, he won't travel these lands without the sheet because he claims it protects him. You must keep him safe as I am his teacher. If they come veiled, it is because he is with them."

"Ah damn." He glanced at her. "Sorry, I didn't mean to curse."

"Curse?" She covered her mouth. Could he curse them? How powerful was he?

"I shouldn't say bad words in front of a lady."

She relaxed. This was a different type of curse. He meant some things a delicate lady could not hear. She scanned the area. Where was the lady? Did he mean her? She looked down at herself. No one had called her a lady before. She'd seen ladies in Moose Jaw. They were nothing like her and she believed they might die if someone told them words that cursed them.

Sacri was a warrior with no desire to be a lady. She wasn't sure which word was a curse. "I understand bad words. Slave is bad and those cursed with it are hard to free. Very bad. Get your people together to a safe area. I will fight."

"Fighting I do when necessary. Let me talk to these guys. Run back to the wagon and tell Wali to hide Lacey. I'm Alex, by the way."

"Ale-aches." She repeated his name several times, as she hurried to the wagon because the word didn't sound the same coming from her lips. It was a hard name. He was bossy, but she let it go this time because his confidence meant he understood the importance of his task and she was curious how he planned to get the ghosts off Sacred Land without a fight.

She paused to watch his steps. He didn't have a determined walk but a grounded one. He wasn't leaving, that was clear in how his bare feet met the earth and the idea should have terrified her yet it was a relief, almost a comfort to know he was here to stay.

She ran to her bow and arrow, forgetting about the others at the wagon, forgetting what Silver had told her about protecting the woman.

–SEVENTEEN–

Alex couldn't believe what he saw. Men sitting on horses, wearing white sheets they must have stolen off their beds. They approached as if their bizarre cloaks were normal. They'd cut in holes to see. He tried not to smile because clearly, they meant this to be serious, but it was amusing and he planned to laugh them off his land.

What was going on? Were these men the ones everyone feared and called ghosts? Why was Clement with them? Why was that earth goddess teaching him?

Alex trekked toward them, hands in his pockets. He didn't bother to check where Wali was or what he was doing but he'd better have a shotgun handy in case things went askew. Heck, maybe he didn't even know they were here.

"You're trespassing," Alex said calmly, but every inch of him wanted to pull them from their horses and pound sense into them. "I assume it's with good reason. Are you lost or searching for your own land, or is this some type of costume party I wasn't invited to?" Despite his anger, Alex chuckled. It rolled out of him until he was laughing with his whole body. He had to lean against one of the horses. "I'm sorry but this is the funniest thing I've ever seen. You boys are riding around on horses, wearing sheets with holes you cut..." His howl roared over the prairies, surprising him with how easy laughing suddenly was.

When he calmed a bit he said, "Take them off and join us for a round. We're celebrating because tomorrow we start breaking our land. Join us. Come laugh with me."

They glared down at him and a strange silence settled on the prairies. "Land around here isn't for you," one of them said, as he shifted uncomfortably on his horse.

"Ah yeah, this is our land. I don't mind if you boys come by for a round or two, but these sheets…" He chuckled again. "I'm sorry but if you come in these sheets, I'll laugh my ass off every time. What are you thinking? This is weird." He dropped the smile. "Frankly, it's disrespectful to a bunch of real ghosts." He grinned at his own joke since no one else laughed. "Join us. Dismount and toss the sheets aside so we can talk like men. Forget this." He searched them, wondering which one was Clement. Surely, he could convince him to…

"Not gonna happen." A gun clicked.

His insides tightened. Alex hadn't had a gun pointed at him in years, and back then, he'd been so drunk, the idea had amused him.

"Then you best move on. I enjoyed the chuckle but I do have work to do." Alex picked out the details he could. Despite the sheets, he noticed shoes, pant cuffs, eyes, and hands. One had a black teardrop tattoo and even though the warrior goddess had prepared him that Clement was among them, Alex felt like he'd received a blow to the gut. Why would Clement run with these men?

The wind picked up and Alex turned his back on them. His hand shook. He needed to carve or paint. Do something to get his thoughts in order.

He remembered the tattoo on the goddess' leg. With this image in his mind, he turned back to face them and took a better look for things he might recognize, in case he knew others in this group. The sheets made these things jump out until they were far from invisible.

Blue cuffs peeked out from the rider on the brown horse. His dirty black shoes had a broken heel like the man he'd met at the train station. He focused on him because he couldn't talk to Clement. It felt like a betrayal to Mattie that he was there but Alex had no idea why. It wasn't as if they were friends. Yet Alex knew how she loved her cousin and he would never do something so horrible to Clement. Not even if he deserved it.

"Heard you had a woman with you. Came to see if she was the girl our friend is missing."

Alex approached the guy with the chunk missing from his heel. Alex stood so that they looked at the camp together.

"None of us are missing. This is where we belong." Alex spoke to them all, and nodded. "We are all hiding from something that ails us, but unless Clement here wants to take his sorrow out on me like a man, I have no business with you guys. 'Fraid he brought you out here just to spite me."

Clement turned toward Laroche, but his silence made the other riders shuffle uncomfortably in their saddles. Alex glanced at each one, desperate, but no one acknowledged him, all eyes on Clement, waiting for him to make a decision.

"Clement. Come on," Alex pleaded when Clement started a trot back to town. "Tell me why you're goofing around with these guys." Alex raced beside him. "Maybe I can help you." Some desperate need was always in him to help this guy.

Clement slowed his horse to a stop and leaned down toward Alex. He lowered his voice. "I come for Sacri. That's all."

"Sacri? And who's that?"

Clement looked down at Alex with a deep breath. "She's none of your business. She'll fight and end up dead." His voice croaked. "I came to get her out of here."

"Fight what?"

"You'd better clear out. My uncle wants this land."

Alex grounded himself. "See, I knew you were a good guy. You're here to protect a woman. Is she a tribal? Your girlfriend? Join us. Introduce me. Clement, you're all I have left of Mattie. Don't leave. I want to meet this Sacri."

Clement looked back at their camp and for a moment, Alex thought he might join them, but then a click made Alex pause. He glanced over his shoulder. The guy from the train station was right behind him, pointing the cold metal of his pistol at Alex.

Alex was ready to run, yet couldn't. He planted his feet. Something about people telling him how to live always made him stand firmer. Like with the cougar, even when he knew better, he couldn't help it.

An arrow flew past Alex and lodged in the arm holding the gun. The gun dropped. Alex picked the weapon up, ignoring the scream.

The others didn't stay to chat. "Savages! Get!"

Clement was the last one to leave. He stared long and hard

at Alex but finally followed the others.

Alex watched them gallop away. Strange bunch. Still, a few fools in sheets, he could handle. Suddenly, the girl was at his side, watching them with him. Her bow was across her back but he was sure she'd shot that arrow.

"I had it under control. Let me handle idiots." He gave her the gun. She took the weapon with ease and slid it along the leather lace that tied her dress together.

"You laughed at them."

Alex nodded. "I did."

"They were not funny."

"They were a bit funny."

"This does not mean you can stay."

"As long as it means we don't have to go." Alex went to check on Lacey and Wali.

–EIGHTEEN–

It was too quiet to sleep. Was such a thing possible? Alex stretched out on the thin blanket. Tomorrow he'd start building to put a roof over their heads, and it was probably a good thing. The nights were cold and the mosquitoes annoying. He missed a warm bed.

"You smell that?" Wali asked in the dark.

The anxiety at seeing Clement riding around in a sheet tore at Alex, distracting him. "Huh?"

"You smell that?"

"You mean the stench of you needing a bath? Not sure how Lacey stands our company."

Lacey slept on a cozy moose hide. A lovely lilac fragrance came from her direction. Alex glanced over. A large pile of lilac flowers rested at her feet. Where the heck had she gotten those?

Alex planned to stay awake and see if anyone joined her on her cozy rug. He rolled over and inhaled deeply. The earth aroma was potent. As if someone dug. He yawned, sleepy. Despite his desire to stay awake, he was pulled into a deep, restful sleep.

When he opened his eyes, the sun was directly over his head, burning a hole into him. Noon? He'd slept until noon? He had a strange taste in his mouth. Why did he feel like he was…floating?

"Wali, why didn't you wake me?" Alex rolled into icy water. He leapt to his feet, shocked. The water was up to his waist. What the heck? "Wali, this is not funny." How far had he floated down the creek? There was a strange canoe behind him. His initial, wild fury vanished as he saw the humour in this. When had Wali made this?

The carvings along the side of the canoe were rough, but clearly a language and not like Wali's carvings.

The girl.

Why was she bent on annoying him? One minute she saves his life and the next she tries to drown him.

This doesn't mean you can stay.

Someone else bossing him around. This reignited his rage. No one would scare him off this land. Dragging the empty canoe behind him, he splashed in the water toward a large oak. In front of it, the reeds were gone, creating a shore that he now aimed for. Anger drove him forward. He hadn't done anything wrong and didn't deserve this treatment.

He cursed and swore vengeance, his feet sloppy and clumsy as he trudged through the unfamiliar territory.

As he approached the shore, a woman slipped from the shadow of the tree. "You storm around like a bull in water." Her smooth voice taunted him in French. She stood in the sunlight, nothing but a shadow to him. A slender goddess judging him from a distance. She could be a ghost.

Her.

"Leave this land. It can't be owned," she ordered.

"If this land can't be owned, you have no right to kick me off it. We'll learn to live here together."

He loved how she wore each emotion for the world to experience with her. Or maybe this display was just for him.

She bent and drew something in the dirt with her finger, then she was gone. Alex walked over to see what she'd traced in the dirt. It was a stick man in a canoe with a spear in him. Nice. Clear. He understood the warning. He glanced around, but there was no one for as far as his eyes could see, and the land was so flat that, standing on the bank of the creek, his pants dripping wet, he imagined that he could see all the way back to Winnipeg.

She was probably in the grass, he told himself. Yet the grass wasn't as long as where they'd set up camp.

He leaned against the tree. The oak was huge, at home yet out of place. He liked how it symbolized his own out-of-place feeling about being on the prairies. "How do I not get dead?" he asked the air in front of him. "Because that looks painful."

"Go home." She was in the water behind him, pulling the canoe up onto the shore. How had she got behind him?

She flipped the canoe and dragged it further up the shore, then slid it along the reeds and the bank, making it disappear. His anger vanished as he went to see how she had done that. There was a perfect hole dug into the bank. The canoe slid into it, out of sight. A shelf for a canoe.

His excitement showed on his face as he stepped closer to her. Even her stance was serious. This woman was used to men listening to her.

"I am home," he whispered the secret she wouldn't believe.

"This is my home. Go to your home." She pointed to the east, in case he was so dense that he didn't understand her. Then she babbled in a language he'd never heard, yet many of the sounds were like Cree and French mixed.

With his hands out he said, "Slow down, I can't understand you when you speak so fast. Use your hands to show me your words when you speak your language. It'll take me time to learn it."

She frowned and for the first time met his eyes.

Wow. Her eyes were golden. "I'm Alex," he said again, his mind numb.

"You wish to learn my language and not make me learn yours?"

"You clearly know mine. Your French is better than Wali's." Alex chuckled. "You said something about earth and wind, but I didn't catch it."

She said it again. The same word she'd said while he sang.

"Peace?" He nodded. "I won't disrupt your world. It is peaceful. Too much perhaps."

She went off again. Pointing to the tree and the boulders.

"Sorry, I touched your tree and rocks. Show me what to use. I need rocks to build myself a shelter, trees would be good, too, but I don't have to touch yours."

"All these rocks are sacred. No using them. And stay away from Sacred Oak." She crossed her arms. "Go home."

"I am home." The more he said the word, the more he knew it was true. This was where he would raise...everything. He smiled at her and her golden eyes seared into him.

"Cannot stay. You must go. Elders will not allow this. You are bad for this land."

"Me? What did I do wrong?"

"You..." she pointed to the rocks and the tree again. Finally, she looked at the creek and the mud for support. She blurted out, "You breathe wrong."

"Now my breathing offends you?" He watched her chest. She wore a tight pelt dress that brought her cleavage together and the cross around her neck spilled into her breasts. He shouldn't be staring at them but her bosom rose slightly as her chest filled effortlessly. She was right, he didn't breathe like her. He wanted to breathe with her. It looked so...peaceful.

"It hurts when I inhale. Teach me to breathe like you."

She stepped back. "I... No."

Still, he watched her inhale and stepped closer. This close he had to glance up a smidgen to meet her eyes.

"Each breath has a past, a reason, and leads to the future," he said.

He matched her breaths. They were slower. Longer. Each one filled him with her earthy fragrance. "I like breathing with you. But sometimes, I don't deserve to breathe."

"No one does. Breaths are earned until they never end."

"Where are my friends?"

"Your companions left."

"Why?"

She smirked. "*Cîpay.*"

Was it the name of her tribe?

"Wali wouldn't leave me. He'll be back."

"I will make him leave again."

Maybe she was right. Maybe they should leave. Yet the more she wanted him to leave, the more planted he felt. He would prove to her that he could do this.

He followed her, curious as she headed north. "How do you find your way? Everything is the same out here. Well, except the tree." Being lost didn't frighten him. The idea was actually kind of fun. What would he do? How would he survive? It was a challenge he liked.

As this daring quest for adventure came over him, she broke into a run. Excited where she might lead him, he chased behind her. They ran north, into land he hadn't explored yet. They were beyond the land that he and Wali owned. Maybe she was leading him to Wali. He pushed on with that hope.

After only about fifteen minutes, he was hot and tired of running, his wet pants were uncomfortable, yet she continued. He was too stubborn to stop. He wasn't sure anymore if they should stop. Maybe they could run like this forever.

They passed surveyed land. By the stakes, cut path, and railway ties scattered about, Alex expected that rail lines would come through soon. Which was good. They'd be close, yet far enough. He thought these things, but something inside him didn't care. That was another world he could easily leave behind.

His burdens melted off him with each step. He ran with her, free and blissful. She was ahead of him, but he didn't mind. He secretly enjoyed not knowing where they'd end up, or what they might see. His adrenaline spiked when he thought about maybe running into a bear or a wolf, or even another cougar.

He stepped into the different types and lengths of grasses, and closed his eyes for a minute to feel the wind whip at him. It was warm, and had a smokey taste to it.

She stopped.

He caught up to her, ready to ask where they were but his words wedged in his throat. The grass was healthy and green at his bare feet, but inches away, life was gone. He didn't dare move. What had happened? A panic swept over him as if the darkened grasses might suck him in and destroy him.

Maybe it was because he had no idea where Wali was, or maybe it was because looking at the death inches in front of him was too familiar, but the freedom from moments earlier crashed from him. This lifelessness was how he felt inside.

Alex stared at the death before him.

"What do you see?" Her voice implied that this was a test, but he had no answer for her.

He checked to the south, knowing that his land was not far, ready for him to build a house on it. The creek flowed through it. "It's... What happened here? Why is this grass dead, and this grass healthy?"

"When the fires start, head for the creek."

"Start? They'll be more? Will they come to our camp?" He found it hard to believe they'd been this close.

"Maybe. This fire touched the Sacred Oak, but it healed quicker. This was burned deep and will take longer to find new life."

The idea terrified him. Everything was open. He could almost see flames eating at the prairies in rapid hungry gulps. How would they survive the destruction? What had stopped this fire?

"It's not the fire that kills you, it's the smoke," he told her numbly, remembering how limp Mattie had been when he'd hauled her out. She'd been feet from the door. So close.

The woman knelt to touch it but he pulled her back, afraid the death would suck her in.

"It's fine. The fires passed through and are gone." She brushed aside the black and underneath was green grass. "Life returns. One blade at a time. Come see." She pulled him down with her but Alex didn't dare touch the grasses.

She showed him her soot-covered hands.

"Fires are good. They bring new growth."

"They kill. This is dead."

She smiled. "Bad things happen yet the joy inside can't be touched." He listened to her carefully, searching for some sense of reason. "The secret is that Mother needs fire to give new life. Besides, nothing will damage the roots. They are deep and protected by Mother."

She rubbed soot onto her fingers from a pile of ash that was probably a cluster of bushes before the fire. Then she brought her hand up to his face. He didn't move as she smeared the soot on his face with two fingers. She moved slow and warm against his cheek.

She prepared to do the same to her face but he stopped her.

"Let me." He stained the soot on his fingers and brushed them to her skin. She closed her eyes, making him pause with his fingers on her cheek. Her head rested in his hand and they sat, her with her eyes closed, resting her cheek in the palm of his hand, him on his knees admiring her lips. In his mind, he saw his lips on hers. Desperately searching her for answers.

He didn't even know her name.

He edged in closer, until her lips brushed his with her words, "Your touch is…full of honey."

He pulled away and looked at the handprint he'd left on her cheek. "Honey?"

"Yes, honey. It's difficult to get, sticky to my skin, and sweet to my soul. Honey."

He smiled. "I have a honey touch?"

"Very much so. I never felt that before."

"Why did you bring me here?" He smeared the soot on his shaking hand. He needed to draw. "Give me your leg so I can draw on it."

She sat on her bottom, her long legs in front of her. "I didn't bring you anywhere. You came on your own."

Alex appreciated the canvas of legs in front of him. Her sensual skin was golden and he rubbed the soot on her legs, tracing over them with his vision. Drawing wind and water over the ground, coming together. Images exploding onto the world. He traced the soot over her tattoo wishing he had made it for her, adding in details to it.

"It was nice to run with you," he confessed as he worked. "I usually plant myself and fight. Running for no reason was freeing. Were you going somewhere? To find Wali?"

"Why must I need a reason to run?"

"Well," he glanced up from her sexy legs, "most people do." He slid her feet together and drew an image that connected along the top. It was a long blade of grass made of soot.

He worked, energy flowing in his movements. Then he wiped his fingers on the grass to clean off the soot.

He studied his work.

He was never a good artist, but he loved making symbols.

She stayed relaxed on the grass, her legs his masterpiece. His. He met her eyes.

"Each image tells a story," she whispered.

He wanted to share his journey with her. "Yes, a story." His words stuck in his throat as she peered into his soul.

He forced his eyes back to the images on her legs. He doubted they made sense to her. He was ready to explain it but she pointed to the swirls by her knees. "This is me swirling with life. You are these grasses, set in your ways.

The fires came." She leaned in and traced the air over the fires spreading over her ankles. "Something burned you inside like this, but there is a tiny blade of hope that grows." She pointed to the blade spread across the tops of her feet.

Despite himself, he smiled. "These swirls aren't you. That's me fighting, me dreaming, me wanting things the fire destroyed."

She nodded. "Those same swirls are trapped in the blade of grass. Is it me?"

"That's the dreams, the fights, the want locked inside me. I won't dream, fight, or want anymore. It's making me...not me."

She rubbed soot on her fingers and linked the swirls he'd drawn until they looked like the tattoo on the side of her leg and he was amazed at the transformation. He caught her hand and whispered, "You are not in these images for you are the canvas."

She said, "The fire changed these swirls and now they are one. They are new. You cannot go back, but you'll grow stronger with these beliefs inside you. This is how you earn an earth symbol."

He considered her teachings and his hand shook, needing to draw more. Giving into these urges was so satisfying. He was tempted to ask her to undress so he could cover her in the images his mind wanted to see on her.

"Look." She moved a few more blades and there was a strange plant. "This is a tree. It was not here before, but now it grows, new. Different because this fire changed things, brought to life new things, made the old things new."

He watched her lips move, lost in them. "Now I want to draw a tree on you."

She nodded, as if such a thing might be possible. "A tree so strong it will shade this blade of grass. The blade will look up and wonder how you grew so strong. Only you will know the fire burned you inside to make this happen." She smiled. It was so full of hope that he almost asked what she meant, but a part of him didn't want to know. She spoke in images.

"Your words imply that I'm stronger for my battles, but I feel so lost," he admitted.

"Lost? I thought you were home?" She stood. "What if I

told you, that these images are from my dream?"

Alex rubbed the soot between his fingers. It smeared on his skin. Something in him itched to draw more. He'd always been this way, impulsive and compulsive. Needing to do things when his thoughts jumbled.

"I'd say that's strange, wouldn't you?" He gazed around at the open prairies. "Then again, maybe not. Everything is so connected here. I have to confess, I know your tattoo. I draw that symbol all the time. It's from my cross. The one you're wearing."

"Then it is settled, we are both strange and you are in fact not lost but exactly where you are meant to be."

He chuckled, then a pang of guilt washed over him. How could he find joy while Wali was missing? "I need to find Wali."

"Walll-ee? Is this your friend?"

Alex nodded.

"Silver brought him on a healing journey."

"Will Wali come back?"

"This is how healing journeys normally work, yes."

Alex frowned. "What happened to Lacey?"

"The woman who blesses? Is she your mate?"

"No," he snapped.

"I did not see, but Silver says she went for supplies."

"Did she take our things? Our wagon?"

"Last I saw, all these things you brought were at your camp."

He was relieved. Wali would be back, and she'd let them stay or she wouldn't be talking to him like this. She wouldn't be letting him draw all over her. Gosh. Did she feel this connection between them?

He was about to ask her but touched the blades of green grass hiding under the soot. Life was here, fighting for growth.

He stood amazed at how at home he felt. "Can I learn your name?"

"I am Sacri."

"Sacri?" So this was the woman Clement wanted to protect. She had called herself his teacher. He frowned, trying to figure out what was going on. "Are you..." He didn't want to talk about Clement, so he said, "What language is that?"

"French."

"No."

"Yes." Her eyes sparkled in the sunlight.

He fell in step beside her, enjoying her company.

"A priest wandered through when I was born. I was screaming, screaming for my mother who died in childbirth. Nukum asked the priest what was my name. He didn't know what she said and he answered, 'ça cri', meaning 'it cries'. They assumed he spoke my name. I am Sacri, protector of the cross."

Alex couldn't help himself, his grin exploded to life. He loved wild tales like this and she told it with such liveliness. "It's a fun story. Would you like a tea? I'll warm water and well...that's about all I have. No, I do have maple syrup. If you add a drop to the tea, it's magical."

"Hunt if you are hungry."

"Oh? Am I allowed to hunt on your sacred land?"

"The land is here to feed and nourish those who respect it. Respect your kill with a prayer so his soul finds the light. I won't deny you life."

"Perfect. And you'll teach me to hunt?"

She frowned. "What type of man comes to live off the land but knows not hunting?"

"Well. You see, in my old world, we have jobs. A task we get money for that we exchange for food."

"Yes, I know jobs and money." She nodded and pulled a twenty-dollar bill from her satchel.

"Whoa. Where did you get that?" He studied it while they walked.

"Found some bills in the tunnels in Moose Jaw. I have a few more. Do you want them?"

He handed it back to her. "They're yours if you found them."

"I use them for traps in the tunnels."

Alex shivered. He didn't like the idea of tight areas or being trapped underground. Open skies were more his thing. "What do you trap with money?"

"Men. These bills will be their demise."

He burst out laughing but she looked serious.

"I see. And what do you do with these men you trap?"

"I ask them questions, and teach them to respect the land."

"What type of questions? You searching for something?"

"I hunt for a man."

"Oh. Any man in particular?"

"Yes. The Man of Legends."

He paused. Clement had used the expression once when talking to Mattie. "Legends, eh? Well. Good luck with that." A bitterness seeped into his voice he couldn't control. He didn't want her out trapping men or searching for some hero they told stories about from generation to generation.

"So I can teach you to hunt?" she asked.

"I don't need a man of legends, I have Wali."

She giggled and her joy bounced off the prairies.

He bowed his head, "I don't eat meat. I don't use animals for anything I don't have to." Of course, he might need them to survive out here, she had a point.

She frowned. "What else will you eat?"

"I'll manage."

She surveyed the prairies and pointed to a prairie hen. "There is supper."

It waddled peacefully in the grasses. "I'm not killing that thing. Look at it all happy, getting ready for a date."

"That is my supper, beside it is yours. That tall plant with the big leaves has delicious roots." She smirked. "What job did you do in this other world of yours?"

"Lots of things. I don't like to label myself or limit myself. I was a translator, a carpenter, a farmer, a store clerk. I love to sing and draw…" He shrugged. "Not much of anything, I guess."

She considered this. "Words and building? That won't work on a hen or finding roots. They don't like words or building, and drawing even less."

"I don't suppose."

"Do you have a weapon?"

"No."

"Do you fight?"

"Sometimes I find things worth fighting for."

"What do you use to fight?"

"My fists."

"Fists won't work on a hen and aren't for digging." She slung an arrow and pulled. The arrow vibrated through the air and the prairie hen was dead instantly. "I hunt and dig, you cook."

"Sounds fair. Will you teach me to cook it? Will you be insulted if I don't eat it?"

"A hungry man eats."

She grew silent, staring off into the distance as they approached the area where the train tracks were destined to be. A ghost appeared on the horizon. Not a real one, Alex promised himself, but as he stared at a white sheet blowing around a man, he had to wonder if maybe it was a ghost.

"Clement again," she said.

"How does he know you? You said you teach him… What? Did he give you my cross?"

"Oh?" She looked at him shocked. She reached for the one around her neck. "He gave me one like this."

"It had a gold chain."

She nodded. "I gave it to Silver."

"Well, I want my cross back. I met this Silver. He told me I could have it if I brought Lacey here. Can you get it for me?"

"The pendant is Silver's to give. If he told you this, he will keep his word."

Alex relaxed. "Why did Clement give it to you?"

"It was a gift. He told Silver he wishes to marry me in the ways of your tribe."

A strange panic gripped Alex. "And did you?"

She swallowed a lump. "His offer haunts me."

Alex didn't like the idea of other men haunting her. Clement even less. "If your answer is no, I'll make it clear for you."

She studied Alex. "This is not what I mean. Regardless, I must teach him. He must learn how to be a respectable father. I have to consider the offer because he could make things much easier for my people."

"Easier isn't always right. Sometimes you have to fight to get what is right." Alex frowned and looked at her belly. "What you said about him learning how to be a respectable father… Do you want to have his children? Are you pregnant?"

She studied Clement. "He is a child himself. He will grow up and needs a good father to teach him how he should act so that he will make someone else a good husband." She closed her eyes with a regretful sigh. "Did you have a kind father?"

"I did. He was a farmer. He always stopped what he was doing to spend time with me. Why?"

"If he agrees to meet you, will you be his father?"

"How old do you think I am? Geesh, Sacri. I'm only twenty-seven."

"He is lost, Alex. At a troubled spot. He lost Mattie and she was his last hope. I must help him understand that I am not what he wants. I need his help." Sacri's hand shook. "I must go."

She bolted.

"You knew Mattie?" Alex called after her, but she was too far and didn't turn around.

What the heck was going on?

Alex headed back toward his land. He was about to leave the hen then he figured it might insult her so he picked it up and checked the plant she'd shown him. He dug up the roots and brought them with him back to camp.

-Nineteen-

As he approached the camp, Alex caught sight of his wagon. A fire burned beside it. He ran, hoping Wali and Lacey were back, but the camp was deserted.

Hungry from the run, he made porridge while munching on the roots of the plant. They were sweet and he decided to try boiling them next time.

He had no idea what to do with the bird, but he drew the line at boiling it in his porridge pot. So he pulled off the feathers and cut the meat into pieces he arranged on stones along the side of the fire.

He hated to admit it, but as the tender meat sizzled, it looked appetizing.

While her supper cooked, he hauled out the shovel and pick, and began the hole for his house. The rocks he'd used to outline it were gone and he was tired of Sacri moving them, so he dug. It didn't matter where he built it, he had to dig down and plant roots. He'd been doing nothing for too long, and doing things with his hands always felt right.

He cut out the sod carefully so he could use each piece, amazed how it came out like a brick about a couple inches thick with stringy roots sliding through it. They would stack nicely.

Alex cut them in rectangles so they were about two feet long and a foot wide, give or take, and piled them along the edge of what would be his house. He saw exactly what he wanted to do in his mind. He knew from experience to build bigger than his initial judgement so he doubled his outline. He imagined enough room for three or four beds, a table, a stove, and a few extras. There might be three or four living in his house for a couple years, since he didn't know what the situation was with Lacey or how long it would take him to build a barn and a decent house. Winter might be long on the open Plains with no trees for shelter. He considered these things while he dug into the ground making a long wide hole about two feet deep.

He used the dirt to build up the sides, not in piles, but he packed the soil down along the edges, adding height to his hole instantly.

It was late when he felt the hole was deep enough. The sod lay in heavy clumps around it, leaving him pleased with the progress, yet he found stopping hard. A part of him wanted to continue until he was done. Like with the drawings on Sacri, he had more to do and he could see the work that was needed.

Yet he knew the hole would be waiting for him in the morning. Unless Sacri filled it in. This made him even more determined to get his house done before she returned. He moved the wagon closer to the foundation and set up camp in the hole.

The hen was cooking. Someone had turned it and added branches or twigs, from the bushes by the creek, to the fire. He was so caught up in his work he hadn't noticed.

The stack of dry twigs and sticks by the fire was new. He also noticed a pile of dried bison dung. He wasn't sure what the bison chips were for so he shoved them aside and added twigs to the fire. The bird sizzled, and the smell intrigued him. He was hungrier than he'd thought.

When he stopped, he pondered where Wali could be. And what about Lacey?

They'd be back soon, he promised himself.

It smelled delicious but he mixed flour with water and fried himself supper. The longer it cooked the more Alex wondered if he should taste the bird. Breaking free a piece, he rolled the meat between the fried flour, then bit into it. And another. The taste was interesting, a bit wild for him, but then he remembered the poor bird standing there. The idea of it now being in his mouth made him gag. He probably wouldn't have swallowed except Sacri appeared beside him, so he forced it down.

She dangled an onion in front of him. "Found you this."

"Thanks. You'll have to show me which plants out here I can eat and how to prepare them. I'm not familiar with any of them, but I do have seeds and will make a garden. Until then, little treats like this are wonderful. Thank you." He peeled it.

She picked the skin off the ground and hid it in a satchel she had around her waist.

Alex rinsed it off in his bowl and cut the onion to eat with his fried flour. It was delicious and he ate guilt-free.

Sacri mumbled a prayer with her hands in the earth. She used the dirt to wash her hands and arms, then her feet. Once she was as dirty as possible, she pulled meat off the bird and ate.

She still had soot on her legs and he was about to comment on it when she said, "Your fire needs life." She pulled a bison chip from the dirt and tossed it on. The dung smoldered but didn't flare up. Alex smirked. Yeah, it might work. She knew secrets to survive.

"Did the ghost leave? Or is Clement coming for me to father?" Alex asked when he couldn't eat another bite.

"Louis spoke to him. Clement will not come see you. He is jobbing for money and his job is to get you off this land so his uncle can own it. Clement does not like you."

Alex shifted. How much had Clement told this Louis? "I suppose I don't like me sometimes either." He glanced around, feeling like a million eyes were on him.

"He wants to please his uncle, like he would his father." She touched her neck but the necklace was gone.

"Did someone take your necklace from you?"

She glanced away from him. "I broke it in anger when Louis told me what Clement said."

"Does it need a lace? I have one." He unlaced the leather tie from his bag to show her it would work. "Don't let him upset you. He hated me long before I met you."

She pulled the cross out of her satchel and handed the pendant to him. Such a simple gesture full of trust that made him work quick to fix her necklace and hand it back. "Is it weird that this is the same as mine?"

"Legends say there were two. I always believed this." She didn't take it from him. She turned around so he could tie the lace around her neck. Again, a simple gesture, but he couldn't move. He swallowed hard. Breathing was impossible.

She waited.

The leather weighed a ton as he moved his arms around her.

She lifted her hair for him.

Her neck was long and he saw himself slowly making his way up it with gentle kisses.

Against the warmth of her neck he whispered, "What legends?" The necklace dropped around her and he came in too close to tie the lace. They sat like this, not moving, even after it was done up.

She told him a story about some curse killing off settlers and their crosses saving a couple. He barely heard her, watching her lips. This close, the words embraced his soul.

She brushed her cheek against his before pulling away. "Thank you," she said with her hand on the pendant. "It never feels right when I am not wearing it."

"I know what you mean. So how did you meet Clement?"

"He saved me. Long ago. About ten summers past. Now I must save him."

He'd never understand her ways so he settled on accepting them. If she had to save Clement, so be it. "I'll help you save him. You…you mentioned Mattie. Was Mattie with him when you knew him ten years ago?" Despite himself, his voice crackled on her name.

"Of course."

Alex edged in closer to her. "What was she like as a child?" He wanted to share that he had almost married her, because he was proud of this, but his past suddenly felt like a meaningless secret.

Her voice was a melody as she talked about Mattie as a child. Sacri saw the world differently and her passion amused him. She spoke about the teachings Mattie needed and not her personality or her looks.

Yet by the things she wanted to teach this young girl, he could paint a picture of Mattie perfectly.

"You taught her to sing." The idea gave him comfort. "The world feels so small. I can't believe I found you. Everything I loved about her…well…you taught her these things." He smiled. "I used to wonder how a guy like Bellecoeur could have such a wonderful daughter and now I understand. She lived by your teachings. You touched her life, Sacri, giving me a moment of happiness."

"Mattie was the girl you were to marry?"

He nodded.

Then her hands fell on his shoulder and he pulled away from her warm embrace, even if her touch was needed. He didn't deserve it.

"Oh Alex, I am so sorry."

"Doesn't matter. That life would have been perfect." He studied his new world. The hole he planned to sleep in tonight. "I lie. That life would have been a horrible lie. She was marrying me to make her dad mad and I wanted to matter. I was lying to myself and I still am. Now I live here and talk about her with someone who taught her how to be so wonderful and I wonder if maybe this is my true destiny. Is it possible to matter here?"

"Everything that matters is here." She stood to pace around his hole. "So you know Mattie's father?"

He sensed there was more to her question.

"Yeah, I worked for him. He hates me."

She turned her back on him as if his answer was not the one she wanted.

"Sacri?"

"Are you building an altar or a trap?"

"This is my home. Well, it will be. I see the house in my mind, but I've never actually built anything like this before. It's temporary, because we need shelter. I'll build a real house once we get seeds in the ground, and a barn up. I can work on it this winter."

"Looks like a hole and will fill with water when the snow melts."

Alex hadn't considered that.

"How do I keep the inside dry?"

"Ask Silver. He likes holes. Digs them for warriors all the time. But you cannot dig your hole deeper."

"I don't plan on. It's as deep as I need it." He wondered who Silver was to Sacri. Was he her husband or Lacey's? Maybe he was the chief and had several wives or something.

Alex didn't know why he cared but he needed to know. Sacri was close to Alex's age, she could have a husband and several children for all he knew. She'd turned down Clement and he was well off.

Finally, he blurted out, "And Silver would be...someone you care about?"

"Yes."

"Your boyfriend? Husband? Lover? Mate?" What did he care if she was married? He didn't, he promised himself, yet he waited for her answer as if the fate of the world depended on it.

"No."

"So...will he care that I drew on you today and want to draw on your entire body under the moonlight, breathing so close to your skin I might be able to taste it?"

Her eyes grew big and in a breath she said, "Yes, this would be important to tell him."

He was breathing weird and it bothered him that she had this effect on him. He needed to distract himself. "Tell me more stories. I need to hear you talk."

"Words. Yes. I forgot your job is words. I like words, too. Silver says I speak too much. Listening is important. Feeling the earth is hard to do when I am always going off at the mouth. I respect his teaching. But between us, using words is better."

So Silver was her teacher. A brother? "Talk as much as you want with me. In any language you want. I love hearing you speak different languages."

He sat against the wagon, full, warm. His only problem was Wali. If he left to search for him, Sacri would be throwing them off the land. "I won't leave. That's what you want, but I won't. You bring my friends back. Lacey isn't safe in Laroche. Those ghost-fools who came were searching for her because she's in love with a shadow from your tribe. I assume it's Silver, but I don't know that for sure. He might be the guy sent to keep her safe. All I know is that she's safest here."

"Yes, we don't go to Laroche and I doubt Lacey went there for supplies."

"So there are other towns?"

"Supplies are all around us, no need to go to a town." Sacri bowed her head sadly.

"What's wrong?"

She studied his bare feet. "Sometimes, I wish you were the Man of Legends."

"Why? What's so special about him?"

"He is the man I wish to raise my children with. He would be able to stay."

Alex rubbed his jaw, thoughtful. "Is he around here? Can I meet him?"

"Not tonight." She shook her head sadly.

Alex wanted to leap toward her and bury his head against her neck but instead, he closed his eyes. "It'd be nice to know I have a purpose and it's that simple. Find Sacri, be her Man of Legends, and marry her." He smirked. "What did he do to be the Man of Legends?"

"Mother has not sent him yet, but he will come. Legends say he protects Sacred Land when all else has failed. I believe this. I believe it is time for him to come. There can be no settlers on Sacred Land, it is for spirits only."

Alex glanced around expecting a warrior to leap out and kick him off the land. "How will he keep them off it?"

Eyes closed, she released a long breath. "The Man of Legends will know what to do."

"Yes." Alex studied her. "I suppose he would be at least that smart, being legendary and all. Do you have a lot of legends in your tribe?"

"We have many about Sacred Land."

"And this would be the ground we sit on?"

She nodded. "Under us is a Ceremonial Chamber. Our ancestors are buried here and our future will be born here."

"Underground?"

"It is from here they emerge into new lives. Every part of Sacred Land has a purpose and *Cipay* tribes protect each part from destruction. There are many dangers to Sacred Land, but this new danger is not one we know how to fight. What do the white tribes want with our land?"

Alex shrugged. "To farm it, I guess. It's rich soil."

"This is the most holy of the lands. My dream made me feel that I could protect my home by finding the Man of

Legends." She pulled a yellow flower from the grass and studied it before shoving the flower into her satchel. "Of course, finding him is hard."

"I suppose this might be true, but from my experience, sitting around waiting for a hero to show doesn't really work. Legends are usually stories about things that are past not future because no one wants that type of responsibility. Safer to take care of things yourself."

"If any of us understood how to protect it, we would not need him. These legends might sound like the future to you, but to Mother, our future is so set, it is already the past."

Alex reflected on what she meant. "So, you'll marry the Man of Legends then what? All will be good?"

"No. That will keep Sacred Land safe, but my actions will not end the curse."

"Curse?"

"My brother called on the Cursed Lands to protect Clement and me from a shadow, but it was not enough. This curse must now be stopped. Only my family will be able to do this, but we have lost this knowledge." She studied her hands. "Perhaps we never had it and Mother will bless our children with it."

Alex glanced around uneasy. "What exactly are you talking about?"

"No one believes me," she mumbled.

"I wish I didn't, because it makes me nervous to think my life might be controlled by some curse your brother made and that I'm living on some destined path that's pre-set." He thought for a moment. "What about if you forgot about legends and curses for a bit and had some fun with me?" He smirked.

"I have no time for fun. My people will die."

Responsibility weighed on him as if her destiny were his own. "I just mean… Forget it. What do I know about being responsible?" He tossed a small twig on the fire, frustrated. "I do know a few things about impossible goals, though. I did this with Mattie and moving forward became unbearable. She saw this wonderful perfect life for us, where I had to be someone I was not. Everyone moved me around as they wanted and I was far from happy about it. I wasn't myself. I didn't even feel comfortable sleeping with her." He glanced shyly at her, cursing himself for telling her that. "Yet I pretended to be because I wanted to prove to everyone that I was more. I won't make that mistake again. I don't think you should either. It's too much responsibility. Marry who you want, and enjoy having children."

"What if my children are the ones who will end the curse? Shouldn't I prepare them?"

She was so blasted serious, it frustrated him.

"How? You said yourself, you don't know how. Let your children be young and enjoy life, learning as they need. Besides, maybe it's not your children. Your brother might train others, or raise someone else's brats. Heck in this one story I know, this brave man, Jesus, gave his life for mankind and left behind disciples to spread his beliefs. They were his warriors, handpicked for this task. He came back from the dead and guided them."

Her eyes grew huge. "You can do that?" She let out a long puff of air. "Are you *Cîpay*?"

"No, but the Man of Legends might be able to do something that crazy."

She stood. "You make fun of me."

"Sacri, sit. I just know how it feels when others think you're something you're not. It's hard to move, to breathe. Every time you do, you're sure you're about to disappoint them. I believe in men and women capable of changing the world, the afterlives, and even of raising the dead, but if I wait for one, I'll be wasting a perfectly good life where I could be one."

She stormed off.

He called after her, "For the record, I like your stories." He hadn't meant to insult her and wasn't sure why he'd said anything.

In the middle of the night, she returned with a bear hide she placed beside him. "This is my mat," she announced so matter-of-fact as she made herself comfortable on it.

He adjusted the jacket he used as a pillow and turned over so as not to face her but a smile grew on his lips. Her action was symbolic. "What does it mean?" he asked the air in front of him and glanced over his shoulder to see her. She had her eyes closed. "Sacri, what does it mean that your mat is by mine?"

Eyes closed, she said, "It doesn't mean you're right."

"Well...goodnight then." He watched her sleeping, a curious happiness inside him.

-TWENTY-

The next morning Sacri was nowhere in sight but her mat was by his. Alex touched it. The fur was still warm. She couldn't be far.

While he washed his face in the creek, a shadow appeared over him. Alex watched the reflection in the water. Silver looked different by the light of day. Or maybe it was the scowl on his face. The arrows in his hand had silver tips that shone in the sun, making Alex nervous. Silver gripped a knife in his other hand and was clearly ready to scalp him. Alex focused on the cross around Silver's neck.

"Paws off her," Silver said.

Alex studied his hands. "You her brother?" Only a brother would be this distressed about him sleeping by Sacri. He'd met a few angry brothers in his day. Anything he said would make things worse.

Alex watched the reflection, ready for an attack.

Silver said a bunch of things in his Native language. Alex listened closely. His brain automatically counted beats, syllables, intonation. He was working out the words. Finally, Alex faced him. He wasn't talking about Sacri. Was he talking about his house? The one he was building? "I am home. That's my house. Well, it will be."

Silver growled and repeated his first comment. "Paws off her." He threw his blade and it dug into the earth between Alex's feet.

When Alex glanced up, Silver advanced toward the wagon to talk with Lacey. Alex didn't know anything about her, yet he felt relief that she was back.

The horses grazed in the distance. Lacey stood with Silver. Her hands told him a story. Silver looked distressed by her actions. He glanced at Alex several times.

Why wasn't Wali back? Should he go searching for him? Now that Lacey was back, he might be able to.

Alex glanced at the wagon. If he left, he might come back to find his things tossed in the creek.

He had a lot of work to do today. Wali would return soon, he promised himself. He believed Sacri when she said he was on a journey, even if he had no idea what that meant. Really, she had no need to lie to him, if Wali was dead, she would have told him, unless a journey was how she described death...

Lacey left, holding hands with the warrior, and they vanished by the creek.

An uneasy worry settled over Alex as he unloaded what he needed from the wagon. Then he piled the wood to build the frame. He only found one bag of nails so he figured out a way, using a saw, to arrange the wood so it slipped together and wouldn't need nails.

He'd need more wood, though. He had enough to build a frame around the door and about half a roof. Any type of trees would do. He surveyed the area. Far in the distance was the oak.

Sacri had called the oak sacred so he dismissed it. It was hard enough to work with her stupid rocks; he wasn't touching a tree she was in love with.

The sod would make insulation but the frame he had in mind needed wood. Unless...could he use these rocks and sod? What if he piled the sod upside down like bricks and used rocks for support? He needed to practice because it'd be a lot of work. Wasting a day trying things and building his foundation right was better than building it wrong and having to start over.

Using the sod he'd cut from the hole he'd dug, Alex piled a row, lining them side by side. He added another row on top, making sure the center of the 'brick' was where the bottom two met. He found rocks and pushed them between the bricks for support. He added some around the foundation of his pretend wall.

A shadow blocked the sun and he glanced up. The warrior watched him work with a frown.

"Silver! You scared me."

Silver tilted his head to both sides and inspected the wall. Then a smile crept on his lips. "A house rising up from the ground?"

Alex nodded. "I hope so. If I figure this out. I want sod bricks but how do I stack them so my home doesn't flood come spring?"

"Build it wherever you came from and leave Sacred Land alone."

"You telling me to leave, too?"

"You asked me how to keep it from flooding, and that is the solution. I know not how to ask a tree to leave. It changes with the season but only moves to dig itself in deeper and grow higher. If I help you, will you allow Lacey to live with you when I leave? She is frightened by herself and not fast enough to run with me." Silver rubbed a hand over his jaw, distressed.

"Sure. She's been helpful and keeps to herself. If she wants to stay, she's welcome. You sick?"

Silver fell on his knees, grabbed a sod brick, and flipped it upside down so the grass was on the bottom. "I will be fine." He stared at Alex, swallowing a lump. "I shall be a father. Not sure why, but my entire world changed with that news." He piled an entire row.

"So, you and Lacey?"

"Now another. A boy. He will be named Bernoit after her."

"You know he'll be a boy?"

"Yes. I see this." Silver beamed. "He is like you."

Silver smiled so that must be a good thing. He pulled more bricks from Alex's pile and stacked them the same way making a third layer.

"What do you mean by 'he's like me'?"

"You see," Silver picked up dirt and dropped it like a waterfall, "this is what a *Cîpay*'s soul looks like. It blends downward endlessly communing with the dirt. Yours is grounded. He will live up here, with you. You will teach him things he needs to learn so he can blend in with the settlers. He needs you. I need you." He nodded as if it made sense.

"How do you see this?"

"With my eyes." He pushed each layer down hard with his

weight. Then he moved his hand from the top brick to the bottom one diagonally and pointed to the sod. "Now you do this. Think about the winds, the rains, and most importantly, the snows."

Alex checked to see.

He'd piled them so they'd slant toward him, making an angle. A slight one. Alex smiled. "This is good. You know your stuff. I plan to build walls like this around the hole. Put a roof on it. Think it'll work?"

Silver nodded, dusted off his hands. "You will raise a home out of the earth itself. I will gather a few warriors and we will help you."

"Thanks. You aren't afraid to leave Lacey with me or even Wali?"

"Alex." He pronounced his name as All-Ax. "Sacri moved her mat by yours." He paused as if this explained things.

"About that, I don't know what having her mat beside my blanket means. I like it there, but it was her idea."

"Your soul is tied to Wali and Sacri. Lacey is safe with you. We all are." He relaxed his shoulders, clearly relieved to admit this to Alex.

His soul? Alex thought about this. "How can you know that about my soul?"

"I know this because I see it. With my eyes. Like I see how you want to kiss Sacri but stop yourself because you are afraid, not of her but of yourself. It is written all over you." He motioned with his hands at Alex.

Alex studied the stacks with a tragic sigh. He should have kissed her. What kind of idiot sits in front of a goddess with his hands on her legs and doesn't kiss her? "Think she'll kiss me back?"

"I do not think about those things." With that, Silver abruptly turned and walked away.

"This means I can have my cross back and stay?" he called out to Silver.

He was by the creek and answered, "I never said otherwise."

Alex chuckled. He liked Silver. He was an interesting guy. "Congratulations on the baby."

"Yes. A boy is good news. A boy is incredible news." He

didn't sound half as happy as he should have been and Alex stopped building the wall to make his hole a bit wider so that there was room for Silver and a baby, too.

He returned to his trial wall. The sod had piled nicely. Alex was impressed. He'd planned to use it like a blanket on the frame but what if these could be the walls?

He grabbed a pail and headed to the creek for water.

He trickled the water over his wall to see how it held up. Dirt crumbled between the cracks, but overall, it was sturdy. The roots from the weeds and grass helped. He considered going for a stroll to find sod with roots running through it that were even longer. Maybe Sacri knew where he could find some. Or Silver.

He liked the idea of lining the walls along the bottom with rocks for added support, so he shoved a few more rocks in the holes and piled some on both sides of the wall.

Sacri arrived while he was piling rocks. She had a bunch of purple flowers in her hands that she dropped. "No!" She pulled the rocks from him and dropped them back where he'd found them, saying a prayer for each rock. He watched her, amused. She was almost frantic. Finally, he helped her replace them. Despite himself, he apologized. He wanted to see her smile again.

She left once the rocks were all replaced, too flustered to talk to him more than that.

Disappointed that she didn't stay to help with supper, Alex worked on his wall.

He was so caught up in testing the wall for endurance and trying new techniques to see what made it stronger or weaker that he jumped when a man covered in a sheet rode past. Alex leapt to his feet, shocked. The man stopped by the wagon to snoop through it.

"What are you doing?" Alex demanded. "Clement? Is that you? Come sit with me. I miss Mattie and I know you do."

"Don't talk about her."

He rode off.

A strange chill washed over Alex. What had Clement been searching for? He touched his neck, as if his cross protected him, but it was gone.

–TWENTY-ONE–

It was three days since Wali went missing. Lacey didn't return. Neither did Sacri nor Silver.

The only time Alex had seen Sacri was when she took off on a white horse, headed north.

A few others arrived to help him cut and stack sod around the house. They worked fast, hauling sod from a distance. They talked to each other, ignoring him. Alex picked up words. One commented on Sacri's mat as it lay so innocently by Alex's blanket. It was some internal joke that only these guys understood, and he felt like an outsider.

Alex had folded his blanket each morning and arranged it by her mat; not sure why he did something so foolish, but it was exciting to see them side by side which was probably why their comments bothered him.

One of the men in the group was a priest and introduced himself as a friend of Sacri's. No name, just 'a friend'. The priest gave him a playful slap on the back and chuckled.

Alex got an evil glare from Menashen. His eyes were piercing, so dark they were almost black. He was about twenty, in his prime, with thick arms. They were probably the size of Alex's head. He wore mud in streaks on his bare chest, like paint. The leather band around his head kept his hair out of his face and his hair was dark like Sacri's but with a light curl. He had a long scar down his cheek.

He didn't have as many tattoos or scars as Silver, but he stood off to the side to study the group every now and again, ready to kick everyone's ass. He carried a spear and looked ready to use it on Alex if he turned his back on him. Watching him work was intimidating but he didn't stay long. Once they started about the mat, he stormed off.

Alex spoke to them in many languages but they always answered in their language. He suspected they understood though, because one cracked a joke he caught about him having more words than muscles.

Despite the odd one giving him a hard time, most were friendly. The priest even offered him food.

Tonight, he sat around the fire with Louis and his two sons. They were four and seven, but they'd worked hard all day, copying what Louis did, learning how to build a house from the ground. Alex invited them to stay for supper even if he had no food to give them. He warmed oatmeal, poured it into bowls and gave them each some. Louis tasted it and leaned forward. "You eat this crap?"

"Oh? So you do speak French?"

Louis watched his boys gobble the mush down, starved. "My father was French, a Dubois. My oldest is Michel and his younger brother is Gilles."

"Nice to meet you, boys. Is it good eatings?"

"What is this mush you enjoy so much?" Louis demanded.

"It's better with maple syrup but I can't find any maple trees around here."

"There are some to the north. Along the creek. Here." He handed the bowl back to Alex. He was so hungry he almost ate Louis' share, too, then he decided to offer it to the boys. They cleaned the bowl in moments, using their fingers to finish every drop.

"They seem to like it."

"They're growing. They'll eat dirt if I let them." Louis stood and walked about ten yards from the camp. It grew dark and he got on a knee to touch the ground. Then he headed east for a bit. He knelt again and headed north. Alex stood, curious what he was doing. The boys followed. Louis stepped to his right, his left, then he scooped something up.

He showed them a wild hare.

The boys didn't look impressed. They had the same indifferent expression on their face no matter what happened around them.

"You caught that with your bare hands?" Alex was shocked. "Did you boys see that?" he asked them in their language and for the first time they both glanced up, their faces giving away their surprise.

Louis ignored his poor attempt at speaking their language and explained, "A hare goes one way, you go the other, and they fall right into your hands. This is supper, and I'll add the fur to a blanket for my...for a baby." He handed it to his oldest son, teaching him how to hold it by the neck with its head buried under his arm. The boy tried. Then the other did the same. He passed the hare to Alex who copied them. The hare wiggled and scratched his arm but Alex held on.

"Now snap its neck," he told Alex.

Alex almost dropped it. "What? I can't do that!"

"Boys, it's getting dark. Warm the fire so we can eat soon. Your learning is done for the day. Oh, and here." He pointed out a few plants in the dirt among the weeds. They cut the leaves and ran off with them, giggling for the first time that day. They shoved each other and Alex was amazed that the well-behaved boys he'd seen work all day stacking and learning had vanished so easily. It reminded him of Wali and him as children.

Louis stepped up to Alex and gently took the hare from him. "Sacri's mat is beside yours, no?"

Alex nodded.

Louis snapped the hare's neck. "She moved it there?" His eyes fixated on Alex's.

"I'm not stupid enough to touch her things."

"Silver know this?"

Alex nodded. The tension around them was new.

"If I die, she promised to raise my children."

"Don't die. She isn't reliable or as good at teaching as you. She kinda likes to lounge around and have men draw on her."

"Yeah, right." He chuckled. "She's like the sacred relic no one is allowed near. Drives the guys nuts that she moved her mat for the first time and it's by yours. I wanted you to know about my boys because she is bound to the promise."

"How is it any of my business?"

Louis was telling him something important.

"Well, her mat is by yours."

Alex frowned. "Are you saying if you die, she raises your boys and since her mat is by mine if she dies I raise them?" His frown deepened when Louis nodded. "Why would you trust me? Even by default?"

"I don't have to trust you, I trust her. No idea what she sees in you, but if I end up seeing something I don't like, I tell Silver, and he won't let you stay."

"This Silver seems to have a lot of pull around here."

Louis raised his eyebrows. "Don't ever mistake pull for respect." He left him to prepare the meal.

While the food cooked, Louis worked on the hide from the hare and Alex paced around the 'house'. The walls grew thicker and taller. He wasn't sure what to do about a roof and was thinking about this when one of the boys brought him a fistful of berries. "Thanks," he said in their language and they giggled and repeated the word with a better pronunciation. Alex tried again. He was having a bit of trouble with certain sounds, but it would come.

Louis sent them off with the hare's hide.

"Where are they taking it?" Alex asked.

Louis sighed. "I have a story to share. It happened many years ago when I was a stupid boy who wanted to be a man. That mistake brought us here, at war with settlers."

Alex settled in by the fire, eager to hear this story.

"We kept settlers off this land for generations by blending in and scaring them off it. Things have changed and I fear it's my fault. Why I sit with you and hope to find an answer."

Alex watched the small fire.

"My friend Silver and I were on a journey to find ourselves a mate. We planned to travel from one end of the blessed lands to the other if needed."

Alex listened closely now that he'd mentioned Silver.

"We stopped for the night in a tunnel. The chamber we found had out a mat and a pipe full of sacred plants." He smirked. "Being young and stupid, we eyed it up and sat on the mat waiting to see what was going on. No one showed and it was late when we decided to smoke the pipe. Why not, right?"

"I would have."

"Well, we shouldn't have. We weren't thinking clearly when a woman appeared."

Alex sat, curious.

"This is normal for the smoke to draw out women, and the

smoke does make us desire companionship." He sat silent, thinking about his story. "I'd like to say I listened to Silver. Given what I know about him, if this would happen today I would have listened. But back then, I was a stupid idiot and this was a woman dancing in the smoke. Just for me. She joined us. Silver was furious and tried to send her off, but I told him to leave if he didn't want to look at her because I did. He said something that haunted me forever. He said she was linked to another. Linked. I had no idea what he was talking about, but I was about to find out. That morning, I met her husband." He stared at the fire.

"Oh boy. I know that feeling."

"If Silver ever tells you that you're linked to someone, I don't understand what he's seeing, but it means this someone is who you need to breathe. A guy like me, he can't come between that. So anyway, Silver got us the hell out of there and explained things once he calmed. He told me her husband had an accident and could no longer give her children. Yet she didn't want others to know this. She wanted to couple with warriors until she was with child. I was so naïve I didn't know what he meant. I believed women were blessed with children from Mother."

Alex smirked. "I take it your friend educated you on the subject."

"And then some. I learnt the hard way that some women use men. Our encounter put us on our guard and we returned home without wives after a long journey all over a world unlike ours. We learnt how to tan hides better. We taught how to burn fires without wood. It was a great journey." He studied his hands as if seeing a miracle in them.

Alex settled back, at ease with Louis. "On our way home we stopped in the same room. There was no pipe this time. In the night, screaming brought us to our feet and we came on a woman giving birth." He sighed. "I was there when Paniya was born and I held her in my arms. Her name came to me and terrified I shared it. Her father was thrilled."

"This was your child?"

"Silver figures, and like I said, it's hard to argue with him. I have no idea if her husband understood how these things worked. The idea that the tiny child could be mine haunted me and I went many times to see her. I became great friends with her father."

"Must have been hard."

"She was spoiled and it frustrated me that they didn't teach her things. Unlike us, they feel a warrior should learn in the moment, as needed. Which is fine, but she never needed to learn. She grew up sheltered and when thrown into the real world, she was shocked. I spent a lot of time teaching her. Each time, Silver found me and forced me to leave her, but I was never the same inside again. I wanted to do right by this. It goes against everything we believe in this tribe, but I can't help how I feel.

"Of course, I met my wife and life was going swell, then Paniya shows shortly after my wife died. Her father had passed on. She was alone and scared and her journey was dangerous. I am her teacher and so she sought me out. She didn't have the skills to survive. I don't know how she even made it to me. Silver told her she could stay here."

"Silver is your…leader?"

Louis smirked. "He's all we have. He warned the warriors he would decide who was worthy of having her as a wife when the elders told him she was ready. I spent time with her and taught her things. But she came to me terrified, saying a man attacked her on the prairies while she gathered berries."

Alex glanced around, uneasy. "Did he hurt her?"

"She's with child." Louis turned the meat.

"Oh."

"Silver stormed around demanding to know who had attacked her. He found many who offered to take care of her, but he says it wasn't a Ghost tribal who did this to her."

"Maybe they lied?"

"No one lies to Silver."

Alex believed it.

"He says Sacri knew the truth and he grilled her a bit about it but the best he could guess was that Sacri saved her from someone who got away. She sent him after a Bernoit who farms a section of the Cursed Lands…"

"Ah, and this is how he met Lacey?"

Louis nodded. "I've never seen him so enthralled by a woman. The guy is nuts about her."

"So now you'll be a grandpa and it is a possibility that this child is Lacey's brother or sister."

"Silver says Lacey's father is a rotten man, and he wants him off Cursed Lands. He's hoping you can help with that."

"I don't see how. Does Paniya have a husband?"

"Silver told the tribe that the elders announced her as a Chosen One."

"May I meet these elders?"

"There are no elders. We know this, but Silver says he talks to ancient spirits, *Cîpay,* and they guide us. He's never led us wrong. Means no one will go near her until the baby is born. It means the warriors will help raise her child. He said it was the best he could do for her." He rubbed his eyes. "She's a child herself. She's afraid. I believed it was a good idea, but the women shun her."

"Why?"

He shrugged. "Could be anything, women are impossible for me to understand."

"I take it you're finding it hard to keep her happy."

"She hates it here. Thinks no one wants her. Do you believe she asked Silver to share her mat?" Louis shook his head. "He was so stressed he won't even look at her. Yet he told me she'll have a boy."

"Silver sounds like he knows strange things."

"He comes in handy. If he tells you something, listen. He doesn't talk to talk."

Alex understood the warning and nodded.

That night, Alex lay down to sleep with a new sense of hope. He was building a house. He'd made a friend. He tossed around on his thin blanket, glanced at Sacri's comfortable hide, and decided to snuggle into hers. If she appeared, he could roll off it. It would be worth her yelling at him if he sneaked in a few hours of sleep. He needed sleep. Tomorrow, he'd search for Wali.

–Twenty-Two–

Alex couldn't sleep, even exhausted as he was. He rolled over and there was Sacri sitting at the edge of the bear hide, cross-legged, watching him sleep on her mat. Would she kick him off? He didn't care, it was comfortable, and he was tired.

"Sacri, what are you doing?" He spoke her language, imitating her quick snap with the words, but he was sure they came out slurred and dull compared to her lively way of speaking.

"I watch you sleep. You look worried." She spoke French.

"I am. Wali has been gone for too long. He gets tired, you know. His nose bleeds—"

"Your friend will be back soon. Silver brought him to our most gifted healer."

"Really?" Alex was excited. "Did this healer help him? May I meet him?"

"He is not from this part of the blessed lands. The journey takes days. I know not if it helped."

"So when he comes back, will Wali have to leave or can he stay?"

"Silver says you can stay if you do what he says."

Paws off her, or *look after Lacey when I have to leave?*

Alex smirked, admiring the stars. "You know what he wants me to do?"

"Be the Man of Legends."

He refused to get into it again with her. "Paws off her. He thinks because you placed your mat beside mine that we're sleeping together."

"We are. I sleep there. You sleep beside me. Together."

"I don't think it counts. I sleep this close to Wali."

"I thought your mate was Mattie not Wali?"

"Wali is my brother. I am…mate-less and hoped to remain that way to avoid this hurt again. But…at the same time, I don't want you to leave or move your mat…is that confusing?"

They were silent.

"Think you could stay and…be here?"

She nodded.

"I met some of your tribe. I don't remember all their names, but I liked Louis."

"Match names to traits. Pick one thing about them that stands out and match the name to that, this way faces mean something."

He liked that idea. "Like how Menashen wants to kill me because your mat is by mine."

"Yet he did not." This news pleased her. She edged in closer so she grazed his legs. "Alex…" She brushed his cheek. "You seem to have memories clouding you tonight."

He nodded, casting his eyes away from her. He'd forgotten to sing these past three nights.

"Remembering is easy," she said. "Knowing what to forget is hard."

"I suppose. What about you? Who else did you move your mat beside?"

She frowned. "No one."

"No one, not ever?"

"This is the first time I move my mat."

He looked at it. "But I'm not the first guy to sleep on it, am I?" His stomach turned, because he wasn't good with innocent women.

"I only allow warriors to share my mat." Her voice implied this was a great honour and she had her pick. He glanced around expecting a slew of suitors to storm them and kick his ass. Maybe wildman Menashen would spear him.

"Yet you never found one worthy of moving this mat to?"

"Yes, I moved my mat beside yours."

He smiled. "Could you maybe explain to me what it means? What's the difference? You shared your mat with these warriors…so what would have changed if you'd moved your mat beside theirs instead? This isn't how things are done in my world. Your blanket has everyone wound up.

Some are lined up to kick me out, while others are teaching me things I will never do."

She touched the fur. "A warrior can share any mat as long as there is no mat beside his. But once I move my mat, no one will share my mat but him."

"Oh. You're marking your territory." He was relieved. "No worries there, I have no interest in sharing any mats."

"You are on my mat," she pointed out.

"Well…it's warm."

"I could keep you warmer."

He opened his arms to welcome her. She pushed her back against his chest. He warmed up inside when she pulled his blanket over them.

He was sleepy, but wanted to talk with her. "How does marriage work in your tribe?"

"A woman chooses a warrior to teach her children. He must protect them when she cannot. He must work with her to raise her children and if he does not meet her standards, she will send him off and move her mat beside a more suitable mate."

"And what? You decided not to follow tradition? You don't wish to raise a family?"

"I know something they do not."

He hesitated to ask, afraid she'd go off about the Man of Legends again, but he had to know. "And what might that be?"

"Souls link."

"Oh yeah, Silver mentioned something about my soul being tied to Wali and you. Doesn't sound like something I want."

"I want this." She lazily ran her fingers on his arm, sending warm shivers through him.

"Silver told me to keep my paws off you." He held her for dear life. The idea of her moving her mat terrified him.

"Off me? No. Off the earth. You are messing it up with your digging."

Oh, he doubted Silver meant that. Everyone dug.

"And what will your Man of Legends think about our link?"

She shrugged. "What can he say? It is there."

"He'll probably get in line behind Menashen to kill me."

"Menashen cares not who I am with. Nichena has her mat by his."

"Well, maybe he needs someone to remind him."

"You plan to fight Menashen?" She sounded sleepy and not at all interested in his battles.

"No. I don't need my face rearranged."

"Warm?" she asked.

Sleep was coming. "Yes. Perfect. I could sleep with you in my arms every night. Sometimes, I think the scariest thing is being alone." He closed his eyes, relaxed.

She whispered, "Slip your hands in the dirt." He reached over her and did as she said. Their bodies met. The dirt was cold around his hand and he pushed it in deeper. The top part was dry but his hand sunk in finding the ground moist.

"When I am not around, we will still be connected through the earth. You are never alone." She turned around in his arms to face him.

Their lips caressed. When her hands rested on him, his heart picked up.

Sacri's breath had a sweet smell to it and he tasted her as she whispered, "Respect the earth for it keeps us linked."

Alex brushed a kiss on her cheek and rubbed his cheek along hers. She snuggled into him. "I'm trying. I have seeds to plant once the sod is off and I get it ploughed. I want a place to live when the winds blow, and well, I hoped to use the earth to build it. It's just displaced, really."

She kissed his neck and his breathing sped up. Could she feel how he wanted her?

"From the earth, he will raise a house," Sacri said.

"A quote from scripture you believe in?"

"Yes."

He pulled away and fell on his back. She did the same. They stared at the stars. Talking was suddenly impossible. Undressing her was all he could think about and he wasn't sure if either of them were ready for that. He took in a deep breath. Making love to her would mean something and he wasn't sure what yet.

"What does it mean?" he asked himself, but she clearly thought they were talking about the scriptures.

"Honovi said: '*From Her womb, Mother gave life to warriors and welcomed them back in their death. She surrounded Her womb with magical lands that Her warriors protect. One warrior was so special to Her, he was not left to live and die, but remained with Her. She promised to unleash this warrior if ever Sacred Land was in danger, and because their connection was so strong, he would commune with Her how to save Sacred Land. He would travel far to gather this knowledge and return to Her and plant roots so deep, Mother would rejoice at his return by raising a house from the earth to keep him safe in Her warm embrace.*'"

He had no idea what to say. "And this man is The Man of Legends."

"Yes. We need him."

He wasn't so sure they did. "Until he shows, we can keep others off this land. Show me where Sacred Land runs and I'll make sure we own it all. I can move my house off it."

"If Mother lets you build here, you are welcome, but remember this gift is not a right."

"Many things were taken from me in this life, Sacri, but if I can only have one gift, this is the best one I could ask for."

"Your troubled heart needs peace. Close your eyes." She sang softly, moving so she was against him. He wrapped an arm around her, and pulled her closer.

Alex stopped breathing to listen. The words were in her language. He didn't understand everything but the song had him entranced. He fell asleep as she wrapped him in a warm blanket with her quiet voice.

When he woke, Silver towered over them. Dang it. One order and he couldn't even follow it. He didn't care what Sacri said, he was sure Silver meant paws off *her*. He should apologize, yet Alex couldn't let her go. "We were talking and got tired. I swear nothing happened." Still, his paws were clearly around her waist, clutching her for dear life and he did not intend to let her go.

She fitted against him perfectly.

Sacri stretched beside him and mumbled something.

"Sacri," Silver snapped.

She flew to her feet so fast Alex couldn't reach for her. She was gone into the morning light.

Alex stood slowly and faced Silver whom everyone respected as if he were some god. He towered over Alex ready to tear him in twelve.

"I should kill you."

"No reason to kill me. I fell asleep with her. We're both exhausted, and she was singing and warm." In his panic, he spoke English.

"Warm?" Silver repeated the word, confused. Alex touched his forehead and Silver grinned. Alex nodded, repeating the word Silver used.

So he liked to learn. With his hands, Alex gestured to the dirt. "Dirt."

Silver repeated it and spoke a word in his language. Alex repeated it.

They did this for several things. Each time, Silver smiled which was better than tearing him in twelve. Then he glanced around as if he heard something. "No one teaches me anymore. Thank you. Come, now I will show you something."

Alex studied Silver. He waved for Alex to follow, got on his knees by a bush along the creek, then vanished in the long grasses.

Alex went to the area, got down on his knees to see how he did that. The ground sloped under the bushes full of berries and separated into a hole big enough for him to roll into. Should he follow Silver into this hole?

"Alex?" Wali called.

Alex glanced around surprised. Wali was at the camp. He rushed to meet his friend, forgetting about Silver.

Alex wrapped him in a brotherly hug. "I have never been so glad to see you. Where have you been?"

"You won't believe this." Wali had colour to his cheeks, which was rare these days.

"Underground?"

"Yeah." Wali asked, "Where's Lacey?"

"I told you about Silver, well, Lacey will mother his child."

"A baby? Oh. That does explain a few things."

"So what happened?"

"I woke up in this strange room. I'd had the weirdest dream. You were a tree." Wali shared stories about the tunnels he'd travelled for days following a shadow who left him food and who led him to another room that gave him even stranger dreams. Alex asked several times about the healer but Wali blew him off and changed the topic. He said it was dark and damp underground and when he found his way out, he then had to figure out where he was. The tunnels stretched far under their land. He made it sound like a light adventure, but Alex wasn't sure the journey had been so easy on his friend. Regardless, he was back, and he looked better.

"You got quite a bit done while I was gone." Wali helped him stack sod. "Did you search for me?"

"I was sent down the creek. Leaving meant I'd come back to our stuff gone, and I wouldn't let her toss us out. Plus, where the heck would I look?" Alex scanned the prairies. "I had no idea where to start, forget underground. She told me you were on a healing journey, and frankly, it sounded like something you needed. Feeling better?"

Wali glanced around. "She who?"

"Sacri. She's a local. I met a bunch of them. Silver is the one with Lacey, and I'm guessing Sacri's brother, but he might be a chief or something because everyone seems on edge when he's around, but he's a good guy when he stops threatening to kill you. There's Louis, who has two boys he's raising alone. And Menashen, who wants to spear me for some unknown reason. And I liked this priest but he didn't give me a name, and I got the impression he was passing through because people asked how things were." He told Wali about the others and how fast they worked.

"Never heard of them." He frowned and inspected Alex. "There's no one here, Alex. Look around. Bet this Silver stole Lacey and we'll never see her again." He looked miserable at the idea.

Alex wanted to say they lived underground in those tunnels Wali had been in, but he knew how stupid it would sound, because they weren't mole-people. They were…warriors. "They seem to have a deep connection with the earth and it annoys her yet makes her excited that I'm building a house out of it, but as long as we get our seed in the ground shortly, she might let it pass."

Wali groaned.

"What?"

"I know that crazy look you have. This 'she' you talk about...you're falling for her. How off limits is this one?"

"Sacri? No. Maybe. I mean she's..." Alex smirked. "She let me draw on her."

"You drew on a woman? You are one of a kind." Wali chuckled. "What was it like to draw on someone?" He leaned in, curious.

"It was a connection. Does that make sense?"

"I know how connected you get to your canvas. I can't imagine." Wali let out a puff of air. "Sounds fun. I might have to try it sometime..." He shrugged. "If I find someone worth drawing on."

"Could we get a few seeds in the ground today?" Alex asked.

"Sure. I feel great. I could move mountains...well, if there were some to move."

"So you're better?"

Wali stared off in the distance. "The coughing is better." He was quick to change the subject. "I'll test out a few areas to see where the best dirt is. Plus we have to plough a fire-ring."

"A what?"

"Well, you need sod, right? We'll make a ring around our home quarter, then keep the soil ploughed so it's always black dirt. This way if a fire blazes through, the flames won't—"

Alex cut him off, excited. That was perfect. Why hadn't he thought of that? "How thick? I wouldn't want flames to leap over this ring. I saw the mess the fire made of things northwest of here."

"These rings work. I'll start on it tomorrow. I'll pile the sod in the wagon and haul it back for you to build the house with." Wali scratched his head. "You sure a girl was here?"

"She brought the bear hide to sleep on." He pointed her sleeping blanket out to Wali but it was gone.

Why had she taken the mat away?

–TWENTY-THREE–

Sacri had her basket full of flowers and walked through Alex's camp. She was surprised to see that the friend Alex called brother was back.

Wali measured a board and dropped it when he saw her. "Holy hell. You must be Sacri."

"I am. You enjoyed the Healing Chamber?"

He inhaled deeply and glanced around. "The dreams I had were weird. I saw my death."

"This is common." She dropped the flowers and felt his head. He was fevered. His skin wasn't well. Explained why so many healers were suddenly in the area. Such a sickness would have them curious. "This is a painful illness that has the healers confused."

He ignored her. "Who brought me there?"

"Silver wanted to thank you for bringing Lacey here. He was impressed you did so without being challenged. He thinks it must be because you had everyone so wound up, they didn't notice her. He hoped the healers could help you feel better, but he says it wasn't good news."

"And where are you going with these flowers?"

She had more than flowers. The white clay was very rare and she couldn't wait to work it and pray over it.

"To make Alex paint. I had to travel far for these." She pointed out the wonderful red onions. "He'll love the onions and their skins will make purple." She expected him to laugh but he winced.

"Do me a favour and wait to give it to him until after I die." He looked solemn so she nodded. "And be careful. After his parents died, he broke everything he owned. Smashed it all. Then when he lost Mattie, he sank into a depression. I had to drag him home several times from the pub after he'd got in fights he had no hope of winning." He took a deep breath. "I worry about him. He feels pain and anger too deeply. He's too hard on himself for no reason. Of course, the painting helps and I carved with him, too. I'll teach you how. He needs to keep his hands busy doing something worthwhile. It's about having control of things."

She liked how he understood his friend so well. "Did he hit you?" She'd had a man swing at her once while grieving.

"No. It's more God he blames and when he drinks he fights to get back the control."

"Thank you for teaching me." She bowed and gathered up her things to dry them out.

Wali called after her, "I saw it."

"What?" She faced him.

"Love. I saw passion in his eyes when he spoke of you. So...don't get dead on him, because he can't lose us both."

"We are both here, Wali. If you live your days worrying about what others will do without you, you won't be enjoying the moments you have with them."

"Yeah, but still I worry."

"My father told me that when I worried, it was because I needed something to do, so he found me work to make the worry stop."

"Good plan. I have a fire-ring to make. I want to leave him something worthwhile. You're a smart one. I like you, Sacri."

"I like you, Wali." He was a teacher, like her. She could see them being good friends.

–TWENTY-FOUR–

Later that day, Wali had hitched a horse to the plough he'd bought and now he worked in the distance, probably trying things out.

Alex couldn't focus. He needed to find Sacri. At the creek, he peeked in the hole where Silver had rolled. A soft humming echoed somewhere down that hole. What if she was down there?

Alex glanced over his shoulder at their camp before he rolled toward the shrub.

He landed on Sacri and a bunch of flowers exploded around them. "Alex." She squirmed under him. "That is not how you enter a tunnel. What are you doing?"

"Sorry." He stood. "I had no idea the drop was so sudden." His shoulder throbbed. He glanced up. He should have rolled then got back to his feet immediately. He'd know for next time.

"Do you need stairs?" she asked, playfully.

He said, "Were you spying on me?"

"Maybe, if you twist as you fall, you could land on your feet." She sounded worried.

"I'm fine. I can drop into a hole. It was deeper than I assumed. Actually, I didn't think or I wouldn't be here. I'm not a fan of tight areas." He could stand, he felt airflow…maybe it wasn't a tight area. "I wanted to see you and figured this might be where you hang out. This is impressive."

She was on her knees gathering the flowers, sorting them in piles that he couldn't make out in the dim light.

He fell to his knees to help her but she slapped his hands when he grabbed a flower so he dropped the stem and watched her gather them frantically.

"Is this your home?" The light entering the cave wasn't much but he could make out her features. The cross gleamed around her neck. Her eyes shone.

"Yes. Home. Mother protects us." She stood and left the flowers in their piles. "Come, I'll show you."

"Do you want help picking up your flowers? I'd like to stay in the light not wander around and get lost down here."

"Touch not. They must dry. I was about to hang them in the sun. Come. You must travel in the dark, Alex, or you will never leave that spot."

"Great. Lead the way."

She led him out of the chamber and down a shadowy tunnel, but to his surprise light filtered in through high slots about every thirty feet, giving enough light for them to make their way. The dark wasn't so bad if he stayed by Sacri, but next time he planned to bring a lantern.

Alex touched the walls, amazed. "These are manmade or natural?"

"Both."

The corridor had other passages leading out. Some were thin fissures in the earth. She vanished into one. Alex was too broad to slip in behind her. "I can't fit in this crack."

"It gets bigger, suck in your breath and come. If Silver fits, you fit."

Alex glanced around, nervous. He couldn't see much. So he crammed himself in behind her and to his relief the opening had only the appearance of a fissure; the gap opened immediately to a slightly bigger tunnel. It was cramped but Sacri was against him. She was warm and he stepped closer to her.

"See? Safe."

They travelled like this for some time. Every tunnel looked the same and she led him around too quickly. "I'll get lost down here," Alex complained. "How do you see in the dark?"

"One does not see in the dark."

"How do you know where to go?"

"The walls tell me where to go. Use your fingers. Your taste. Taste how different the air in this tunnel compares to the last. Like I told you with faces, give each tunnel a name based on what your senses tell you about it."

Taste? Was she serious? He smashed his tongue around his mouth. The air was damp. Maybe more so than the last tunnel. He touched the wall. Her fingers came over his and she pulled him away.

"This chamber is where we store things." Overhead, she reached for a cubby.

"Up there? In the hole?"

"The hole is for grabbing." She grabbed it and pulled. The wall moved and, to his surprise, behind it was an entire room stocked with containers of all types. Some were made out of glass but most had been made from clay and earth.

"Is this yours?" He was shocked.

"These things belong to everyone. If you need something you take it, but you must place something new in the spot. We never leave an empty spot. That would be disrespectful to Mother."

He nodded, loving the simplicity of it. "Not that I'd ever be able to find my way."

She leaned against the wall. "I will make markings for you. Feel them." She placed his hand over the marking. The way the carvings dug into the wall was familiar.

"You carve in this stone?" His heart leapt. These were like the markings from his cross. It dug deep into the rock wall. "Will you show me how to do this?"

"Of course. This is the symbol for *Where the Crow Flies*. You will take this path to your burrow."

"It's a house." He moved in closer to her until her lips brushed his when he spoke. "I should get back to it. I have a lot of work to do but..."

She grasped his hand and it warmed as she placed it over the cross around her neck.

Alex rested his head against hers. "Thank you for sharing your secret. Will you live here after I build my house?"

"Where else will I live?"

He had no idea, but it was weird that he'd have a house above ground and she'd be living underground. He couldn't see himself living underground. He needed air, sun, wind.

"I live at one with the earth."

He wondered just how important air was. Maybe he didn't need sun. Wind was overrated. "I could make a cellar that leads to this tunnel and we could meet there and talk. Let our necklaces brush. When I get mine back, that is."

"If you must build an entrance, make steps so you do not get hurt."

He chuckled. "With steps. Our own secret room leading from your home to mine. Maybe you could keep your mat on my bed."

"It is where it belongs."

"Yet you moved it." The pain seeped into his voice even though he didn't want it to.

"I did not." She sounded offended. "Silver moved my mat because he said warriors were coming to challenge you. He cannot allow this."

"Why?"

"He promised Menashen he could kill you if you needed killing."

"Oh great. You didn't come last night…"

"My friend needed me."

He pinned her against the frigid tunnel wall. "I would have gone with you." He nudged her lips with his, playfully. "Sacri, breathe with me."

Her lips parted, reaching out to his, softly at first then he pushed into her deeper, his tongue searching for her sweet savours. She was so earthy the fragrance made him dizzy and Alex relaxed into her, their bodies hugging.

While their lips danced, he pulled her hips in closer, then he slipped his suspenders down one at a time. His clothes were restricting. He needed out of them but he couldn't pull his lips off hers to ask if she was ready.

The kisses turned savage as she held his head firmly against hers, her breaths pushing her chest into his.

She flipped him so he was backed into the cold wall.

Alex pulled away from her lips to catch his breath. Lost to her. Hers to do with as she pleased. Sacri ripped his shirt open, attacking his neck with kisses, melting him into the wall. When her hands slid down his lower back and into his slacks he snapped back to life, scooping her into his arms. Their lips met again.

Everything blurred as her legs wrapped around him, trapping him to her. He ran his hands up her legs and under her dress, then gripped her naked ass so he could roll her toward the wall and into… Wali?

He'd come around the corner and they'd smashed into him. "What the hell is going on down here?" Wali snipped, getting back on his feet. He held a lantern on them. "I see why you didn't search for me." He chuckled. "Don't stop on my account, I'll just back out gracefully."

Alex dropped her as if caught doing something forbidden. She flung herself against the wall, brushing her lips and pulling her dress down frantically.

"Sorry, I don't know what came over me." Alex bowed his head, afraid to look at her. "The earth pushed me to do it."

"The earth?" Wali chuckled. "Yeah, let's blame it on the earth. She took off. Sorry."

Alex rested against the wall, his shirt open, his suspenders down. He tried to pull himself together but his breathing was wild.

Wali snooped around the storage room. "Show me around down here. This is amazing."

Alex couldn't move.

"Alex? You want to go after her?"

"Did I hurt her?" His voice shook.

"She looked fine to me. Not sure I can say the same about you."

"I lost control," Alex admitted. His heart raced so fast he was dizzy.

Wali smiled. "Or maybe you just gave her control for a moment. I like her. Shall we go find her? Or do you need a drink?"

A drink? He ran a hand in his hair. "I feel drunk already." He was shaking. What the hell kind of kiss was that?

–TWENTY-FIVE–

Six days later, they had a garden planted. Alex was close to finishing the walls of the house, and he'd even built an outhouse, for privacy reasons. Wali was still working on the fire-ring, determined to get it done. Tomorrow he planned to get supplies for the roof.

Alex told him to check how much lumber and cement mix would cost for a barn, too. The price would determine which way they went. Of course they both hoped for lumber. Hauling rocks was something Alex didn't want to explain to Sacri.

Sacri hadn't come to see him since the kiss. He'd only seen her once, riding her white horse in the distance, headed to Laroche. He didn't know what that meant. Had he scared her off?

All six nights he'd forgotten to sing to Mattie. He promised himself to go by the creek tonight. Maybe Sacri would return. Not that it mattered if she didn't, he lied to himself.

Another problem was Lacey. Alex would have to talk to Silver about Lacey because how could he know if she was safe if she kept vanishing?

Trying to distract himself from where these gals got off to, Alex planned to start a well today. The more he thought about it, the more he felt using a hole already half dug made sense. The hole Wali had stumbled into was just sitting there. He figured he could dig it about another ten feet and see if there was water under the ground. He jogged from his house out to the hole. It was a distance but hauling water would do him good and would be easier than starting a new hole. He'd build their next house closer to the well.

Before they'd left, he'd gone by the library and read about

how to build a well. On paper, the plans had looked easy, but standing over his future well, he could see that even with a hole half dug, it would be a job.

He returned to camp for supplies, pulled the lumber off the wagon, made the ladder longer, then he grabbed a hammer and some extra pieces to make a tripod over the well. He needed a pulley and rope, which he found at the bottom of their supplies.

He brought the shovel and a crowbar for prying rocks and with his load in the wheelbarrow, he headed to the hole.

Before he built the tripod, he wanted to dig a bit, see what he'd do to stop the sides from collapsing.

He was hauling dirt up and about halfway up the ladder when a shadow blocked the sun. He caught his breath and paused, waiting for Sacri to say something. No movement came from above. Squinting, he glanced up to see Silver glaring at him and he didn't realize how eager he was to see Sacri until he knew she wasn't there. Disappointed, he asked, "What?"

Silver growled.

"Now my well annoys you?"

"My hole," he yelled in French.

"Oh." Alex looked down, then up at Silver. "I didn't know this hole was yours. It's a decent hole. I was just thinking it would save me time to use a hole half started."

"Not started. Finished." Silver shook his head and banged his chest. "Mine."

Alex climbed up and sat on the edge of the hole. Silver hesitated, then joined him, so Alex sipped from his flask then offered it to Silver. He smelled the drink and sipped.

"Water," Alex told him in English. Silver repeated the word, but in his language and Alex was quick to repeat it and pointed down the hole. "Water."

Silver shook his head. "My hole. I worked hard on it, so keep out."

Alex nodded. "This hole will fill with water to drink," he said in French. "We call it a well."

Silver shook his head and in his language he said, "My burial hole," while banging his chest, clearly too frustrated to explain.

Alex pulled out his ladder. He journeyed twenty feet over and said, "My hole." With that, he started his own hole.

Silver sat with his hole until Alex was about four feet down. Then he pulled something from his pant leg and fell to his knees to help Alex dig his hole.

They worked side by side in the hole, filling the bucket and hauling it up. They dug all day, were about ten feet down, and had a good width. Silver was a great teacher. He taught Alex to smooth out the edges and line them with rocks so they stopped collapsing. Alex wished there was something clever that he could teach Silver.

They were discussing life when Silver stopped and touched the wall. He scrambled out.

Alex was on his heels. "What is it?"

Silver faced Alex and gripped his shoulder. "A storm is coming. Get in the tunnel and wait for my return. Tell Lacey..." He met Alex's eyes but didn't finish the message. Alex nodded. Silver didn't have to finish it, his message was clear.

"I don't ever know where Lacey is."

"She's learning the lay of the tunnels."

The sky was blue and Alex didn't see any reason for alarm. "I'll go with you. I don't see any signs of a storm."

Silver pulled out his blade and stomped his feet three times. He pointed to the west, where Wali worked. "The wind is strong, the hot from today and the cold from tonight will mix. There is no shelter or no place to hide from winds. Stay underground, and if the hail hits, you are in a safe place, but if all goes quiet then winds...you had better be in those tunnels."

A horse walked up to Silver as if he'd called her. He flung himself up.

Alex felt like a child being left behind as he watched Silver ride off. Still, he'd left him in charge, kinda.

–Twenty-Six–

Sacri took her necklace off and handed it to Clement. "You gave me a cross and believed this would bond us, so I return it." He hadn't given her this one, but Silver had promised the other to Alex so it was no longer hers to give.

"I don't want your stupid necklace. I want you. I always have. You have to come with me before my uncle kills off your tribe."

"I am not yours to want." She knew now, there was never a choice to make; she belonged with Alex. No vision, no promises, no one would change that. "You deserve a wife who will live with you on your land. A wife who would be proud of you, not shadowed by your mistakes."

Clement's jaw clenched and he got off the horse. "Then I'll live with you."

"This is not possible. You are marked for judgement."

"I'm the Man of Legends. I'll protect you."

"Then do it," she challenged him. "A hero will not admit that he is such, he will show the world, and they will call him this."

"It's him, isn't it? Alex." His face distorted in anger.

"You dislike Alex, but he could teach you things."

"Like what? How to get slobbering drunk and toss women around. You're blind, Sacri. He's not good for anything, never was, never will be. Mattie was terrified of him. Only stayed with him to get her hands on the necklace for you. Didn't want to be alone with him. Said he was rough with her." He snagged the necklace from her. "I will take this and save the trinket for when you come crying back to me. I won't ever be far, Sacri."

He grabbed the reins of the horse and rode off.

She was sad for Clement but had no idea how to reach him. Menashen stepped beside her. He'd been waiting in the grass because she needed a man to talk to Clement. Silver said if she'd linked to him, her duty was to save him. Menashen was brave and about to be a father. He would do just fine.

She glanced at him, and was surprised that he wasn't as hard to look at as usual. His wild animal-charm was tame as he stood bravely beside her as if this were a battle and they were equal. He kept his focus on Clement.

"Thanks for coming with me," she said.

"I see what you mean. He's cursed. I'll talk to him, but killing him would be easier." He studied Clement as he rode off. "Why not get your Alex to set him straight? He's got a fatherly way about him."

Sacri was surprised Menashen would say this. He was usually very bitter toward the men she talked with. "You like him?"

"I never said that." He chased after Clement and they stopped to talk. She watched. Clement stared at her while Menashen talked to him. Was he listening?

Sacri was so focused on Clement she'd missed the man rushing at her on a brown horse. When she noticed the man in a sheet, he was almost on top of her and she stumbled back then rolled aside to avoid the attack from his long knife. He rode past her, glanced over his shoulder as he slowed his horse, then came back for her.

His blue eyes gave him away as they peered into her like daggers. She would forever know those eyes—Gavin Bernoit.

He turned his horse and rushed her again.

The entrance to the Healing Chamber wasn't far but she didn't want to lead him there, so she ran toward Clement and Menashen.

Bernoit threw the blade, just missing her.

Menashen and Clement noticed him now and Menashen shoved Clement out of the way, ready to tackle this man from his horse. Sacri changed direction to lead Bernoit away but he saw Menashen as a challenge and ran his horse that way, ploughing into Menashen.

Sacri scrambled to change direction.

Menashen wasn't getting to his feet. Was he dead? She'd never seen someone taken down by a horse. Menashen didn't move.

Stories leapt to her mind about men who had gone crazy on the prairies and no one could stop their rampage. This was real, and she understood what Alex meant. She had to find a *real* way to stop Gavin Bernoit.

Clement was by Menashen and the crazy man on the horse rode back for her. She had nowhere to run so she faced Bernoit, her knife in hand.

He got off his horse, slowly.

Sacri stomped for her horse, but she wasn't around which was strange, for the mare shouldn't be far. Gavin Bernoit approached. Sacri leapt for him. He now had a gun in his hand and shot at her. His aim wild, the bullet tore the flesh along the side of her leg. She leapt for him. Her body rammed into him, knocking him over, giving her an advantage as her knife dug into his shoulder.

Bernoit flipped her, pinning her to the ground, tearing savagely at her dress.

She was surprised to hear Silver yell. Where had he come from?

Bernoit pointed his pistol up, without looking, he shot toward Silver's voice.

Clement appeared over them and wrapped a rope around his neck. He strangled Bernoit and pulled him off her. Sacri yanked her blade out of Bernoit's shoulder and slammed it into his neck so his life was over. She was tired of this man and needed to see how Menashen and Silver were. She was sick of Clement thinking he had to protect her.

She wiped the blood from her cheek and reached for the necklace so it would guard her from his evil soul.

The necklace was gone.

She'd given the cross to Clement.

Sacri dropped to her knees, as Bernoit's soul appeared in front of her. A spectre surrounded by angry flames. Bernoit's ghost dived for her and she screamed as the pain cursed her.

"I got ya," Clement mumbled against her ear as she fell against him. "Walk with me. Walk. Your horse shouldn't be far. I'll get you somewhere safe. There's a storm raging this way." His voice was underwater, clouded. Blurry.

She leaned on Clement, her legs too burning to move. She had to stop moving, stop breathing.

Then Clement was ripped from her and she fell to the grass.

–Twenty-Seven–

Alex threw heavy rocks on anything that might blow away. It annoyed him that his house didn't have a roof yet, because it would have been interesting to see how the roof fared in a storm. When he rushed into the tunnel, the sky was miserable and he saw a twister playing in the horizon. It wasn't big, but he went underground, as Silver had instructed. Wali was already down here somewhere, with Lacey.

He had no idea where to go in the tunnel so he leaned against the wall, peeking out from under the bushes. It rained and he expected water to rush into the hole, but it didn't. The air was damp and he could almost taste the rain, but he remained dry.

Someone sighed down the tunnel causing him to jump. "Louis?" Alex lit his lantern.

Louis leaned against the wall like him. "I hate not being invited to battles anymore."

"What battle?"

He stared ahead, listening to the storm.

"Louis? Where is Sacri?"

"She was determined to talk to Clement."

"Alone?" Alex was ready to climb out of the tunnel, but Louis hauled him back.

"No, Menashen went with her. What has you so wild?"

Alex faced him. "What?" A frantic fear flooded Alex. "Do you know where?"

Louis was calm. "No, but I know how Sacri is. She would have invited him to meet with her on Cursed Lands, so she was close to a tunnel."

Alex thought about how Clement had hidden under that sheet. "Clement is afraid of something. He wouldn't be meeting with her without others. She'll be attacked. Let's find her."

"Best to wait the storm out." They watched the skies through the hole. Lightning was constant.

A long painful roar echoed down the tunnel.

"Silver?" Louis stammered. "Lacey, I'm going. Alex is with me," he called over his shoulder as if she were right there, and he took off. Alex stayed tight on his heels.

"Is Silver hurt?"

"A warrior doesn't call for help for fun, Alex."

"I should have ignored Silver and gone with him." They rushed through the never-ending tunnels in silence.

When someone moaned from up ahead, Alex whispered, "Did you hear that?" He almost dived around the corner, the lantern held high, but there was already one lighting the area. Silver was on his knees, with a man in front of him.

The walls were a light orange and the room left a strange taste in his mouth, almost metallic. Even stranger, one of the walls had plants growing out of it, and in the middle of them was a dent in the wall, like an altar.

Silver glanced up at Alex.

"Oh no," Louis sat beside Silver so they were shoulder to shoulder.

Silver hung his head. "He's dead." He'd discarded a muddy sheet beside them.

Alex ran the lantern over the man. He was stabbed. The wound in the neck was probably the fatal blow.

Silver bled from a bullet wound to the shoulder. He was drenched, too. Water streamed down his face like tears...or mixed in with tears.

"Who is this?" Alex asked, joining them on the dirt floor of the small room.

"Gavin Bernoit," Louis said as he scooped up dirt and rubbed it on Silver's arm.

Silver kept his head down.

"As in Lacey's father? What happened?"

"He shot me so I didn't see what happened. The blow knocked me out and when I came to, the storm was on us. But...his was a cursed soul, so someone will suffer the curse."

"You know who did this," Louis said. "You know who suffers."

Alex looked from one to the other trying to understand what was going on. "Is it Sacri?"

"I don't know where she is. Clement was here…"

"So why the hell are we sitting here?" Alex checked the area. A ladder led to a trapdoor. "Let's go."

Silver stood. "If I could have saved him, it would have saved her." He looked like he might puke. He handed Alex his golden chain with the cross dangling from it. "I no longer need it. I'd planned to do this myself."

"You needed my cross to kill him? If you wanted to kill her old man anyway, what are you so upset about?"

"Shadows." Silver climbed the ladder, leaving the man in the dirt. Louis followed so Alex joined them in the storm.

"I suppose if I could see souls I might understand what the hell you're talking about, but you know what I see?" Alex said as he faced the wind and pelting rain.

"What?"

Alex had to get closer to Silver to tell him what he thought. The wind jabbed the rain at him, stinging him. "If Monsieur Bernoit only had Lacey as a child, she inherited his land, and from what Louis told me, it's land you guys didn't want him to have."

Silver glanced from Louis to Alex and wiped the rain off his face. "Are you sure this is how it works?"

"Yeah."

"All of it? All?" Silver's voice shook. "Cursed Lands are hers?"

Alex had no idea. "Anything he owns or is about to own she'll take over. Where did you find this bloke? Sacri won't be far."

Silver moved his arm and dropped to his knees with a moan.

"You're hurt?"

Louis was over him. "The Healing Chamber had his pain numbed. He needs to stay down there."

The rain pounded on them so hard Alex could hardly open his eyes.

Alex had no idea how a room could numb his pain but

maybe it had something to do with the orange walls or the weird plants growing in the dark. Regardless, he helped Silver back into the healing hole where he collapsed on the dirt floor. Alex moved the light over his arm. "He has a bullet in him. We need someone to operate."

"I'll get Lacey." Louis rushed off, leaving him alone with Silver.

Silver opened his eyes. "It wasn't supposed to be like this, Alex. She tried to help a child and now, I have unleashed a curse that will destroy her."

"Not if I can help it." Alex pushed up the trapdoor that led to the prairies.

"Will you be able to find your way?" Silver asked.

Alex didn't care, Sacri was out there. He had no idea what was going on, but that much he knew.

Wild winds ripped the trapdoor from his hands.

Cold rain stung his face as he emerged into the world again. He couldn't see anything. His lantern was useless so he left it by the tunnel entrance.

He needed help… He pounded his foot on the ground three times as Silver had done earlier.

He waited, feeling crazy.

Silver's horse appeared in the assaulting rain and nudged him. Alex paced around her. "Do you know where Sacri is?"

Despite the rain and the lightning exploding the skies, the horse watched him patiently.

"Will you take me to her?"

She waited. He had no idea how to talk to a horse, they'd always terrified him, but he hadn't ever admitted that to anyone, least of all himself.

Alex peered into the shadows but he couldn't see anything.

Then, over the roaring of the storm, a scream pushed him onto the horse and together they rode into the rain.

Head down, Alex breathed against her mane. Silver liked to ride bareback and didn't have a saddle anyway, but Alex had never ridden a horse bareback. She moved under him, listening to what he wanted. "Find Sacri," he whispered along the mane he gripped. The horse galloped, on a mission that ended rather quickly when the mare stopped abruptly and stomped around something. Alex dismounted and was shocked to see the body of a young man. He was dressed in deerskin pants. Tattoos like Silver and Sacri had. He flipped him over. Menashen. Alex shook him but he didn't respond. He couldn't leave him in the rain so he tried to sit him up to heave him onto the horse. He was heavy and slippery and fell back in the mud with Alex sliding on top of him.

Menashen groaned.

Alex had no idea how to get him onto the horse.

He wrapped Menashen's arms around his neck and flung him up but he fell forward in the mud, pinning Alex to the ground.

Dang it.

He flipped him off and tried waking him again. "To your feet, warrior. Stand."

He didn't move, so Alex grabbed his feet and dragged him through the mud.

He trudged beside the horse, using her to guide him in the stormy winds and rains. "We can do this," he told the horse in case she cared. Still, she was with him, and all he had.

Rain pelted them.

They shuffled in the downpour for about thirty minutes. He promised himself only thirty minutes had passed yet somehow it felt like forever.

The mare came to a halt.

Alex expected to see the tunnel entrance, but nothing was familiar. He had no idea where they were. "Stupid horse." He searched the ground for signs of familiar things and left Menashen with the horse. "At least try to help me find her." He blamed the horse, as if it even cared about his plight. "Argh. Stay with Menashen. I'll search the area myself." A shadow in the distance caught his eye. He approached, cursing himself for not bringing a weapon.

It was Sacri's white horse. Her neck sliced. Dead. No wonder Silver's horse was upset. Who would do this?

"Sacri?" Panic gripped him. Where was she?

Lightning lit the sky and he spotted a huddle of bodies in the distance. Alex rushed to it and dropped to his knees. Clement jumped when Alex knelt beside him. He had used his shirt like a blanket to protect them.

"Storm came out of nowhere," Clement told Alex. "She

passed out and I'm lost."

Seeing them together made Alex's stomach tighten. When lightning struck again, he looked at Clement. His lip bled. His eye was swollen. Damn. What had happened? "You did well," Alex reassured Clement then he felt Sacri's neck for a pulse. Her skin was freezing but the necklace wasn't there. Alex took off his gold chain and placed the pendant around Sacri's neck. Her laboured breathing ended almost instantly.

"How did you do that?" Clement wiped the rain from his face. A cross dangled from Clement's neck, the leather strap that Alex had given Sacri rubbing his skin.

Why would she give her cross to Clement? A deep uneasiness settled in him. Did she choose Clement?

With a deep breath, Alex set his pains aside and focused on her. He wiped the hair off her forehead. "We'll take her and Menashen to a hole. We'll wait out the storm there." Alex pulled her in his arms and stood.

Clement didn't seem to know what to do. "I saved her." He tagged after Alex.

"You did well."

Clement followed him to the horse.

Sacri was limp in his tired arms.

The horse came to them and offered shelter from the wind as Alex trooped beside the mare with Sacri in his arms, trying to pinpoint where he'd left Menashen. He looked closely at Sacri in case he might see her in the dark. It took a few moments before lightning lit the sky. Her dress was torn open. He couldn't detect any blood or wounds needing attention. He wanted to get her to Silver. To the room that might heal her, because he was willing to try anything to save her.

But he was lost. His sense of direction gone.

As terrifying as it was to think about, he needed the Man of Legends right about now to whisk in and save her.

Her chest moved peacefully. Then again, maybe his mind played tricks on him. When he'd carried Mattie out of the burning house, he could have sworn he saw her breathing, too.

They travelled about ten minutes. He needed a break and had to admit that he'd lost Menashen. Wind tore against them the entire way. He settled Sacri next to the horse. "I need a quick minute. To catch my breath," he lied to Clement.

"I'll carry her if you know where we're going," Clement offered. "She's breathing better."

"The cross will help. She should have never taken it off. She knew better. The pendant protects her from some stupid curse." Despite himself, bitterness drowned his voice.

Clement touched the cross around his neck. "You're... You're blaming me?" Clement ran off into the storm, leaving Alex. Argh. Why did he always say the wrong thing to the brat?

"I never said that," Alex hollered. "Clement, come back here. You'll get lost." He waited but Clement was gone. Alex looked out into the dark after him. Seeing Clement leave was always a relief. Alex usually liked having people around, but he could do without Clement shadowing his life.

Alex lifted Sacri in his arms again and continued. The horse kept pace beside them, leading the way. A moan came from somewhere to his left, so they headed that way, blindly.

"Menashen?"

"Silver?" Menashen groaned.

"He's in the healing hole. Help me with Sacri."

Menashen melted out of the storm and was on him like a ghost. He stared at Alex for a long time and finally said, "Did you move me?"

"Yes. I'm lost," he admitted.

"Follow me." To Alex's relief, he didn't offer to take Sacri.

-TWENTY-EIGHT-

The trapdoor was before Alex and Menashen, with the lantern still beside it.

"Open the door to the tunnel," Alex ordered. "Silver should be there."

Menashen wiped his arm along his jaw. When lightning flashed, he glanced at his arm then did as Alex instructed.

"Are you hurt?" Alex demanded.

"I'm fine." He spat at Alex's feet as lightning flashed again. Blood. Great.

"Get in this hole, you need healing, too. I'll pass her to you."

"I'll carry her." Menashen looked like he could probably even carry Alex, hurt or not, but Alex refused to hand her over.

They stared each other down.

He got closer to Alex but Alex stood his ground with Sacri in his arms.

Menashen snapped, "Hand her to me."

"Help me lift her on my back, then go first and guide me down."

"I'll carry her."

"You're hurt and you risk hurting her. Stop acting like a jackass and help."

Menashen let out a long rumbling growl, then he helped Alex drape her on his back and vanished down the hole.

Alex started the awkward descent. Menashen tried to pull her off his back, so Alex paused. "Guide. Help. Don't hurt her."

When he was almost on the bottom step, Menashen took her in his arms and gently placed her on the ground.

Overhead, lightning lit the skies. Alex brought the lantern in and got it going. Then he climbed the ladder and shut the trapdoor, sealing them in.

"Silver's gone?" Alex checked the ground for any trace of him and it dawned on him that Lacey's father was missing, too. "I'm sure this is the same room. Maybe." He looked around confused. Maybe he'd found another room.

"We only have one Healing Chamber." Menashen snapped a leaf from one of the plants and placed it on his chest.

How long had Alex been out in the storm? His clothes were soaked and the hole was damp.

Menashen rested in the dirt, too, with the leaf on his chest. Alex sat on the other side of Sacri. The lantern beside him.

Alex took off his own wet shirt and was thinking about taking off his pants, too. After a quick glance at Menashen, he changed his mind. With Sacri between them, he didn't want Menashen getting too comfortable.

Menashen rested on his back, his breathing sounded painful. "How did you move me?" he asked in his language, eyes closed.

Alex explained how he'd dragged him.

"Why move me if I was too heavy for your puny arms?"

Alex clenched his fists, responding to Menashen's bullying. "I couldn't leave you, but I couldn't leave Sacri either. I did my best. I was careful with you. You look like you were run over by a bull."

"More like a horse." Menashen glared at him. "I would have left you." His breaths entered slowly now. He reached for Sacri's hand and closed his eyes. "We must sleep. Go."

"I'm not leaving her. I'll wash her up. Want me to clean you, too? Are you hurt? Do you need anything? What does the plant do? Why are you holding her hand?"

"I need the healing sleep. Touch me and I kill you."

"Fine." Alex moved the lantern over Sacri. Her dress fell open, exposing her skin underneath. She was covered in bruises. Seeing them ignited a wild rage in Alex. He needed to rush out and tear the bastard who did this limb from limb. Yet seeing her so helpless also created a surreal calm in him, pushing him to sing to her until she was better, making him promise to never leave her.

The difference in the two emotions numbed him and he set to work cleaning her. He placed a leaf on the wound on her leg, not sure what it would do, but desperate to try anything.

His gold chain fell between her breasts. She shivered against him, but there was nothing in this hole to make a fire with so he pulled her closer to Menashen and himself, using their bodies to keep her warm.

Menashen didn't move, lost in a deep sleep. He didn't let her hand go either, which for some reason annoyed Alex. He tried slipping his fingers between their hands but Menashen clutched tighter, then Alex was stuck between them. With a sigh, he freed himself and let it go.

When she stopped shivering, Alex cleaned her legs, using his undershirt, wiping gently at the mud and blood. She hadn't moved. He glanced down at her, sprawled out in the dirt. She looked so innocent, holding Menashen's stupid hand.

Restless, he cleaned the undershirt outside. Rain fell but the winds had died. The sun was fighting to light the sky. He'd been up all night? Just outside the hole was a bush covered in berries. He picked a bunch and cradled them in his shirt to carry down but he didn't dare eat them. He'd have to ask Menashen or Sacri if they were safe. He was out of his element, looking after two sick people. He didn't know who owned this land, or even where it was. What if Sacri needed a doctor? How far were they from one? Could Lacey help her, too? And where was Silver?

Exhausted, he fell beside her and drifted off. A strange dream came to him. Sacri's beautiful white horse watched him load a gun that he had no idea how to use. The horse said in a deep voice much like Alex's father's, "*Revenge clouds your judgement. It was smart what you told Silver about Lacey. Be smart. Look around, my boy. Your temper will get you into trouble out here.*"

Alex crossed his arms in front of the horse and answered, "They hurt her. They hurt you. They disrespected land. Someone needs to set them straight."

"*No one can. Best you can do is divert their attention long enough to get the land in safe hands. Besides, if you get rid of the troublemaker, you get rid of the trouble.*"

He had lots that he wanted to tell this horse who talked like his father, but reading his mind, the horse shook his head. "*You worry too much, Alex.*" He pronounced his name like Sacri always did, which made him think about Menashen holding her hand.

"*Oh?*" The horse looked smug. "*Sacri will pick who she wants. Nothing will change that.*"

"She wants a Man of Legends."

"*That's right. Not the bravest nor the strongest, he must only be legendary.*"

Alex forced out a disgusted sound. "And how does a guy be something so impossible?"

"*He just is.*"

Alex woke with a burning in his arm. No, not in it, against it. Sacri burned up against him as she slept.

It sounded like the storm was over and much to his surprise, natural light shone through tiny pinpoint streams from overhead. They bounced off the plants and reflected off the walls making the room come alive with sparkling dancing lights.

He took a deep breath. The air was damp and smelled fresh.

Alex leaned over to kissed Sacri's forehead and promised her that not one of those cowards would ever see a tunnel on Depaix Land. This was a magical place, and he'd find a way to protect the land that they wouldn't expect. He liked the idea of Lacey getting her father's land, then marrying Silver. It was a start.

Menashen was on his side, watching him. Their eyes met. Menashen said, "You look serious. What did you dream about? This stupid chamber always gives me weird dreams."

"Just a talking horse giving me grief about nothing. You?"

"I have to get back to my wife, she's to birth soon. You have food?" he asked Alex, removing the leaf and looking at the nasty bruise on his side.

Alex showed him the berries. "I found these. Can we eat them?"

Menashen glared at him and Alex expected him to make fun of him or mock him but he nodded. "Give me a fistful, and thank you for asking and not eating something that will make you sick." He sat and Alex noticed he favoured his right side.

"Does it hurt to breathe?" Alex asked.

"I'm fine."

"Stop acting like you're invincible. Does breathing hurt?"

Menashen glared at him. "Yes. And what magic will you do to help? I must breathe."

"Lift this arm up a bit. I'll feel your ribs to see if they're broken."

"Don't touch me."

Alex sat in front of him. "If you want to return to your wife, you need help. I don't know anything about healing, or being out here, but I'm all you have." He searched his pocket and pulled out a salve he had in a silver tube. It was for burns and bug bites but he didn't tell Menashen this. "I'll rub this on, it might help." If he could touch his ribs, he'd know more.

Menashen grabbed the tube and smelled it. He pulled away shocked. "This is for girls."

"It's for healing. Like the leaf. If it doesn't work, it doesn't work, but what do you have to lose?"

They stared at each other.

"If it hurts that bad in this healing hole, how intense will the pain be when you leave?"

Menashen struggled for air, flat on his back. Alex rubbed a bit of salve on his fingertips and slid them over each rib. Only the one wiggled. "This rib is loose. If you run or lift heavy things you could send a fragment into your lungs and die."

"Every warrior must die." Then quietly he added, "How do you know this?"

"I was in plenty of fights growing up. Wali was always pushed around. I don't take that shit. Means I broke a few ribs. I know how much pain you're in. It hurts to move, to breathe, and you'd better get home today, because tomorrow it'll be worse. When you get home, rest. Let it heal. Once it doesn't hurt to breathe again, you'll be back to being crazy."

"You fought?" he asked, skeptical. "Did you win?"

"A guy who wins, doesn't usually know about broken ribs."

Menashen chuckled. "If we fought, what would you do to win?"

"I don't fight to win. I fight to protect those I love. You plan to hurt my friends, or be my friend?" Alex met his eyes.

Menashen inspected him. "Silver said if you must die, I can do it."

"You see that's the difference between us, Menashen. If I wanted you dead, I wouldn't need his approval."

The tension between them was stupid and Alex decided to end it. "A smart guy doesn't fight someone like you, they ask them for help. Thanks for that, by the way. I couldn't have gotten her down without you."

He nodded. "What if we had to fight?" Menashen's tone implied he'd considered it.

"Why would I ever have to fight you?" Alex forced a smile.

Menashen glanced at Sacri. "We could fight for a woman."

Alex shook his head. "Nah, they either want me or they don't, and anyone brave enough to marry you, I do not want to deal with."

Menashen chuckled again. His laughter came from the depth of his soul and Alex relaxed. "You will like Nichena. She is a powerful warrior, like Sacri, only she likes me more. Will you come when her child is born?"

Alex nodded.

"Your magic lotion is warm."

"Keep it. Have your wife rub the lotion on your chest when you get home. It sounds like the storm has cleared. Feel better?"

"Yes." He stretched his left arm. "Sacri feels hot. This is good. Means she'll be better soon."

Alex wasn't so sure. He'd never heard of a fever making you better.

Menashen got up. "I am leaving. Thank you, but know this doesn't mean I like you." The corner of his lip curled up in a quick crooked smirk. "But I will think twice before I kill you."

Alex stopped him. "Before you go, I have to ask something, and I suggest you choose your words carefully because if I don't like your answer, I will hit you right in that broken rib."

Menashen waited.

"When you slept you held Sacri's hand. I mean, it's… You're clearly…" Alex squinted. "Why?"

Menashen's jaw went up and he met Alex's eyes. "*Cîpay* find strength in each other when in pain. I needed her strength."

"Oh." Alex nodded. "So if Silver would have been beside you, you would have held his hand?"

Menashen mumbled as he left, "I don't expect you to understand."

Alex rubbed his jaw, thoughtful. "I wouldn't hold your wife's hand if she was hurt unless you told me to. That much I do understand. And really, what more do I need to know?"

Menashen considered this, his shoulders tense. "Won't happen again. Be safe, Sacri's mate."

"I'm not…" Alex glanced at her and back at Menashen. He was gone.

–Twenty-Nine–

Alex lay beside Sacri. He pulled her into his arms and held her. She had no life-threatening wounds so he promised himself she would be fine while he listened to her breathing peacefully in the quiet chamber. He fell into a deep sleep, talking to the white horse again, and woke with a start because Sacri was gone.

Gone.

The berries were missing. His shirt was stained with blood and mud, and the leaf he'd placed on her leg rested on it.

Panicked, Alex went above ground. The creek wasn't far. He walked beside it, west, toward his place, feeling it was safer than the winding tunnels that he'd get lost in. When his camp was within sight, he ran, hoping she was there.

Wali must have left for town as planned, since there was no sign of him.

Alex was relieved to see his walls stood firm.

He called for Lacey, but she didn't appear.

Louis and his boys were walking through the grasses, headed north.

Alex caught up to them "What's going on? Where is everyone? Did you see Sacri?"

Louis let out a long breath. "Wali went south for supplies. Lacey and Silver were tagging along."

"South?"

"Yes, the town across the border is closer and has what he'll need. Our friend the priest is there and can help them. They should be back late tomorrow. Nichena is labouring. We're about to leave to get word to the Ghost Healers, since she is of their tribe and they will bless the child as one of their own."

"How long will you be gone?"

"Couple hours. Just need to give word to her sister and she'll have her husband bring them the message."

"And Sacri? How is she? Her leg…"

"She looked fine to me, but I wasn't checking out her wounds. Mad like she was, I just let her go."

"Mad?" He searched Louis' face for answers, but Louis avoided meeting his eyes.

"Follow the creek south until you see the cemetery. The priest there will help you. We have to go."

"This the same priest Wali will meet? Why would she go there?"

"She made it very clear that it's none of my business."

"Louis?" Alex wanted to shake the answers from him, but Louis' stance was firm and he knew he wouldn't say any more.

"Wali should be the one to tell you, not me. He left early by horse. It was still raining. I doubt he's still at the priest's but Sacri wouldn't listen to me and made me swear I wouldn't tell you anything. You might catch up to her if you hurry."

"Tell me what's going on. What the heck was the big rush for Wali to leave? Why would Silver and Lacey go with him? And what has Sacri upset?"

Louis sighed. "Some idea they had that Sacri says you won't like." He grabbed Alex by the arm. "You're probably safer staying with me. They'll be warriors coming and going. It's a big deal when a child is born."

"Yeah." Alex studied his hand on his arm. "I might be safer with you, but you know I have to go after her. I don't like the idea of her mad, chasing after Wali. Whatever trouble he's in now, can he handle it?"

Louis nodded. "He'll be fine. But I agree that she shouldn't be running after him. You'd better hurry."

Alex didn't waste any more time with Louis. He took off in a light jog.

He was hot and sweaty but he continued, watching the horizon for signs of life. In the distance, he spotted a herd of buffalo and a few deer, but no people. No Sacri.

It was late afternoon and Alex was beginning to wonder if

this was such a good idea. He didn't have a clue how far he had to go, but he was annoyed that Louis wouldn't give him a straight answer about what was going on. Wali was always doing things that got him into trouble, but really, what kinda trouble could he get into out here that Silver and Lacey would encourage?

And why would Sacri chase after them, leaving him behind? He was tired of her taking off but had no idea how anyone could make a gal like her stay.

A cemetery came into view on his right, hidden in trees. Lots and lots of trees. A small shack hid in the shadows of the woods. A church was visible down the path. Wali had said there were no towns...unless... Had he crossed the border to the United States of America?

The idea thrilled him. Did their land really run right to the border?

He rushed to the shack and knocked on the door. No one answered so he peered inside at a bed, a table covered in books, and a wall with prayers written on it in chalk. A lantern, a small stove, and a few pots on the wall by a cross, gave the place a homey feel.

Maybe someone was at the church? Alex was heading that way when movement in the cemetery made him turn around.

Sacri was climbing out of a plot.

"What the hell?" He rushed to help her but she pushed him toward the shack.

"Alex. Good. I need help. Get me a blanket from the house. Water. Hurry."

He did as she instructed and hurried back to the grave she'd been in. It had a tombstone only it wasn't a tomb. The wood in front of it flung open like a trapdoor.

Alex dropped into the hole. He was expecting to see a woman in labour. It was dark and cold, but these tunnels reminded him of the ones by his place. "You guys need lanterns down here," he complained to Sacri who was further down the tunnel, on her knees, working on someone. He stayed back in case it was Menashen's wife in labour.

"Feel the walls, they guide the way. Come help. This is my friend. He protects the entrance from this end. I protect it from the other. He taught me many things."

He?

Alex knelt by her, trying to make out who was on the floor.

"Help me with him," Sacri pleaded.

It was too dark for Alex to argue. "What happened?"

"I just found him like this."

He knelt by the warm body. "I'll pick him up the best I can, you guide me back." Alex ran his hands over him so he'd know where the wounds were. His neck was sticky and warm. Blood. He tried to cradle him, but he was too big so Alex dragged him with his hands under his arms.

Sacri helped and Alex admired her strength. He'd never met a woman as brave or as strong as her.

"What are you doing out here?" she asked as they walked.

"Searching for you. You left me. Last I saw of you, you were in rough shape, and here you are being a hero."

"You were dreaming," she said. "One cannot wake a dreamer in the Healing Chamber, but it is not good to stay there too long. The dreams linger."

Alex couldn't get him up the ladder so he arranged him on the blanket Sacri set out. Light poured in, revealing that the man Alex was hauling around was the priest who'd helped him build his house.

Sacri offered the priest water. The gash on the side of his head was bleeding into his long hair making it sticky.

"What else can I do?" Alex asked, not sure what to do or touch.

"Find me something to make a stitch. Keep watch up top."

Wanting to be helpful, he did as she instructed, finding a needle and thread in the shack. Then he sat over the hole with the trapdoor open. Sacri worked, saying prayers, her voice a comfort in the quiet day. The world was heavy with anticipation as if something serious was happening and it was only a matter of time before their lives changed.

Alex pulled out the two carving tools he liked to keep handy and started to make letters on the wooden grave marker. Slowly he wrote, *Here Rest the Ghosts of the Earth*. He was carving symbols around it when the earth shook.

The earth actually moved under him.

Alex jumped up and looked down, shoving the tools in his back pocket. "Are you hurt?" he asked Sacri and the priest.

She was on her feet and stared up at him, shock on her face. "The earth has dished out a punishment."

Alex was ready to leap down the hole but Silver appeared from the tunnel. He glanced up at Alex and whispered something to Sacri. He wore a strap to keep his arm against him. His scar was visible with new marks from a tattoo around it.

Whatever he'd said upset Sacri. She wept and clung onto him, making Alex leap down to hold her. Silver handed her to him, and told Alex, "Three men came through here. Hurt our good friend, the priest."

"Wali was coming here, is he…" Alex held his breath.

Silver said, "Wali and Lacey were through before they arrived. They are safe. Alex…" Silver winced. Before he could open his mouth again to share what troubled him, a roar echoed through the tunnel. Like a man in pain or out for vengeance.

Alex bowed his head, clutching Sacri tighter. He knew the agony behind the roar. "Menashen has lost his wife."

"And child," Silver whispered. "I came to block this exit, because those murderers will not leave this tunnel."

Sacri sobbed against Alex.

The priest leaned against the wall, exhausted. "Sorry you have to see us like this. When we lose one of our own, our connection through the earth pulls at us. The pain is unspeakable."

Alex could feel it, but he said, "Menashen will be crushed. Let's find the bastards."

The priest shook his head. "There won't be life to find. The earthquake you felt was Mother reclaiming their souls."

They couldn't know that, yet Alex didn't argue. Instead, he made himself useful and helped the priest out of the tunnel. He was their age and in excellent shape but he'd clearly taken a beating. Sacri ordered him to bed and even tucked him in.

She had a limp and Alex worried about the wound on her upper thigh but she focused on helping her friend. She kissed his forehead and said a prayer with him while holding his hand. Alex was intrigued by how motherly his tough warrior could be.

Once they were outside the shed, Alex rolled her into his

arms. "I am so sorry about your friend."

She rested her head against him, no longer the fierce warrior but a woman needing him for strength. She pulled it from his soul and he stood stronger for her, but her pain was so intense he had to close his eyes as tears washed over him.

She brushed them lightly from his cheek. "Alex, I am still feeling weak. The pain was horrible when I killed Gavin Bernoit. His soul attached itself to me, sucking me down." She touched the gold chain Alex had placed around her neck. "I woke with your pendant on and I don't dare remove it. I feel the protection it offers like a warm blanket of hope."

Alex held her, watching Silver close the tunnel entrance and carry what he could with his one good arm.

"We shouldn't leave Menashen alone," Alex told Silver when he approached them, still huddled, by the shack. "He's not so bad."

"He's with his mother and brother," Silver reassured him. "We are never alone." Silver headed out, so Alex and Sacri followed.

-THIRTY-

"Tell me when you're tired and we'll rest," Alex told Sacri, loud enough so that Silver heard. Silver did slow his step a touch.

"I'm fine. Slower than I'd like." Yet she kept up with Silver just fine.

They hiked a bit, with Silver in front. The sun began its slow descent and Alex doubted they'd make it back before dark.

Needing something to talk about, Alex asked, "Sacri, does it bother you to be linked to Clement?" He didn't want her linked to another man and had no idea how to say he was jealous without sounding like a baby.

She shrugged. "Clement is scared of turning out like his father."

"Well, your link to him isn't like ours, is it? I mean, you gave him your necklace..."

Silver chuckled, but Sacri kept her head down.

"It's not funny, Silver. I don't like the idea of her soul being tied to his."

Silver waited for them and stepped beside Alex. "You're linked to Wali. Should she worry about that?" Silver wiped the smile from his face and in his stern teaching way, he said, "Every link is different. Your link to Sacri is earthy. Sacred. One of desire. Her link to Clement is as a teacher."

He felt better, but really, if he could help Clement figure out his lesson, he would.

Silver added, "He killed his father."

"That's horrible. Here I was feeling sorry for him because I missed my pa and assumed he must, too. Why did Clement kill him?"

"He pretends his actions were to protect Sacri. His soul confesses to me that he was only protecting himself in hopes to win Sacri as his bride."

"So he's in love with her?"

"No, it would have angered his father, he thinks only of this. His father is a shadow on his life, even after all I did to help him, he suffers."

Sacri sighed. "I have much to teach him."

"Do you guys know that Bellecoeur has targeted your land?" Alex asked.

"He has no qualms about taking our land since I took his slaves," Sacri explained. "At first his threats were meant to spite us, but now I suspect he sees value in Sacred Land."

"Slaves?"

"Yes." Sacri's tone was firm.

Silver shook his head. "It was long ago and he paid them, so the deal is on the up and up."

Sacri cut him off, furious. "Paid them little and charged them to room and feed them. They could not leave and were told not to speak of their work. They slept and ate when told. They were slaves."

"The guy was always up to no good," Alex agreed.

"What Sacri says is almost true. Our enemy wants more than revenge. The value he seeks is not something he will let go. He loads things from tunnels in Moose Jaw on trains that will soon travel to Sacred Land. These things will be hauled across the border through our tunnels and to the next train. No one will know."

"What things?"

"Barrels. These barrels will bring disgrace to Sacred Land and money to them. This is the dream many had while in the Healing Chamber."

Alex felt the weight of what Silver said. It was too late. If Bellecoeur had it in his head that he wanted the land to store his dealings and smuggle them across the border, he'd get it. "Clement could help us. I mean, he usually sided with Bellecoeur, but we might be able to talk to him about this."

"Clement could help us," Silver agreed. "But why would he? The only thing he wants is Sacri."

Alex grabbed her hand, coming between her and that dumb

idea. Yet he suddenly understood why she was so distressed. He quickly searched for another solution. Anything else. "He loved Mattie. Ask him what she would want. He'll see it. I know he will." Alex knew nothing. This was what he wanted and hoped it would be so.

They travelled in silence for a bit, each lost in their own stories.

Sacri asked, "Alex, do you believe in legends?"

He thought about her question. Perhaps he did. Not that he was a part of her legend, but he did believe in stories influencing or changing lives. "Maybe. I love the parables in the Bible and I believe that they apply to my life, at times. They're not really the same, but want me to share one?" No one argued, so he continued. "A man had two sons. He was a respected father and since his boys were important to him, he hired servants to do the dirty work. They worked the fields and helped, but weren't asked to clean the pigpens. Well, the youngest one gets it in his head that life could be better and asks for his inheritance."

"Inheritance?" Silver cut him off. "Doesn't that mean his father was dead?"

"Well, asking meant he wanted his father dead, but the father was calm, handed it over, and watched his son leave." Alex was quiet for a moment. "I feel like that son sometimes. I mean, I was that greedy guy. I asked Bellecoeur for a bunch of things and disrespected him, spending his money wildly while showing Mattie a good time. Meanwhile Clement worked and respected him."

Silver looked proud. "Your story teaches."

Alex forced air into his lungs, not feeling so good but wanting to talk just the same. "Well, tragedy hit their lands and the son was forced to return home to beg his father for help. My kingdom was less vast and Bellecoeur wasn't as full of joy to see me. I asked Bellecoeur for help even though I didn't want to face him again. It was humiliating, and frankly, he should have turned me away, he owed me nothing."

"But he didn't?" Sacri asked.

"It was probably hard for him to offer me a job in a town he was moving to, but he did. Like the father took the foolish son back."

Sacri was against him, and he gripped her hand.

"But, the brother who had remained felt cheated," Silver offered.

Alex liked how Silver was always figuring things out. He was probably one of the smartest men he'd ever met. He waited for Silver to explain to Alex what he meant. "In your story, Clement is the loyal brother. You wonder why he doesn't like you, but it's clear. Bellecoeur took him in. How did Clement feel about you walking in and getting things he was entitled to?"

"Bellecoeur even called me 'son'. Mattie was always out with me..." Alex bowed his head, ashamed that he hadn't noticed that Clement felt left out.

Alex asked, "How could the foolish brother explain that these things were out of his control, that he suffered, too, that he..." Alex rubbed his forehead, "that he needed to start over? He was a broken man. He was no longer the fool who stole shamelessly from his father. He was humbled by guilt so deep it was a shadow keeping him from finding joy in his father's efforts to help."

"He had a shadow." Sacri covered her mouth, seeing more in the story than he did.

Silver placed a hand on his shoulder while they walked. It was a gesture of a teacher and he said, "You will live the change, and they will understand when ready."

They marched a bit more. Silver's stride was determined and Alex wondered if anything bothered this warrior. "What troubles you, Silver?"

His stance changed. "My worries are with Lacey." Silver had a shake to his voice. "Now she will own land. They will ask her for it..."

"A young woman isn't a worry to them. They'll leave her for last; confident she'll be easy to sway. What they don't know is that you'll be beside her."

Silver wouldn't look at Alex. "I worry we made a mistake. I don't always understand the ways of your tribe, Alex."

"What do you mean?" Alex wondered. The skies were dark, but the moon gave enough light for them to keep travelling. Still, a blackness loomed before them and he didn't like it.

"While Lacey worked on my shoulder, Wali listened to what I had to say about Lacey inheriting land, and he offered to marry her in the ways of your people so she could inherit his, too."

Alex stopped. Silver kept his head down.

"What the hell?" Alex snapped. "You sent Wali to marry the mother of your child?"

"It is already done. The priest has helped us."

"What the heck is wrong with you? With him? What if he lives to be a hundred? Or do you plan to kill him?"

Silver kept his head down. "It was not an easy decision."

Sacri stepped back.

Was this why she'd left after them? To stop them?

"Talk to me," Alex demanded, glaring at him then her, understanding why Louis wouldn't tell him this.

Sacri met his eyes firmly. "It is done, Alex. Silver felt this was the right thing to do. If Sacred Land is lost, so are we. This is where our souls connect and come back. Without this land, the Ghost Tribes are no more. We will vanish. Do not question what Silver does to protect this land."

"Yet you went after him to stop him."

She wouldn't look at Silver. "I knew this was not a plan you would like. I hoped to bring them back to discuss this with you but I was too late. I must stand by my brother's decision now."

"So this…" Alex motioned to Sacri and himself showing her the invisible connection. "You placing your mat by mine, that his plan, too? He hoping I'll marry you and you'll get my land? When Clement realizes what it'll take to win you over, will you give him my cross, too, and marry him?" He stormed off anger pushing him forward.

"Alex, no."

He turned around. "No? So what? You get your brother to kill me in my sleep?"

"Sacri, give us a moment." Silver rushed up to Alex and with his good arm, he shoved him toward the creek. Alex stumbled forward and scrambled up to face him. Did Silver want to fight him?

"I'm not about to fight you, you're a cripple."

"I could still kick your ass, but I have something more important to teach you." He pushed him again and this time Alex was ready and didn't budge.

"What?"

"See the boulder in the creek. I want you to remove it."

Alex didn't move. It was too dark to get in the water. He could make out the shadows in the gloomy night. "I can't. Not with my hands. Not in the dark. It'll take work."

"Take a closer look at how the water runs around it and tell me what would happen if the boulder was removed by force."

Alex climbed on the rock and stood over the water with it rushing around him, it was quiet along the sides. The moon reflected in the water as it emerged in the sky. He tried to see what Silver wanted him to understand. "The large rock created this calm area where the water sits peacefully. If I remove it, the torrent will rush through here."

"If Sacred Land is full of farms, and travellers, this peaceful connection will be washed out. I will not kill Wali, his time here nears its end, and all we can do is plan for this."

Alex rubbed his forehead. He refused to imagine a world without Wali.

"Your link is tight. I am sorry. It will be painful for you to let him go. You make firm connections. I can hardly refuse the one you offer me, but it is in our best interests if I do."

"I don't know about these links but he's my best friend. My brother. Family. Like you and Sacri, and I don't like you using him like this. I'm not impressed with you."

Alex jumped from the boulder back to shore.

"Let me show you how your link works." Silver walked to a plant. "Pull this tree out without destroying the roots and without digging it up."

Alex bent and yanked. "It's stuck."

"Use your muscles."

Alex heaved. It moved a bit but he couldn't break the roots from the ground. "The roots are too deep. I have to dig it out."

"This is what your soul does to others. It digs deep into it." He offered Alex his knife. "Cut it and these deep roots, they know not that the top is cut and they will keep digging, searching for more life. This is you. If I kill you, Sacri will have those roots in her soul and the sorrow will destroy her. So I should kill you, but I cannot. I will ensure you live a long life, Alex. But we have a problem. You must keep your soul away from hers."

Keep away from Sacri?

Sacri was curled up, sleeping in the grass and he didn't want to bother her, yet he wanted to wrap himself around her and keep her warm.

He changed the subject because this wasn't one either of them would win. "I just can't understand why you don't use those bills you all seem to have and buy the land yourselves."

Silver stepped past Alex to sit by Sacri. "I cannot own land."

"You can. Sacri has money, let her use it. Once it's sold, they won't look twice this way and your land will be protected. Take your warriors and buy up what you can. I'll go with you to teach you how to buy land. No one will be able to use it or bother you."

"Sacred Land must be earned and I cannot buy it," Silver grumbled.

Alex sat by Sacri and she moved so that her head was on his lap.

To Silver, Alex said, "Put your name on a title for show and pretend to them you bought it, just like you let Lacey pretend to follow us, and pretend to hang with us, when we know she wants you. It's better than having her marry Wali and pretending to be his wife."

After a long silence, Silver whispered, "I am not allowed either."

They were silent. Finally, it dawned on Alex what Silver meant. "Are you saying you tried to buy this land and they won't let you?" Rage pounded inside him.

"Yes."

Alex was shocked. This man went against his beliefs and tried to buy land but they refused to sell it to him. Why? Because he was Native? He almost jumped up but Sacri was warm against him so he whispered, "What did they say?"

"They said I stole money. They said I am a savage. They said to go back to my hole and leave the land settling to real men. They said a few things before I broke their jaws.

Thanks to Wali, my son will have his name on the Cursed Lands and parts of the Sacred Lands. I think only of him."

A shiver passed through Alex. He played in Sacri's hair. "I don't understand why you'd want cursed land."

Silver sighed. "Cursed Lands act like that rock I showed you. It keeps Sacred Land safe from the torrent of settlers. I am to blame for the present curse. Clement's father shadowed him. Sacri took the burden of this shadow on her soul, so I banished him to the Cursed Lands. He leeches on those who travel that land, like Bernoit who lived on the Cursed Lands, and he drives them mad."

Alex studied Sacri. "Will Monsieur Bernoit make Sacri crazy?"

"The pendant will protect her, but he will try to get to you, through these roots you have planted in her soul."

Sacri stirred. She slept on her side, and the tear in her clothes reminded him that she was hurt and they shouldn't push her so hard.

"Silver," Alex said. "I'll get a bit of sleep. We can head out in the morning."

Silver didn't argue.

–THIRTY-ONE–

Sacri woke from a deep sleep, surprised to be resting against Alex. He stared at the night sky. "What keeps you awake?" she asked.

"The kiss we shared." Alex cleared his throat. "Thing is...I can't see us not doing that again. Yet I got Silver telling me I can't, as if it's dangerous or something. I got you vanishing for days after. I learn that Clement is linked to you. None of it I like. What's going on with us?"

She caressed her lips. "I like the way your soul fits next to mine, but it is too dangerous for us to be together, now." She leaned on him to study his face in the dim light.

He raised an eyebrow. "Dangerous? Do you think I would hurt you? Was I too rough? I...I have no idea what happened but that kiss consumed me, took over."

"I like you claiming me. Besides, I kissed you. It's not the kissing that is dangerous, it is the shadow on my soul."

"I won't let a shadow come between us."

"It already has."

–THIRTY-TWO–

Alex, Sacri, Louis, and Silver sat around the camp fire cooking a pheasant when Silver asked Alex about the roof of his burrow. He had a playful tone.

"It's a house," Alex snapped. "When you build one, you can make fun of mine."

Silver faced him. "Is that a challenge, my friend? You know the land on the other side of my burial hole? I will make a home there for Lacey and me, but I will make a real home."

"You do that, smarty pants. Let me know if you need help so your home doesn't flood come spring."

Silver glanced at Alex. A deep smile lit up the lines around his eyes.

"When you smile, I forget you have to kill me," Alex teased.

Silver's smile faded. He turned and walked away, without another word.

"Now what did I say?" Alex asked Sacri and Louis.

"You reminded him that he has failed this task. He cannot kill you," Louis said.

"Good. So Louis, you and your family can stay with us in the house you helped build. Once we get a roof on it, I mean."

"Seriously, what we gonna do for the roof?" Louis wondered.

"I need wood, branches…anything to put across then we'll pile the sod on top."

"I'll see what we can find."

Silver broke into a run, headed south. He was so fast, Alex could hardly make him out against the horizon.

"Where is he going?" Alex asked.

"Wali returns with his gal," Louis said as if it was old news.

Alex went to meet them, too. He hiked for ten minutes before he saw Wali with the wagon full of things. He was getting good at spending Lacey's money.

Lacey rushed through the grasses with Silver, but Alex ignored them to yell at Wali. "I see your wife bought you more things." The bitterness rolled off his words.

"So you know." Wali slowed the horse, keeping pace with Alex as he walked beside them. "I have lumber to build Lacey dressers."

"Wanna tell me what you were thinking?" Alex demanded.

"Nope."

"You'd better behave because Silver will kill you if you touch her."

"I have no intention of touching her. You know that."

"Just talk to me."

"Dawned on me, that I'll die and won't leave anything behind except a memory, and most days you'll be trying to forget that. So I decided to spend the time I have helping others find a moment of happiness. Then, when they're happy, my life will have mattered."

"This is why you're always getting screwed over. What happens when you meet someone you do like and want to live with on your land? How will you explain a wife who sleeps with a warrior? Or what if Silver decides the land can go to Lacey and kills you?"

"Alex." Wali closed his eyes. "It's fine. Calm down. I'm glad to help them and Silver trusts me as much as I trust him. Let it go."

"I want you to be happy, Wali, but this is stupid. Talk to me before you make bonehead decisions like this. There are eyes and ears everywhere and this is not the time nor the place for you to wear your heart on your sleeve."

Alex walked in silence by Wali and his horse until the camp came into view.

Wali said, "I bought cement mix for the barn."

Alex couldn't imagine how Sacri would react to him using rocks to build a barn.

Wali shrugged. "Everyone is building. Wood and nails are hard to come by. Who's at our camp?" Wali sat higher to get a better look.

"Louis."

"Oh, from here he looks like a settler."

Alex studied Louis. Maybe he could pass for a settler. Alex smirked, a plan forming.

Part Three

Two Weeks Later

"You see the truth in my soul, yet you love me anyway."

–Lacey

–THIRTY-THREE–

Alex's place had been crowded since they'd put the roof on, the week before, which meant he hadn't gotten a moment alone with Sacri and stealing her all to himself was suddenly all he could think about.

Silver had travelled to the States for wood. He was incredibly proud of the little shack he was building, and came to Alex several times for advice as if he were some type of expert.

Sacri sat on the edge of the bed. Alex had thrown it together using long grasses stuffed inside fabric that Lacey had prepared. It wasn't comfortable but Sacri had placed her mat on it, so he enjoyed it, even if he was dying to be alone with her.

Sacri watched him pace the house as he listened to Wali go over the list of things they needed in the city.

"Why don't you come?" Alex asked Wali, frustrated because he'd never remember everything Wali had listed off.

"I'm staying here. I'd like to finish the internal fire-ring. Go. A break will do you good. Visit the city. Have fun. You need to unwind." He lifted his eyes, teasingly and nodded to Sacri, with a playful smirk. "I know you don't like to be alone, but spending time with just her might make you more bearable for the rest of us to stand."

Alex sighed. "Silver doesn't want Sacri to leave Sacred Land." He hated the idea of making this trip without her. Yet he wanted to try out his plan.

He shook his hands, needing to do something creative, useful.

Alex had no idea what to take with him. He had nothing for travelling, yet heading to the city empty-handed was foolish.

He searched for a bag, but they had nothing.

"I don't care what Silver says, I am coming," Sacri insisted.

"Silver is being difficult about this and I don't like to irritate a guy who has to kill me but didn't yet. Do you have a bag I can pack a lunch in?" he asked her.

"We eat what Mother provides. We go by tunnel until the train," she insisted. "A few days hike. Faster if you take the horses." She played with the cross around her neck.

He couldn't see himself going without her. Wali was right, he needed time with her. "Dammit." He tossed a spoon in the basin. "I'll talk to Silver."

She nodded. "We leave now. You need nothing but me."

Everything in him screamed not to leave her again. Ever. It wasn't an idea or a hope. It was a fact.

He found Silver by the water's edge where he was showing Lacey something, but stopped to approach Alex.

Alex spoke firmly, "Sacri is coming with me and we're leaving right now. You'd better not kill off Wali while I'm gone."

Silver stared at him, silent.

Silver's arm now had a tattoo running over the entire shoulder, and the scar was no longer visible. Alex tilted his head. "Who the heck made that?"

Silver smirked. "Wali." He added, "Sacri must stay." Silver crossed his arms. "This is not me telling you what to do. I do not expect you to understand the seriousness of her responsibility or the danger she could put you in."

"I can understand. You don't want me to."

Silver raised an eyebrow. "Sacri is supposed to protect this land. This is not her duty, this is her destiny, and one does not escape such things because you are a horny fool."

"Stay and take care of things so she can come with me. She's not running from her destiny. We'll protect this land in the only way I can think of: together."

Silver squinted and Alex got the impression he was peering through his soul. "I see it is impossible to talk to you today. You're a mess. Go if you must but heed my warning; do not couple with her. Your soul is vulnerable and the shadow following her is eager to leech onto you."

He didn't care. He'd damn well couple with her the moment they were alone. He couldn't take having her near him anymore and not doing anything. He'd rather die with her in his arms than never get the chance.

Alex glared back. "What do you do to marry someone in your tribe besides ask them to marry Wali?"

"What does it matter? You are not from my tribe. Do things your way, and leave my way alone."

Sacri rushed out to them. Silver wouldn't speak to her until Alex stepped away, so he left them and went to wait for Sacri in the tunnel.

–Thirty-four–

Alex and Sacri were heading north. These tunnels were dark, so Alex held his lantern like a lifeline.

Sacri hadn't said much since her talk with Silver.

"Did Silver upset you?" Alex wondered. "He annoys me lately, never leaving us alone."

"He tied the soul-line that links us in a knot, hoping it would protect you but he thinks if we connect physically this shadow will still find you."

Alex didn't want to be linked to anyone anymore.

"It means nothing." She glanced at her hands, avoiding his eyes.

"What does he think we should do about this link since it's too dangerous for us to act the blasted way I want?"

"We could talk about something else. What about Mattie?"

The urge to throw something gripped him. "I don't want to talk about her, that's even more frustrating."

"Why would talking about her frustrate you?" Sacri rushed ahead, forcing him to almost jog to keep up with her. "The other night you were content to talk about her."

"I have days when I go without thinking about her and those days are worse. Isn't it weird that a woman I planned to marry can be so easily forgotten? Why would you be with someone this shallow? I have no idea how to cope with losing her and suddenly feeling something stronger for you."

She stopped walking to study him. Then she kept going. "She is not forgotten. She shadows your thoughts. I see her in how you dress. In the way you sing. Her imprint was left behind and is a part of this new you. You cannot un-know something. I like this you. I cannot imagine you without this shadow on your life. She is remembered. Yet you learn to breathe without her again. Like Louis does. See how he teaches his boys and makes new friends? This is him finding a way to breathe on his own. There is no wrong way, no right way, but you have to accept what is done and not forgotten."

"You say it like it's a good thing she's gone." Alex tasted the dust of the tunnels in his mouth.

"It is a good thing she lived and met you. She made you who you are, and I like this you. You are brave. Very smart."

"Me brave? Smart? Sacri." He watched her move in the dim light. Every curve called out to him. "Stop for a minute. I desperately need to hold you. What am I doing? I had my entire life planned out. I mean, I had every detail figured out. Now I'm facing a new life I don't understand and I don't even belong in, yet this is all I see."

She faced him, pausing in his light. Her smile danced the light off her lips. "We have to keep moving."

He set the lantern down and leaned against the roots behind him to study her.

"Do not lean on those roots," she grabbed him and pulled him toward her.

Their bodies smashed and the heat between them was like a magnet. Alex slipped a hand around her and leaned in to touch his cheek against hers. He whispered, "Why?"

"They are from the mysterious maple trees along the creek bed."

They were by a creek? Explained why the air was damp. "I want to see these trees," he lied. He wanted to undress her and his hands were ready, waiting for an invitation, but she got on her knees and in the stream of light she drew symbols in the dirt.

"See them. They are right in front of you."

"This is just the roots."

"They are a part of the tree. When Silver was born there were five trees, now there are four. This is a holy place."

"Where did the other tree go?" He knelt beside her, too close.

"The earth gobbled it up." She drew a triangle pointed sideways in the dirt with a line beside it like a half tree. Then next to it, she made a tiny horseshoe, then a P and a plus. She prayed over them and blessed herself with the dust.

He'd seen these symbols before. They were tattooed on her arm. "These protect you from something?"

"*Wîhtikow*."

The word was new to him but the way she said it was full of reverence and fear. "Scary monster?" he asked.

She nodded, a shadow in the dim light. The dark forced his other senses to be more aware, and he enjoyed her earthy fragrance.

"He comes from the earth to reclaim those who suffer."

He took a closer look at the roots, an excuse to rub his shoulder against hers. "Sounds evil."

"This is how Mother heals those with a broken heart." Her hand slipped into his and she squeezed gently.

"She uses a mud monster to suck people into the dirt?" Alex wasn't sure if she was serious.

She bowed to the root and Alex was quick to copy her. Underground, listening to the fear in her voice, he believed in legends and curses.

He turned toward her. "How can you be this close to me and not want to do things? It's all I think about. I know you're trying to teach me something important, but if I don't undress you soon and kiss every little inch of you I might rip my limbs off in frustration."

She kept her head down, holding two rocks. He brushed her lips. Just a caress, skin against skin, and the life inside him fought for survival. He was dizzy. Did she feel this pull?

"Let me show you something," she said, still looking down. In the light, she showed him the rocks. "Two souls are like these rocks. They sit side by side and are happy. This can be any two souls. This comfortable is perfect." She dropped one and picked up a black rock. "Our souls are not content side by side. We need a touch." She struck them together and Alex was shocked when a spark shot from the connection. It left an echo of light in the dimly lit tunnel.

Her eyes sparkled. "When you touch me, our connection burns away all I was and makes me new. Each time. No one else sparks me like this. It is impossible not to act on it, but I must not. I felt this shadow on my soul. It is not your burden to endure." She bowed her head. "The problem is that this connection makes me forget. I forget about Sacred Land and my responsibility. I forget about those I have to teach. I even forget about the dangers to you." She took a deep breath and he watched her chest heave toward him. "You make me forget." Her voice was a whisper. "Because when I am with you, I feel hope. I can do anything, nothing is impossible."

He let out his air, no clue why he'd held it in. He had a hand in her hair along the back of her neck and stared at her lips in the dim light while the fire she spoke of burned his soul and left behind ashes for him to rebuild.

"You are not alone to suffer this." Their lips met and he gave in, seeing the spark explode in his mind. He tore into her dress and she flung him over like a wild beast, right there in the tunnel. Rough. Fun. The dirt floor was cool against his back, bringing him comfort as he explored her body.

A long groan rumbled the earth. Sacri shot to her feet instantly, torn from him in a painful flash. The earth softened under him and it sucked him in.

"Did you hear that?" Sacri demanded.

"I'm sinking." Where had their light gone? He needed to see her.

"He got you?" Sacri gasped and her hands wandered over him, sinking in the warm earth around him. Why was the ground so warm around him? He sank deeper when he moved.

"I'm sinking. Give me a hand." He was desperately trying not to panic but any movement made the earth grab him tighter.

A firm hand snapped around his wrist. "Do not struggle. Relax in my grip." Menashen? Seriously?

Alex grabbed his arm. He was like a brick wall he could pull himself up with. Sacri's hand slipped around Alex's neck and it made a strange sucking sound as she freed his head from the mud.

"Think happy things," she ordered.

"Happy things? You're naked! Menashen here could run off with you while the mud sucks me in and I wouldn't be able to do a blasted thing about it."

Near his ear, Menashen whispered, "You can't steal my happy thoughts." He chuckled. "Relax. It's just a mud bog. We'll have you out in a jiff."

Alex closed his eyes and imagined Sacri riding her white horse. She'd looked so free and full of joy when she rode.

Menashen and Sacri rolled Alex's upper body toward Sacri. Instantly, mud gobbled his legs and yanked him back. A monster was sucking him in bit by bit.

"I'm sinking," Menashen whispered. He growled and the walls answered, growling back.

Alex reached up, grabbing for anything. He snagged the roots of the tree, not sure how or why they were suddenly so close to him. He pulled. Menashen and Sacri worked the mud around him as he freed himself an inch at a time.

He fell backwards and the root came down fast on him in a crushing landslide. Hands moved against him in the dark.

Shoved him.

A loud crash flooded the eerie tunnel and an explosion propelled him into Sacri. They landed on their clothes.

"Menashen?" Alex called blindly as he scrambled off Sacri. She pulled him back. The only light was in the distance.

Darkness engulfed them.

"This tunnel is lost," she whispered.

"Menashen," he called again over the rushing of the cave-in. "We have to get him out of there."

She held his shoulder, pulling Alex back. He bumped a wall in front of him. Had he lost his sense of direction?

"The tunnel has caved in and will continue to crumble." The ground shook, making her stumble against him.

Alex was covered in cold mud, but he jogged with her as she dragged him away. The mud caked around his muscles, making him tired. Things they couldn't see crashed behind them. Confused and numb to what had happened, he kept a hand on her. She ran easily in the dark tunnels. It was several minutes before a faint light streamed in, and he was able to assess the damage they'd suffered. They were a mess, but he'd learnt that these rays of light meant a way out was close, and this was a relief. He wanted out of these tunnels.

Sacri handed him his clothes and they dressed. His shirt was torn, and his slacks ruined. His hands were raw and he must have hit his head because it bled. He forgot all that when he saw Sacri crying. She tried to hide the tears from him, but he pulled her into his arms and rested his head against hers, sharing her loss.

"I'm sorry, I only knew him for a bit, and I feel pain at losing him, too. I don't understand what happened."

"He is not lost. He is one with the earth. It is sad, because sometimes joy is that way." She cried against him, a hand on his muddy chest and the other on her heart.

Alex added, "He was a warrior."

"Yes," she agreed. "He was smart and brave. I am proud he agreed to share his mat when I asked."

A wave of jealousy came over him, yet he held her anyway. Finally, he mumbled, "You asked him?"

She pulled away and wiped her tears, standing in the stream of light she looked at the cut on his forehead. "Yes, this is how it is done."

"Not in my world. I want to ask you." He frowned. "Why didn't you ask me?"

"As long as my mat is with yours, there is no need to ask. When you are ready, I am there. If I move it, then I must do the asking. I am yours, Alex, and you are mine."

Oh. Alex didn't realize that she was waiting for him to ask.

"I don't like the idea of other men looking or thinking about you. I don't even like to think about Menashen touching you."

"You cannot control how other men think or look. Nor can you control what happened before I met you. These things will not happen now that my mat is beside yours. You must stop trying to control everything and live in this moment, for right now might be all that matters."

He clenched his jaw. What she said was a vow. A promise to him, like a ring. He wanted to give her a symbol like this back. The ring Bellecoeur had given him for Mattie weighed heavily in his pocket, but he couldn't give her the gaudy thing. "You told me you wait for some predestined legend. What if he shows up all heroic and is gonna give you these legendary children? What then? Will you move your mat then? I have to know, Sacri, because a vow like this…will mean something to me forever." They stood inches apart and his body warmed up to hers.

She pulled away from him and ran off, disappearing in the gloom of the tunnel.

He chased after her, a hand on her back so not to lose her in the dark that gobbled them up.

When Sacri stopped running, he crashed into her. "I cannot deny him when he arrives. He will be everything I am not. He will be my angry breaths when I am too tired to fight and he will cry my tears when I am too proud to feel pain." She stepped against him and caressed his jaw. He couldn't see her, but they somehow breathed the same air. He could smell her words as she whispered them on him. "His touch will make parts of me come alive and he will remember everything I am forgetting."

When she said it that way, what she asked for was already hers.

Her breasts heaved up when she breathed and he wrapped a hand around her waist naturally.

"When the Man of Legends finds me, even you will not stop me from placing my mat by his."

She spoke of leaving him, yet her tone was seductive as her body talked to him. By the hunger in her touch, she wasn't going anywhere.

"I want to be this man you speak of this way." He waited in front of her lips, for her to tell him this magical man would never be him.

She whispered, "Then my mat is where it belongs."

It was.

His buttons were undone and her touch was light against his skin as she pushed the mud around his chest. He pulled her hips against his. "I hope to never disappoint you, Sacri, but I can't be something I can only hope to be." Alex rubbed his head against hers. He licked her ear. "I can only be me. With Mattie, I tried to be someone I wasn't, and that life was all a sham. I don't want to lie to you."

"I don't ask you to." She pulled away from him, leaving a gap between them as she climbed out of the tunnel, opening a trap door that let in an engulfing light. "I don't ask you to be anything you aren't already."

He stood in the shadows, staring at where she left as if she might rematerialize. *"Go after her."* A ghostly Menashen breathed behind him.

Terrified, Alex rushed after her.

–Thirty-five–

Alex had left Sacri at the hotel while he went to the titles building. He was side-tracked into a store selling rings. It had Chinese symbols over the door, which is probably what had sucked him in.

He checked out every ring in the shop. They were incredible and each one was very different but nothing felt right. "Who does your designing?" he asked the gentleman behind the counter. He was Chinese, so Alex spoke to him in his language.

He chuckled. "Your Chinese ain't bad."

"I like to learn my languages from those who speak it. I need practice, but I learnt Chinese with my friend when we were young. His father is Chinese and he wanted to learn in case he ever ran into him. Beautiful language to speak. Did you make these rings?"

"I did. I made everything in here." The guy was behind the counter, watching Alex closely. "I'm Gui."

"I'm Alex. You're very talented." Alex knew how hard carving into the delicate molds would be. He chatted with the artist a bit, discussing some of the finer details. "What I really want for Sacri is a ring with specific symbols on it."

"You know Sacri?" He beamed, and stood a little taller. "I'd be honoured to make her a ring."

"How do you know her?"

"I owe Sacri." He smiled, but it was clear that was all he'd say on the subject, so Alex let it go and drew him the symbols he wanted on the ring.

"That can be done, but not until fall."

"Should give me enough time to get the cash together. Unless..." He pulled out Bellecoeur's ring. "How much would you give me for this ring?"

The jeweller examined Mattie's ring and he rubbed his hand on his pant leg. "Where did you get this?"

"My last fiancé died the week before our wedding. Her father had wanted me to give it to her."

The jeweller swallowed so loud that Alex heard the action from over the case. He looked Alex over. "My question to you is what value do you put on it?" He studied Alex.

"I suppose, I should return it," Alex admitted. "Forget it."

The jeweller glanced around, but they were alone in the shop. He pulled out a paper. "An arrogant man was in, showed me a drawing of the ring you're holding. Claimed it was stolen. I was to contact him if anyone came in to sell it. Would be a nice reward."

Alex looked at the picture of the ring and the words accusing him of stealing a family heirloom to support his drinking problem. "Too proud to ask for it back so he stoops this low. Bet he went to every jeweller in the area."

"Not hard. Only two of us until Winnipeg."

"Why are you telling me this? If you think I stole it, just turn me in."

"He was a pompous ass. I make my own opinions about who I help and who I send on a wild goose chase."

Alex smirked.

"Get out of here, I'll see you this fall. Bring me some new ideas and I might cut you a sweet deal. And make sure you tell Sacri I was good to ya."

Alex left, feeling good about Moose Jaw.

The title's office was his next stop. The gentleman there was a skinny fellow with a monocle. He studied the map with Alex. Alex found the land and marked off the numbers he wanted. They didn't make any sense to him, but he thought about them as if they were names of each section. He found the creek and the maple trees. It was north of his place to the east of Wali's. That was land they would want, too.

The man left and came back moments later. "Every one of these is on hold, pending a sale to a corporation."

"What does that mean?"

"Well." He adjusted his monocle. "A Land Colonization Company will buy the lot. They do this, and sell it off as a sponsored scheme."

Alex looked at the map again. "This area? It's farmland."

The guy shrugged.

In stumbled Louis, dressed in clean clothes. He had his hat in his hand, had combed his hair back, and had visited the barber.

"Monsieur Dubois," Alex said in English to Louis while trying to hide a smirk. "I was talking to this fine gentleman about the land to the east of mine by the land of the poor sap who went missing in the storm. He says it's locked up in some corporation."

The man with the monocle squinted at Louis. "You know this…gentleman?"

"Of course," Alex said. "He's been checking out the land. We explored the farmland in the area. He's French like me. Yup. We have a lot in common."

Louis rubbed his chin. "Need to buy some land for me and my boys." His English was excellent; Alex had made him repeat the phrase until he spoke flawlessly. Louis stared at the map with them so Alex pointed out where his land was and Louis nodded. He traced the creek, seeing how this map resembled Sacred Land. Alex pointed to where he'd built his house.

Louis said, "This here, along the creek, I'd like that stretch of land for my eldest boy. My son Gilles might be thinking about setting up a store after he finds a…after he marries and he'll need something closer to the creek, maybe along here…" He pulled out a ring to reinforce his lie. "He bought this for his gal. I'm proud of him."

The guy's face lit up. "Where are your sons?"

Louis couldn't say his sons were still young children or this guy wouldn't sell them land. Alex had coached him on what to say. "You know boys, off gallivanting."

"As I told Monsieur Depaix, this land is on hold until the government accepts this project, but I do have a name to pass on if I find acceptable candidates. The corporation is Bellecoeur Enterprises."

Great.

Alex tried to remain calm. "We should talk to this corporation; see if we can buy the land from them, or if they can take the hold off it. This is decent farmland. We could build a town and farm around it. Show us where the rail line is going down."

He explained the railroad plans then scribbled a name on a paper for Alex and handed it to him. "Here. Good news is that, depending on the project, you might not have to follow Homestead Laws. But it will be expensive." He smiled.

Alex frowned. "We have money."

"Well, if you need more, we give loans. You don't have to pay a cent on them for five years. Interest rates are marvellous. We take land as collateral and keep payments low by making them a twenty-five-year term."

Twenty-five years? Alex almost dropped the paper. A lot could go wrong in twenty-five years, then Bellecoeur would get this land back and could sell it again. Alex glanced at the paper then snapped it up.

They left.

Louis' boys hid along the side of the building and joined them.

"How did I do?" Louis asked.

"Good."

"You look ticked," Louis said. "What's wrong?"

"Bellecoeur will make money off your land. Highest bidder will get it. You won't be able to get a loan or even afford half what he'll ask. It'll be aristocrats coming in, drinking, partying, and making him a small fortune."

"I don't know what that is, Alex."

"It means not us. It'll be out of our price range. Even Lacey won't have that kind of money. If I use my land, they'll put a hold on it and give me the cash for a price. If I miss paying, they'll take the Sacred Land I own as payment." He rubbed a hand over his jaw, terrified. He risked losing it all if he did that but he couldn't see another way.

"That legal?"

"Very. Whatever price he gives us, don't even blink."

Louis frowned. "I don't know how to negotiate."

"Me neither. We need Wali. He knows a guy in Winnipeg who might help us." Alex thought about how shaken Wali had been after that deal. Dammit. Could he do this without Wali? "We'll come back with him to work out a better price.

I can't believe Bellecoeur is still slithering around, making my life hell."

"You know this Bellecoeur fellow? Isn't it helpful news for us? You can talk to him."

"I should have punched him when I had the chance."

"Oh. One of them relationships." Louis' shoulders leaned inward. "We can't have artsy cats on our land."

Alex nodded. "It'll be worse. Silver suspects he wants your tunnels for illegal smugglings across the border."

"That won't happen. Mother would collapse them." Louis studied him. "Listen Alex, it's not my business but I noticed you get mighty irritated lately. What's really wrong?"

"Silver says I can't go near Sacri, but I figured if we got married, he couldn't say much about that, now could he?"

"Look at you always finding another solution."

"I hoped to give her a ring but it won't be ready for months."

"Why does she need a ring?"

"A wedding ring is a symbol."

"I mean, why does she need one? She moved her mat. Can't get more symbolic than that. Wake up man, you're married."

"Easy for you to say, I don't know how these things work in your tribe so Silver said to do things my way, but I can't."

Louis held up the ring he'd shown off earlier at the land title office. The gold band had the strange symbol of a house with a flat roof carved into it. "Take this ring temporarily. Give it to my son, whichever one finds a gal first. You should have a ring made by then, no?"

Alex snagged the band from him. "It's perfect. Where did you get this?"

"Silver gave it to me. Told me to give it to you if you went berserk."

"Where would he get a wedding band?"

"From me. It was my mother's. My father gave her the ring. I gave it to my wife. When she died, I was upset and gave it to him. He returned my ring, asking me to give it to you. To make the energy around it happy again, and this would somehow help my soul. I trust him when it comes to my soul. Ya know?" He glanced at Alex. "Now give this to

Sacri, until you get your special one made. Tell her it's a loaner."

Alex felt better. A ring from her tribe was perfect. It bore symbols they needed. He would tattoo the others on her. "You guys make nice tattoos. I like to draw. Think you could teach me?"

"Yes." Always that simple. These guys loved to teach.

They found the place on the paper easily and wandered in excited. They both removed their caps and greeted the gentleman at the desk. An office was behind him but the door was closed.

"Good day. We heard your company has a hold on some land we were fixing to buy."

The gentleman pulled out a large book and flipped it open on the desk. "Names?"

"This is Monsieur Dubois and I am Jacques Grenier," Alex lied.

"Where?"

Alex pointed to the creek on the large map that covered the entire wall. "Somewhere in here, I suppose."

His nose scrunched up. "We're selling that in lots or acres."

Alex glanced up. "I'd like to farm. I was thinking the quarter section."

He stared at Alex blankly.

Alex tried again, "How much for an acre?"

"Nine hundred."

"Dollars?" He forgot what he'd told Louis about staying calm. Were they nuts?

"Any acre you want or a lot is only two hundred dollars. We're settling a town there. You just have to build around the tracks when they make it there. We'll lend you what you need to build any business you want. It's free rein."

Yeah, as long as he brought cash to the table. "Show me where the town will go, I'll farm around it. I can get land for ten dollars a quarter section at the Dominion Office."

Again, the guy had an indifferent look on his face. "Then I suggest you do that. The land we're selling is for a town." He pointed out where it would go, showing them the land between his and what Lacey would inherit—where the Healing Chamber was located.

Louis tensed beside him.

"A town would be better down here. Then the tracks could go—"

"This is the land we're selling."

"Would you sell me the entire quarter section?"

"One hundred and sixty acres at nine hundred each." His tone was flat.

Louis was quick to say, "My son wants a hardware store, but I agree, we can't afford that." To Alex, he said, "We could buy up all the land you said and sell it ourselves."

Alex and Louis went to leave, talking about how they planned to start their own town. The guy called them back. "Wait. Maybe we can make a deal. I need to talk to Monsieur Clement. Come back tomorrow. He'll want to meet with you."

"Why?"

"Well, there are some boys on this land here." He showed them their land on the map. "Clement would like them off the land. We could build the town there instead and you could have your farmland. A gift from us."

How many others had been offered this deal?

"Why do they have to go?"

He lowered his voice. "One of 'em is a Coolie, that'll bring down the value of the land, so we need them gone."

Alex frowned when Louis tensed beside him. "Coolie? You'll have to enlighten us a bit, 'fraid we never heard the term before."

"You know, a Chinese dog."

Alex hit him.

–THIRTY-SIX–

Alex stormed out.

"Why are you giving up?" Louis demanded, following him out. "You are supposed to fight for Sacred Land, not hit the man who can help us."

"He spoke of Clement. He's the guy Sacri wants to help. He saved her life or something."

Louis frowned. "I talked to Clement. He wants her hand in marriage. Is this coming down to a competition between warriors?"

"I won't fight for her, Louis. She has to choose me."

"But you'll mark her up, put a ring on her, and make damn sure he knows who she's moving her mat beside, won't you?"

Alex gave him an evil glare. "So maybe I will."

They found the boys along the side of the building, listening at the window. They came running when they saw Louis.

Michel's eyes were big. "What's a Coolie?"

"What did I tell you about using those words?" Louis snapped.

"I'm saying it like him, is all."

Alex frowned. "I can't deal with that guy, but you go back and get land. Get a piece in each of your boy's names. When he asks to see them tell him they went ahead to check it out and you'll bring them back to sign but you want it saved for them. If he offers to let you sign for them, take the offer, but wait for him to offer. I'll get ya nine hundred but see if he'll make it at least three acres for that price."

"What if he insists my boys come in?"

"Come back next week and tell him they're working the

land and will be by next week, keep doing it until he lets you sign. Wali says these guys do this all the time."

Louis grabbed his shoulder. "Alex, why don't you give him the land and go be safe? It won't even grow weeds for you. This is not your fight."

One of the boys said something about legends but Louis gave him a glare and they remained silent, waiting for Alex to talk.

Alex considered what his friend meant. Why was he doing this?

He had no real answer, he couldn't walk away and this was just something he had to do. "I plan to marry Sacri, then the land will be hers if they kill me off, and we both know she won't give Sacred Land up, ever."

"Sacred Land will be safe," Louis agreed. "We will be safe, if you marry Sacri."

Maybe it was just that simple. Still, the idea of losing even a lot of her land to Bellecoeur annoyed him. He didn't care how much debt it put him in.

–THIRTY-SEVEN–

Sacri left the room while Alex was gone to buy land. She went to the front desk. Alex said she had to stay on this side of the desk so she waited patiently for the gentleman to notice her. He wore many clothes and worked, ignoring her. She ran a hand over her dress, out of place in this strange hotel.

"Excuse me."

He kept working.

"May I help you, Miss?" A young man with wild orange curls approached her.

"I was searching for your dirt, so I can pray."

"Our dirt?" He glanced around. "I suppose it's outside."

Someone chuckled off to her right. He was an older man with a beard covering his face. He looked wise, and Sacri rushed to him as he stood to meet her, but she backed up when they were closer because he smelled funny.

"I'll show her to the park," he offered, and stumbled forward a bit.

"That won't be necessary." The young man stepped between them to protect Sacri, but she peered around him.

"I am Sacri," she told the wise man, eager for his teachings. Elderly were very rare in her tribe and their wisdom was of great value.

"Nice to meet you. I'm drunk, and I could use some fresh air." His eyes were red. He needed more than fresh air.

"Yes, dirt will do you good, too."

"Miss, I don't recommend you go outside alone with this…"

Sacri waited patiently for him to find his word but perhaps his English wasn't that strong, because he never did find it.

"You come, too. We will find dirt."

"I…" He ran a hand in his curly orange hair and looked ready to leave, so Sacri gave him a polite nod.

"Where are you from, Drunk?" she asked the man.

He chuckled. "Oh, I'd like to forget."

"That will be hard."

He nodded.

"And you?" she asked the young man.

"I'm Gerry Levigne, I was born here."

"In Moose Jaw?"

"Not exactly. My parents were coming to Regina and I was born on the prairies, before they made it."

She took a better look. His face was covered in freckles. "Born on the prairies like me." She smiled and he gave her a charming smile back. "I like your city, but it needs more dirt. You like living here? It is the most prosperous of the blessed lands. Perfect for trading and dealing."

"It's fine, I guess. I have a job, but it doesn't pay well."

"Are you slave?"

He stepped beside her, thinking about this. "I don't know what you're asking."

Drunk chuckled. "She wants to know if you're a slave. But you see, Sacri, this is a trick question, because in a way, we are all slaves to something."

She nodded. He was most wise. She was a slave to her duty to protect Sacred Land.

They left the hotel together, and she confessed to Drunk, "I am slave to my destiny. It weighs heavily on me these days and is why I invest so many efforts to help others shed the burden of what enslaves them. I wish one day to stand on Sacred Land and feel the freedom that it promises my soul."

"That is a wonderful goal to have," Drunk agreed.

They were silent as they walked beside her, finally Gerry pointed to an area to his right with trees and a bench. "Here's the park."

It would do. She fell to her knees, praying with her hands in the dirt.

–Thirty-Eight–

On his way back to the hotel, Alex rounded the corner. Louis had gone hunting, sure that Alex would come up with a plan, but Alex had no idea how to get the land from Bellecoeur without digging himself a financial hole. Would he even sell it to Alex? How could he convince Bellecoeur that owning this land was a bad idea when he'd see Alex wanting it? If he told him it was sacred or haunted, he'd want it even more to prove to Alex that he was a fool to believe such things.

Alex stopped by the park, shocked to see Sacri on her knees with two men watching her as if she were crazy and putting on a show for them. He strode over to them. "Get lost. She's praying and doesn't need you idiots watching her." He shoved the younger man, the older one stumbled backwards on his own, clearly drunk.

Sacri jumped to her feet. "Alex! What are you doing?"

His fists were clenched, ready to fight. "These good-for-nothings were just leaving."

She stood at his side. "This is Gerry and Drunk. I came to pray, but the dirt was too far, and Drunk offered to come with me but Gerry said I was not to go without him. Gerry was born on the prairies, like me. And so, here we are. The dirt here is quiet. I can hardly hear it over the noise. Do you have time to join us for a blessing?"

He gave her a sideways glance. She'd invited these guys here?

Gerry was already leaving.

"Take your drunk friend," Alex ordered him.

Gerry turned around. "He's not my friend. I was just making sure he didn't do nothing to Miss Sacri, but I see she's in safe hands."

The old man smelled like whiskey. He glanced at Alex. "Sorry, I was amused by Sacri and wanted to see what she'd do with the dirt. I'm Doctor Harold. Well…I was. I haven't practiced in a year. Sacri was telling us about Sacred Land. Sounds fascinating." The drunk offered Alex a hand for him to shake.

"A doctor?" Alex glared at him when suddenly something Sacri had said smacked into him. "Gerry, wait. Were you really born here?"

Gerry was about a hundred yards away but he nodded from the side of the road. "Why?"

"A doctor and local…" He studied them. Clearly, Sacri trusted them. Alex needed more time with them before he sought their help…yet time wasn't a luxury he had, he needed them to make a deal for him. Like Wali had Xavier do in Winnipeg.

Alex pulled out his pocket watch. "Sacri, it's lunch. Doc needs something to eat. Lunch is on me. You too, Gerry, as a thank you for looking out for Sacri, but in the future, know that a gal like Sacri looks out for herself."

Now Doc evaluated him with those inquisitive eyes. "Why the sudden change of heart?"

"Come for lunch and we'll see what happens."

They walked into a new café with a fancy veranda. They were the only customers and picked a bench by the kitchen.

Gerry slid in first. "I'm working. I should get back." Yet he pulled the food listing from the side and read it. Alex watched him, amused, then Alex sat across from him. Gerry blushed when Sacri poured her dirt on the table and slid in beside Alex with Doc across from her.

The server approached. Doc ordered a tomato sandwich, Gerry a turkey one.

"Any rabbit?" Sacri asked, excited.

The waitress didn't miss a beat. "Not yet, but I'll check before you leave."

Alex glanced at the menu. "You have to order off this list." He showed it to Sacri. "No rabbit."

He was ready to read it to her when Doc asked, "Do you read English?"

Sacri studied him for a long time. Finally, she said, "Yes.

Would you like me to read it for you?"

Alex smirked. He enjoyed how Sacri interacted with people.

"Who taught you?"

"My friend. He is a priest. I was taught to free slaves, reading is a skill I had to master."

"Slaves? Again with that." Doc sat up taller. "What slaves are you talking about?"

"All kinds."

Alex turned to the waitress and said, "Bring us each a soup and something cold to drink."

The server looked like she was about to pull up a chair and join them. "Whiskey?"

Alex glanced at Sacri then Doc. "We better stick to water around this table."

She nodded and waited to hear what Sacri had to say.

"Mmm. I love soup," Sacri told the waitress but the woman still didn't leave with their orders.

"How old are you?" Gerry asked.

"Since my birth, twenty-seven summer seasons have passed."

She was the same age as Alex This added to Alex's comfort with her.

Alex glanced at them. Strangers. Yet he was desperate. He couldn't imagine what would become of Sacri if her land were torn apart for train tracks. "Her land is in serious trouble." He glanced at Sacri and back at the men. "Sacri's tribe lives there and because of certain natural elements, they can't move. They can't plant roots anywhere else. They are bound to this land in a very sacred and magical way." He studied them, waiting for questions.

Doc rubbed his hands on his shirt. "What is it you need help with? I'm not sure what we can do."

"We? There's no we. What I need is minimal involvement from you guys. The land Wali and I own is right in the middle of the path this businessman is buying up. Means he'll be paying me a visit to get the land. Means he knows who I am and won't let me buy up the rest. Plus, I kinda hit the guy selling it today, so I might not be on their welcome-come-on-in list."

Both boys smirked. Sacri didn't say a word. The waitress finally left.

"He wants this land for a reason." Doc was clearly used to solving problems. He sat excited. "What?"

"Doesn't matter," Alex pointed out. "He can't have it or an entire tribe dies."

Doc frowned, worried. "Tell him that."

"He knows that," Sacri mumbled. "It is what he wants, because he blames me for the death of his brother."

Gerry sighed. "Did you kill his brother?"

"I was there when he died."

Doc said, "So what is this minimal involvement?"

Gerry was silent, studying Alex.

"You go in, make the deal, get the land. I pay you what you had to borrow plus a nice fee for your trouble and you sign it over to someone from her tribe."

An uneasy silence settled on the table and the server brought their waters and hovered a bit too long, staring at Sacri as if she had something exciting to share, then she left.

Gerry said, "What if I wanted this land for me? Could I move out there and do like you, farm and stuff?" He glanced at Sacri and blushed. "The idea never occurred to me, but this sounds like excitement. Something I could use in my tired life." He smiled. "I want to do my own things, too. I like the idea."

"Besides him asking prices that will make your skin crawl?" Alex shook his head. He didn't want more people involved. "Where you gonna get that kinda money?"

"Where will *you* get it?" he shot back, and his brass impressed Alex. Maybe he was the right guy for this.

Doc asked, "What is so special about this land?"

Sacri started to tell him about the tunnels but Alex cut her off. "They only need to know that it's a burial ground. Anyone who lives on the Sacred Land and doesn't respect it risks living the curse." He lowered his voice and spoke to Doc and Gerry. "This land is not something that we can take from them. I will be the only one to live on it." Alex wanted to make that clear. "The land around it offers some type of magical or spiritual protection, so we need people living there who will respect this land. I'm not one to believe in legends and curses lightly, but I'm starting to think there's a fated path for each of us we can't ignore."

"It would be nice to know we're here for a reason," Doc agreed.

The waitress was back, empty-handed. She hovered over them. "We do have rabbit after all."

Sacri smiled. "Excuse me, Alex. I will be back shortly."

Alex glanced at the waitress. "Why?" Still, he got to his feet, ready to follow her. "We'll be right back," he said to Doc and Gerry. "You two think about whether you want to help me. It's just transferring money, signing a few documents. If you do, we'll talk some more when I get back." He paused. "I suppose if you do want to come out, I could show you around. We could use a doctor and your energy is something I like, Gerry."

"I'm afraid, I'm not much of a doctor these days."

Alex nodded. "I was at that point, and walking on those prairies changed my life. I got a second chance and I'm glad I took it. There is no booze out there to tempt you and every breath you take is a new start. Think about that, Doc." Alex rushed after Sacri.

The waitress led them to a back room. "The boss stepped out for a few minutes, we have to be quick."

Alex was nervous. What was going on? The tension was high.

She glanced around and brought them outside by the back door. They were in a back alley. She ran her hands over the brick wall and slid a brick that opened a fake door.

Alex glanced at the brick she'd pushed. He ran his hands over it. In the corner was a tiny fleur-de-lys chiseled into the brick.

He followed the others into a dark room and pulled the door shut behind him.

They were in a storage room.

–Thirty-Nine–

The waitress led them to the entrance of the blessed tunnels concealed in the storage room. They walked around boxes and crates. The area felt cramped. "Is it Shu?" Sacri asked her friend. Tally was married to the local doctor and she worked at the restaurant as a waitress to help those in the tunnels. Sacri thought of her as an angel and no one would ever know what a good person she was.

Tally nodded, wiping her hands on her apron. "I checked every day since you left." Her grey eyes sparkled. "She must have arrived an hour ago and left...well... See for yourself." She pointed Sacri to the back of the storage area. There were many crates lined in the dark. She grabbed the lantern and lit it.

Shu had been dealt a poor hand. Her husband had helped lay the rail lines that joined the west to the east. He'd died after bringing her from China to start their life together in Moose Jaw. Alone and afraid, Shu had taken a job in the laundry. She was paid poor wages from which were deducted ridiculous amounts to pay for her room and board. She was told this was how things were done. Sacri enlightened her and promised her a better way, if she wanted such a life for herself and her unborn child. Of course, running to a new life with a baby on the way was scary, and she refused. So Sacri took the time and showed her the path to freedom in case she changed her mind. Tally kept an eye on her in case she needed help.

"So rabbit was code for something?" Alex asked, blocking the doorway.

"Yes, for someone needing help in the tunnels."

"Moose Jaw has tunnels, too?"

Sacri searched the crates, curious what Shu had left for Tally. Movement in a crate caught her attention and Sacri peered in the box to find a baby. A newborn baby girl with no clothes, wrapped in a soft white blanket.

She gently brought her to her chest. The infant whimpered, searching for her mother.

"That's a baby," Alex said. "What the hell, Sacri?" He paled. "What's going on?"

"Her mother is probably in the tunnels," Sacri said. "I should check them. I'll have to talk to her."

"You know her mother?" Alex sounded stunned.

"Shu. She is a slave in the laundry." Sacri handed the infant to Alex.

He took the child dutifully. "What will we do with a baby?" He met her eyes. "Do you plan to keep her?"

"If I must."

Tally spoke, "My husband is the doctor in Moose Jaw. If needed, I will ask him to find her a home."

"Find the mother. I can hold her." Alex stared at the child. "She's adorable."

Seeing Alex hold the baby made Sacri's stomach flip. Maybe they could keep her. She wasn't sure she could even have children and...

"I'll be right back."

"I'll come," Alex promised her. "You aren't alone, Sacri." His stance was determined. "Let me get the lantern."

She didn't like to be left behind either, and understood his need to do things.

Sacri went to the far wall. Behind a barrel was a trapdoor she opened. She jumped down the hole. They always kept the lanterns to the south of each entrance so she felt for it and found the light easily. She lit it and checked the tunnel.

Shu was crumpled in the corner.

"She's here. I need a healer." Sacri felt her neck for the movement of energy. It was faint.

Alex was still in the storage area and he asked Tally to get Doc.

Shu grabbed Sacri's wrist and, in Chinese, whispered feebly, "My baby. I won't make it, Sacri."

"I have her. She's safe." Sacri squeezed her hand. It was

swollen from working with the chemicals in the laundry.

"Bring her to this life you told me about. Promise me she will be safe."

Doc and Alex joined her in the tunnel.

"Step aside and let me have a look." Doc lifted the lantern and Sacri ran down the tunnel. She needed to find the Healing Ghosts. Someone who could help.

"Sacri?" Alex called after her, but Sacri ran, she wouldn't have much time.

–FORTY–

Sacri felt the markers etched into the rock walls to locate herself. She rushed north, taking the tight passageway, running in the dark toward the Healing Lands.

The passage ended suddenly. Sacri pushed on the trapdoor overhead. It opened easily and she slid up to the tunnel overhead. She felt to the south for a lantern but it was missing.

The chamber exploded in light. "Sacri?"

"Chogan! I need your help." The elder of the Healing Ghosts nodded and followed her without a question.

"What are you doing here?" Sacri was curious. It was rare for him to leave the Healing Lands.

His jaw firmed and he said nothing.

Sacri knew that look. Someone in his tribe had died and he was passing through the Trading Lands to get to Sacred Land to spend the night in the Healing Chamber. There he would dream of this soul he missed and they could talk. They all did this, but no one liked to admit it.

"Who has Mother reclaimed?" she demanded. She knew everyone from the Healing Ghosts tribe and the thought of losing a friend made her stand taller, as she prepared for the news.

"You never met. Who do we go to?"

"The woman I told you about. She has had her child and there is a complication."

"Kanti was resting. Go back for her and let her know I am helping you. Where did you leave the woman?"

"By The Way The Water Rises."

"Kanti is by Where The Eagle Soars." He grabbed Sacri's arm. "She grieves. I grieve." He swallowed a lump. "Our son died last night from a strange fever that sucked the life from him." His jaw shook.

Sacri met his eyes. "Your pain is shared, my friend." She bowed her head and they parted ways.

-FORTY-ONE-

Alex watched Shu hold her child. She'd fed her and was staring at her, lost in the infant. Was this the friend Sacri had been helping? He suddenly felt selfish for wishing she would stay with him. She was clearly needed, helping people.

"What is her name?" Alex asked her in Chinese as Doc checked her and tried to make her comfortable with the blankets the waitress had brought down. Doc had sent her for other things. Much to Alex's surprise, Gerry was helping her, excited.

Shu smiled. "Shuang." In English she said, "She is my joy." Her smile sank to a tragic mournful face as she handed the baby back to Alex.

He held the tiny infant by her mother. The ground was cold but he settled close, hoping having the child near would help. Doc kept telling him to back up, but there was nowhere else to go.

Where had Sacri gone off to?

Shuang slept, content. She was so dependent on them. Alex pulled the blanket around her to keep her warm in the damp chilly tunnel. Joy. He understood what it meant. He felt so peaceful looking at her.

Doc cleared his throat, reminding him that he was here to help.

"Does she want to hold her child?"

Doc faced Alex. The lantern danced light around them. Worry etched around his eyes. "Alex, she…she passed on."

Alex glanced at the baby in his arms. Who would feed this baby? Panic seeped into him. "But she was talking a moment ago. Are you sure?"

"We were too late, Alex. This is how life is. One moment

you are talking and the next you are a memory." Doc took out a flask. He offered some to Alex. "Have a sip in honour of her life."

Alex shook his head. He felt like puking. The world crowded him and he wanted out of the tunnel but he couldn't move. The baby weighed a ton in his arms. "Why did she die?"

"A birthing complication that could have been prevented had I been there." Doc put the whiskey away without taking a sip. "Maybe it's time I made myself useful. I think I will help, Alex." He nodded, thoughtful while he looked at the mother of the baby Alex held.

Alex put his head back. "I miss the warmth from the sun that blesses the prairies. I feel cold and hopeless here. A shadow has fallen on me." He took a breath. "I'm sorry. Death is a hard thing for me to understand. This isn't right, Doc. This child needs her."

"Yup."

"That's all you're gonna say?"

"What do you want me to say, Alex? Go marry the earth goddess and find joy like Shu did. Life is too short for us to be pondering it here in a hole."

"How can I marry her? She took off and didn't even think to tell me where she went." He sounded bitter. Alex sighed. "I blame her, but why would she tell me anything? I can't even tell her the truth."

"Which is?"

"I want to hold our child like this. I'm terrified when she runs off doing God knows what. When she's around me, I feel powerful and powerless all at once. I mean..." He glanced at the baby. She slept. "In her eyes, she believes I am some type of hero a legend promised her. I would like to be this hero she needs, but let's face it, I am a lot of things: a drunk, a sleaze, a poor friend. That's not heroic. What will I do when he shows? A part of me really wants to meet a guy who has them this wound up and the other part just wants to prove to them that they don't need him. We can do this without him. I'll just find another way."

"I don't have answers, Alex. Look at Shu. Her last moment was a happy one, despite where she is, or the pain she must have felt. She is at peace and doesn't look like she regretted anything. Why? Because someone touched her life. That baby isn't some great hero. She's just a tiny creature needing love. Shu found that in her own heart, and that is what gave her peace in her final moment."

Alex frowned, not sure he understood what Doc was saying but the message felt important. Like the answer he needed, only he had no idea why. "What are you saying, Doc?"

"You can't see into Sacri's heart. Maybe she thinks you are legendary, or just wants you to protect her land. Does it matter, if you know your own heart? Because the question that allows us to be happy, even for a moment is not how much does this person love me, but how much do they mean to me? That's the only question you have to answer every day, and it won't matter if some brave warrior shows up. Besides, do you really believe there is some arrogant hero out there walking around thinking he'll fulfill a prophecy? No. A real hero, he doesn't even know he's one. A real hero, he's just happy to breathe the same air as her."

Alex placed his head against the cold tunnel wall. "I would quit breathing for her."

Doc's hand was on his shoulder. "If you quit breathing for her, it's because she's breathing for you."

A shadow appeared over them. Doc jumped to his feet. A tall warrior who took up the entire area glanced down at them. "How is the child?"

"Who are you?" Doc stammered.

"Chogan. Sacri sent me. You must be the healer." He bowed to Doc. "I welcome your wisdom."

"Well, don't. We were too late. Shu has left us."

"You saw Sacri?" Alex scrambled to his feet.

Chogan moved the blanket aside and looked at the infant. A warm smile came to his lips. "A baby without a mother."

Why did that please him?

Chogan glanced from Alex to Doc. "Kanti is a mother without a baby." He took a deep breath. "Her son died last night." He took another breath. "My son."

Alex felt the hand of God at work and the panic that had settled on him eased back. "Where is Kanti?"

"Sacri has gone to get her. She suffers and the journey was

hard on her, but she insisted on making it with me." He knelt by Shu. "I will bury this blessed body by my son and raise her daughter as my own."

There was no doubt or fear in his voice and Alex felt much better. This was a warrior—what a Man of Legends should look like. It pleased Alex to hand the sleeping baby to him.

From the dark tunnel, Sacri emerged with a woman wrapped in a fur shawl. Chogan carried the infant to the woman ceremonially. "This child has no mother. Who will feed her?"

The woman raised her head and met his eyes.

Sacri rushed past Alex and fell to her knees by Shu. She held a hand against her cheek while saying a prayer. Then she faced Alex. "You were with her?"

He nodded. "I'm sorry we couldn't help your friend."

"But we have. She asked me to find her child a home among the Healers, and they are here. They will love her as Shu wished."

-FORTY-TWO-

Sacri entered the hotel room, carefully. Alex pulled her in and slid her against the wall, moving in too close, too fast.

His movements exhilarated her. She was his entire focus, and his intent was clear.

"Alex," she breathed his name against his lips. "What has gotten into you?"

He dived for her neck and her body responded, too eager for him. "Silver said we mustn't." She struggled for air, needing more of it.

The force and strength he used appealed to her as he claimed her, his lips melting against her neck, his hands roughly exploring her. She tilted her body toward him, unable to stop him. Fingers slipped into the lace along the side of her dress while his form trapped her to the wall. When the dress wouldn't cooperate, he ripped it open, breaking the lace with a satisfying snap that deepened her hunger for him.

His fire excited her and she slipped his suspenders down and tore open his shirt. Buttons flew off and Alex glanced at the wall where one hit. His eyebrow went up playfully.

She didn't bother fumbling with the button on his pants, but pulled that one off, too. "Too many buttons," she whispered, making him chuckle.

Then she slid her hands into his slacks and moaned into him. He was warm and ready for her.

"Sacri." Her name came out a roar as he tossed her onto the monstrous bed with soft blankets.

She let her dress fall open, an invitation.

He growled like a beast, starving for her. Mud streaked his cheeks and arms. Alex removed his pants, his eyes locked on her.

Her body heaved up to him, sinking in the blankets. "Take me," she pleaded.

"First, I must tell you something…" He breathed, staring at her. "I like your mat beside mine. It means something to the others in your tribe that makes me feel like I belong in your world." He brought up his hand. Between his thumb and finger, he had a tiny ring. "I wish for you to wear this ring as a symbol to those of my tribe that you belong in my world. It's a symbol my father used, as did his father, to let others know that a vow was made that no one could break. And so I vow to the heavens, to the ghosts watching over us, to all the world, that I love you in this moment. You taught me that who we were matters to this moment and who we want to be matters, but in the end, isn't it just the present that matters?" He placed the ring on her finger. "Will you wear this ring as my wife? When you feel the gold around your finger, no matter where you are, remember what brought you to that moment, and where it might lead you, but more than that, remember that in that moment I love you."

A ring? He wanted her to wear a ring like the women of his tribe. Others would see this and know she belonged with him. "Right now is always a really really good moment to be loved." She flung him over, tackling him into the soft blankets until he surrendered.

-FORTY-THREE-

Sacri woke with a start and almost leapt out of his arms. Silver would kill her.

She crawled out of bed and gaped at Alex. He looked fine. Would Silver know what they'd done? Of course, he would. He always knew when she'd coupled. Drove her nuts. Silver was clear about her not doing that with Alex until they figured out how to protect him from the shadow on her soul.

They needed the other necklace.

Alex slept peacefully, but what if she'd hurt him?

He opened his eyes. "What are you doing? Get back in bed with me."

"How do you feel?"

He grinned and stretched. "Pretty damn good. You?"

"Silver said if I coupled with you my shadow could move down our link and hurt you. He didn't know if the knot would hold."

"Oh yeah, I forgot about Silver and his annoying rules. I'm fine, come on." He leaned on an arm to admire her. His naked body appealed to her and she let her eyes dance from his chest to his legs freely while he talked. "Get back in bed with me." He stared at her naked body. "Wanna play a game?" he added with a teasing grin.

It was fun to tease and he looked fine. Good. *Delicious.*

She went to the window, naked. It had a heavy grey curtain. Sacri pulled the layers of fabric aside to let in light and was shocked to see a brick wall. Well. That was just wrong. Where was the light, the nature?

Alex got out of bed and she hoped he'd come for her but he leaned against the door to the next room, arms crossed, waiting for her. Watching her. "They have a shower here," he said. Again, his tone was playful. He had ideas.

His skin drew her closer.

She peeked into the bathroom with him. Already, he had a hand around her waist, almost pulling her in with him.

"Do you wish to be alone?" she asked, knowing she wouldn't leave.

He stared at her. Too serious. Had the evil spirit infected him? The danger weighed on her soul because she did not want to hurt Alex. Now he was so stern, not like his usual happy self.

"Alex, we shouldn't. I might hurt your soul." She touched the gold chain he'd given her. If he cried out in pain, she would return it. "Silver says Clement won't give us the other pendant unless you leave the land. Leave me."

Alex touched his neck and she knew the feeling. He needed the protection it offered.

Then, his warm hands brushed against her back and arms, exploring her. She was powerless to fight him, mud in his hands to explore. "You're safe, all that matters. Let him have it. He'll think he won some battle against me and move on."

"If you feel any pain, promise you'll tell me. I will give you this necklace."

"You're not safe without it, either." He swallowed a lump and she was surprised at how deeply he believed this. "You're my necklace, my hope," he promised her. "Stay with me and it'll be fine." He rested his head against hers. "We'll find other ways to protect our souls. The crosses have symbols on them. I ordered you a ring with them on it. We'll use those symbols and tattoo them all over us. We'll be protected."

She looked at the ring he'd given her. He was making her another? No one had ever given her so many gifts.

"Louis gave me that one to give to you until the other one is ready. He wants me to give that ring to one of his boys when they're older. Sounds symbolic, almost brotherly."

Sacri relaxed with this news. Louis accepted him, this meant the others would, too. They looked up to Louis and his teachings.

Alex was so smart and she liked how he naturally took control of things. This was a quality Silver and Louis found important. Besides, he didn't look like he suffered.

He would be fine.

"Alex." She spoke in a quick breath. "You'll send this shadow to the Cursed Lands. You are so strong you fight evil spirits."

She took a deep breath when his lips brushed against hers. Weak in his arms, yet so powerful.

He picked her up by the bottom and walked her into the washroom. "We need a shower. I will behave, but I'll wash the mud off every minuscule part of you, and you will ignore my desire for you for as long as you can." A strange gleam in his eye made her think he was slowly turning evil.

She rubbed him roughly since he responded to physical power.

He caught her hand and gripped it. "This time we play gentle. Teasing. Hardly touching."

She nodded, excited.

"We'll marry before we leave Moose Jaw."

"I see this as if it were already done," she agreed.

He looked relieved. "Then it is. I haven't had a shower in a long time." He turned a lever and to her shock, water gushed out like at the water pumps.

"How did you make the water do that?"

"It's a shower. It'll wash the dirt off us. Surely, in your travels you've seen a shower?"

She leaned over him, her naked breasts brushed against him. He caressed them softly and his gentle ways were as exciting as when he was animal-like. She came to life under his fingertips. Magic fingers. Gosh.

"Where does the water go?"

"Back to Mother," he explained, and she liked how his explanations were just for her. She knew he could go into detail on how these things worked since he was clearly educated in such things, yet he spoke for her.

"This is wonderful." She climbed in, letting the shower rain down on her. "Can you do this in your burrow?"

"Yup, I can figure something impressive out for our home."

The dirt felt wonderful while it mixed with the water. He stood on the side watching her, and for a moment, she wasn't sure if he'd join her, then his hands smeared into her, exploring her without fear. Slowly, he wandered around her thighs and she opened them for him to dip into.

–FORTY-FOUR–

Alex burned inside. His stomach was on fire. He sat on the edge of the bed with his head down, fighting the pain with thoughts of Sacri. The warm air burned his lungs. He didn't want to wake Sacri; she'd think his pain was caused by the curse and give him her necklace.

Slowly, he stumbled to the bathroom to check his right side. The pain pierced there yet it ached right to his navel. He couldn't touch it.

He felt dizzy and was thankful that Sacri slept on, unaware. He wasn't so sure how long he could pretend that this pain was nothing. The burn in his gut grew worse and worse.

A heaving came over him and he threw up in the sink, running water from the tap to muffle the sound.

His reflection was pale and sweaty. Something was wrong and getting worse. Gripping the side of the sink, he tried to fight the crippling pain but dropped to his knees. Then he curled into a fetal position.

"Alex?" Sacri's fingers were cold against his neck. "You are fevered. Show me where it hurts."

He wanted to tell her that he was fine, but couldn't talk. Why didn't the pain ever stop? Was this how he'd die?

"Here?" She touched his right side under his rib and he screamed, not meaning to. "This is where your soul connects to the body. When did this pain start?"

He couldn't remember. It had suddenly become something he couldn't ignore.

A knock came at the door and Sacri vanished.

Alex lay there, breathing. His breaths were short and every movement hurt.

"Get me a pillow and sheet."

That was Doc's voice. When did he show? Alex rolled over and air went in easier when he was on his back. "What are you doing here?" Alex forced out.

"Heard you scream."

He didn't remember screaming.

"My room is across the hall. Thought you were dying, but I know that scream. Sacri says it's your side and she'd like to make you a tattoo. I assume her rituals are fine with you so she's off to find Gerry to gather the things she needs. You have an infection, swallow this." He dropped liquid in his mouth and Alex swallowed. "I'll give you a shot of morphine to help with the pain. Does it hurt here?" He pushed on his side and Alex bent in agony.

"My guess is appendicitis. An infection of one of your organs. Surgery is needed which means I have to get you to the hospital. When the drugs kick in we'll find your pants."

Alex wanted to argue and tell him it was a curse, but he was too weak.

–FORTY-FIVE–

Two weeks later, Alex and Sacri were married and on their way home. They were camping above ground under the maple trees where Menashen had died. Three trees remained on a sharp drop that reminded Alex of a cliff. Sacri had pushed on each one to see how sturdy they were. Everything looked so normal that it was hard to believe a tree was gobbled into the ground. Now Sacri was underground, checking the damage.

Alex investigated the biggest rock. He'd picked up some tools to carve in stone and took them out to try them. He made symbols on the rocks to remind him of Menashen. He enjoyed the peacefulness. Breathing was easier.

On his wrist was a silver arrow tattoo. Sacri said it meant that he was *Cîpay* and ghosts were to respect this and pass him by.

Doc said his appendix had been removed, whatever that was, and that he'd be fine. He had no idea whether Sacri or Doc was right anymore, but he felt better. He eyed up the mud along the banks of the creek and considered collecting some. He could use it to draw on Sacri. She might enjoy him smearing mud all over her.

"The path is blocked. The cave-in permanent," she announced, materializing from the north.

"So is there another way to get to Moose Jaw by tunnel?"

"No. If Mother cut us off from the city, She has contained the blessed lands. Sacred Land and the Cursed Lands are separate from the Trading Lands and the Healing Lands."

"We can't use those names anymore when we're above ground. We'll call our home Depaix Farm." From his pocket, he pulled out the marriage certificate and the will he'd had the courthouse witness because he wasn't leaving anything to chance. They were just papers but these documents meant a lot. He arranged them under his hat so he could draw on Sacri and get as dirty as he wanted without messing them. "I want you to hide those papers in the vault you guys have underground. The land is yours. When we die it will belong to our children, and if we have none it goes to Louis' and Silver's. Bellecoeur will never get it." He inhaled deeply trying not to think about the strangers he was trusting, or the loans he'd taken, or even how close he'd been to death before making the deals.

She nodded.

"Now come here so I can paint on you with this mud."

She smirked and lay so innocently at his feet with nothing on. With her under his fingers, forgetting the responsibility he'd signed on for was easy.

He painted the tree going under and Menashen giving his life to protect Alex. He drew, smearing the mud around her naked body until the stars brought the skies to life. Then he promised to love her in the moment and she promised him this moment was a happy one.

They made love in the grass, locked together, at one with the world.

Free.

The sun brought a new burden and he slipped on his pants and checked on the wagon and ox. He was amazed at how at home he felt on the prairies. "You know," he told her. "It used to terrify me to be alone, but I always feel so crowded out here."

The grasses blew. Sacri sneaked behind him. "This is the Cursed Lands. What Lacey protects begins over there." She pointed to land that hadn't been touched. A couple of bison grazed by a big rock. "It is worked to the south and Silver wants you to teach him to farm so he can teach his son."

Alex nodded. It'd be easy to teach a guy like Silver.

"What Wali protects is straight ahead."

"Let's check out your brother's place on the way." He was curious to see if Silver had finished his house. "I bought him a housewarming gift."

From afar it looked like a shack, which made him smile.

Would Silver live above ground in that house? Alex's father had told him once, *"What a man gives up for a woman he loves is hard to imagine. Only he understands the depth of his sacrifice yet only he finds value in it."*

Something blew around on the front door. Alex rushed to the house. He snapped the white hanky from the door.

Fear gripped him. What was wrong?

He pulled out his knife, scanning the area for any signs of danger, but all was calm.

"What?" Sacri demanded, scrambling from the wagon, sensing his terror.

"I told Lacey to display that hanky when something was wrong."

-FORTY-SIX-

Something was wrong. Sacri noticed the unease in the air when they got closer to the tunnel entrance by the Sacred Oak. The pendant against her neck warmed, and her breaths were harder to find. She took several deeper breaths wondering if she could fight a spirit she couldn't see or a link weighing heavily on her soul. She rushed to the creek, something drawing her to the tunnels. She stopped before the entrance and glanced at Alex, at a loss for words. There was a footprint of a shoe leading into the tunnel.

"What?" Alex demanded.

"Someone is in the tunnels."

Before she could stop him, Alex rolled into the hole. Sacri followed. Darkness welcomed them. She listened, but focusing was hard, the rage pounding inside her was distracting; this anger wasn't from her. Had her shadow decided to attack Clement instead of Alex? What if Clement was no longer wearing the cross? Would her shadow latch onto him and make him crazy?

She needed Silver to tell her what was wrong with her soul. Why was the necklace burning against her skin?

Whispers came from Louis' room. "The boys are this way. Maybe they saw someone." She touched the cross around her neck, the heat unbearable.

Alex said, "The cross is glowing. Why? It's warm. What's going on?"

"It's protecting me." She didn't want to tell him that her soul was straining. "The link I have to Clement is full of torment." That was the simplest way for her to explain it.

Alex didn't question it. She'd never met an outsider who believed in their ways so easily.

She pushed on and slipped into Louis' room. His mat was rolled up. The boys had a lantern going that Gilles held while Michel searched through a basket for something. She signalled with her hands, instructing them to be quiet. They were on their feet and by her side instantly, then much to her shock they stood by Alex.

He knelt. "Do you boys know where Wali is?"

They nodded.

Michel said, "Papa sent us to get this for him. He said he couldn't leave." They held up a fabric satchel. Sacri peeked in the bag, shocked to find a leaf from the Sacred Plant. Leaves weren't supposed to leave the Healing Chamber. The fact that Louis had one in his room meant he was drying it out to use in case the healing plant might help Wali. The boys looked worried.

Alex glanced at Sacri. "Maybe we should have gone into the house."

It grew harder to breathe. If Clement was down here, she needed to find him quickly and talk to him, calm him. She told Alex what she'd seen by the entrance to the tunnel. "There was a struggle in the mud. Lacey against a man in shoes." She sucked in air. "I fear it is Clement. If he hurts Lacey, Silver will kill him, regardless of who he is linked to."

"Don't you think if Lacey was in trouble Wali and Louis would be down here? Where is Silver that he'd even leave her?"

Michel answered. "He went for a healer and Pa can't leave the house."

"Is Wali hurt?" Alex demanded. He tensed beside her.

Gilles said. "He just fell over."

"I need to get to him," Alex said.

"Yes, take the boys. I will find Clement."

Alex glared at her. He touched the necklace. "No, something is wrong with you. You're not breathing like you usually do. You take the boys, I don't like them alone down here with Clement running wild in these tunnels. I'll find Clement and meet you at our house. Tell Wali I won't be long." Alex left.

She was too weak to argue and watched him vanish in the dark, a sense of dread washed over her. He should stay with her, but Sacri was not one to tell a warrior how to act. She looked down the main shaft, the sun filtered in through the lookouts. Not all their tunnels were this close to the surface or had light. Would he venture further underground?

"Come." Sacri guided the boys to the exit leading to Alex's burrow. "Go to your father and warn him there is danger in the tunnels."

They went up and she watched them enter the house safely.

Sacri had no idea where Lacey would hide. The vault? Silver had told Sacri when they were young to hide in the vault if strangers were in the tunnels. It had weapons, food... She wasn't far and made the vault her goal.

When she approached the vault, she heard Alex speaking from around the corner. His voice was fatherly, in-control.

Sacri waited, her knife handy, ready to help, yet trusting the Man of Legends to keep her safe.

"She's pregnant, Clement, with Sacri's nephew. Think about your actions here, because this is not the way of a friend. If what you say is true, and you came here to warn Sacri, what are you doing with Lacey's neck under your knife? This isn't you. Mattie once told me you were her hero. That's a lot to live up to, but I believed her. You're upset about something, and clearly drunk. Breathe, just breathe."

"She attacked me, and took the pendant Sacri gave me. I want it back," Clement snapped.

"She can't speak, Clement. If Sacri gave it to you, it's yours. Lacey didn't know and was looking out for her family." Alex sounded so calm, even Sacri relaxed. "See, all is fine. Thank you, Lacey."

Lacey suddenly flew around the corner and into Sacri's arms. She glanced at Sacri, touched the cross on the gold chain. Jaw tight she motioned to Alex and Clement in the other room. Sacri nodded. "You were brave to try and get it back, but Alex is right, we cannot take it from him, he needs this protection, too, or the evil spirit shadowing me will travel our link and infect him." She hoped it wasn't too late.

Alex was talking, "I have something else that is yours. Bellecoeur gave me a ring. The heirloom was from his grandmother, which means it is rightfully yours." There was a long pause. "Take it. Mattie would want you to give it to your wife one day."

"Sacri is—"

"Safe with me," Alex cut him off. "She's made her choice, doesn't change the fact that she still cares about you. We both do."

Lacey tried to pull Sacri to the room but she shook her head. "Alex is the Man of Legends. I trust him. Are you hurt?"

Lacey leaned against the cold tunnel wall and took a few breaths.

"Clement," Alex spoke again, his voice still calm, "what did you come to tell Sacri? Will you help her?"

"Uncle is coming. He wants to meet the men who bought the land. He doesn't know it's you yet. He won't like this." There was a desperate edge to his voice. "I don't know what he has planned, but he said he'll show me how to get savages off land he wants. Nothing can happen to Sacri." His breathing was so heavy, Sacri heard it. "I won't fail him, but I don't want to see her hurt. There is only one solution."

A strange gasping made Sacri more alert. She rushed around the corner, too late. Clement pulled his short blade out of Alex and leaned over him as he fell to his knees. Clement glanced up to see Sacri, and the evil she'd seen in him as a child flashed in his eyes. "It had to be done. Now come with me."

He'd stabbed Alex where he'd just had surgery. She knew the spot was delicate.

Alex bent over, struggling for air.

"Put the cross on, Clement," she breathed, afraid of what else the shadow would make him do.

Clement gripped her arm, pulling her but Sacri had her small blade in her hand and she rammed it in his arm.

Shocked by her attack, Clement stumbled out.

She let him go.

He was lost to her, and the weight of his betrayal was heavy on her soul. She wiped tears that materialized, and knelt to help Alex in his final moments.

This was all her fault.

-FORTY-SEVEN-

When Alex woke, he was in his bed. His side hurt so bad he couldn't move. "I'm alive," he mumbled.

"Makes two of us," Wali said from the bed on the other side of the curtain.

Alex shot up. He regretted it instantly when pain tore through him. "Wali!"

Wali coughed.

Slowly and carefully, Alex got out of bed to talk to his friend. Wali's hair was plastered against his forehead with sweat. His skin was drawn against his bones.

"You don't look so well."

"Thought I'd die while you were gone and wouldn't have to see you look at me with that fear. But God has an evil sense of humour. Shit, Alex, when they hauled you in here, I thought maybe He'd make me watch *you* die. Sacri brought in a bunch of people to heal you. Even promised a doctor from Moose Jaw that he could live out here with us. Silver almost smacked her."

He coughed, and much to Alex's horror, blood splattered into the hanky. Wali wiped it, slowly. "Dying sucks from both ends of the deal. I just want the pain to end."

Alex sat on the bed by his friend. "You're not dying."

"I am. All those healers coming and going through here and not one of them told me differently." He closed his eyes.

"Want me to bring you outside?"

"I would like that."

Alex pulled back the blankets. Rancid sickness swelled into his sinuses. Wali was in his slacks but they were clearly too big for him. He'd lost a lot of weight.

Gritting his teeth against the pain in his side, Alex helped

Wali to his feet and together they walked, making their way outside at a snail's pace. They settled along the creek to watch the ducks.

Where was everyone? How long had he been passed out?

Wali clutched his hanky.

"Need anything?"

"Nope." He forced air in. "Nice day, eh?"

"It is," Alex agreed.

"I never heard you sing, but Sacri sang to you a lot these last few days. They'll be back shortly. Some young settler arrived and was asking for you, so Sacri went out to calm him. He refuses to step on Sacred Land." Wali smirked. "What kinda trouble have you been up to?"

Alex's stomach rumbled and he was dizzy. He lay back. "I'll sing you the tale of my foolish ideas." He let the Song of Sorrow dance over them.

Each word told of their journey. Of the people they'd met. He took his time and sang of his hopes, his happiness, how each breath had a new purpose.

Wali rested beside him, eyes closed.

-FORTY-EIGHT-

"Wali?" Alex watched his breaths. They were gone.

He looked so peaceful resting under the oak tree.

Alex had no idea what to do. He got up and wandered aimlessly, searching for Silver, until he came to his hole. He climbed down and sat on the cold ground. The sun was directly overhead yet the wind was cool.

The world was suddenly so different; he had trouble moving. Wali was dead, but he couldn't bury him alone. He had to find the others. Was this a nightmare?

It was hard to imagine a world without his best friend. His brother.

Alex sat in the dirt wondering why he wasn't crying. Or drinking. He should at least have a drink for Wali. He thought about the housewarming gift he'd gotten for Silver and still hadn't given him. Was the wagon even unpacked? He had no idea what day it was.

The pain in his side reminded him that all this was very real.

Head against the side of his hole, he waited for...the ache inside him to numb so that he could move again. Think again.

Silver came down the ladder.

Alex thought about kicking him out of his hole, yet his shadow filled the place with warmth. Silver grabbed the bucket to fill it with dirt. The hole was cramped but he worked in silence. When the pail was full, he dumped the dirt on Alex.

Alex shot up. "What the hell! Silver!" His fists clenched.

"Oh, you are alive. I thought you were dead and I came to bury you." His lips drew back in a serious way. "Good, then maybe we could share a drink in honour of our friend." He went up and came back with the bottle Alex had brought for him.

Alex took the booze from him. It was from Bellecoeur's and had the Sacred Land label. Alex had thought Silver would get a kick out of that. "It doesn't feel fitting to drink today." He held the bottle with both hands. He desperately wanted to tear into it and drown his sorrows.

Silver snatched the bottle from Alex and admired the label. "You're right. Today is for digging." He handed Alex the pail.

On his knees, Silver dug a hole that he placed the bottle in. Then he buried it.

Alex helped him, not sure why they were burying a good bottle of booze, but the idea gripped him. Burying it would help.

Both on their knees in the tight hole, Silver whispered, "His pain has ended. He did not wish to burden you with his death, but your grip on his soul was so tight, he could not let go until you did it for him."

"Is Lacey hurt?"

"She's fine. Thank you."

"Did you find Clement?"

"There is nothing we can do with Clement. If he dies, so will Sacri. She bears the weight of his sufferings. She is not well."

"Then I need to talk to him, ask him to forgive me."

"Forgive you? He stabbed you."

"He was trying to win Bellecoeur over and he wasn't himself. Booze had him not thinking straight. I understand the grip both can have."

Silver returned to the wall and scraped the sides with his digging rock. He ran the rock slowly over the rough surface, and his face tightened in pain. "Alex, your soul wants a fight. If you want to hit me, you can. It might make us both feel better."

Alex studied his hand. He'd balled it into a tight fist that shook. Wali usually carved with him when he felt the urge to hit things. Cutting into wood felt right.

Much to his surprise, Silver handed him Wali's carving tools.

Alex used a chisel to dig images into the soft earth. Images from the Bible he loved to read.

They worked in silence for some time. Alex continued to draw on the walls. Working slowly, making each one perfect, which was stupid to do in a well, but he needed to release the pain through these motions just the same.

Silver climbed the ladder and dumped the bucket around the top, building the ground around the well up. From up top he said. "You and Sacri coupled."

Alex fumbled with the chisel and finally dropped it. Crap. She told him that?

He glanced at the chisel and it was strange but a chuckle tickled his lips. "Silver. I am not talking about that with you."

"I was making an observation." He came back down the hole.

Alex faced him. "Why?"

Silver held the pail against his chest with both hands. He stood still and Alex watched his actions so he understood exactly what Silver was worried about, because his body language spoke what he wouldn't say. "Sacri is a warrior of the earth. You are a farmer of the earth. She lives under it. You live over it. How will you come together? This is what Wali answered me when I asked for his help with Lacey. He did not understand how we would find joy, but he helped me anyway because he believed we would. It is how I feel about you."

"Oh."

They returned to work.

Alex closed his eyes for a minute, until Silver spoke.

"Sacri gave you a tattoo that summoned an ancient belief."

Alex glanced at the silver arrow on his wrist. "She was afraid some curse was killing me, and if this type of action makes her feel better, I feel better."

"Well, it's serious to wear such a marking. Means you have been chosen to protect *Cîpay* and all we believe in."

Alex nodded, he would never allow anything to hurt Sacri. This was an easy vow to uphold.

"The shadow was trapped in her links, travelling them, looking for a host," Silver explained. "The darkness infected Clement briefly and this was why he attacked you." He glanced at the bottle they'd buried. "You somehow transferred the shadow to that bottle. Very strange. I suggest you leave it buried. The shadow will be cursed to the earth."

Funny guy. "I decided to live from one blissful moment to the next, but this sorrow crippling me is making such a promise hard to keep." Alex rested his head against the wall. "I keep promising myself there will be another moment of happiness if I wait for it."

Silver crossed his arms. "If you wait for only the good moments, you will miss the sad ones, the scary ones, and all the other moments. Any fool can be content in the happy moments, Alex, but a real hero finds teachings in all moments. We have a legend that says a white horse roams the prairies in search of her happiness."

"Legends. I'm sick of them."

"They are based on truth and since the legends annoy you, I will tell you the true story. It is about three tribes fighting over land. The one tribe lived there forever. It was their home. The chief of this tribe had a beautiful daughter who he felt might help end the battles. So he approached the tribe who used the land as their hunting ground and the tribe who used this land as their fishing ground and offered each her hand in marriage. Only, both opposing tribes had warriors who wanted to win her over, making things worse. He decided not to use her to end the war. But one of the suitors came forth with a trade so incredible; his offer blinded the chief with greed. It was a white horse. Unlike any he'd ever seen. He wanted this horse desperately and in his greed, he made a deal with this warrior and the two tribes agreed to peace. They would go to war against the other tribe the next day."

"So he made a deal knowing the other tribe would flip out?" Alex was curious and sat in the dirt to listen.

"Greed will be the demise of men. Like all moments, the bliss of owning such a horse was short lived and rumours say he regretted the deal forever."

"So two tribes teamed up against one? I can see this ending well."

"The other tribe didn't wait for them to end the celebration. They attacked. The newlyweds fled on the white horse and were killed. Her soul did not move on. She shadowed the horse, cursing it to eternal life and legends say that when men trade their future for one happy moment she intervenes and shows them a glimpse of what eternity without love feels like."

"You almost sound like you've seen this horse with your own eyes."

"I have. They robbed her of happiness. I welcomed her soul into mine so when I am one with the earth, she will be free of this curse."

Alex pondered this. He was implying that God had bigger plans for him, but he had to trust Him.

"You took this spirit in your soul? How?"

"The same way you transferred Sacri's shadow to a bottle."

"But I don't know how I did that."

Silver stared at him, a stone statue, and he knew he wouldn't get more out of him.

On his knees, Silver gathered loose dirt in the pail. Watching him work, Alex wondered how he thought and if he'd ever understand a guy like Silver.

"Why did you pick Wali to marry your gal?"

While Silver considered this, he hauled the pail up the ladder for Alex.

Alex continued to dig, feeling better now that he was doing something.

Silver joined him, digging into the sides.

"I mean, I would have done this for you."

"You linked to Sacri. I could not ask this of you."

"Did you know he was dying?"

"Wali was near death when he arrived. Our healers bought him time. Wali gave me everything, not because he liked me, but because he wanted me to let you stay. He never once said that, or made it part of the deal, but I could see his wishes in his soul." Silver stopped digging and leaned against the wall. His face was inches from Alex's. "What will you do now?" Silver frowned. "This anger I do not understand. You direct it at the sky."

"I'm angry at God," Alex confessed.

"God? He was not involved. Is this Wali's burial hole?"

Alex shook his head. "I'm making a well."

"Not here. No water here. These are burial holes, Alex. Warriors dig them on Cursed Land so they can protect Sacred Land in their next life. It keeps us at one with the earth, near the tunnels. Your carvings will protect his soul."

"So you're helping me dig a grave? One that means eternally the buried soul will haunt these lands?" Alex quit digging and rested his head against the wall. His tears were close but he refused to cry in front of Silver. "Cursed Land? I thought I was on my land."

"I will walk the lands with you and show you where Sacred Land begins. It is not the same division as your surveyors marked off."

"No, I don't suppose."

Silver dug, ignoring him.

"Sacri married me. We plan to have one happy moment after another," Alex confessed, needing to tell someone.

"That would be happy forever. Do not call a burial hole a well, Alex. Say what you mean."

Alex sighed. "I made a bunch of other dumb decisions. Louis bought land from Bellecoeur. He paid extra to have them keep the tracks off it. And a local was actually able to make a deal for him and his brothers. They bought everything else. I'll trade them land so anything sacred is mine and Sacri's. The lands I trade them they can sell in lots for a town and hopefully make some of their money back." He didn't burden Silver with the depth of debt that he was in.

"I met Gerry." Silver smirked. "He's welcome on Cursed Lands. I will see what I think of his brothers."

Alex picked up the pickaxe to break the earth up a bit more but Silver grabbed it from him.

"Do not hit the earth in a burial hole. This is where Wali plans to spend eternity, show respect."

Alex didn't even question it. He dropped the axe. He could do that when Silver wasn't around. "Teach me how to dig through this hard stuff then. I think I'll keep this hole for me. Wali should be buried by the creek. By the oak tree, so he isn't tied to Cursed Lands but free. This feels more like my burden than his."

"Then this hole will be yours. We will be at peace facing each other. You are a brother to me."

Alex smirked. "Yeah? But what will I do for water?"

"No need for water when you are dead."

"I meant now."

"You have water, an entire creek full. Stop making yourself more work. Be content with what Mother provides."

"I want fresh drinking water that will fill the hole. I'll pump it out. In the cold months, too. Fresh water tastes better, it's cleaner, and I can rely on the well storing water in the winter."

Silver looked up. "That would be wet."

Alex laughed, and the release freed the aching trapped inside him. "Yes. The water will collect along the bottom and I'll line the well with sand to filter water and add a bucket at first but later a pump so we can pump it by hand. We'll have drinking water."

"I mean it would be wet in our tunnels. This will not work here." Silver touched the wall and dug his feet into the soil. He contemplated the sky then a slow smile spread over his lips. "Lacey will like this idea. I want to tell her about it. A well must be dug where there is water. I will show you where and help you dig."

"You know where water is under here?" Of course he did. Why hadn't Alex asked him?

"Silver…we should get out of this hole and dig one for Wali."

"If you're ready."

–FORTY-NINE–

Sacri hurried to set things up for Alex while he prayed over Wali's grave. They'd spent all day out there preparing it, and tonight she knew he would need to use his hands to create something.

Alex returned as Sacri slid the last of the jars onto the shelf. She almost dropped it when she saw how strong he was. He was dirty and a haze of sorrow surrounded him, but he looked at her like the last tree on the prairies. He'd survived. He knew the weaknesses inside himself yet had found a way to overcome them.

Days ago, he had been close to death and she'd vowed to never think him invincible again, but as he stood in front of her now, she caught her breath, shocked by the transformation.

She wished to wake to this man every morning. He was vulnerable and pale, tears still marking his dirty cheeks. Yet he was grounded and home.

From the table, the lantern danced light around them as if they interrupted it. She glanced at the shelf she'd been stocking. Wali had made it for Alex. He'd invested work into the details carved along the sides, even while bedridden. She'd told herself that the shelf was perfect, but it was the oddest shelf she'd ever seen and she wasn't sure why Wali had built something so weird. She hadn't wanted to insult him so she pretended that it was acceptable, but it was slanted and crooked. The wood was beautiful, though, and she'd always loved polished wood. On it were the painting things she'd made. She was almost done setting things up.

The lantern continued to dance shadows around his place, almost touching each jar. She'd worked hard on each one.

Dozens of containers she'd prepared especially for him. Sacri was thinking about how to improve them when he touched her. She jumped from the realness.

He gently guided her chin up. "What is this you're doing?" His voice was soft and she threw herself in his arms, unashamed by her sudden weakness.

"A gift," she mumbled against his cheek. "Alex, I vow to the heavens, to all the ghosts watching over us, to the shadows on Cursed Land to love you in this moment."

He held her, resting his head against hers. "A sad moment? It's a good moment to be loved."

She nodded. "Very sad. Wali made you this and we added to it. He said you were to paint him a picture."

"You made paint?" He gently pulled a jar from the shelf, opened it, and smelled it. She'd made the yellow pigment from marsh marigolds. He pulled back, shocked at the scent.

"I prepared each colour from the gifts Mother provided."

While he checked, she searched for the canvas hidden under Wali's bed. It was large but she brought it out and stood proudly with it.

He clutched another jar. "I don't need that canvas." He eyed up her body.

His tone was firm and not a piece of her could say no.

She couldn't move.

He held the purple. It was the hardest to make. No words found her while she watched him open the jar to stick a finger in the paint. He admired it. Then he brought the finger to her chest and drew a symbol on her skin. She closed her eyes, standing still, unable to breathe while he drew on her.

Her clothes were too tight. She wanted out of them.

"Do you like them?" She clasped her hands on the canvas but he slowly pulled it away from her.

"All the things you hid in your satchel…they were to make paint? For me?" He set the canvas aside and grabbed the pot of brown paint. She'd stolen his tea to make that one. It turned out perfectly and she'd make him more so that he could paint dirt. The paint had a wonderful smell to it and he was lost in the aroma.

His movements were so slow, as he dipped his finger in it and stared at her intently. "Why make me paint?"

"Because death is not something you can fight but you will want to. Because…"

He stared at her chest where he'd used the purple. His finger swirled in the paint, teasing.

"Because I wish for you to paint on me," she admitted in a quick breath and pulled out the container with the white clay. "But first, I must paint on you."

−FIFTY−

Alex was exhausted. All his sorrow and fears were poured out in those images.

He rested his head against Sacri's belly. "Thank you," Alex mumbled as sleep consumed him. Peaceful, restful sleep.

He woke alone, covered in white paint. Even his hair was sticky, but he threw on pants, eager to search for Sacri. She was probably cleaning up, and if he hurried, he might be able to help her.

When he stepped into the world, all was silent, even the birds watched him as he wandered to Wali's grave. The long grass brushed against his bare feet, making them itchy under the thick paint.

He bent to scratch the clay-paint off, but in the dirt by his foot was something… Grass grew around the object as if it had been hidden forever. Kneeling, he brushed the dirt off the cylinder and finally pulled the relic from the weeds.

Staring at it in awe, he marvelled at the oldest thing he'd ever held. Carvings decorated the long cylinder and both ends were open, stuffed with a dry weed. Was it a pipe or a piece of something more complex?

Silver would know what it was.

Along the sides, images were carved in the wood. He had no idea what any of the symbols meant, but he'd carved them many times into things. Maybe this winter he could sit with Sacri and have her explain this language of symbols to him. Maybe he'd figure out why it was so familiar to him.

He ran his finger over them and smelled it. The strange scent made him curious. He trudged to the grave with the find in hand, and was surprised to discover Louis beside it. His boys stood in the shallow creek, catching fish. They were quiet, focused.

Louis had slipped his hat over his eyes, probably sleeping. He peeked but kept the hat over his eyes. "I am sorry you lost your brother. Your shroud is a strong reminder of our loss."

His shroud? Did he mean the paint Sacri had put on him? "I was painting with Sacri." Alex rubbed at the dry paint on his cheek. "I found this."

Louis peeked uninterested, then leapt to his feet. "Hide that."

"I found it." Alex shoved the cylinder at him but Louis wouldn't touch it. He glanced around, panicked as if it might get them in trouble.

"It's the bonding pipe." Louis let out a long breath. "It can be smoked once per moon cycle. Unless you want to bond with someone, you'd better hide that thing."

"Bond? Like marriage?" He sat by the grave. "I know who could use it."

"Deeper than some paper saying you're married." Louis ran a hand in his hair. "How can I explain this to you? The guy who finds this pipe gets to choose one warrior in the tribe he wishes to smoke it with. He will be forever entrusted to this man."

"A man?" He frowned. "Like he'll owe him?" Alex squinted.

"More than owe him. He will take care of his wife if he dies. He will teach his children when he cannot. He vows to be by his side and with him in every battle. He is a brother by choice."

Alex turned the pipe over in his paint-covered hands. He had more than white on his hands and arms, from when he'd painted Sacri. He thought about how Silver had called him a brother. "That sounds like a serious promise."

"The secret is, once you light it up, this pipe will be passed from warrior to warrior who vow to each other in such a way."

Alex liked the idea. It was like having many brothers. Family. "So I smoke with you and you pass the pipe to someone and they pass it to someone else?"

Louis nodded. "Until the women warriors show." His voice dropped. "They circle their men and see the real them." Louis rubbed at the tattoos on his chest that Wali had made. "One will get to see his girl dance. She must be with child and she must have her mat beside his."

"Dance?" The idea of Sacri dancing for him was intriguing. "What kind of dance?"

"A dance done before all the men in the tribe but meant for him. He will be swept into the magic, his eyes seeing the secrets she hides. Everyone witnesses this bond because such a connection means he will share her mat, raise her children, provide for her, and be loyal to her. The other warriors promise her that if their brother doesn't live up to her expectations, they will kill him or disgrace him. They are free to challenge him any time during the dance."

"Wow. That's better than marriage." The pipe suddenly weighed a ton in his hand. "Will you smoke it with me?"

Louis let out a long puff of air. "That pipe is the most sacred of relics on these prairies, and if you ask any *Cîpay* about it, they will tell you such a pipe doesn't exist. The fact that a guy like you is even touching our most sacred of ritual tools terrifies me. Why did the pipe choose you? We both know it was not to smoke it with me. Someone here needs to bond with you and needs you to promise him you will have his back and raise his son when he cannot."

Alex felt a lump in his throat. Louis was telling him something he couldn't right out say.

"This pipe has never touched the hands of someone who was not *Cîpay*," Louis told him, his face stone serious. "Show as much respect for this tradition as possible."

"What do I do with it after we smoke it?"

He smirked. "Legends say the pipe will vanish in the smoke."

"Yeah?"

"This is not a tradition we take lightly. It unifies us as a tribe and keeps us strong. Mother chooses you to be a part of this."

"You ever have a woman dance for you?"

A smile lit his entire face. "She saw every secret I kept and chose me anyway. Love like that is rare."

"So, what will the others say when someone who isn't *Cîpay* lights it up?"

"That won't happen, Alex. Only *Cîpay* can light it."

"What if I do?"

"As I said, only *Cîpay* can light it. This will never change." Louis stared at him. "Never."

Was he telling him that he was one of them or that he'd be blown to bits if he lit it?

Louis glanced at his boys. They were suddenly beside him, studying the pipe that Alex held. Michel tilted his head for a better look. Gilles shoved his hands into his pockets.

Louis whispered, "The smoke is magical and will draw out the warriors to celebrate or compete."

"Compete for what?"

"The heart of the dancing woman warrior. No one knows who will dance or for whom she'll dance. What if she chooses a warrior who is not worthy? They might stand a chance."

"So if you're married you don't smoke it? And if you don't have a wife can you smoke it?"

"You smoke it to bond to the others. Let them know you support them. Your mating status is only important to the women. I might even challenge a guy if he has a woman dancing for him whom he doesn't deserve." He stepped closer to Alex. "How I met my wife and I might do it again. Think if I stood by a guy like you, with the truth-smoke around us, think she'd still choose you?"

Alex swallowed a lump. "If you came between Sacri and me, I'd have plenty to say."

"Ah but, Alex, that's the thing about these rituals, there are no words spoken. The smoke speaks for us and cannot lie. Think before you pull the pipe out and light it. Because if I stand beside you, challenging you, who is best prepared to raise her children and provide for her?"

Alex stepped back. How many warriors would stop him from being with Sacri? A paper some court gave him meant nothing to guys like this.

"Actually," Alex said, "I am. The world you see is changing. There will be a town near Sacred Land. Either your tribe works with these settlers or it loses Sacred Land. Your father might have been from the outside, but he blended in completely with the tribe. I can't do that, Louis, or Sacred

Land will suffer. I have to build a house and act like you don't exist, to save your tribe." He stepped closer to Louis. "I almost hope you do challenge me."

Louis slapped him on the back. "No one will be that crazy, but truth is Sacri already turned away every warrior possible and now you walk out here like this." He motioned to Alex's face as if he had a message on it.

Alex rubbed at his cheek again, not remembering much of what she'd said when she'd rubbed the thick paint on him. The night was a blur.

"Of course, they might come see what the heck makes you so special." The tension between them vanished. "We'll see what happens when you find the courage to light it. Wait too long and it will vanish, but I suggest you clean up first. When you're ready."

Alex held it. The pipe was solid in his hands yet he expected it to wisp away.

"Think Silver will smoke it with us?"

Someone screamed.

They paused and looked around.

A second scream chilled them and Louis made a low whistling sound. His boys dropped and weren't visible. Louis scanned the prairies.

"Paniya."

–FIFTY-ONE–

"What?" Alex listened with his entire body, not sure which way to run.

A woman stumbled in the distance and Louis tensed. "She's labouring."

"I'll get Sacri."

"Sacri?" Louis glanced at him. "Women do not help other women labour."

"Why not? They know what's going on better than us."

"How my mother explained it was that men see strength where women see weakness. I didn't ask her for details because my father whacked me on the back of the head and told me to shut up and learn because out here, if I plan to raise a child as my own, I better know how to birth him." He rubbed his arms. "I will have to help her, she has no one. Look at her... She's a confused child." He sighed. "I don't know where to start raising a girl who is supposed to be a woman."

"Louis." Alex stopped him. "Your problem, all the problems in this tribe, is that you insist on teaching everyone. Sometimes, people need to learn the hard way. It's how I spent my entire life, and the value of what I learnt is what makes me strong." He frowned, not sure if Louis would understand, but he nodded and went out to meet the girl.

Alex panicked when she stumbled and cried out again. "Will others help us?"

Louis marched toward Paniya calmly even though she screamed. "Us? What makes you think you're helping?" He faced Alex. "Do you know how to birth a child?"

"No." This wasn't something he wanted to learn either, yet he followed Louis in case he needed help.

"Oh. Well then, come on. Remember to look and act calm, no matter how afraid or confused you are. She will respond better if we at least pretend we know what we're doing."

She stumbled toward them.

Alex slipped the pipe along his back and chased after Louis. They helped Paniya to her feet. He spoke to her calmly and Alex understood what had Louis concerned; she was too young. Would she survive childbirth? Was she even fifteen?

"I see why you wanted to kill the bastard," Alex mumbled. Louis glanced up, his face cold.

In the distance, a cloud of dust brewed from several directions. Louis pointed them out. "Warriors are coming. Silver has invited them to witness the birth of their next leader," Louis promised her, but Alex had his doubts that this was why they were coming. "Paniya, what are you doing up here?" Louis demanded. "I told you to stay where it was safe."

"It hurts." She wouldn't look at Alex. "My back. Make the pain stop."

"This grieving soul is Alex. He will help me until the others arrive. He's the Man of Legends Sacri goes on about. He's safe. All the colours in your dream, he brought them in his hands. See? Everything will be fine."

She glanced at Alex's hands quickly and looked away, her face warming.

Alex ran his hand over his hair. The paint had dried hard and his hair stuck up. "I am not…" Alex was about to correct him, but Paniya calmed. Did they really need to believe this? He had no idea what to say. "Nice to meet you. Louis told me you're brave and smart. He enjoys teaching you."

She gripped Alex's arm and squeezed. "Make the pain go away."

He checked his pockets and found one of the containers for paint Sacri had given him. Blue. There wasn't anything in the jar, but he could wipe enough off the sides. "I have something to draw on your belly with. It'll help," he lied. "Let's get her under the tree."

Silver rose up from the grass. Alex glanced around confused. How did he do that?

"We'll have every warrior on our land tonight, Louis." Silver rubbed his hand over his jaw, concerned. "What will I tell them?"

Alex answered, "You'll give them hope. You promised them a leader, let's deliver one."

He stared at Alex, his eyes taking in his messy hair, his face, then sweeping over the smears on his pants until they rested on his painted feet. His face remained serious. "And if I'm wrong?"

Hearing Silver doubt himself made even Louis pause his steps. Alex was quick to shove them all toward the tree; they needed shelter from the sun. "If you believe he is the leader you're waiting for, the others will, too. They will fight harder to protect this land until he's old enough to make them proud." Alex grabbed Silver's arm. "You'll teach him. This'll be fine. You can share your doubts with Louis and me, but in front of our people, you stand firm."

Louis gathered Paniya in his arms and marched her to the tree.

"Do you see him? Her baby?" Alex asked Silver.

Silver's eyes rested on something to his right. He bowed. "Yes. We must hurry, he's impatient."

"He's not even born," Alex pointed out.

"It will be an honour to meet a soul this wise and this grounded."

Paniya stopped her noises and reached for Silver. "Tell me what you see."

Silver marched by Louis, explaining the soul he saw, calling the image a vision. Paniya calmed.

Louis sat against the tree and pulled her onto his lap. He pushed on her belly. "This baby is in position."

Silver knelt beside her, watching carefully what Louis did.

"Alex, you must go." Silver didn't glance up. "This is a sacred moment, our leader is about to be born."

"No," Louis ordered. "He must know what to do when his mate is labouring. Unless you plan to help Sacri?"

Silver closed his eyes, gathering strength, but he didn't ask him to leave again.

Alex planned to get a doctor if his wife was labouring. Of course…Sacri would expect him to do this.

Needing to do something, Alex headed to the creek to wash, but he never made it. Louis whistled and the boys jumped out of the reeds and ran to them.

"Head to Alex's burrow for my knife, the rabbit blanket, and a towel we can bury. Ask Lacey for some blankets and towels, she had things put aside for her," he ordered and they ran off.

"They listen well," Alex said.

"Well, they'll be back and they will learn with you what to do. Just keep your mouth shut. I'll answer all your questions later."

Alex rubbed his messy hair. "You'll teach your boys…" Really, learning how to help a woman through labour didn't seem like a bad idea.

Paniya screamed again. She got to her knees and wrapped her arms around Louis' neck, her head against him.

"She needs to breathe with you," Alex said, surprising himself with his understanding. "She's breathing wrong and it's hurting her. Actually, get comfortable and listen to how Louis breathes. Silver, she likes it when you talk about her son. Talk to her. Focus on his breath, Paniya." Alex came beside her. "And relax, you're in safe hands. Make each breath count. Turn around to sit on Louis so he can feel the baby with you. He'll tell you when to push. I'll draw symbols on your belly to bless this child."

Silver nudged Louis and they exchanged a look that implied Alex had done something to amuse them, but they did as he instructed and he felt in control. Better.

She relaxed. Alex drew the symbols from his cross along her tight belly and Silver talked about how brave, smart, and respected her son would be. When the boys returned with the blankets and towels, Silver put a towel under her and a blanket over her legs so she could have some form of privacy.

Alex knelt by Wali's grave and glanced at the cross Louis had planted. WALI MONTAGUE was carved into it. He bowed his head. This was a strange week. Once again, he marvelled at life and death.

"Paniya, you will have to catch your child," Silver ordered as if this was a normal event.

"She can't," Louis told him. "Find someone to do this for her."

Men approached carefully, heads down, not looking at her, yet each made eye contact with Silver and Louis. Silver scanned the crowd and picked one from the bunch. He was as young as Paniya. His father stood behind him and approached with him.

"Just him," Silver pointed to the young man. "She is too tired to guide her son. You will do this for her. Reach under the blanket and catch our leader."

The young man glanced at his father who said, "Remind her of her strength, or be it."

The young man nodded, stepping forward, bravely. Alex was terrified yet amazed by the entire scene.

On his knees, the young guy blocked her from view of the gathering men, and he only peeked under the blanket once. Gently, he took her hand in his and promised, "It is time to push. I am Kohana, and I will not leave your side. You are tired but your will is strong, any moment where I feel it wavering, I will be there, you are not alone." He nodded to Louis who then coached Paniya when to push by what he felt along her tummy.

The warriors fell to their knees and kept their eyes down, so Alex copied them. One pounded the ground in a slow beat that several others joined, until Alex felt his pulse matching the rhythm. It slowly increased with her panting and screams, as if they were one with her and when relief washed over her, the pounding softened. Paniya rested against Louis bringing a silent hush to the prairies.

Alex was ready to get up and run for a doctor. No one breathed.

Then the baby screamed. Warriors jumped to their feet, called to war by an infant. Somewhere in the distance, women sang. Their voices were soothing, welcoming.

The young man held the slippery child in fright, but his father approached with a blanket, and whispered something to him. Together they wiped the newborn off, taking extra time so he could collect himself while Paniya rested. When his hand shook, his father gripped it and they breathed together for a moment before he continued.

Paniya was spent but the energy grew as the singing in the distance came closer. Alex saw the women now. About thirty of them, waiting. He had no idea what for, but their singing drowned out the cries of the baby.

Kohana handed Paniya the child and she put him to her breast while Silver knelt by Kohana and his father, waiting for something.

Alex was the closest and the only one watching, but he didn't want to miss anything. If he had to do this one day, he would need to look that confident. Silver folded the towel under her and left with it.

The warriors were on their feet ready for action, yet, heads down, they didn't move while the women sang.

When Silver returned, more men had arrived and Silver met the eyes of each one before they took up a spot with their heads down. Alex counted them quickly and stopped at thirty-five. There was at least double that in total. It terrified him to think that these guys might one day watch him do this.

Silver took the child from Paniya and waited for the singing to stop. He spoke to the newborn, but he spoke loud enough for all to hear. "A boy knows only what his father takes the time to teach. A man grows only from applying those lessons in his own way. A leader lives to protect the beliefs he must teach." He got on his knees and everyone followed his actions, but the circle around them grew tighter, so that each man was shoulder to shoulder.

The singing started again, this time the women were closer. Sacri was with them and Alex waved to her, but she just stared at him, as if he weren't there. She wore very little clothing to show off the paintings covering her entire body. She was a goddess mixed with a tree. A walking canvas. He stared at her proudly. Gosh, she was beautiful.

Alex got on his knees like the others.

Silver said, "I promise you: the wisdom of our ancestors, the strength of your mother, the courage of your warriors, and the love of your friends. I can promise this for I see this passion in the eyes around us, and so it is already done."

He handed the silent child to Kohana who looked at the baby boy, smiled and said, "I promise to tell you about how strong your mother is for each warrior has a hidden strength that amazes me. I can promise this for I was there when you were born, and even as an infant, I felt the powerful hope you brought our people."

Alex wiped Paniya's head with his hanky while he listened to such promises. Each man in the group took a turn cradling the infant.

The melody the women sang vibrated the earth. As the song grew louder, the infant was passed silently from warrior to warrior. Some promised to teach him to hunt, to fish, to talk to settlers...

Alex and Louis' boys were the only ones who hadn't held him. The last warrior handed the child to Michel.

He looked up at Alex, panicked.

"I'll help you hold him." Alex whispered to Michel. "It'll be fine."

Together they took the child, Alex showed him where to put his hands so that he was safe and they waited. "I think you're supposed to make a promise," Alex urged him.

With a deep breath, Michel said, "I promise to show you a secret I protect. I can promise this because I trust you."

Alex smirked. He did it. Proud, Alex took the infant from him, prepared to let Gilles hold him, too. He glanced at the baby. He was so small it was hard to imagine him a warrior like these men. His eyes were blue. They sparkled in the sunlight as Wali's always did and Alex chuckled. "Yes, Michel, it's safe to trust him. He has the eyes of a Montague."

It was a joke but Louis gave Kohana a little jab with his foot and he shot to his feet. The singing ended abruptly, then Kohana announced. "We welcome Montague to our family. He is our hope." Cheers erupted in the group, men rushed to the women.

"No, Silver. I didn't..."

Silver ignored Alex as everyone hugged and celebrated. Alex held the baby, lost at what had just happened. Kohana was beside Alex, as if he might run off with the infant. Silver approached Kohana, energy colouring his cheeks. "His mother needs rest. She is no longer a Chosen One, so take her to safety, warrior."

Kohana nodded and scooped Paniya up from Louis' arms

as if she were a blanket. Alex followed with the baby, not sure what to do with him.

Kohana told Paniya in a gentle whisper, "I find your strength impressive. Paniya, I'll walk you to safety for the night. Tomorrow we head to our home, if you want to join us, you and your child are welcome. I would love to show you our lake. We aren't many but we're proud to call ourselves Ghosts of the Forests."

Silver followed, too. The boy's father joined them to speak to Silver. "Of course she's welcome, but Kohana is too young…"

"Yes, he is. But he is the one the elders trust to raise our leader." It was that simple. Silver walked away. The father sighed and took the child from Alex.

"I didn't mean to name him," Alex told him. "It was just his eyes…"

He wouldn't meet Alex's eyes but bowed slightly. "Your pain is shared."

"Bring them to my place," Alex offered. "You'll be safe there."

Louis grabbed his shoulder and spoke so only he could hear. "You did well for your first. I was older than Michel my first time and I threw up." He smirked. "Never gets easier."

"Why the promises?"

"He is destined to be our leader but has no father. So if we each promise to teach him, he will lead with the wisdom of an entire tribe."

"I didn't mean to name him. I'm not sure what happened." Alex was dizzy. How mad would Silver be? Why didn't he keep his mouth shut?

"You didn't name him. Montague is his name. We all know this, no one was brave enough to say it, not even me." Tears rimmed the corner of Louis' eyes and he looked away. "Wali will protect that boy. This was his promise to me. Montague Dubois. Sounds like a leader. If you don't mind, I need to throw up before I talk to Kohana's father. I'm sure he's panicking right about now."

He whisked his boys off with him.

Slowly, the crowd thinned as they led Paniya to his home.

Alex sat beside Wali's grave and leaned against the oak tree, taking all the experience in.

Silver watched him. Alex closed his eyes. How bad had he messed up their ritual?

"I like how you took control," Silver said, his voice too calm. "You're a natural leader, and will do well as Sacri's mate." Silver climbed the tree, and Alex was too tired to ask him what he was doing.

Eyes closed, he sat thinking until he couldn't take it anymore. He pulled out the pipe and peeked in the end. Dry leaves were stuffed in it. He smelled them. They had a very sweet scent.

Alex turned the pipe around in his hands. Should he light it?

Silver fell from the tree onto Wali's grave. He scrambled to his feet, went to grab the pipe from him, then retreated as if he wasn't allowed to touch it. "What the heck are you doing?" he demanded of Alex.

"Found this pipe and hoped I'd smoke it. Care to join me or were you busy in the tree?"

"I was searching the distance. More warriors arrive." Silver sat facing him, Wali's grave beside them. "You found it? Today?" He closed his eyes as if this news was horrible. "Maybe you should clean up instead."

"It's just paint." Alex scratched at his cheek. White paint flaked off. "Sacri and I were goofing around." He shrugged. "I like hiding behind this paint, I feel protected."

"That's because it's a barrier blocking your grief. If you are not ready to remove it, you are not ready to smoke this with me."

"If I remove it, I might never find the guts to light this up."

"This is serious." Silver pointed into the distance. "A bunch of warriors are coming."

"Good. A strong tribe is impenetrable. Clement told me Bellecoeur was coming, too. It might do him good to see how strong your tribe is."

Silver nodded sternly as if Alex was a great council on war. "I found this pipe once, you know, when Louis was danced for." He pulled his long hair back and sat taller. "You plan to light it up?"

"If you'll join me."

"We'll be vulnerable."

"We'll be stronger. If this pipe magically appears, it's because we're to use it, today." He said it this way, but in his mind, he was sure that Wali had left it for him and he wasn't about to disappoint his friend.

Silver rubbed his hands in the dirt over the grave, then on his pants. "You must choose who will stand beside you and bond with you. If he accepts the pipe from you, the others will know you are one of us. If someone offers it to you, remember who, this will be important."

Alex nodded, nervous. "Can I refuse?"

"I can, but you'd better think twice before you turn down the pipe from *Cîpay*. There's no hiding once we light it. I haven't done this in years. Ready for some magic?" He bit his bottom lip, then gave in and smiled. His eyes sparkled. The warrior washed off him. Alex sat with a friend about to smoke something they shouldn't.

Alex nodded once but it was a lie, he wasn't ready. He had no idea why this pipe was special. But when he held it, he was powerful, better, where he belonged.

Silver looked as nervous as him.

"I want Lacey to dance for me. I know she has no idea what any of this means…but damn, Alex… What if she does show?" He let out a long breath. "Then everyone will know I gave in to our enemy. Everyone will know how weak I really am. Sometimes, I think that by loving her, I have let a lot of people I respect down. Yet I really don't care, because at the end of the day, I'm proud of her and the me she inspires."

With a big breath, Alex lit the pipe.

–FIFTY-TWO–

Eyes closed, Alex's next deep breath was from the pipe. Smoke gathered around him. It enveloped him in a cloud that danced like a white horse stomping the ground.

He passed the pipe to Silver. Louis stood not far off. Alex nodded to him but he waited and showed Silver what he had in his hand. It looked like an acorn.

Silver copied Alex. When he blew out the smoke, Louis was beside him. Time was suddenly measured in breaths not movements.

Silver passed the pipe to Louis without a word. Before taking it, Louis passed the acorn to Silver. Using a flat rock, they moved a bit of earth at the foot of Wali's grave to start a hole for the acorn. Then Louis placed the rock beside the line he'd dug in the dirt and Silver placed the acorn beside it.

Louis whispered a silent prayer, then reached for the pipe that Silver held out to him. Louis held it for several breaths and finally, eyes closed, copied them by taking a deep breath. When he blew out the smoke, another had joined them and marked the soil, digging the hole deeper.

The hand was familiar and Alex glanced up, shocked to see Wali. He was see-through, a ghost. Alex squinted, sure he was seeing things, but the cloud of smoke swirled inside Wali for all to see and turned into a cougar that leapt from him and into the pipe.

Wali passed the pipe to another see-through man, this time the ghost was Menashen. He took it eagerly and transformed into a cloud of a tree holding the pipe. He passed it to a man with a scar on his chest. Alex knew his name but he couldn't remember it, the smoke was making him dizzy.

Had the scarred man helped him build his house?

The ceremony continued this way until they were two men sitting in a circle of men, smoke uniting them, a hole between Alex and Louis being slowly made deeper at the foot of Wali's grave, as each struck the earth with the rock before finding their place.

Alex tried to count them but couldn't. Most were real, but some were ghosts shifting into beasts or clouds or wind. But like the tree he was resting against, Alex was planted.

Things looked strange to him. Everything danced in mysterious forms. He touched a blade of grass and twirled it between his fingers. It was real, like him. Planted. Things moved slowly, yet too fast. They were between times. In a place where nothing but souls existed and new souls gathered.

Excited souls…

Alex glanced up at the change in energy. What was coming?

Not what. Who?

Women.

They appeared through the smoke like goddesses hunting.

He searched the smoke for Sacri but she was missing. No one sat in front of him. No one held his hand or looked into his eyes.

He scanned the crowd.

Silver was alone, too. Not Louis. A ghostly woman sat before him and he had his eyes closed, imagining her touch as she stroked his face.

Many others were alone.

Yet the humming, the energy grew.

One of these women would dance. It could be anyone…

Lacey appeared, materializing on the prairies beside them. How she travelled through the circle of appearing women and shifting men was beyond him, but there she was, beside them. One minute they were surrounded by smoke then the air was clear and Lacey was there with her hair pinned up. Her eyes were on Silver, and he reacted, leaping up, floating in the air above them.

Alex pulled him down before he floated away, but he let him go when Sacri's hand came out of the smoke and embraced his.

Sacri?

Alex sank deeper into his spot. She came.

He had no idea where she came from but she was like a fire ready to consume him and all he could do was wait for her to burn him alive. A goddess shining on him. She still had paint on her and Alex wanted to take her to the creek to wash but he couldn't move. He was planted where he sat.

Silver floated before him, a silvery shadow of who he should be. Alex tilted his head for a better look. Was this Silver's soul hovering around Lacey? Alex wanted to see what they'd do, but the smoke from the pipe curled up and blocked them.

Why was there so much smoke?

He stared at Sacri. She sat against him, so he wrapped her in his arms. It warmed him inside so he waited for the smoke to clear. Slowly, it danced toward the sky and fell to the earth, swirling up. Lacey and Silver were gone, a wisp of smoke.

He wanted to ask Sacri what they were doing in the clouds, but it didn't matter. He'd sit and enjoy this peace with Sacri in his arms, his friends around him, his home not far.

Someone pounded the ground with their feet, creating an echo that demanded he join in. Boom. Boom.

Sacri stood and he followed her up, so they could pound in unison, stomping the ground.

Lacey and Silver were back or maybe they'd never left. It was the pipe or the smoke making him see things weirdly.

Much to Alex's delight, Lacey danced for Silver. He was lost in her.

The pounding was at one with his heart as Alex searched the settling smoke for Wali. He was still there and offered a hand to greet him. Alex reached for him and Sacri clasped his outreached hand and grabbed her brother's, too, forming a chain. Silver pulled Lacey in with him. She tumbled forward and put out her hand, which Louis grabbed. The chain of people grew.

Alex didn't know if they saw Wali, but he wanted to talk to him before he left. He pulled them forward. They snaked behind him as he bolted for Wali. Wali didn't seem to move yet he was always too far. Alex weaved, to sneak up behind him, but he was just out of reach. The chain grew as they danced around the prairies, with Alex leading, chasing a ghost.

When Wali melted into the earth, Alex stopped running, only to see that he hadn't moved. He was exactly where he'd started. How could that be?

Pounding extended outward and Alex saw everyone clearly as the sun set to the west. Hundreds had gathered on the prairies. With each stomp they backed off, leaving Silver and Lacey kneeling by Wali's grave. He had her in his arms and together they planted the acorn in the hole the tribe had scratched out.

Sacri led Alex off.

"Maybe we should wash," Alex whispered, kissing the skin on her shoulder.

"If you're ready."

He wanted to scoop her in his arms, but his side ached, so he walked her to a quiet spot along the creek. Darkness fell on the prairies, yet the moon was full and bright. They undressed and stood in the moonlight to study their reflections.

"I'm a tree," she said and the revelation seemed to mean so much more to her.

"I look like a ghost. No wonder your brother was freaked out."

They stepped into the cold water. "Stay close to me, I'll keep you warm," he promised her.

Sacri rolled into his arms as they melted into the chilly water.

She brushed his face, washing the paint from his skin gently. "I saw you. In the smoke. I saw the real you."

He closed his eyes. Would she now understand that he wasn't from some legend?

"It changes nothing," she promised him.

He opened his eyes. "What did you see?" He expected disappointment, but her eyes sparkled in the moonlight.

"I saw you. You were one with a tree."

Her acceptance was a relief that washed away the fears. She knew who he was and she wanted him anyway.

–FIFTY-THREE–

It was early morning and Silver stretched in the long grasses by Lacey. A few stars were still in the sky, but the sun was starting to light the day. A good day. Everyone knew the truth and had accepted it. Lacey was a Ghost of the Earth, as was Alex.

Silver's world was balanced. Everything was perfect.

He watched Lacey sleep. Her thick brown curls fell on her shoulders. She breathed peacefully. He propped himself up on one arm to memorize every detail of her. She looked so vulnerable and innocent as she slept quietly, wrapped in the cougar fur. Her soul danced full of vibrant colours, sharing all her secrets with him, entrancing him.

Silver was ready to caress Lacey's cheek when her eyes shot open. Everything in him reacted to her fear and he jumped to his feet.

A fire roared, blazing their way.

Lacey was at his side, wrapped in the fur, watching the fire with him.

Alex stood in the distance, by the fire-ring Wali had put so much energy into. Several times Silver had teased him about making something so foolish and every time he'd answered, "Doing something to put your friend's mind at ease is never foolish."

Like when Alex had faced the cougar, his soul was now planted, ready to endure whatever this fire might deal.

Silver sighed. "Why does he do that? He'll be burned alive. Fool."

Lacey gathered their clothes and pushed them at him. Silver glanced at her pleading eyes. So blue they made it impossible to look away.

"You think I should save him?"

She raised an eyebrow and her soul-light intensified.

"Fine, but one of these times he'll have to do something nice for me."

She smiled, while he put on his pants. Then he marched toward Alex, curious as to why he grounded himself like that in moments of fear. Sacri ran toward them and he signalled her to get Lacey to safety.

Still, Alex stood. Silver had never seen another do this, and Alex's soul-light was a wild mess of fearful greys. He hadn't moved a muscle as he waited for the fire. Silver had never seen a fire-ring before, and even though Wali had explained the protection it would offer, he wasn't so sure a layer of dirt would keep a fire from jumping. Heck, Silver had seen fire jump clear across the creek.

Alex stood between their burial holes, his soul digging deeper, so Silver sidled up beside him and watched the fire grow and move, raging.

"I see you cleaned off your grieving shroud."

Alex focused on the fire. "We should get the horse and hook the plough up to go around again," Alex said as if something so stupid might be possible.

They didn't have that kind of time. "Your horse has already put the creek between her and this fire. What we should be doing. The fire might not cross the creek. We'll be safer." The smoke was thick and he could taste it. Must have been what woke Lacey. She could always sense things like that before him. A wild spectre flew past them and Silver glanced around for others. Spirits rose from the ground and rushed to the sacred chamber. What was going on?

Silver glanced toward his home. Wali had even ploughed an extra fire-ring around each house. This was why building above ground was stupid. All their work would be gone by nightfall.

The wind picked up, blowing at the fire as the flames approached. "Alex. We must move. The flames—"

"It's the smoke that kills. I don't know how."

The air was warm. The fire was ten yards from them. Nothing but ploughed soil between them. Dirt. The only thing Silver ever trusted and now he relied on it to keep them safe.

The fire had no place to go. Flames raged back and forth in the wind looking for a way over the ring until the fire lost its momentum and shrank.

"It worked," Silver whispered.

Alex watched the flames. "Sacri told me that fire was healing, but this close, I taste the smoke. I feel the pain in my lungs. Fire took my parents from me, my Mattie, and now I was prepared to watch these flames take my life."

"Wali taught you how to protect yourself from it, and as much as I doubted the simplicity to this plan, it worked. Let's walk the ring and make sure it worked the entire way. If flames jump, we can dump dirt on them. We can let the others know. They'll be at the creek." The smoke was too thick, Silver couldn't see beyond where they stood. If fire jumped the ring and came at them from another direction, he wouldn't be able to see flames until it was too late. They had to keep moving.

Silver turned and stumbled back into Alex. Two men on horses materialized in the smoke. One wore a sheet, the other was Bellecoeur.

Alex steadied Silver and glanced up. "Who is that with him? Clement?"

Seeing Bellecoeur always terrified Silver. He was the only man he'd ever met without colour to his soul. It was an invisible shimmer. He'd sold his soul to the evils of mankind, leaving him nothing but a wisp of a man. A shell trying to find hope in others who had it in abundance. Worse, when guys like Clement were around Bellecoeur, Clement's soul clouded over and turned grey, as it poisoned his hope, draining the life that fought to survive. "We need to keep that boy away from him," Silver told Alex.

The bright hope that was always in the heart of Alex's soul dimmed. Silver watched it, concerned. "Alex, we have to get to the others, make sure Sacri is safe. We have no time for these two."

"They did this," Alex accused. "He knows how fire terrifies me. He did this so I would give him this land."

"Bellecoeur wants nothing more than to see my tribe suffer for the death of his brother. That is all, Alex. I see his soul. Everything he does, every choice he makes revolves around this vengeance that has eaten him away over the years."

Bellecoeur dismounted. His eyes fixed on Alex, which Silver found amusing. What would Alex do to him? The real threat here was Silver.

Alex stormed toward him. He shoved him and Bellecoeur stumbled back, not used to physical people. It took him a moment to pull himself together. He had his hands up to ward Alex off.

Alex's soul was in flames, matching the fires around them. He shoved Bellecoeur again, making Bellecoeur land on his ass by Silver's hole. For a moment, Silver thought he might slither down it and vanish.

"Watch the hole," Silver warned, not wanting to see Alex tumble into it with the fires this close.

Alex stopped inches from the hole and looked down as he probably considered tossing Bellecoeur in. His ladder was on the ground beside it.

Smoke surrounded them. Silver glanced around, nervous. If fire crossed that ring, they were trapped...

Clement coughed but stayed on his horse.

Rising from the dirt, Bellecoeur said, "Always a loose cannon. My nephew told me you were romping around on the prairies, cavorting with squaws, giving him a hard time about some dame he wants. Mattie was that easy to replace, was she?"

The flames in Alex's soul died as he stared at Bellecoeur. Then something happened. The tiny beam of light in his soul grew, reaching out to help Bellecoeur up.

"One can't replace something as valuable as a promise of happiness. It can only be lived."

Silver was amazed at how Alex stood before this man who stole light from others, and fed Bellecoeur light with his soul, as if he might save such a monster.

His soul kept growing out, cloaking Bellecoeur.

Perhaps he wasn't reaching out but planting roots, like a tree. There were legends about men who'd give their souls to save others. They would link with them, as Sacri had done to Clement, but not in life, in death. Fear gripped him. What if Alex was such a warrior and died to save this horrible shadow of a man?

Silver approached, ready to intervene if Bellecoeur did anything unexpected. It was hard to tell in a soulless man what he might do. He was also prepared to stop Alex from doing anything…rash.

Alex's soul grew into a monstrous tree. Maybe it wasn't Bellecoeur he planned to save but all of Sacred Land.

Shocked, Silver gaped at his soul. How was he doing this? Alex's face was placid as he faced Bellecoeur. His fists unclenched. Like when he'd faced the cougar, there was an acceptance to his stance that he was exactly where he was meant to be. The respect in Silver was so intense, he bowed to the light.

The horses jumped, jarring Silver back to the men facing off. Clement was still on his horse and out of sight, lost in the smoke but he called out to his uncle in fear. Flames had crossed the fire-ring and exploded from the smoke, jumping for Alex.

Silver dived for Alex, prepared to flip with him into the burial hole, giving them a chance against the raging fires.

A deafening roar pierced the air as they collided. Silver fell out of his body and landed by the hole. He looked down at his body as Alex landed on it.

He was dead? Was it really just that easy to die? He checked his worn hands and rubbed his fingers together. He felt alive. The lifeline from between his soul and body was still there. Maybe he wasn't dead, just displaced. He'd seen this before in an injured warrior. Silver tugged on his lifeline gently. It flung up, and much to his horror, attached itself to Bellecoeur. Silver yanked on it wildly, trying to release himself from the soulless man, but their connection was fixed.

Panicked, Silver glanced down the hole again at Alex and his body. When Bellecoeur dived for Alex's burial hole, Silver felt the pull and landed in the hole with him. *Great. Would he have to go wherever this fool went?*

Bellecoeur watched the flames overhead, oblivious to Silver standing beside him. Silver reached over and stuck his hand in Bellecoeur's invisible soul. All his knowledge, all his fears and wants became his, giving Silver a great advantage. Bellecoeur was terrified of Alex. He was the one man who had surprised him. Bellecoeur had classed him as a lost cause, but countless times Alex had stood up to him with beliefs that were firm and well-founded. When Bellecoeur had fought back, it cost him his daughter. Now Bellecoeur feared he'd turn Clement away with his need for revenge. The thought of dying alone in this hole had him rattled. His thoughts sang loud in the hole and Silver paid each one special attention because they were vindictive and fearful, but he sensed they were covering for something more terrifying.

Every time I face that boy, he pushes me. I almost died. He looked up. *I still might. First Mattie, and now Clement didn't even find it in his heart to come back for me. This boy will take everything from me if I'm not careful. And I'm always careful. I need to bide my time. Wait for him to make a mistake, return to his drunken ways. They always do.*

Yet he hasn't and God knows I gave him more than enough rope to hang himself with. God. What I wouldn't do right now for a bloody drink.

Silver crossed his arms, watching the man who'd just taken his life. His gun was in the dirt.

The gun. What if someone finds out I shot them? Which one did I hit? Neither was good. If it was Alex...

A strange sorrow filled the area and Bellecoeur wiped tears on his sleeve. Silver moved in quickly to feel his soul. It was full of respect for Alex. This emotion seemed to confuse him. He respected how Alex pulled himself out of the dirt, because this determination to survive was something he himself had found, but not until it was too late. Not until his mistakes had cost him his wife. Every day Bellecoeur walked into his distillery and made booze, because alcohol was his only blasted weakness and he wanted to bring everyone down with him.

If it was that savage, his thoughts continued, *others will hunt me down. Will Clement return for me?* He picked the gun up, studied it, and finally went to bury it, but his digging revealed the bottle they'd buried. He clutched it thinking about drinking the booze and the cursed soul that was clinging to the bottle found a new host. Silver tied a knot in his lifeline so the cursed spirit wouldn't travel to him, but Bellecoeur's strange soulless mess absorbed it with ease. He sat quietly, holding the bottle, watching the smoke and flames overhead. Silver heard his thoughts and relaxed. As long as Alex stayed on Sacred Land, Bellecoeur was convincing himself to leave them alone. Alex had him afraid, afraid he'd do something that would ruin him or something that would push him back to the bottle.

I'll leave him out here, to rot on the prairies.

He threw the bottle and it exploded, spraying booze and glass at Bellecoeur.

Silver yanked on his lifeline and was relieved when the connection expanded out. He flew up, testing how far he could go before being sucked back to his murderer.

Huh. Maybe being dead isn't so bad.

–FIFTY-FOUR–

Sound was stolen from the world as Alex and Silver landed in Silver's burial hole.

Silver hit the bottom first. Alex lost his breath for a second and rolled off him.

"You hurt?" Alex demanded.

Alex looked up. Flames raged over them but they were safe in his hole. "Silver?" Alex checked him. "That was a nasty fall. You hurt?"

Something sticky poured on his hands. Alex held them up. The flame overhead gave him enough light to make out blood.

He knelt by Silver. "Silver, do you hear me?" Alex found the wound. It was a bullet hole. He'd been shot in the neck. Blood streaked from his nose. Bellecoeur had shot Silver?

"Breathe." Alex tried to get a grip on his cascade of thoughts. There was no breathing. Silver was gone.

Alex dropped to his knees as the fire roared by, leaving a heavy smoke overhead, blocking out the sun.

Alex pulled out his hanky and wrapped it around his face. A weight fell on his shoulders. How would he do any of this without Silver? There had been a certain sense of adventure to coming out here, to trying something no one else was brave enough to do, and if he was to be honest with himself while he was in this hole, he was sure he'd die out here. But now, the weight of how serious life was fell on his shoulders. Dying wasn't an option. Overhead, Sacri would be fighting the fire, and Lacey... His responsibility suddenly doubled. He'd have to look out for Silver's wife now.

Alex leaned against the cold wall with Silver at his feet. Was this responsibility what he'd been avoiding?

Overhead, a peaceful silence settled on the world as light filtered through the smoke in spears. Maybe the fire hadn't been that bad inside the fire-ring.

Alex stared at the wall, thinking of all the things he suddenly had to do. He wouldn't let Bellecoeur run him off this land.

The earth was clay and rocks. His first order of business was to dig deeper and entomb Silver in the wall. Then he'd be at one with the earth forever.

He set to work, using the rocks to dig as Silver had shown him. It was busy work meant to distract until someone found him.

Losing Mattie was a loss of his dreams, a future he wouldn't ever deserve. Losing Wali was more like losing a part of his past. These things stung but the new pain was more as if he'd lost a strength he was using to get by. Now he was on his own. Others would look to him. He had settlers and Bellecoeur in the balance. Lacey would need someone to help her labour and raise a son.

The Song of Sorrow trickled out, this time, while he worked to dig Silver a tomb in the hole he loved. He sang the melody low to the wall in front of him, his hands working in the dirt.

Overhead, others joined in.

"Listen to them sing."

Alex jumped, Silver's voice silencing him.

"It's the first time in years all the spirits are out. It is a real sight, I tell ya. Gives me hope that maybe you do know what you're doing."

Alex spun around, shocked that Silver was talking. Alex took a better look. He was Silver all right, see-through, but Silver just the same. His body was still at his feet, but Silver stood, smiling at him.

"Quicker we get my body in the ground, the better. I really don't want anyone to see me looking that pathetic."

"Silver?" Alex pushed himself against the wall. "You're… But you… What the hell?"

Silver chuckled. *"You look like you saw a ghost, good friend. It's me."*

"You're dead."

"That would be wonderful, but no such luck. You remember what I taught you about killing on Cursed Land?"

"Your spirit is linked to Bellecoeur?"

"Yup. Lucky me, eh? When he dies, I will get to move on. For now, this is my life. I was reborn, a new man. Well…a see-through one." He looked tragically at himself.

Alex tightened his fists. "It won't be for long. I will kill him, give me the strength."

"Whoa." Silver held him back. *"You cannot be killing him out of revenge because then he will be linked to you and where will I go? Besides, we both know you wouldn't even kill a cougar who wanted to eat you. You forget, Alex, I see your soul, and I know you won't be killing anything. You're here to…teach us how to blend into this new world."*

"Louis would do it."

"He will not take that chance with my soul. Smarten up. Surely, I can wait for the bastard to die. You hear them up there? It is a Cîpay ritual known as a Judgement. Bellecoeur will be marked for judgement and no one will be able to take his life. He will live it with me haunting him every day. This is my destiny. I will protect Sacred Land as a true Ghost of the Earth."

"How is it that I can see you?"

Silver shrugged. *"Perhaps because I have the Sight, it allows others to see me in this state."*

"What about Clement?"

"Talk with him."

"He won't listen to me."

"Then maybe it is time you listened to him." Silver filled the bucket with dirt.

Alex was quick to help, still shocked. "So, you're not really gone?"

"Good news is, a ghost ain't that easy to kill." He had a wicked smirk.

"What ya got planned?"

"It is fair to say, Sacred Land will be safe. I will haunt him something fierce. I am actually excited about this. I feel alive. Of course, the other warriors have Clement tied up and they plan to drag him around for a shaming. End it."

"Me? I can't lead your people."

"If he dies during their fun, Sacri's soul will suffer. Like Bellecoeur he is marked and they know better. They are afraid and in pain, forgetting their leader was born."

Alex nodded. His body tensed with determination even though he had no idea where it came from. "No one hurts Sacri," he promised her brother. "Or you."

He worked, burying Silver's body, then Alex added, "You know, Bellecoeur is well-off. Maybe you could get him to send your wife and child some cash as compensation. Give them land we could work."

Silver nodded. *"Yeah. I have ideas."*

Hours later, someone brought a ladder over. When Alex climbed out of the hole, the smoke was gone. Live bodies lay around the hole, their faces or arms painted in white like he'd been yesterday, praying and chanting.

Lacey was on her knees, her hands in the dirt. Soot and mud streaked her face. Her hair was a mangled mess. On her hand was a silver arrow tattoo like his.

Alex knelt beside her and touched it. "He's still protecting you." Alex promised her. "Where's Sacri?" Alex refused to do anything without her. What if he messed up, ruined their traditions, and made things worse?

Head down, Lacey didn't respond.

Alex knelt in front of her. "Lacey, Silver hasn't moved on. He'll be with us for a while. I mean, he's see-through at times, but he's Silver."

She gave him a questioning look.

"Don't ask why, just enjoy the extra time you get with him."

She rubbed her belly.

Alex nodded. "He'll see his son grow. Not like a normal father, but I doubt Silver ever does anything like a normal guy."

She hurried to the creek without more direction than that. Alex followed, not sure where Sacri was.

–FIFTY-FIVE–

Sacri lurked in the shadow of the oak tree talking with her brother. He was *Cîpay,* reborn into a new life and she marvelled at seeing him this way. He was taller, stronger, and looked very much alive, even though Michel said he couldn't see him, Gilles could, so she knew he was real.

She had Gilles and Michel at her side. Their father went nuts when he heard Silver had died and tackled Clement. He had Clement tied behind one of the horses and dragged him through the lands he'd burned. She kept them with her until it was safe to return to the tribe, but she felt weak and exhausted.

Many were singing by Silver's burial hole as they celebrated a new *Cîpay* who would protect the land. Seeing her brother this way was an honour, even though she was unsure what his new life meant. Silver was extremely relaxed.

"How did Alex take it when you died in his arms?" she asked Silver. "Will he leave? Does he blame me?"

"It is not your fault."

She bowed her head, in a way it was. "My choices brought us here."

"Not only yours."

She studied her brother's serious face. "What does that mean?"

Silver looked at the fields. "Alex chooses to stay. Remember the impossible things I told you a Man of Legends would have?"

She nodded.

"I was wrong. The hero we need, he must only love so deeply that he forgets everything else."

She looked around at the loss Alex had suffered. The new wagon was ruined. His plough was made of metal and still intact, but all the hook-ups were burned off. These things could be replaced. But would he see that?

Lacey ran toward them.

"Excuse me," Silver said. "Lacey sees me." He ran to her and scooped her in his arms as if he were real.

"Why can't I see him?" Michel asked for the third time. "I see Lacey flying. I heard him." He studied Lacey. "What do you see, Gilles? Tell me."

Gilles watched, fascinated.

"You don't have to see to believe," Alex said, coming from around the tree. Sacri jumped. She'd been so busy watching her brother, she'd missed him. He was filthy.

He knelt by Michel and pointed to Silver. "Believe that Silver is here with us."

"I want to but I can't see him."

"See how happy Lacey looks in his embrace. Even if you don't see him, you can see him through her."

Michel gasped. "Silver is here."

Sacri told the boys to play by the water so that she could talk to Alex, but they lay in the grass to watch Silver with Lacey.

Alex touched the tree. "I see your precious tree survived." It had suffered from smoke damage, but he was right, it stood.

"All is not lost," she agreed.

He faced her. She was surprised by his stance, his voice, even his eyes sparkled with whatever idea he had.

She was filled with an overpowering hope even if she grew weaker. "Alex?"

He rubbed soot on her cheek. He was filthy but she leaned against his hand enjoying his touch.

He looked at his feet. "The ground is still warm. My house is still standing. Wali would like that. His fire-ring prevented a lot of damage."

"What happened?" She waited for him to collect his thoughts as it was clearly hard for him. Her eyes were heavy, her body ached.

"We're safe. Death is like this fire, just another way to

access new life."

"So you won't leave? Even if they come back and do this over and over again?" Her face tightened with the pain. She didn't know if she could keep doing this.

He looked surprised. "I have nowhere to run. Didn't you promise me that everything that matters is here?"

She grabbed his arm as the cross around her neck burned her skin.

"What's wrong?" he demanded.

She tried to open her mouth but it suddenly hurt to breathe. She needed to get the other pendant off Clement. They were somehow connected. The weight his pains added to her already-weakened soul was tremendous. She gripped her cross. Maybe she should remove hers...

Alex pulled her fingers off it. "Clement. Where is he?" Alex scanned the prairies, ready to fight.

She collapsed against him.

–FIFTY-SIX–

Louis was attaching Clement's wrists to a long leather strap not far from Silver's house. The second fire-ring had held out and his home was intact, too.

Alex stepped up to him with Sacri in his arms.

Louis glanced up but kept working.

"You're not pulling this boy behind this horse. Louis, your people need a leader until your grandson is ready. They're looking to you. If you kill the first white man in front of you, these actions won't leave the settlers in the area with much hope. If you kill a marked man, a man you are supposed to help Sacri teach, it will only show your lack of faith."

"Our leader is dead."

Alex placed Sacri between them. "Do any of you really die? I saw you kiss your wife. Don't tell me death got in the way of that kiss."

He stared at Alex. "I told you love like I had was rare."

Eternal love. No wonder Louis didn't like leaving Sacred Land. How often did she stop by?

"Silver is a Ghost of the Earth, like the rest of you, he won't abandon Sacred Land. Look at him watching you as if you've gone mad."

Louis glanced up and his jaw dropped when he saw Silver with his arms crossed, watching him.

"He sent me over here to demand you act like a leader for our people."

"Ours?"

"I am not leaving."

Clement started to say something, but Louis kicked him and he curled up, inside his sheet.

"Louis." Sacri reached for him, weakly. She wobbled and

Alex held her steady, terrified to see her so weak. "Clement has been beaten all his life. Teach, as is our way."

Louis yelled at her, "The Man of Legends was supposed to save Sacred Land, not make it into something new. Not take Silver from us and defend scum like this."

Alex snapped, "Well, when your precious hero shows, tell him to fix the mess of things I made. Right now, *you* are all we have."

"You were supposed to keep Sacred Land safe," Louis accused him.

"Me?" Alex was ready to yell that he couldn't do anything around here when it occurred to him that Bellecoeur was no longer a problem to this tribe. Silver would keep him in line. They had all the land they needed and as long as they paid the debts, Bellecoeur couldn't fight that. Alex would sell off parcels of land to those he felt understood the tribe's beliefs and respected them. With Silver's help, it would be easy to tell if a settler had bad intentions.

He stared at Louis, understanding why they needed him. Sacred Land was safe and under his control. But he needed them to believe this. "How I protect this land is not for you to question. Just know it's safe. I can't say this to the others, but you can."

Sacri gripped his hand.

"I can't do this alone," Louis whispered. "I can't."

"None of us can. Look around. You aren't alone. Your family is strong, so strong they stave off death. I won't leave you to do this alone, Louis, because I can't do it alone either. I'm terrified all the time. When you say things like I am the Man of Legends, I panic because I know who I am inside, and I will never be this hero your tribe has been waiting for since God knows when. I can't get out of bed in the morning without wondering why I even exist." It felt good to confess that to someone. Sacri held his hand, giving him strength. "Still, I know how to deal with the settlers looking for land. Land we own. They will come, but I promise you, they will respect your ways. No one will live on Sacred Land but my family. This is all I can do. You have to lead your people. And Silver will have to deal with Bellecoeur. We each have our part to play in your legends."

Louis closed his eyes and put his hands in the dirt. Sacri knelt with him. She took Louis' hand with both of hers.

"I want someone to pay for this," he confessed to her.

"Kicking him while he's down is something Clement understands," Sacri pointed out. "Why would you teach something he already knows?"

"Then you deal with him." Louis pulled the sheet off Clement and left them to deal with him.

Clement's clothes were covered in blood. Clearly, Louis had dragged him for a spell.

Sacri touched her necklace and fell against Alex. He guided her to rest in the dirt she loved.

Alex checked Clement's back. It was raw, cut through his clothes. He needed a doctor. Alex glanced up. A few had gathered, but they stayed back. He doubted anyone would help this guy. "Help Sacri," he ordered them. "While I escort him off Depaix Land."

"I will bring her to your house." The priest, her friend, came forward. "I will put her to bed and wait for you to return."

"Thank you."

Alex cut the ropes around Clement's wrists. Clement was still for a moment, head down, then he charged for the priest as he tried to bring Sacri into his arms.

His attack took Alex off guard. He'd thought him weak and suffering.

Alex dived for him and took Clement in a tackle before he reached Sacri. Clement was tough and desperate. He slammed Alex into the dirt, knocking the wind out of him.

Clement hit him across the jaw. "She said she'd be in the barn, looking after the horses. They were to surprise you. It was always about you." He hit him again, this time on the side and Alex screamed out, the pain blinding.

He took several hits to the face as Clement yelled, "He told me to do it. He told me to do it."

Men pulled him off Alex and had him restrained. Clement fought them wildly, but they towered over him, one holding each arm, his feet not touching the ground.

Alex got to his knees trying to breathe through the pain in his side.

"I could snap his neck," one of them offered. "Or did you have it under control?" They chuckled.

"Glad you're enjoying this." He couldn't see who laughed at him. Everything was blurry. Alex raised his hand. "He is marked for judgement. I have to listen to what he needs to say. Let him talk. If hitting me helps, so be it. This is how I teach." They chuckled and shoved Clement toward him.

"I hate you," Clement said, kicking Alex so he flew over.

"Not so fond of you right now, either." Alex lay on the ground, trying to breathe through the pain. Words tumbled out of him, "I'm sorry I came between you and your uncle and you felt you had to prove yourself to him. I'm sorry Mattie went in the house and I didn't make it in time." He took a deep breath. "But I am not sorry I came here or that I love Sacri. These people are my family. I won't let you hurt them."

"You think she loves you?" Clement laughed. "No one loves guys like us. All she wants is your golden cross."

Alex thought about how she'd touched it. Was it important to her? Was there a connection between the two? He touched his own neck where he was used to feeling the comfort and strength that the cross offered.

"What will you do when her Man of Legends shows?"

It was meant as a slap, to sting deeper than the punches, but Alex had spent many nights pondering exactly that. The thought of losing her to some hero made him nauseous, yet at the same time, if this guy would save her from something, who the heck knew what, he would be there to thank him. "I will help him keep her safe." It was really that simple. He couldn't change how she felt or who he was. He could only be there for her. "I don't ask her to stop believing. These strange stories she trusts, they make her who she is, and I don't want her to change. I'm kinda eager to meet him myself."

Clement paced like a trapped bear. His fight was gone and Alex knew how he felt; he'd been there not long ago.

"Sometimes, we think we have to fight, Clement. But what we really need to do is learn. This war you wanted between us is over. Your uncle is now haunted by *Cipay*. He'll learn that this land is not something he can own and his life will be hard. Move on, start fresh."

"Run away?"

"Think about it more like finding a place you can call home."

Clement wiped his sleeve along his bloody nose. "How can I go on? I crave death."

Alex offered him his hanky. "Sometimes, we have to learn the hard way, and death gets in the way of such things."

"So you would welcome death?" Clement demanded.

Alex waited for an attack. He looked to the skies, feeling God all around him. Was there such a thing as death or just another life? He slowly got to his feet and Clement copied him. "You ever read the Bible? When I can't find my way, I find answers there."

Clement tilted his head, listening. "It has answers?"

Alex nodded. "They aren't always what I want to read, but they're always there."

"Uncle forbids it."

"All the more reason to find out for yourself what you believe." It was a challenge.

Clement had something in his fist. He opened it, revealing Sacri's cross on the leather lace Alex had given her.

Alex didn't reach for it. Ready to fight.

Clement dropped it.

Alex had to fight the urge to dive for it.

"I saved her. She should be mine."

"To her family, it looks like Sacri saved you, and at a great cost to her own soul, even to her land. This tribe respects her. Means they won't kill you, but they will make sure you're worthy of raising your son, and if you're not, they'll find someone who is. This is how things work in their tribe. It doesn't matter what you believe, this is how they'll act, so prepare."

"I have no son."

"One day you might. You're wealthy, smart, any woman would be thrilled to have you."

"Yet Sacri refused me. What do you have to offer her that I can't?"

Alex sighed. "I'm just as stumped. But I know that when I walked on this land, I was given a fresh start by the hand of my Father, go find yours."

Clement turned his back on Alex and asked, "Do you know the secret? What is the secret between a father and a son?"

Alex placed a hand on his shoulder, his other protected his burning side. "Don't ask someone to teach something you can have the joy or pain of learning for yourself."

Clement's jaw tightened. With a limp, Clement marched south. Two warriors followed and Alex let him go, sure he'd be back, yet Clement didn't look back, not once.

When he was out of sight, Alex picked up the cross and put it on.

–FIFTY-SEVEN–

Months later—

Bernoit was born to Lacey and a see-through Silver. A healthy boy. Alex had helped birth him, but he'd insisted Doc be there which Sacri found amusing since Lacey wasn't sick or in need of a healer, but having Doc there put his mind at ease.

Silver held Bernoit, talking to Alex while he painted in their home. Sacri had never had a home before and she liked that Alex let her decorate the walls with anything she wanted. She'd hung flowers to dry, and spices for food. She brought in plants with dirt and hoped to keep them alive in the winter above ground, but the best part of her home was that it opened to the tunnels.

Sacri hovered nearby, not sure how safe it was to let Silver hold a child when he was see-through, but he did fine, and Lacey was never worried about him wandering off with Bernoit.

As Sacri watched her brother, pride swelled inside her. He was a good father and an excellent brother to Alex who needed family around him all the time. He didn't do well on his own. She hoped to give him many children. She touched her belly and Silver glanced at her. She spoke to him with her hands, asking if he saw the shadow of her unborn child. He nodded.

She knew it.

Silver said to Alex, "*Now that I see how you place the canvas on the shelf, it makes sense. I thought Wali was nuts for making you something so weird.*"

Alex was proud of his shelf and beamed while he worked

at it. "He left each detail half-finished so I could finish it for him. Sounds like a winter project."

Perhaps this is why none of the markings made sense. "It will be something you both worked on," Sacri agreed.

He nodded proudly and swooped in more colours on the canvas. They were magically hidden and he brought them to life.

"What do you see?" she asked, studying the canvas with him.

"It's beautiful. I must release it. There is a goddess stuck in this canvas."

She wondered how he could see such things. "Show me."

"Look here, it needs dirt." He pointed to the bottom of the canvas and she agreed, searching for the brown. He opened the container, smelled the paint, and slipped the jar into the strange divot in the shelf. He picked up a paintbrush.

"*You like the brushes I made?*" Silver asked. "*Each one is from different hairs: beaver, raccoon, even wolf. When I found out you liked to paint, I put them together.*"

"Yeah, they're perfect, thanks."

"*I can teach you how to make your own.*"

"I'd really like for you to teach me how to make those tattoos."

"*I will, and you will teach me to farm.*" He shone. "*I feel so alive. You have no idea how much a guy gets done in a day when he does not have to eat or sleep. Oh, the boys came up with a name for our town—Eau Claire. It was Gilles' idea, and I like the name, but I told him I would run it by you. What ya think?*"

"Eau Claire," Alex tested it out. "Yup. It'll do. How is Clement?" Alex dipped a brush. He swiped paint across the canvas and Sacri sat on the edge of the chair at the table and watched the painting consume him.

"*When Bellecoeur checked himself into that hospital for hearing voices, he passed everything to Clement. He had no problem starting new. Found a wife, bought a ranch, and refuses to speak French because he hates the idea of being like his father or uncle.*" Silver frowned. "*He confuses me, but is not a danger. You will start your family in peace.*"

Sacri sat quietly, listening to them talk, enjoying the

moments when they were silent and Alex let the work devour him.

Like a warrior hunting or a father teaching his son, Alex gave his craft all he had. Only he pulled a picture from a blank canvas with magic. It was the most powerful thing she'd ever witnessed.

While he waited for the paint to dry, he held the baby so that Silver could study the painting. "He looks like you, Silver."

Silver glowed proudly.

Sacri rubbed her belly, eager for Alex to hold his own child. "Soon it will be your turn," she whispered and touched her golden chain lightly.

"What?" His head snapped up. His eyes swept over her. "Really?" A smile lit his face and it drew her in.

Silver grumbled a good-bye and left with Bernoit.

Alex scooped her in his strong arms and poured love onto her.

Lost in his embrace, she asked, "Is that painting me?" Her voice was a whisper.

He smiled. "You on your magical white horse, flying over the prairies free and alive with a fire chasing you. My beautiful goddess who believes in legends so deeply, I have to paint them out for you."

She touched his cross with tenderness, stealing bits of his strength. If only he could see himself the way she did, then he would know what a legend looked like. "It was a foolish dream. I don't need some Man of Legends who is never there, Alex, not when I have you."

Elsewhen Press

an independent publisher specialising in Speculative Fiction

Visit the Elsewhen Press website at elsewhen.co.uk for the latest information on all of our titles, authors and events; to read our blog; find out where to buy our books and ebooks; or to place an order.

Ghosts on the Prairies

A Sacred Land Story

Tanya Reimer

Some things are worth a fight. Strong words that Antoine's father drilled into him. After his father mysteriously vanishes one night, Antoine must find another income or he risks losing the Sacred Land that his father swore to protect.

On a well-paying ranch, Antoine meets Emma, a victim of underground slavery. Fighting for her freedom costs him his home, his sister, his best friend, and puts in question all of his values. If he succeeds, will she and her son fit into his world?

The prairies of 1916-19 come alive with bootleggers, slavery, fools in sheets, haunting spirits, shifty tunnel runners, and even exploding churches. *Ghosts on the Prairies* is alternative history suspense incorporating the paranormal and infused with romance.

Born and raised in Saskatchewan, Tanya enjoys using the tranquil prairies as a setting to her not-so-peaceful speculative fiction. She is married with two children which means among her accomplishments are the necessary magical abilities to find a lost tooth in a park of sand and whisper away monsters from under the bed.

Tanya was fifteen when she wrote her first column. She has a diploma in Journalism/Short Story Writing. Today, she actively submits to various newspapers, writes and publishes the local Francophone newsletter for her community, and maintains a blog at Life's Like That.

Ghosts on the Prairies, a Sacred Land Story for adults, is her debut novel.

ISBN: 9781908168535 (epub, kindle)
ISBN: 9781908168436 (356pp paperback)

Visit bit.ly/GhostsPrairies

CAN'T DREAM WITHOUT YOU

FROM THE DARK CHRONICLES

TANYA REIMER

Legends say that tens of thousands of years ago, Whisperers were banished from the heavens, torn in half, and dumped on a mortal realm they didn't understand. Longing for their other half, they went from being powerful immortals to lonely leeches relying on humans to survive. Over the years, they earnt magic from demons, they left themselves Notebooks with hints, and by pairing up with human souls, they eventually found their other halves. Humbled by their experiences, they discovered the true purpose of life and many were worthy of returning to the heavens. But many were not.

The Dark Chronicles are stories that share the heartache of select unworthy Whisperers on their journey to immortality after The War of 2019. *Can't Dream Without You* is one of those stories, in which we meet Steve and Julia, two such heroes.

Steve isn't a normal boy. He plays with demons, his soul travels to a dream realm at night using mystical butterflies, and soon he'll earn the power to raise the dead. Al thinks that destroying him would do the world a favour, yet he just can't kill his own son. Wanting to acquire the power that raises the dead before Steve does, Al performs a ritual on Steve's sixteenth birthday. He transfers Steve's dark magic to Julia, an innocent girl he plans to kill. But Steve is determined to save Julia and sucks her soul to Dreamland. From the dream world, he invokes the help of her brother to keep her safe.

Five years later, Steve can't tell what's real or what's a nightmare. Julia's brother wants to kill him, a strange bald eagle is erasing memories, and Steve's caught in some bizarre bullfight on another realm with a cop hot on his trail looking to be Julia's hero. All the while, Steve and Julia must fight the desperate need to make their steamy dreams a reality.

ISBN: 9781908168924 (epub, kindle)
ISBN: 9781908168825 (288pp paperback)

Visit bit.ly/CantDream

LiGa series

Sanem Ozdural

A thought-provoking series of books in an essentially contemporary setting, with elements of both science fiction and fantasy.

LiGa™

Book I

Literary science fiction, LiGa™ tells of a game in which the players are, literally, gambling with their lives. In the near-future a secretive organisation has developed technology to transfer the regenerative power of a body's cells from one person to another, conferring extended or even indefinite life expectancy. As a means of controlling who benefits from the technology, access is obtained by winning a tournament of chess or bridge to which only a select few are invited. At its core, the game is a test of a person's integrity, ability and resilience. Sanem's novel provides a fascinating insight into the motivation both of those characters who win and thus have the possibility of virtual immortality and of those who will effectively lose some of their life expectancy.

ISBN: 9781908168160 (epub, kindle)
ISBN: 9781908168061 (400pp paperback)

Visit bit.ly/BookLiGa

THE DARK SHALL DO WHAT LIGHT CANNOT

Book II

We find out more about the organisation behind LiGa as we travel with some of them to Pera, a place which lies beyond the Light Veil on the other side of reality. There are light trees there that eat sunlight and bear fruit that, in turn, lights up and energises (literally) the community of Pera. There are light birds that glitter in the night because they have eaten the seed of the lightberry. The House of Light and Dark, which is the domain of the Sun and her brother, Twilight, welcomes all creatures living in Pera. But in the midst of all the glitter, laughter and the songs, it must be remembered that the lightberry is poisonous to the non-Pera born, and the Land is afraid when the Sun retreats, for it is then that Twilight walks the streets…

ISBN: 9781908168740 (epub, kindle)
ISBN: 9781908168641 (480pp paperback)

Visit bit.ly/Darkshalldo

ABOUT THE AUTHOR

Born and raised in Saskatchewan, Tanya Reimer enjoys using the tranquil prairies as a setting to her not-so-peaceful speculative fiction.

She is married with two children which means among her accomplishments are the necessary magical abilities to find a lost tooth in a park of sand and whisper away monsters from under the bed.

As director of a non-profit Francophone community center, Tanya offers programming and services in French for all ages to ensure the lasting imprint and growth of the Francophone community in which she was raised. What she enjoys the most about her job is teaching social media safety for teens and offering one-on-one technology classes for seniors.

Tanya was fifteen when she wrote her first column. She has a diploma in Journalism/Short Story Writing. Today, she actively submits to various newspapers, writes and publishes the local Francophone newsletter for her community, and maintains a blog at *Life's Like That*.

Legends on the Prairies, is her second *Sacred Land Story* for adults and the prequel to *Ghosts on the Prairies,* her debut novel.